THE LIFE CHEST

GREED LOSES WHAT IT HAS GAINED

THE LIFE CHEST : AFRICA

THE LIFE CHEST

GREED LOSES WHAT IT HAS GAINED

BY KIM YOST

With Terie Spencer,
Agata Wysokinski and Donna Yost
Illustrations by Kristen Trawczynski

AFRICA

THE LIFE CHEST : AFRICA

Life 2000 Ltd.
3331 W. Big Beaver, Suite 118
Troy, MI 48084 USA

Copyright © 2015 by Kim Yost

All rights reserved. This book may not be reproduced in whole or in part, stored in a retrieval system, or transmitted in any form or by any means - electronic, mechanical, or other - without written permission from the publisher, except by a reviewer, who may quote brief passages in a review.

Library of Congress Control Number: 2015959773
ISBN-13: 978-1-4951-8488-8

First printing, December 2015

Printed in Canada

Contents

Foreword by Bill Comrie 7

Introduction 9

Dedication 11

Acknowledgments 13

Prologue: Adventureland and Real Adventures 15

Part One: Riches Found and Lost 41

    Chapter 1: Treasures in the Traveler Chest 43

    Chapter 2: Blood Diamonds,
                    and a Tribe Divided 61

    Chapter 3: Mapping a Plan to Help Africa 81

    Chapter 4: Bernie and Josh: On the Road Again 109

Part Two: Quest For the Diamonds 121

    Chapter 5: The Lion Chest:
                    The Puzzle Comes Together 123

    Chapter 6: The Rhino Chest:
                    Good Beginnings 159

    Chapter 7: The Zebra Chest:
                    Shaking Off Trouble 175

    Chapter 8: The Giraffe Chest:
                    Unexpected Help 193

Chapter 9: The Cheetah Chest:
　　　　　　　Kosey Gets Schooled 213

Chapter 10: The Buffalo Chest:
　　　　　　　A Narrow Escape 229

Part Three: Battle For the Diamonds 249

Chapter 11: The Leopard Chest:
　　　　　　　The Clues are Complete 251

Chapter 12: Mount Kilimanjaro:
　　　　　　　The Dream Within Sight 271

Chapter 13: Greed Loses What it Has Gained 299

Chapter 14: Hard-Won Rewards 319

Epilogue: An Appetite for Adventure 351

Appendices 355

Appendix A: Journey Map 357

Appendix B: Character Map 359

Appendix C: Photo Album 363

Foreword

Kim Yost has gone from writing advice books to writing adventure books, and I'm not surprised. Kim makes adventure happen wherever he goes. I know, because I was there for many of those adventures. During the years we worked together, our adventures included trips to Europe, the Americas, China and Africa.

Kim came up with the idea of building life chests on his first trip to the Far East. I became involved in the project several years later when Kim and I traveled to China together. I was thrilled to read that story in *The Life Chest: China.* My trip to Africa with Kim is recounted in this book, the second in the Life Chest series. We went on safari together, along with my son-in-law Jay, nicknamed Jumbo. I must admit I'm a bit of a practical joker, and I played an elaborate trick on Kim and Jumbo which might have put them off safaris forever, or at least going on safari with me. Josh and Bernie, the main characters in the series, find the story in Kim's journal in one of the early chapters of *The Life Chest: Africa.* I never thought that silly joke would be immortalized in a novel, but now it is, and I hope you get a laugh out of it.

Even though the Life Chest books are adventure novels, Kim has a penchant for embedding powerful lessons in the stories he tells. Learnings from his *Pumptitude* books pepper the pages of *The Life Chest: China*. In *The Life Chest: Africa,* he continues that tradition using African proverbs.

I assisted Kim with the initial launch of the first life chest company, Life 2000, back in the days when we were working together. His enthusiasm for the project was contagious, and I've been a life chest fan ever since. I'm as excited as Josh and Bernie to see the life chest idea expand as it travels around the world, with the book series and the revitalization of the life chest business.

THE LIFE CHEST : AFRICA

Kim's wife Donna, whom I introduced to Kim on a blind date, is now the CEO of The Life Chest and is taking the project to new heights. She's gone so high with it that she's even jumped out of a plane on behalf of The Life Chest, with the All Veteran Parachute Team.

Donna's website states that there are three reasons to keep a life chest: for the past, for the present, and for the future. That's the beauty and the magic of the life chest, and it's why I've given them to everyone in my family. It's not just a place to hold keepsakes— it's a way to stay focused on your goals and get energized for the future.

I treasure the memories of my friendship with Kim and Donna Yost. Here's to the life chest— may we all be inspired by its message!

Dr. William Comrie
(Bill Comrie)

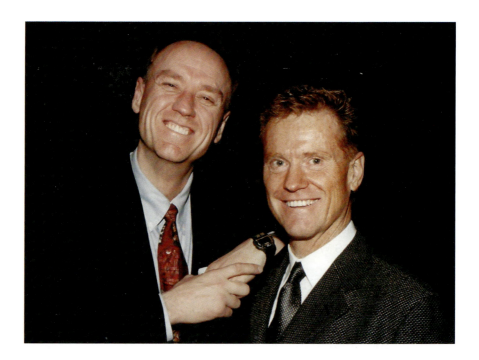

Introduction

Here we are, back on the road again! In *The Life Chest: China,* we followed our main characters, Bernie and Josh, on their trip to China to experience the origins of the life chest. It was a life-changing journey for our characters and our writing team.

After *The Life Chest: China,* the question naturally arose, "What next?" Just like Josh's granddaughter April, readers were anxious to hear more of the cousins' adventures. We're happy to tell the story. *The Life Chest: Africa* puts Bernie and Josh in the middle of another mysterious and life-threatening adventure. They travel from a safari camp in South Africa to the foot of Mount Kilimanjaro in search of life chests that hold clues to an incredible treasure. Along the way, they encounter the beauty and grandeur of Africa and the diversity and resilience of the African people. All the characters in the book experience the power, mystery and magic of the life chest.

The Life Chest: Africa continues my personal story as well. We tell of my travels in Africa, where I collected unforgettable memories for my life chest, and relate the story of how I befriended a famous painter of African landscapes. Simon, the painter, figures in Bernie and Josh's adventure as well.

After creating the concept of life chests, I began to see the length and breadth of their possibilities in every aspect of life, in every part of the world. We started the life chest legend in China, but it didn't stay there. It spread to the Americas after I met Mr. CC in Bangkok and took my first life chest home to Canada. That was one of the stories we related in *The Life Chest: China.*

The Life Chest: Africa imagines the growth of the life chest movement in Africa as generations of characters are affected by the magic of the life chest. They learn to preserve their past accomplishments, focus on the present moments, and become inspired for the future by making the life chest philosophy a part of their daily life.

To learn more about the life chest, go to thelifechest.com. As we have encouraged you to do throughout this journey, take steps to acquire your own life chest and begin to realize first hand its significance in your own life story.

A life chest is for everyone. All of us deserve to have our stories told, whether we live in Beijing, Vancouver, Detroit, Cape Town, or anywhere else on the planet. Where will the life chest take us next? One thing for sure: it will be exciting. Keep reading!

Kim Yost

Dedication

We dedicate this book to the military men and women around the world who guard our freedoms and have spent their careers and lives as liberators.

The Life Chest: Africa features the fictional General Erasto, who leaves his legacy in the original Freedom chest. He also encourages his soldiers to keep life chests, preserving their memories and inspiring generations to come.

Today, the mission of Donna Yost and The Life Chest team is to capture and share the stories of inspiring individuals impacted by military service, illness, tragedy or triumph. The present-day Freedom chest was designed with the input of U.S. Army Special Forces.

To our active duty soldiers and veterans in all branches of service: thank you, from the bottom of our hearts. We enjoy the freedom we have today because of you.

THE LIFE CHEST : AFRICA

Acknowledgements

I'd like to thank our artistic team of Terie, Agata, Donna and Kristen, who once again worked together to create an exciting and inspiring adventure for Bernie and Josh. They used their wealth of imagination and creativity to make Africa come alive in Book 2 of the Life Chest series.

We have so much appreciation for our family members who have life chests, and for the Life Chest team who continue to share the stories that help people preserve their legacies.

Our dear friend Dr. William (Bill) Comrie deserves a special mention. He wrote the foreword for this book, was in on the life chest project from the beginning, and planted the seed for Book 2 when he sponsored our first adventure in Africa. We appreciate his support, both past and present, in spreading the life chest philosophy around the world. He is truly an inspiration to many.

Kim Yost

THE LIFE CHEST : AFRICA

The African elephant: the largest animal that walks on the earth today

Prologue

Adventureland and Real Adventures

In our first book in the Life Chest series, *The Life Chest: China,* we meet Josh. We learn about his life through the stories he tells his young granddaughter, April. In 2151, 70-year-old Grandpa Josh does his best to keep up with and entertain eight-year-old April, who he calls Blossom.

As a young man, Josh's life was changed by what he discovered in his great-great-grandfather's life chest. The lessons he learned gave him purpose, a passion for living, and the tools to live his best life. Josh went from being an aimless 19-year-old dropout engaged in petty crime to a hopeful young man, eager to engage the world.

His older cousin Bernie, who had already learned many of the life chest lessons, encouraged Josh on his journey. Together they traveled to China, and using a map they found in Great-Great-Grandpa Kim's life chest, recovered a lost treasure of ancient Chinese gold coins. They returned the coins to their rightful owners and received a generous reward. Josh also discovered a love for Chinese Opera (not really—just the swords) and Bernie discovered a love for a beautiful, thoughtful young Chinese woman named Chen Li.

The Life Chest: Africa begins with Josh telling nine-year-old April more stories of the past, many of which are prompted by treasures or journals in Great-Great-Grandpa Kim's life chest. After a trip to Disneyland and a ride on the Jungle Cruise with April and Grandma Leah, Josh begins to recall his second adventure with Bernie. He shows April some African keepsakes and journals from Gramps' life chest. We learn their history, and then move into Josh and Bernie's adventure: in 2114, three years after the China trip, the cousins reunite for a trek to Africa.

Bernie is now married to Chen Li, and Josh and his wife Leah have an eight-year-old daughter, Meg.

Josh and Bernie's families help them prepare for the journey, their excitement tinged with a little, "Here we go again!" The China trip was incredible, but Josh and Bernie have a feeling that the African adventure will provide even more excitement, more danger and more reward.

"Hurry up, Grandpa!" called April as she ran ahead of Josh and Leah on the path leading out of Fantasyland.

"So whose idea was it to come to Disneyland on one of the hottest days of the year?" groaned Josh. He took off his new baseball cap, which was topped with Mickey Mouse ears, and wiped his brow with his handkerchief. Leah smiled and took Josh's hand. "That little girl can talk you into anything," she laughed. "Look what you've got on your head!"

"Hang on there, Blossom. You're running on nine-year-old legs. Give us old folks a minute to catch up." Josh walked to a shady spot with a bench. "I thought after we met Mickey, she'd be done," he said as they sat down. April ran back to join them.

"We should probably think about heading back home soon," suggested Leah, making room for April on the bench. Her granddaughter thumped down with a sigh. "Aw, Grandma," she said. "Can't we go on one more ride?"

"Your grandpa's pretty tired, honey," began Leah, but Josh interrupted. "Who, me? I'm game for one more. As long as I can sit down, that is." Leah looked around and pointed to their right.

April, Josh and Leah on the Jungle Cruise in Disneyland

"The entrance to Adventureland is right here," she said. "How about the Jungle Cruise?"

"Ooh, yes!" agreed April, jumping up. "Let's go, Grandpa!" she said, pulling him to his feet.

The trio headed to Adventureland and the Jungle Cruise, and Josh was more than ready to sit down again after a 20-minute wait in line. "Take lots of pictures, Grandma," April commanded as they settled into their seats on the boat.

Josh got a kick out of the Jungle Cruise. The ride operator told corny jokes as the boat traveled along the winding river. April giggled at the animatronic chimps and pointed at the huge elephants spraying water from their trunks as Leah snapped pictures of her wide-eyed expressions.

"Pretty good, pretty good," nodded Josh as the ride passed by a family of lions feeding on a zebra. "Looks authentic." As the boat rounded the next corner, though, Josh shook his head and laughed. "Look, Blossom. See those safari-goers? That rhino has them trapped up in a tree."

"Would a rhino really do that, Grandpa?" asked April.

"Maybe," answered Josh. "Rhinos are pretty dangerous animals."

"They're one of the big five, aren't they?" offered Leah.

April started to ask, "What's the big five?" but she was interrupted by a drenching from the waterfall the boat had gone behind.

"Well, that was refreshing, anyway," said Josh as the ride ended and the damp passengers stood up to disembark. "Hopefully we'll dry out by the time we get to the car. Oh, no!" he exclaimed. "Leah, did our tickets get wet?"

"No," answered Leah. "Don't worry. They're in my purse."

"Good." Josh was reassured. "Don't forget to put your Disneyland ticket in your life chest, Blossom," he said as they headed to the parking lot.

"I'll remember," said April. "I love my Zen Blossom life chest, Grandpa. I've put a lot of things in it since I got it for my birthday last year."

As they drove home, April wanted to hear more about the big five. Josh explained, "The big five are the five most dangerous animals in Africa. Let's see. The rhino is one, and the elephant."

"Are lions in the big five?" asked April.

"Yes," answered Leah. "And leopards."

"Ooh, I love leopards!" said April excitedly. "I think they're my favorite."

"What's the last one?" asked Josh, trying to jog his memory.

"I'm surprised you forgot," said Leah. "It's the Cape buffalo. That's the animal that killed Simon Lyons, remember?"

"I do now," said Josh wryly. "But maybe we shouldn't talk about it in front of Blossom."

"What happened? Can you tell me the story, Grandpa?" asked April soberly.

"Another time, honey," said Leah. "But Grandpa has lots of adventures he could tell you about right now."

"Did you see a buffalo kill somebody, Grandpa? Or a rhino?" April asked with wide eyes.

"No, not me," answered Josh. "That story is from one of Gramps' old journals. I can show it to you when we get home. Gramps went to Africa way back in 2002."

"I'm so glad he recorded all his trips in those journals," said Leah. "And kept them in his life chest for us to discover."

"That's for sure," agreed Josh, turning to smile at his wife. "Gramps' China journal got me and Bernie on our first adventure. It was a life changer. And after that; well, it was adventure after adventure!"

"And it wasn't just you and Bernie that went," Leah reminded him. "Chen Li and I had our share of excitement too!"

THE LIFE CHEST : AFRICA

"You did?" asked April. "When is it my turn to go on an adventure, Grandma?"

"You don't call Disneyland an adventure?" asked Josh. "The Jungle Cruise was pretty scary. Remember the lions?" Josh tried to imitate their roar while Leah laughed.

"Oh, don't be silly," said April with a frown. "That's pretend. I mean a real adventure! Hey, Grandpa, that's your house! Don't miss the turn!" she called out.

"I got it, I got it," laughed Josh as he turned into the driveway. "I promise, someday you'll have your very own adventure, Blossom." After setting the levicar in hover mode, Josh turned to his granddaughter. "Let's go dig through Gramps' life chest and find that Africa journal!" he said excitedly.

Leah gave him a look that changed his mind. "Oh. I mean after I cut up the vegetables for supper like I promised your grandma," he sighed. "Your mom and dad are going to eat with us when they come to pick you up, and there's a lot of zucchini to slice."

"Thanks, dear," said Leah as they got out of the car. "It shouldn't take long. I know how much you two enjoy looking in the life chests." She smiled, amused at her husband's newfound exuberance. He was so tired an hour ago, and now he had almost as much energy as their granddaughter!

The helpers got the zucchini prepped and deposited in the sauté pan about a half-hour later, and then made a beeline for the study. Josh opened Great-Great-Grandpa Kim's life chest and soon found the Africa journal. April dug into the chest for more treasures.

"Is this from Africa?" she asked, picking up a small bottle filled with white sand.

"No, that's sand from a beach in the Caribbean Ocean."

"How about this horn thingy?"

"That's a rhino horn trumpet, and yes, it is from Africa. Here, this is from Africa too," said Josh, holding up an ebony bust of an African tribeswoman. "Zulu, I think. Isn't it beautiful?"

The rhino horn trumpet

"Yes! Was she a queen, Grandpa?"

"Maybe. Oh, here's that little rosewood elephant. But it's not from Africa. It's an Asian elephant. Now give me a minute to look through this journal."

"Didn't Gramps have an e-tablet to write on instead of this old paper?" asked April as Josh paged through the book.

"Not the pocket-sized ones like you have now. He preferred writing on 'this old paper' anyway," said Josh.

"Okay," said April with a shrug. "Did you find a good story yet?"

"The whole thing's a good story, Blossom. You remember that Gramps was a furniture buyer for a while, right?" asked Josh. April nodded. "Well, he went to South Africa with his

THE LIFE CHEST : AFRICA

boss Bill Comrie and Bill's son-in-law Jumbo. In Cape Town, they went searching for big pieces of slate to use as tops for coffee tables and dining tables. South Africa is famous for its beautiful multicolored slate and stone. Anyway, they decided they couldn't leave Africa without going on safari. That's when you go on a trip into the wilderness to see the animals in their natural habitat."

"Did Gramps see a lot of wild animals?" asked April.

"Yup. Their safari was in a huge nature reserve, where the animals are protected. They saw all the big five. Do you remember what the big five are?"

"Hmm." April pursed her lips thoughtfully. "Lions, leopards—hippos? No, not hippos. Elephants, buffaloes and— oh! Rhinos! Like that funny scene on the Jungle Cruise!"

"That's right. The wild animals are so important in Africa that they even have them on their money. Gramps must have kept some," he added, lifting a tray from the chest and rummaging through it.

April looked over his shoulder. "Wow! Gramps collected lots of different kinds of money! That one there, Grandpa," April said as she pointed to a bill. "Is that African money?"

Josh picked up a 20-rand note. "Yes. See the elephants on it?"

"Cool," said April appreciatively. "Anything else with pictures of animals?"

"Well, take a look at this, Blossom." Josh held up a large book with a beautiful cover: a painting of an African savannah with a pride of lions in the foreground. "Of course, it's just made out of old paper. You probably don't want to bother reading it," he kidded.

"Oh, Grandpa! Can I please see it?" April asked. "Old paper's not so bad. The picture's pretty."

"Okay, I guess," said Josh, still teasing a little. "Just be careful turning the pages."

"This book is full of pictures!" said April as she gazed at the expansive landscapes and vivid renderings of African wildlife. "And here's a picture of an elephant with big ears. That's an African elephant, right? But there aren't very many words, Grandpa."

"It's not really a storybook," explained Josh. "It's a catalog of paintings, all done by Simon Lyons." He looked at the page April had been pointing to. "Yup, that's a big African elephant, Blossom. Gramps collected a lot of Simon Lyons' artwork. See that painting on the cover? It was one of his first, called Migration of the Wildebeest, and Gramps bought the original when he was in Africa."

"Wow! Where's the real painting? In the life chest?"

"No, it's in a museum now. It would be much too big to fit in a life chest anyway. Gramps discovered it hanging in the Great Hall at the safari camp he visited. He fell in love with the painting and bought it right off the wall! But there was something else— something really special— that was even better than the painting itself. Gramps found it when he got home to Canada and had the painting reframed."

Just then, Leah called from the hall. "Josh! Meg and Nathan are here! April! Time to wash up for supper!"

"What timing!" laughed Josh as April groaned.

"I want to hear the story!" she complained.

"I'll tell you after we eat," said Josh. "And then your mom and dad can hear it too, okay?"

"Okay," April sighed. "We would have had more time if we didn't have to cut up all that zucchini."

"But your Grandma tops it with fresh parmesan," said Josh. "Come on. I'm hungry!"

After dinner, April begged Josh to continue the story. "Go ahead, Dad," called Meg from the kitchen, where she and Nathan were starting the dishes. "If you sit on the loveseat, we can hear you just fine."

"And use your storyteller voice, Grandpa!" suggested April.

"Will do," agreed Josh. "If my wife sits down to rest instead of cleaning up, I'll tell the story."

"We won't let her in here," Nathan assured him. He laughed as April blocked the doorway with her best ninja pose.

"Now where was I, Blossom?" Josh asked as Leah settled in next to him.

April ninja-kicked her way over to the couch as she tried to remember. "I'm thinking. Oh, now I know! You were going to tell me what was special about the painting that Gramps brought back from Africa."

"Yup," Josh nodded. "Gramps took the painting to a local gallery to get it put in a new frame, because the original had been cracked in transit. A woman from the gallery called him later that same day. She asked him to come back down to the shop to take a look at something she had found."

As Josh talked, April's imagination took her right into the gallery, where she could hear the conversation as if she were in the room.

"Did you know there was something behind your painting?" Susan, the gallery owner, asked. "I found it behind the canvas when I took the painting out of the frame. I'm not sure what it is, but I'd like you to take a look at it before I reframe the painting."

Kim had no idea what it could be, and he hurried to the gallery. The owner took him into the workroom, where she had the painting carefully laid out on a table. Beside it was another large piece of canvas. "Here it is. It looks like another painting, sort of," she shrugged. "I found it behind the original painting when I took the backing off the frame."

They examined it together. It was a much older piece of canvas than the painting, and it wasn't decorated with watercolor or oils. A pattern that looked like winding paths had been drawn on the canvas, along with pen and ink renderings of several African animals. The top left of the map had some kind of written instructions, and names of cities and regions in South Africa, Zimbabwe, Zambia, Malawi and Tanzania were drawn on the paths. There were other small drawings of African artifacts, shaped to look like numbers, and sketches of diamonds. Kim laughed in delight.

"Did you know this was here when you bought the painting?" asked Susan.

THE LIFE CHEST : AFRICA

"No, I'm just pleased," said Kim. He knew a map when he saw one, and what a great surprise this was! Another antique map to add to his collection! "It looks like someone made a map and hid it behind the painting," he explained to Susan. "But it doesn't even look like it's finished. See, there's a big space in the middle that's entirely empty. Well, go ahead and re-frame the painting. I'll take this map home. Maybe I'll put it in my life chest."

"You certainly do bring interesting things back from your travels, Mr. Yost," Susan chuckled. "I'll let you know when the painting is ready."

"Grandpa," interrupted April, "What was the map for? What were the pictures on it? Was it a treasure map, like the one from China?"

"Gramps couldn't quite figure it out," answered Josh. "It looked like a treasure map. But it was sort of a puzzle, and all the pieces weren't there. Ever play snakes and ladders?"

April nodded.

"Well, that's kind of what the map looked like," explained Josh. "Curvy paths here and there, nothing really connecting, and a blank area in the middle. And all the animals— he figured those were just decoration. There were drawings of diamonds on the map, too. It was quite a mystery, but Gramps loved his odd treasures. He stored the map carefully for quite a few years."

"He was quite a collector, wasn't he?" commented Leah with a smile.

The puzzle map with the plate on top

"He sure was," agreed Josh. "And after buying that Simon Lyons painting, Gramps wanted more of his work. Susan, the gallery owner, helped him get more paintings, and eventually Gramps had an impressive collection. They reminded Gramps of the beauty and majesty of Africa and became some of his most treasured possessions."

"Speaking of treasured possessions, was Gramps married to Donna yet? What did she think of all this?" asked Nathan from the kitchen.

"No, he hadn't met Donna when he went to Africa. By the time they married, Kim had a house full of African artifacts and artwork. Donna loved his collections, though. Especially the Simon Lyons paintings," answered Josh.

"They got lucky one year," he continued. "I think it was 2004. Simon Lyons was planning an American tour to promote his artwork. Since Gramps had bought several of his original paintings, Simon agreed to take a detour to Canada and make a stop in Edmonton. Kim and Donna were thrilled, and I suppose Simon was excited to meet one of his biggest fans.

From what I read in Gramps' journal, he invited Simon to his home for dinner, and it was a great night. They had a wonderful meal in Kim and Donna's special wine cellar, enjoying South African red wine and trading stories for hours. Gramps sure loved to entertain in the wine cellar! Eventually they decided to stretch their legs and take a tour of the house. Gramps was eager to show Simon all his treasures from Africa, and he hoped Simon would approve of how his paintings were being displayed. I can just imagine Simon's surprise at what he saw on the wall."

As they walked around, Simon told Kim and Donna details of how each painting had come to be and what his inspiration for them had been. When they came to Migration of the Wildebeest, hung in a prominent place in the family room, Simon smiled but then sighed.

"Ah, you were certainly lucky to get a print of this painting. It was one of my first large pieces, and copies are very rare."

"But it's not a–" began Kim.

Donna interrupted. "Why is it so rare?" she asked curiously.

"Very few prints were made, that's all. The original's been hanging in the same place for decades. It's hard to get to– too much trouble to go out there, take the painting down and get more prints made. I've got other paintings that are much more popular, especially my elephant works."

"Simon, wait!" called Kim to the artist, who had already started down the hall back toward the wine cellar. "I was trying to tell you– it's not a print. It's the original."

Simon stopped and turned. "Sorry, my friend, but that can't be. If you paid for an original, I'm afraid you've been swindled. That painting is hanging over the fireplace in the Great Hall of Tanda Tula, in South Africa."

"Come on," said Kim, moving to join Simon at the other end of the hall. "Let's go back downstairs to the wine cellar and have another glass. You might need to sit down for this."

"Oh, no! Is Gramps going to get in trouble?" asked April worriedly.

Her mom and dad were done with the dishes. They came into the living room and sat on the couch next to April. Meg gave her little daughter a quick hug. "Don't worry," she said. "This just makes the story more exciting."

"It's getting pretty tense, anyway," said Josh as he turned the page of the journal. "Here's what happened next. Gramps just laid it on the line."

"Look, Simon," said Kim as he replenished their glasses. "I was in South Africa back in 2002, and my boss, his son-in-law and I went to Tanda Tula for a safari. We spent the afternoon before we went home looking for trinkets and souvenirs. At least I did. As you've seen," he said with a grin, "I do love collecting. Anyway, I wandered into the Great Hall and saw an astounding painting hanging over the fireplace. It was your Migration of the Wildebeest. I wanted it then and there, but no one was around to ask about it. Finally, I found a little boy behind the counter in the souvenir shop. He was excited when I told him I wanted to buy something, but when I took him into the Great Hall and pointed to the painting, he hesitated. Just for a moment, though. When I offered him $500, his eyes lit up and he soon figured out a way to climb up onto the mantel and hand the painting down to me. We both sneezed from the built-up dust that flew when the painting came off the wall. I gave him the money, he gave me the painting, and that was that," Kim finished with a shrug.

Simon looked stunned. "Senwe Zuma," were the only words that came out of his mouth. He said them again, louder and angrier. "Senwe Zuma!"

Senwe Zuma taking down the painting to sell to Kim

Kim and Donna looked at each other, confused and worried. What did those words mean? Were they an African curse or something? They didn't know what to do. But Simon composed himself. He sighed and smiled before saying, "Well. This is certainly a surprise. And a funny one, too. I found a painting I didn't even know was lost! And I'm pleased it's in such good hands."

Gramps was relieved that Simon seemed glad. And wasn't the painting better off in his climate controlled home than in the dusty, drafty old Great Hall at the African safari camp?

Simon stood and spoke, a bit of anxiety in his voice again. "Let's go look at the painting once more. I need to ask you something else. It's important."

THE LIFE CHEST : AFRICA

There was no more conversation as they traveled back down the hall to where the painting hung. Simon seemed to be deep in thought.

Gramps spoke up as they reached the painting. "I did have the painting reframed when I got it here," he said. "I hope you like the new frame."

"New frame?" said Simon with a start. "Oh, I see now," he said as he ran his hand over it. "I hadn't noticed it before."

"What was it you wanted to ask us?" wondered Donna.

This time Simon was the one who cut to the chase. He took a deep breath and said, "Did anyone look behind the backing when you had the painting reframed?" His voice rose a bit. "Did you find something there?"

"Yes, I did," said Kim. "It's in my life chest. Come on. I'll show it to you."

"What?" whispered Donna to Kim as they walked. "You never told me you found anything behind that painting. What in the world is it?"

"Be patient. You'll see," said Kim when they reached his office. "Come on in, Simon. Go ahead and sit down while I look through my life chest. You too, Donna," he added pointedly.

"I don't know any more than you do," murmured Donna to Simon as Kim pulled item after item out of his life chest. "Here it is," he finally said and turned around.

"That's it, all right," breathed Simon with a sigh of relief. "May I see it?"

"Sure," said Kim, moving a stack of books and spreading a large canvas drawing out on the table.

"What is it?" asked Donna impatiently. "I'm out of the loop here."

"It's the map," said Simon. "Thank goodness it's safe."

"So you know what it is?" asked Kim. "Is it a treasure map? What's it for?"

"Did you make it, Simon?" Donna wondered.

"No. I got it from an old South African soldier, a general, who I served with in the army when I was just 24. I was a pilot for the RAF," explained Simon. "The general's name was Erasto. He had this puzzle map stored in a chest somewhat like yours. He called his the Freedom chest, and got it when he was a member of the King's African Rifles. General Erasto kept all his military keepsakes in it, as well as treasures from his native village. Erasto founded Tanda Tula back in 1970 after he retired. When he died there in 1989, he left the chest and the map to me. Anyway, now that I have the map back, I can try to decipher it, finish the puzzle and find the treasure."

The Tanda Tula safari camp

"Wait," said Kim. "What do you mean, now that you have the map back? It's been sold. It belongs to me." He grabbed the map and began to roll it up.

Simon stood. He tried not to sound desperate as he spoke. "It was never meant to be sold! That boy Senwe Zuma– the little monster– he sold it without my permission! And the original painting is worth tens of thousands of dollars! Until just now, I had no idea the painting was gone from the Great Hall at Tanda Tula Safari Camp! I thought the map was still safely hidden behind it. And yes, it is a treasure map. It could be the key to the location of a large horde of diamonds."

Diamonds! I knew it, thought Donna. I saw those little diamonds drawn on the map. Now that's my kind of treasure!

"I've planned for years to decipher the map and search for the treasure. In fact, I hope to do so when I get back to Kenya. So hand it over, if you please," said Simon.

"Nope," answered Kim firmly as he held the map more tightly.

Simon was taken aback. "You really won't give it to me?" he asked. The artist sighed and then suddenly seemed to deflate, sitting down with a sad thump. "Oh, what's the use?" he groaned. "I'll probably never find the diamonds anyway. I'm still trying to get enough money to finance the expedition, but even if I could manage it, then what? Look at it. Go ahead; I won't try to take it. Look." Kim laid the map out on the table once again.

"See?" said Simon, gesturing to the random-looking paths on the canvas. "The parts don't connect— and I don't know how to solve the puzzle." He leaned back in his chair, face in his hands.

Now it was Donna's turn to scrutinize the map. "There's a whole section missing in the middle," she said, circling it with her finger. "It's like a piece that someone erased."

"When he was on his deathbed, my old friend the general told me two more clues that were supposed to help me put all this together."

"Did you write them down? Where are they?" asked Donna gently.

"I've never forgotten them," Simon answered. "But even if I could decipher the map, there's much more to the puzzle. General Erasto set up a complicated scheme to find the diamonds, but it was so many years ago. I don't know. It's probably impossible." Simon dropped his head again. "So keep the map for your collection. I guess I don't care anymore."

Kim spoke up. "Simon, you misunderstood me," he reassured the artist. "I'm certainly not the kind of guy to discourage an adventure. I'll give you back the map when I see you in Kenya. Donna and I are going to join you on this trip! We'll help you fund the expedition, and figure out the puzzle!"

Kim and Donna with Simon in their wine cellar

"Are you serious?" asked Simon in surprise. "This could be a very dangerous adventure."

Donna was a little surprised at Kim's announcement as well, but she hid it with a smile and a laugh, saying, "We've both traveled around the world, Simon. And not always in luxury hotels, believe me. We're up for this."

"Well, all right then," said Simon. "I'm delighted at this new development. Especially since five minutes ago I thought our relationship might come to blows."

"Not a chance," said Kim, shaking Simon's hand. "Let's drink one final toast for the night. Everyone still have their wine glasses? To the adventure of a lifetime!"

"And the diamonds!" added Donna.

"That's not the end of the story, is it, Grandpa? What happened next?" asked April, jumping up and down on the couch.

"April! Grandpa and Grandma's couch is not a trampoline!" scolded Nathan.

"Well, Blossom," said Josh as April climbed off the couch and apologetically readjusted the cushions. "This is where the sad part of the story comes in. They did start to plan the trip, but soon after Simon got back to Kenya, he was killed by a Cape buffalo."

"He was just taking a walk in the hills of the Great Rift Valley with his wife, thinking about his next painting, I suppose," added

Leah. "The buffalo attacked without warning and Simon died before his wife could get him to a hospital. I guess when Gramps heard about it, he must've been very sad."

"I'm sure he was," agreed Josh. "Not only did he lose a chance to search for diamonds in Africa, he lost a man who had become a good friend in a very short time."

"So that's it? The story's over?" asked April sadly. "That's the first story you ever told me that doesn't have a happy ending, Grandpa."

Meg gave her dad a pleading look, which seemed to ask: Wasn't there anything else he could add? Something that would cheer April up?

"Hmm," Josh said thoughtfully, rubbing his chin. "There is one more thing I forgot to tell you. Simon left something behind with Kim and Donna. A big dinner plate."

"A dinner plate?" asked April, brightening up a bit. "Why? What was it for?"

"It's a bit of a mystery, Blossom. On the way to Edmonton, the airline lost some of Simon's painting supplies, including his favorite palette. He wanted to make some color sketches, so he used a hotel restaurant plate for a palette. He had his paints and the palette with him that night at Gramps' house. According to Gramps' journal, before Simon left to go back to the hotel, he painted three mysterious looking shapes around the edge of the plate, did a few more animal drawings on it, and drew an eye in the middle. I think it was a lion's eye. Anyway, he gave the plate to Gramps and told him to be sure to bring it with him when he and Donna came to Kenya. He said the plate contained those two missing clues that Erasto told him just before he died. After Simon was killed, Gramps had the plate framed, and it hung in his house for years."

THE LIFE CHEST : AFRICA

"Where's the plate now? And the puzzle map?" asked April.

"The puzzle map is back in Africa where it belongs," answered Josh. "And guess what? The plate is hanging downstairs in our family room!"

"I want to see it!" shouted April, hopping up and down.

"Not tonight, April. Better get your jacket. It's past your bedtime," said Nathan.

April and Josh both pouted.

"Sorry, Dad," Meg laughed. "Next time for sure, April."

"But can you tell me how the map got back to Africa after Gramps had it?" asked April.

"Oh, that's much too long of a story for tonight, honey," said Meg. "It really is time to go home."

Nathan picked April up and swung her onto his back. "Come on, cowgirl! Off to the wagon!" he said, galloping to the door.

"Thanks for dinner, Mom and Dad," said Meg as she hugged her parents. "The zucchini was delicious."

After saying goodbye to the family and closing the door, Josh shook his head and laughed. "That Blossom! She really keeps us hopping, doesn't she?"

"Yes," agreed Leah. "And your stories get her even more wound up. When are you going to tell her the next part? About how the puzzle map got back to Africa in the hands of you and Bernie, finishing another one of Gramps' adventures?"

"Oh, one day when she's really bored, I guess," chuckled Josh. "I've got to save some of the exciting stories."

"They're all exciting," said Leah, kissing him on the cheek. "That's my life with an adventurer!"

THE LIFE CHEST : AFRICA

Part One

Riches Found And Lost

AFRICA

THE LIFE CHEST : AFRICA

Chapter One

Treasures in the Traveler Chest

"Hey Mom, we're back!" called Bernie as he followed Chen Li through the kitchen door of his parents' cozy Brooklyn home. Josh and Leah brushed snow off each other. An impromptu snowball fight had taken place between them and their eight-year-old daughter Meg on the walk back from ice-skating. "That was a lot of fun, wasn't it, Meg?" asked Josh as he helped his little girl out of her snowsuit.

"Yes, Daddy!" answered Meg. "And it didn't even hurt very much when I fell down!"

Bernie's mother Ruby hung up scarves and coats as they talked. "I remember the first time your uncle Bernie went skating," Ruby said to Meg. "He just kept getting back up again every time he fell down."

"I took a couple of spills today, too," admitted Bernie. "It was fun, though. I can't believe the pond is still there in back of Martinelli's."

"It's nice that some things don't change," said Chen Li, hugging Bernie. "And it's nice that some things do," countered Bernie, kissing his wife on the forehead. "A few years ago I never would've imagined I'd be married and living in New York City."

"And I never would've imagined that you'd get a catch like Chen Li," joked Josh, punching his cousin on the shoulder. Leah rolled her eyes at her husband's teasing, and laughed as Bernie started a pantomime sword fight that made its way into the living room.

Then Meg sneezed and Leah glanced down at her daughter. "Meg, honey, you're shivering," she said as she crouched down to the little girl's level.

"I'll get her sweater and then we'll make some hot cocoa," offered Ruby. "Okay, Meggie? You all just relax for a bit. We'll have dinner when Bernie's dad gets home from work."

"Thanks," said Leah. "I'd better try to find some hot-cold cream, if you don't mind. Josh fell a couple times too!"

"Are you sure you don't need any help?" Chen Li asked her mother-in-law.

"Not right now, thanks," Ruby answered. "You know I love puttering around the kitchen. I'm really glad we were able to coordinate a few days together during Christmas break."

"Don't worry. I'll help Aunt Ruby if she needs it," Meg chimed in.

A little while later, the two young couples had settled into chairs and couches in the study on the lower level of the house. This was Josh and Bernie's favorite room because it contained all the family's life chests. Ruby was the life chest keeper for her family and the room held chests going back five generations. The keepsakes, pictures and journals in the life chests and the stories they represented were the most precious treasures the family owned.

Bernie and Chen Li shared a few stories from their honeymoon in China the previous summer, and talked about Bernie's teaching job in NYC. "I'm still getting used to life in the States," said Chen Li. "But I love it. It looks like I'll make the dean's list for my first semester at college."

"Congratulations! You two have had a lot of life chest memories in the last year, that's for sure," said Josh.

"It all started with that one, didn't it?" asked Leah, pointing to Great-Great-Grandpa Kim's life chest.

"You know it," said Josh. He got up from the easy chair and lifted the lid of the old Traveler chest. "The keepsakes and the memories in Gramps' life chest are always going to inspire me. Bernie, remember this little Asian elephant?" he said, holding up a wooden figurine. "Our China adventure began right here," he continued, reaching for one of Gramps' journals.

"I'm glad your Gramps kept all those journals," agreed Leah. "They're such a great resource."

"Which one is that?" asked Chen Li. "Is it a China journal?"

Josh opened the cover. "Hey, this one is from a trip he took to Africa, back in 2002."

"Was he buying furniture again?" asked Leah.

"Yes," answered Josh, paging through the small book. "With his boss, Bill Comrie, and Bill's son-in-law Jumbo."

"That book is bound to have some good stories," said Bernie excitedly.

"You guys go ahead and dig in," said Chen Li, standing up. "I'm sure Ruby can use some help in the kitchen now."

Leah got up too. "Especially with Meg to look after," she said. "You'll have kid duty after dinner. Okay, Josh?"

"Sure, Leah," Josh answered. But he and Bernie were already halfway to Cape Town as they read the details of Gramps' Africa trip.

"The safari camp they went to in South Africa—Tanda Tula—it looks really amazing," said Bernie as he paged through a camp brochure while Josh looked at the journal.

"Gramps said here that you really go on two different safaris in Africa. A safari is completely different during the day than it is at night," said Josh.

"That makes sense," said Bernie. "The animal behavior will be different, and unpredictable, and—" He stopped at Josh's laughter. "What's so funny?"

"Apparently the human behavior in Africa is pretty unpredictable too. Or maybe it was just Gramps' crazy friends. Listen to what his boss did!" Josh read Gramps' words from the journal.

Our first day on safari was exciting. We got pretty close to a herd of elephants and saw a lot of impala, but what I really wanted to see was lions. Our guide Dale assured us that there were lions in the area, and if we got out early the next morning, we might be able to spot some. I was ready before anyone else the next day. Bill was the last one in the Land Rover after breakfast. He looked kind of tired. Little did I know why.

The Land Rover started along the road, and we were off. After traveling for a mile or so, Bill pointed to the side of the road. "What's that?" he said. It was a pith helmet lying in the grass. We figured the wind must have blown it off someone's head and they didn't bother to retrieve it. After a few hundred yards, Bill pointed again. "Look!" he yelled. Along the side of the road were a few broken small trees and some tire tracks veering off to one side. It looked as if a Land Rover had gone off the normal trail. "Stop right here," Bill said to the driver. "Come on, you guys," he said urgently. "Somebody might be in trouble. Let's go see what happened."

We piled out of the Land Rover and made our way through the brush, following the tire tracks. We followed the tracks as they made a curve to the left and then saw a terrible sight. A Land Rover was tipped on its side and evidence of an attack was everywhere. "Oh, my God," breathed Jumbo. "There are people here." A mangled leg protruded from underneath the vehicle. Torn and bloody clothes were strewn around. A body, that looked to be half-eaten, laid face down a few feet from where I stood.

"Was it a lion attack?" I turned and asked the guide.

"Of course it was lions!" said Bill. "What else could it be? You still want to see them up close now?"

"Let's get out of here!" yelled Jumbo, running back to the road. I started to follow him, but then turned back to look at Bill. He wasn't running. In fact, he was just standing there with a really odd look on his face. "Well, it might not have been lions," he grinned.

Kim in Africa on a safari with Bill and Jumbo

"What do you mean?" I asked.

"It could have been hyenas," said Bill. "Laughing hyenas. You know how they love a good joke." Bill reached down and picked up the dead body. I was horrified, until I saw that it was a dummy— just a suit of clothes stuffed with grass. Bill looked at my expression and started laughing like a hyena himself.

"Oh boy, did I get you guys!" he said. "I came out here late last night and set all this up. The Land Rover, the bloody clothes, the dummies— all fake. Dale was in on it too. You should have seen your face. Jumbo's was the best. Hey, you!" he yelled in Jumbo's direction. "Get back here, dummy! I got another dummy to show you!"

Jumbo came back, but he wouldn't speak to Bill for the rest of the day. I just shook my head. I guess your average safari wasn't enough for Bill. He had to have a practical joke, too. It was never a dull moment with these guys!

"Wow! That's hilarious!" chuckled Josh, wiping his eyes as he laughed. He set the journal down. "Now that's a level of practical joke to really aspire to!"

Bernie frowned. "Don't get any ideas, funny man. Note to self: do not go on an African safari with Josh."

"Aw, why not?" asked Josh. "Wouldn't it be amazing to go to Africa? Look at all the awesome stuff that Gramps brought back."

Bernie picked up an object from the chest that looked like it was made out of a horn. "Does it say in the journal what this is?" he asked.

"I think so," answered Josh, paging through the journal. "I know he bought a lot of souvenirs at that safari camp, Tanda Tula. He describes an open air market where local artisans sold their goods. Oh, here it is. That trumpet was made out of a rhino horn, believe it or not. And see that figurine of the woman?"

The Tanda Tula market where local artisans sell their trinkets

"This bust?" asked Bernie, picking it up. "It's made of real ebony, I think. He got that at Tanda Tula too? It's gorgeous."

"So are the paintings in this catalog," said Josh. "This is some good art."

As Josh looked through the catalog, Bernie picked up the journal. "Gramps says here that he bought a painting on that trip. He had a kid pull it down right off the wall and sell it to him. It was by an artist named Simon Lyons. Are there any Simon Lyons paintings in that catalog?" he asked.

"Yeah," answered Josh. "The whole catalog is Simon Lyons."

"Hey, look what else it says," said Bernie excitedly. "When Gramps got the painting reframed, he found a map behind it."

"No kidding? What was the map for?" asked Josh.

"What was it for? A map secretly hidden behind a painting?" asked Bernie. "There's only one thing it could be for."

"Treasure! Another treasure map!" shouted Josh. "Where is it? It's gotta be in the life chest, right? Come on, let's look!"

Both Josh and Bernie turned their attention back to Gramps' life chest and the possibility of finding another ancient artifact. "Careful," cautioned Bernie. "There's a lot of fragile stuff in here. Let's just take things out one at a time." Stifling his excitement, Josh took a deep breath and carefully lifted out item after item from the Traveler chest.

"We could spend weeks just looking at everything in here and reading Gramps' journals," said Bernie, as he examined an envelope full of South African paper money.

"I know," agreed Josh. "It's kind of our life's work, isn't it? Here, look at this." He held up a small figurine depicting an African tribesman holding a shield and spear. "I wonder what tribe this fellow is from."

After about 15 minutes of careful digging, the Traveler chest had revealed many of its artifacts to Josh and Bernie, but not an African treasure map. Sitting on the floor, Josh leaned back against the easy chair and stretched. "I don't know, Bernie," he said. "I don't think it's in there."

"Oh, well," said Bernie. "It would've been interesting to look at." He stood up and yawned. "I guess we better start putting all this stuff back," he said as he picked up Gramps' Africa journal.

A piece of paper fluttered out of the book. "What's that?" asked Josh, catching it on its way to the floor.

"Another journal entry?" asked Bernie.

"I guess so," said Josh. "It's in his handwriting. It looks like he wrote it a couple of years after he went to Africa. It's dated 2004. Why do you think he put it in his Africa journal?"

"Let's read it and see," said Bernie, sitting down again. Bernie and Josh spent the next half hour discovering the story of how Gramps met Simon Lyons and made plans with him to go back to Africa after Simon told Kim and Donna about the meaning of the puzzle map and gave them the plate. They learned about General Erasto, the diamonds, and the plight of the African people.

"Wow!" said Josh, shaking his head. "Simon didn't even realize his painting was gone and the puzzle map was missing until he just happened to meet Gramps and found out that the map was in his life chest. How crazy is that?"

"Pretty crazy," agreed Bernie. "Even crazier is the fact that Gramps had another treasure map. This was different from China, though. Gramps really did have a plan to go to Africa with Simon and search for those diamonds. What a tragedy that Simon was killed."

"Bernie," said Josh. "We haven't emptied out Gramps' entire chest yet. Let's keep looking. The puzzle map's pointing to a real treasure. The fact that Gramps and Simon Lyons were willing to set up an expedition to find the diamonds proves it. There could still be an actual treasure out there waiting to be found!"

"And we're just the guys to find it," grinned Bernie. "Hang on," he said as he ran his hand along the inside of the life chest. "I've got a hunch."

Josh looked closely at what his cousin was concentrating on. When Bernie got to the right hand inside wall of the chest, he found what he was looking for. "Right here, Josh," he said excitedly. "There's some give to this section. If I wiggle it, then maybe… yes! We've got ourselves a secret compartment!"

"Way to go, Doc!" said Josh as Bernie carefully lifted out the panel. Sure enough, a large rolled up piece of canvas had been squeezed in behind it.

Bernie carefully unrolled it and spread it out on the floor. "It's the puzzle map— just how Gramps described it in his journal!" Bernie said. "The pictures, the paths—"

"And that part in the middle that's been erased," Josh interrupted.

"Yeah," said Bernie. "That was supposed to confuse anybody who tried to steal the map."

"And now it's confusing me," said Josh. "How are we supposed to figure out what goes there?"

"Well, Simon knew the missing clues, right?" asked Bernie. "And didn't Gramps say in his journal that Simon wrote them down somewhere?"

"Yes!" said Josh, energized again. "He painted those two clues on a plate. A dinner plate from the hotel he was staying at. And Gramps kept it for safekeeping." Josh lifted the last few items from the Traveler chest. "It's not here. What could've happened to it?"

"You'd think he would've kept it with the map," said Bernie. "Maybe it got broken. Too bad."

Josh sighed, deflated. "And I was all ready for another adventure."

"Oh, well," said Bernie. "Let's go show the family the map, anyway. It should make for some good dinner conversation."

"Okay," said Josh. "After we eat, I'll bring Meg down to show her some of Gramps' treasures. She can help me put all this stuff away, too."

Talking that evening, everyone agreed that the puzzle map was an amazing thing to find in Gramps' life chest, especially in a secret compartment. Looking at it really gave a sense of the beauty and grandeur of Africa and its animals. The mystery was intriguing, too. It was obvious from what the map showed that there was a treasure of diamonds near Mount Kilimanjaro, and the clues that a searcher would need to find the diamonds were spread out among the locations on the map. But long ago, General Erasto had rubbed out two of the clues in the center of the map.

According to Gramps' journal, Simon had painted those clues on a plate he was using as a palette. That's where the mystery seemed to come to a dead end. The plate wasn't in Gramps' life chest with the puzzle map.

The next morning, Ruby and Chen Li spent some time in the life chest room while the rest of the family walked the dogs. Ruby opened her life chest to look for a necklace she wanted to give Chen Li. She found a small jewelry box and picked through it. "I hope you like this stone, Chen Li. My grandmother gave it to me. I want you to have it because it's your birthstone." Ruby held up a nicely firing opal that hung on a delicate chain.

"It's beautiful," said Chen Li with a smile. "Thank you."

"My life chest isn't packed with amazing things like Gramps' is," Ruby laughed.

"The guys really have fun going through his keepsakes," said Chen Li. "It's too bad they couldn't find the plate that goes with the African puzzle map."

"Hmm," said Ruby thoughtfully. "Let me think about this for a minute. Didn't Bernie say that according to the journal, Gramps hung the plate in his house as a decoration? It might not ever have been put into his life chest. It might've hung on that wall the rest of his life."

"What would have happened to it after that?" asked Chen Li. "Would it have been sold? Given away?"

"Given away is more likely," said Ruby. "The question is, who would it have been given to? This family tends to hang on to its keepsakes and hand them down from generation to generation, as you can see," she said, gesturing to the life chests that filled the study.

"That's right!" said Chen Li, enjoying the mystery. "Who was the next generation?"

"That would be Gramps' daughter Ashley." Ruby pointed to the Havana chest. "There's her life chest. Do you want to do the honors?"

"Sure!" Chen Li lifted the lid of the sleek Havana chest. "I don't think I've ever looked through Ashley's life chest. Let's see if that plate got handed down to her."

After a few minutes of searching, the two women struck pay dirt. "This might be it!" said Chen Li excitedly, as she lifted a wrapped disc from the life chest. She held her breath as Ruby unwrapped it. Sure enough, it was a plain dinner plate decorated with a hand painted cheetah and three giraffes, as well as a few scrawled phrases and symbols. "I can't believe it!" she said. "Won't Bernie and Josh be surprised?"

"Don't tell them yet," said Ruby. "Let's set it on the table at lunch and see how long it takes them to notice it."

Her daughter-in-law laughed. "Bernie probably won't notice it at all," she said. "He's such an absent-minded professor!"

Sure enough, when lunchtime came around, the family sat at the kitchen table for about five minutes before the truth came out. Bernie couldn't figure out what his mother and wife were grinning about until he looked down at the plate on which he was about to plop a scoop of tuna salad.

"Whoa! Is this what I think it is? Mom! Chen Li! How did you find it?" asked Bernie.

"And where did you find it? We practically took Gramps' chest apart!" insisted Josh.

"Simple logic, Son," answered Ruby. "We found it in Ashley's life chest."

"Good thinking," said Bernie's dad Matt. He picked up the plate. "This is an amazing piece of work. Beautiful art."

"Art, schmart!" said Josh. "This is the key to the puzzle map!" he yelled as he bounded down the stairs to the study. "Let's look at it with the map right now!"

"Let me eat something first!" Bernie called down the stairs after his cousin. "You're probably going to keep me up all night with this thing and I need my strength!"

After lunch, Bernie and Josh laid the puzzle map out on the kitchen table. Josh held the plate carefully in his hands. Leah and Chen Li watched in anticipation. "Okay, Doc. Now what?" Josh asked.

"Just set the plate on top of the map, I guess," said Bernie. "Let's see what we see."

"This is really exciting," said Leah. "It's the first time anyone's put these two sets of clues together."

Josh set the plate in the center of the puzzle map. "I just hope it gives us what we need to know," he said. "I guess it faces this way?"

"With the sketches of the cheetah and the giraffes facing the same way as the others? Yeah, that makes sense," said Bernie.

"And look at those three triangles around the edge of the plate," added Chen Li. "They coincide with the paths on the map."

"That's it, all right," said Bernie. "Now we've got all the locations that were originally on the puzzle map. Look," he said as he followed along the path with his finger. "You start at the safari camp at Tanda Tula, in the Timbavati Game Reserve. Then you travel through all these places and finally get to the foot of Mount Kilimanjaro."

"It was the two cities in the middle that were missing," said Leah. "They're both in Malawi, it looks like. But what do the pictures of the animals mean? And the places that are described on the map? I get it that you start at the safari camp. But what about this next picture on the path? It's a rhino, and it says 'locate rhino hospital.' Is it in Zimbabwe?"

"And the next one is a zebra, and it says 'football club' next to it," said Josh. "And the word 'Lusaka'."

"Those must be the places you have to go to get the clues that will help you find the diamonds at Mount Kilimanjaro," said Chen Li. "Maybe the word 'zebra' is part of the name of that football club."

"Or the zebra is their mascot," added Bernie.

Leah looked more closely at the map. "There's an agricultural school listed, and a cultural center, and another school, and an animal rehab center."

"What's the next animal after the zebra?" asked Bernie. "Is it the giraffe or the elephant?"

"I think it's the giraffe," said Josh. "Look at these little drawings that are scattered all over the puzzle map. See the spear by the lioness? It's a number one. That snake by the rhino is a number two. The buffalo horns by the zebra are in the shape of a three. Can you see it?"

"Oh, sure," said Bernie. "I see it now. There's a four by the giraffes and a five above the cheetah, made of spears and knives."

Ruby and Matt, who was carrying Meg on his back, came into the kitchen. "How's it going?" asked Ruby as Matt put Meg down so she could climb into her mom's lap.

"It's pretty exciting," said Leah. "Meg, don't touch. Use your eyes, not your hands." She pointed to the small sketch next to the drawing of the Cape buffalo. "Do you see this? It's a snake and an ostrich egg, but does it look like a number to you? Trace it in the air with your finger."

Meg did so. "It's a six, Mom!" she said proudly.

"You're right, honey," said Leah. "And here's a seven and eight. I think it's pretty clear the order these clues go in." She turned back to Josh and the others. "But what about the places themselves? I wonder if they're still there. This map was made so long ago."

"Good question," said Matt. "That would be something to research."

Bernie looked at his dad quizzically. "Why?" he asked. "Do you think we should go there? To Africa?"

"Yes!" said Josh before Matt could answer. "Of course we should go there! Isn't that what you mean, Uncle Matt?"

"Well, I just wonder," said Matt. "It might be worthwhile. But it would be difficult. Even if you can find all the locations where the clues are supposed to be, you still have to find the clues themselves."

"There's supposed to be a chest at every stop, according to the map," said Chen Li. "That's where the clues are stored. Who knows if they're all still there?"

"They could be," Josh insisted. "Like we read in Gramps' journal— if these people had a mission to keep their clue safe and wait for someone to come get it, wouldn't they do it? Especially if it meant they would get a share of the diamonds? I sure would. And I'd make sure my descendants knew about it, too."

"Sometimes you make sense, Josh," said Bernie, nodding his head.

"Every once in a while," agreed Josh with a smile. "But listen." He stopped smiling. "I'm serious. It's simple. We follow the puzzle map and go to each city, from Tanda Tula in the south on up to Mount Kilimanjaro. At each location we find the cause. That's the school or the hospital or whatever. And we'll know it's the right one because they'll have their animal symbol displayed somewhere. Once we get there we look for a chest, like a life chest, I guess. The clue, whatever it is, will be inside the chest. Once we've collected all the clues, we'll be at the foot of Mount Kilimanjaro, where the diamonds are supposed to be. All the clues put together should tell us exactly where to find them."

Josh reached for the plate and held it up for everybody to see. "We've got all the information! We've got the puzzle map, and thanks to Aunt Ruby and Chen Li, we've got the plate too. We can pick up where Gramps left off after Simon Lyons was killed. What do you think?"

There was silence in the room for a minute. This would be a really big adventure. It would cost money, probably take several weeks, and would involve a lot of planning. Nobody knew exactly where to start.

Chen Li broke the silence. "I think you and Bernie should go," she said in her simple, direct way. "The diamonds might be obtainable. There is no way to find out for sure unless you go. It's doable, Bernie," she said to her husband. "You told me yourself your department head didn't want to give you any upcoming classes because you're overdue for a semester off. Make him happy and take a break."

"Okay, okay. I hear you," said Bernie with a smile.

"I agree with Chen Li," said Bernie's dad. "You might never get the chance to do this again. Leah, would you let Josh go?"

"He doesn't need my permission," laughed Leah. "But yeah. We've got some investors' meetings coming up for the foundation we started with Catherine, and I can handle those."

"Thanks, Babe!" Josh jumped up and kissed his wife on the cheek. "Last time gold coins, this time diamonds!"

"But Josh, this is different," Ruby reminded him. "If you find these diamonds, they're for a specific purpose: to help all those causes."

"I know, Aunt Ruby," Josh reassured her. "Just the hunt itself will be enough to keep me happy. And did you see what's written on the map, at the top in the middle?"

Ruby looked closer at the map and read the saying out loud. "Greed loses what it has gained." She looked back at Josh and Bernie. "That's right. It's a good lesson."

Meg stared at her great-aunt. "Grown-ups have lessons, too?" she asked.

"Oh, yes," laughed Ruby.

"Hopefully we never stop learning, honey," said Josh.

"We have a lot to learn about Africa now, if we're going to do this," added Bernie.

"Well, get started, Doc! I know you're chomping at the bit to do some research!" said Josh. "I promised Meg I'd play her new video game with her. When she's done beating me I'll join you." He picked Meg up and tossed her onto his shoulders. "What kind of animal am I, kiddo?"

"You're a hippo!" giggled Meg.

"A hippo? Did you hear that, Leah? A hippo. I don't even know what kind of noise they make."

"Find out for me when you go to Africa, Dad! Now giddyup!" Meg commanded as they tromped down the hall, ready for adventure.

Chapter Two

Blood Diamonds, and a Tribe Divided

"The Traveler chest is back from traveling," said Josh, affectionately patting the lid of the old life chest that held the treasures of Great-Great-Grandpa Kim. "At least for now, anyway."

Josh, April, April's dad Nathan, Bernie and Chen Li sat in the life chest room of Bernie and Chen Li's home in upstate New York. "Bernie, I really appreciate you letting me keep Gramps' chest at my house for a while. You're the life chest keeper for the family, and if you wanted to, I guess you could keep all these life chests locked up tight," said Josh.

"He wouldn't ever do that," insisted Chen Li. "Not after he saw what it did to my family in China. Selfishness is so destructive."

"That's true, Chen Li," said Josh. "And you and Bernie are the most generous people I know. Thanks for letting Nathan and April and I stay for a couple days."

"Well, thanks for lugging the life chest all the way back from California. I'm glad it travels back and forth between us," said Bernie. "I know how much you and April love to look at the keepsakes in it."

April looked up from her coloring book to chime in. "I love Grandpa's stories about things in the life chests. They're better than movies!"

"Meg and I love them too," added Nathan. "No matter what Josh pulls out of that chest, there's an amazing story attached to it."

"Yup," agreed Bernie. "That's why we keep life chests. To keep our stories alive and close to us. And to share the treasures, too."

"Remember the African proverb?" asked Chen Li. "Greed loses what it has gained."

"I'll never forget it," said Bernie. He lifted the lid of the Traveler chest and soon found a small ebony bust of an African woman.

"That's pretty, Uncle Bernie!" exclaimed April.

"It sure is, April," agreed Bernie. "This bust reminds me of the woman who was the first to tell us about that proverb."

"Blossom, Gramps got that bust when he was in Africa. I'm not sure when it was made, but it's really old," said Josh.

"I think it was made in the very early 1900s," said Bernie. "Didn't Gramps say in his journal that it belonged to the old general? General Erasto?"

"Yeah, that's right," said Josh. "General Erasto had a chest he called the Freedom chest, Blossom. It was full of his treasures, and it ended up at the safari camp, Tanda Tula, where Gramps went one time to see lots of African animals."

"And then Gramps bought it for his life chest," said April. "Is the Freedom chest like a life chest?"

"Yes it is, April," said Chen Li. "I think people everywhere want to keep their memories and keepsakes safe, just like your family here and my family in Bangkok."

"I wonder if the statue was General Erasto's wife," said April.

"He was never married," answered Josh. "I remember the story now. The bust was made in memory of his mother. It was carved by a wise man in his tribe who helped care for him. This man was a shaman— a healer— who cared deeply about his village and its people. It's quite a story."

The ebony bust carving, made by Duma

In a Zulu village in South Africa, near what would later become the Kimberley diamond mine called "The Big Hole," there was a man named Dumaka Dia, who was born in 1843. He was known to have special empathic abilities from a young age. Because of this, he was trained as a shaman. Duma, as he was called, became a wise, compassionate leader of the tribe.

Life was full and happy for Duma as he served his tribe as healer and adviser over the years. He never married or had children, but felt a kinship to all in the tribe. Everything changed, however, when diamonds were discovered near the village in 1890. Money, greed and big business came into the picture.

British businessmen and diamond miners took over the area. They had no compassion or sympathy for the Zulu people who had been living and working in the same place, in the same way, for hundreds of years. They cared very little about the people whose homes, livelihoods and traditions they destroyed.

Duma's people were forced to work in the mines. They reaped none of the benefits and wealth that the mine owners did. Much of the profits gained from the diamonds were used to finance wars and genocide, giving them the name "blood diamonds." On top of that, the people were forced to work in terrible conditions. Food and water were heavily rationed. Diseases such as cholera and dysentery ran rampant. Many workers died in the mines, including a husband and wife who were close friends of Duma. The day he heard about the cave-in that killed his friends was one of the most difficult of Duma's life, because he had to tell his friends' six-year-old son that his mother and father were not coming back from the mine. Duma cared for the young boy, Onani Madaki, from that day in 1900 on.

Duma hoped that the boy, whom he called Ona, would have the empathy and compassion to become a shaman, like him. Ona, however, was restless and impatient. Duma loved him regardless and did his best to raise the child to be a productive member of the tribe.

Duma's time as Ona's guardian came to an abrupt end, however. When Ona was 10 years old, he was taken away from Duma by the mine owners and forced to work as a child soldier. He was given a gun and the responsibility for guarding the workers in the mines who were being kept there by force. Ona's childhood was cut short, and he grew to be a bitter and selfish young man. Duma could no longer spend time with him. As a result, Ona no longer had any positive influence in his life.

In 1910, when Ona was 16, there came a point of no return. He had watched his people be mistreated for years. As a young boy, there was nothing he could do to help them, and as a young man, his heart became hardened. Instead of wanting to make the working conditions easier for the miners, Ona took money and favors to look the other way while they were beaten and robbed. He graduated from a child soldier to a paid thug. Eventually, Ona worked for a white mine foreman named Bradley, as his assistant and bodyguard. He had fully betrayed his people, and it broke Duma's heart.

Another boy, Erasto Okoro, was born in the village in 1903, to a couple who farmed a few acres of land near the diamond mine. The year that Erasto was 10 years old, Bradley, the mine foreman, showed up at the farm with his young henchman Ona. They told Erasto's father that his land would be taken over as part of the diamond mining operation. A small amount of money was offered as compensation, but it was nowhere near what the land was worth. Besides, Erasto's parents did not want to leave their land. They refused to give up their farm and told Bradley and Ona to leave. They did, but not for long. The mine owners did not put up with insubordination. Ona was instructed to go back to the farm that night and kill Erasto's father. He did, in front of the farmer's wife and son. Ona was 19 years old, and now a murderer.

Erasto's mother was immediately taken to work in the mine. Ona dragged the stunned child, Erasto, through the streets. He would take him to the mine as well, since he was just the right age to be a child soldier. Duma, praying in his hut, heard the screams of the young boy as Ona pulled him along. Looking out at what was happening, Duma was shocked to see his former foster son.

"Ona!" he called as he hurried forward.

"Go away, old man," snarled Ona. "This is my business, not yours."

"This child is of my tribe. It is my business. I will not say your tribe, since you abandoned us long ago. Where are you taking him?"

"To the mine," Ona answered. "He'll guard the workers, like I did at his age."

THE LIFE CHEST : AFRICA

"He will not," countered Duma. "I could not keep you from this life, but I can save another. Where are his parents?"

"His foolish father is dead, and his mother has been taken to the mine. This boy is valuable to me, Duma. If you want him, you must pay. I'll negotiate." With an evil grin, Ona pushed Erasto to the ground. The child huddled fearfully in the dirt at Ona's feet and looked at Duma pleadingly.

"People cannot be for sale," said Duma. "But if it will keep you from taking this boy, I am willing to give you everything I have."

"I have no use for your talismans and trinkets," laughed Ona. "But let's go into your dwelling." He pulled Erasto up, and they walked toward Duma's hut. "I'll take anything of gold and precious stone that you have and I'll leave the boy with you. It's a stupid bargain on your part. I hope you are happy with it."

Duma, the Zulu shaman, pleading with Bradley and Ona

Over the next few years, Duma was much happier with Erasto than he would have been with any amount of gold and precious stones. He watched over the boy and taught him spiritual truths. Duma pleaded with the mine foreman to release Erasto's mother from the mine, but he refused. Erasto rarely saw her. He kept busy helping Duma, who was now 60 years old, and learning the ways of the shaman. Duma was called on to do very little now as the village counselor and healer, since most of the people were virtual prisoners of the mine owners. Duma begged the owners, and Ona, to release the people or at least treat them more humanely. His pleas fell on deaf ears.

Ona relished his role as Bradley's right-hand man and recruited others in the tribe to assist the mine owners in their exploitation of the people. To an unscrupulous man, it seemed like a good deal: to get out of the hardships of working the mine, you just had to be willing to beat someone up now and then who wasn't toeing the line.

By 1917, the tribe had been split into two factions: those who helped the mine owners in exchange for money and favors, and those who worked in the mine and fought for better treatment of the people. Duma and Ona were on opposite sides of the conflict, and Erasto was old enough at 14 to want to get involved. Since he was under Duma's protection, Erasto was not forced to work in the mine. However, he went there often and reported back to Duma about the conditions the people were forced to work under. Duma kept trying to negotiate with Bradley and Ona for food, pay, and medical care, but they dismissed his concerns and even threatened to harm Erasto.

Duma felt most helpless the day he learned that Erasto's mother had died of cholera. They both retreated to Duma's hut for the mourning period, and Duma carved the ebony bust to help Erasto honor and remember his mother.

Several months later, the mine owners received some big news. From far to the north in Tanzania came reports that a child had found a diamond in a shallow stream near the base of Mount Kilimanjaro. There must be diamonds in this area! The greedy owners were determined to get a share of this newfound wealth. It would be a whole new country to exploit, and they'd find a way to do it. The owners put Bradley in charge of gathering people and supplies to travel to Tanzania. The mining camp and the village were soon buzzing with activity. Anxiety was in the air as well as among Duma's people. It would be a long, difficult journey to Tanzania, and once there, more of the same backbreaking work in the newly created mines.

On the day the caravan was scheduled to leave, Ona strode purposefully to Duma's hut. "Old man!" he called. "Come out at once!"

Duma appeared in the door of his hut. "What is it, Ona?" he asked.

"You're going to the new mine," sneered the cruel Ona. "We need all the workers there that we can get."

"I am 75 years old," said Duma quietly. "How can I be of any use in the mine?"

"If you can't work, then maybe you can make the people happy by waving around your little talismans, old man. No more arguing. Come on, or I'll drag you to the caravan." Ona raised an arm toward Duma in a threatening gesture.

At this moment, Erasto appeared around the corner of the hut, carrying a water jug. "Hey!" he yelled. "What's going on?"

"The old man is going to the mine at Kilimanjaro, boy. He's a little worried about the trip, though. Would you like to go with him to hold his hand?"

Erasto set down the water jug, resisting the impulse to smash it over Ona's head. "If you are forcing Duma on this trip, then I will certainly go with him. I'll do the work for both of us."

"You are both so useless," said Ona. "I don't think I'll get much work out of either one of you, but it will amuse me to see you suffer. Now move quickly before I decide to help you along with this stick. You can each take a small bag of belongings. Gather them and join the rest of the workers at the caravan." He looked closely at Duma, whose face was expressionless. "Is there something you want to say, old man?" he said, eyes narrowed.

The Mount Kilimanjaro diamond mine atop an ancient elephant burial ground, as told in the general's story

"Only this," said Duma. "Greed loses what it has gained." Ona stormed away without replying.

The trip north to Tanzania was long and tiring. Although there were a few short railway journeys, the people walked most of the way. As they traveled, Duma pointed out to Erasto the beauty and grandeur of the African deserts, forests and savannahs, and the animals that lived in each place. Duma had a few pieces of teak and some carving tools with him and when he was able to sit, he carved small figurines. He also brought some treasures with him from the village, including a figure of an elephant made of tiger's eye. He gave this to Erasto, who carried it with him always.

Bradley and Ona had their eyes out for elephants, but for a different reason. Besides the discovery of diamonds at Mount Kilimanjaro, they were excited to get their hands on some ivory. There were several elephant watering holes near the mountain and there were rumors of an elephant graveyard as well. Looking to make quick money whenever they could, Bradley and Ona planned on going into the ivory trading business as well as the diamond business.

After almost two months of travel, the mountain was in sight. Looking at it from a distance, Duma sighed. "Such a beautiful vision and such an ugly reason that we are here. Erasto, after we are forced underground to satisfy man's greed, try to remember the beauty we saw as we traveled here," he said sadly.

For the next several months, the days and nights fell into a pattern for Duma, Erasto, and their fellow workers. Days of digging, building scaffolding, blasting holes into the sides of large pits, extracting buckets and buckets of blood diamonds, and enduring beatings from Ona and the other foremen. Nights of exhausted sleep, much too short, till the days began again. Erasto stayed close to Duma's side. He insisted that the old shaman rest as much as possible and tried to do the work of two men to keep Duma from being punished.

The Kilimanjaro diamond operation

The rumors about the elephant graveyard were true. Elephant bones were found everywhere at the mine site, above and below ground. Ona picked up ivory wherever he could. He also organized trips to the elephant watering holes and shot many elephants for the prize of their ivory.

Duma and Erasto were sitting by a fire one evening after having finished a particularly grueling day in the mine. Their breaks were few and far between, and Erasto made sure that Duma rested whenever he could. They saw Ona walk by, laughing and carrying an elephant tusk. Duma could not contain himself. "Ona!" he called. "Do you not know what you are doing? Put down that tusk and stop stealing ivory."

Ona stopped and stared at the old shaman. "Stealing?" He laughed. "A dead elephant doesn't care what I do with his tusks. Shut up, old man. Save your strength. Tomorrow's going to be an even harder day than today."

Duma would not be silenced. "You continue to betray your people, and now you betray our kinship with the elephants." He shook his fist at Ona with all the strength he could muster. "Revenge and regret will come. To you? Possibly. To your descendants? It is certain."

Ona laughed again. "Now I know why I keep you around, old man. You amuse me."

Duma tried to rise as Ona walked away, but Erasto held his arm. "Please, sit and rest," said the young man. "You are right, Duma. Someday, Ona and his kind will regret what they have done, and good people will triumph. You have taught me that."

The following day was indeed a grueling one, as Ona had promised. The miners were working in a huge pit, as big as a stadium. Dug into all four cavern walls were honeycombs of tunnels, with wide ledges below each row of tunnels. The holes were blasted and bored into the walls at various intervals, as a way of systematically searching for evidence of diamonds. If diamonds were seen in a tunnel, that area was excavated fully.

The mine owners were dissatisfied with the week's progress. They pushed the foremen to work the people harder. More and more tunnels were blasted, some tall and wide, and some narrow. Erasto spent all his time crawling into the smallest tunnels. He was so thin that he was the only one who fit into them.

After several hours of blasting and digging and one break for a tin cup of water, the workers moved into a large tunnel. It was big enough for two men to walk abreast and carry equipment. Ona eagerly moved in, and after a few moments called to the men to follow.

The tunnel opened up into a large natural cave. Ona ordered the workers to dig holes in the floor. He stood grinning in the center of the cave as nine slanting shafts were dug in a circle around him. "Don't stop!" he yelled whenever a man paused to rest. "Keep digging!"

Ona's mind raced. I have a hunch about this spot, he thought excitedly. If I find diamonds here, they will be the finest Bradley has ever seen. He will reward me greatly!

Erasto and Duma had stayed outside the tunnel. The shaman was weak with thirst and fatigue, and Erasto would not leave him. They sat on the earthen ledge while Duma rested. Erasto convinced one of the foremen to bring the old man a cup of water, and Duma drank it gratefully.

Suddenly they heard Ona's voice echo through the large tunnel. "Erasto! Boy! Where are you? I need you here!"

Erasto moved to the opening of the tunnel. He turned back, worried about Duma, but the old man had stood as well. "Go, and I will follow you," said Duma. Seeing Erasto's face, he continued. "Don't worry. I am strong enough. And I have a feeling you will need me."

As soon as Ona saw Erasto, he yanked him into the cave. Erasto looked around at the shafts that had been dug into the floor and knew he was going to spend the rest of the day crawling into them with a lamp and small digging tool, searching for what would become blood diamonds.

"Start here!" ordered Ona, pointing to the smallest shaft. Erasto silently obeyed. Duma watched from the entrance to the cave. After crawling for several yards, the floor suddenly collapsed, and Erasto fell into a sort of chamber. He stood, shook himself off, and called out for help. "I have fallen through the floor of this shaft into another open area!" he yelled. "I am not hurt but I will need a ladder to climb out!"

As workers found a ladder to slide into the shaft, Erasto turned up his kerosene lamp so he could see the ladder when it got to the hole in the shaft floor. The light from the lamp created an amazing sight.

Erasto gasped at what was before his eyes. It seemed as if he was in a room full of stars! But it wasn't stars. It was diamonds!

Everywhere! In every direction he turned, the lamp light illuminated diamonds, in the wall, the ceiling and floor of the small chamber. "Idayimani," he whispered. Diamonds!

Erasto was excited beyond belief, but he also felt something else. Was it the presence of spirits? The room seemed to be filled not only with diamonds, but with the spirits of ancient ancestors. Erasto fell to his knees, saying a quick prayer of thanks. Then he looked down. He was even kneeling on diamonds! The young man picked up a diamond from the floor of the chamber, and saw a reflection of something else. It was the little tiger eye elephant figurine, lying on the floor of the chamber. It must have fallen out of my pocket, thought Erasto. As he reached to pick it up, the light from the lantern made it seem as if the elephant winked at him.

Erasto smiled, and then looked up. He could see the ladder at the edge of the hole he had fallen through and he heard the shouts of the other workers. "Yes, one more push and I'll have the ladder!" he yelled back as he put the elephant in his pocket. After a moment of thought, however, Erasto didn't put the diamond in his pocket along with the elephant figurine. He wedged the precious stone between the toes on his left foot, then grabbed the ladder, pulled it down, climbed it and crawled back through the shaft.

Ona was there to meet Erasto when he emerged from the shaft. "What happened? What's down there?" he demanded. "Did you find diamonds?"

Erasto now knew why he felt compelled to hide the diamond between his toes. He was going to do everything he could to keep Ona from the diamonds in that chamber. It wasn't just that they were so numerous. There was something special about them. They were sacred.

Erasto lied for the first time in his life. "No," he said firmly. "It was just a dirt chamber. I barely got out with my life. No diamonds at all." The men that had gathered began to disperse,

Erasto finds the diamond chamber

disappointed. Duma stayed, however, and looked at Erasto quizzically, as did Ona.

"No diamonds?" said Ona. "We shall see." He checked Erasto's pockets. No diamonds. "Only a worthless elephant trinket," said Ona dismissively. "Now raise your arms, and stand with your legs farther apart." No diamonds. "Open your mouth." Ona ran his finger inside Erasto's mouth as the young man stayed silent. "Smarter men than you have hidden contraband under their tongues," sneered Ona. No diamonds, but Ona wasn't satisfied.

"You!" he called to another worker standing by. "Go down the shaft. The ladder is still there. I want another pair of eyes in that chamber!"

The man did as he was told, but it was the last order he ever obeyed. As soon as he crawled in a few feet, the entire shaft collapsed. Others rushed to help. They grabbed the man's feet, which were still sticking out of the shaft, but no one could pull him out. He had been crushed to death.

Ona was furious. "Get shovels! Dig the shaft out!" he shouted, pointing at two of the strongest men. They obeyed and began to dig, not caring about diamonds, but anxious to retrieve their fellow worker's body.

While they were digging, Erasto pulled Duma aside. He excitedly whispered to Duma what he had seen and showed him the diamond. "You did the right thing," Duma said quietly as he examined it. "I have never seen a stone that gives off this energy. These diamonds are sacred. They must not become blood diamonds!"

They looked up as they heard Ona yelling, and Erasto slipped the diamond into his pocket. The workers had been unsuccessful in opening the shaft. It collapsed around the dead man's body whenever they managed to move a few shovelfuls of dirt.

Ona was becoming more and more frustrated. He pulled one of the men away from the shaft and raised a shovel to beat him. The ivory pendant he wore around his neck broke from its cord and fell to the dirt floor. Ona ignored it, intent on his rage. Suddenly, the earth seemed to move above them. Dirt rained down from above. Ona dropped the shovel and ran toward the tunnel entrance.

"Is it an earthquake?" yelled Erasto.

"Just run!" one of the men answered. The workers reached the tunnel entrance moments before it collapsed behind them.

Once outside the tunnel, Erasto, Duma and the others pressed their backs against the wall of the open pit, trying to avoid falling dirt and rocks. They could see hundreds of people rushing about, yelling. The cave-in caused a chain reaction that extended to fully half of the tunnels on the north wall. They saw scaffolding collapse and bodies fall into the maw of the vast pit. After several minutes, it was all over. The shouting began to subside as first aid was rushed to the injured.

Erasto looked back toward the opening of the tunnel. "Duma!" he said. "Look! The cave-in closed most of the tunnels on this part of the wall, all around us! What could have caused it?"

Duma smiled knowingly. "Look up," he said.

Erasto shielded his eyes from the dusty glare and looked to where Duma pointed, at the sloping corner where the north and west walls of the pit met. It was an amazing sight. A herd of 50 elephants was slowly walking to the west. Some were at the edge of the pit, causing rivulets of dirt to cascade down the wall. One huge bull elephant was at the back of the pack, and seemed to be the rear guard. He slowly turned his huge head to survey the damage the herd had caused. Erasto imagined that the old bull looked satisfied as he turned and lumbered on. Erasto turned back to Duma. "An elephant stampede? It wasn't an earthquake!"

Duma nodded. "The mine destroyed their burial ground. Man cannot disturb nature without consequences, Erasto. And fortunately for us, by causing the cave-in, the elephants have protected the sacred diamonds."

Duma began to cough. Dust was still everywhere. "Come," said Erasto, taking the old man's arm. He led Duma to a stool and helped him sit.

"Do you recall where the tunnel was?" Duma asked Erasto.

"Yes," answered Erasto. "Don't worry. I have committed the spot to memory."

Other miners were climbing out of the pit. Bradley had announced that work would stop for the day. Only Ona remained at the wall that had collapsed. Erasto and Duma watched as Ona frantically ran back and forth, searching. "Where was it?" he yelled. "Where was the tunnel? I will blast it open again!" He saw Erasto, waiting with Duma as the old man rested another few minutes. "Erasto! Come here!" Ona commanded.

Erasto knelt at Duma's side. "Are you all right?" he asked. "Yes," Duma answered. "Go ahead."

Erasto approached the angry man. "Where is the spot?" Ona demanded. Erasto did not answer. "The tunnel! You must help me find it!" he shouted.

Erasto shook his head. "I do not remember," he said.

Ona's eyes narrowed. "I don't believe you. There are diamonds in that shaft. Something tells me you lied when you said there were none. Why?" Ona grabbed Erasto's arms and shook his thin frame. Erasto stumbled and fell to one knee. As he did so, the diamond slipped from his trouser pocket. He grabbed it quickly, but not before Ona saw its glimmer.

"Ah!" Ona was beside himself. Diamonds! There were diamonds in the shaft! He lunged for Erasto, who turned and ran. "Thief!" he called angrily, pointing at Erasto as the boy ran toward the scaffolding. His eyes searched frantically for help. "Do not let that boy get away! He must be punished!" he called to a few men nearby as he began to chase Erasto himself.

No one ran. The other foremen were gone, and cruel Ona was the most hated. The men watched Erasto run and couldn't keep from grinning. Good for the kid. Hope he gets away, they thought.

Erasto stopped to catch his breath. Ona ran closer. "You will answer for this, by God! You will help me find the tunnel and get those diamonds or you will be dead by morning!"

Ona stopped to draw his pistol as Erasto grabbed a rope and began to climb out of the pit. "I will never help you!" he yelled as he climbed. A shot rang out and Erasto felt dirt spray close to his head. There was no turning back now. He had to escape. Once out of the pit, Erasto scrambled to his feet and ran, not turning around to see if he was being pursued. Ona, frustrated beyond belief, emptied his gun into the wall and threw it on the ground. The diamonds were buried deep inside the cave-in. He knew for certain now.

Erasto finally stopped running when he reached the forest. He collapsed on a grassy mound and tried to catch his breath while he thought. He couldn't go back. He couldn't help Duma. He had to keep running. He was certain that if Ona ever saw him again, he would kill him on the spot.

When Bradley, the mine supervisor, heard about the tunnel collapse, he ordered the workers to abandon that particular wall. The owners had noticed the increasing death toll in the south pit, and they wanted to lose as few able-bodied men as possible. There were other areas of the mine that were producing a satisfactory amount of diamonds. They could afford to chalk up that section as a loss. The miners had their theories, too. Whispered conversations took place about that pit being unlucky, even cursed. After all, the old elephant graveyard was practically right on top of it.

Ona was beside himself with rage and greed. He begged Bradley and the mine owners to keep digging in that section of the wall.

He knew there was something there! Something incredible! His pleas fell on deaf ears, but Ona wouldn't give up.

Ona was obsessed with the idea that the diamonds in that particular shaft would turn out to be the finest ever discovered. He secretly took his own men there several times in the middle of the night. They dug and dug into the wall, creating tunnel after tunnel in spots Ona always hoped was the right one. Every time Ona ordered a man to crawl inside the tunnel, however, it collapsed and the man was killed. Eventually, Ona's men abandoned him. He was left alone with his anger and his obsession.

Word of what Ona had been doing got back to Bradley, and he fired Ona from his position with the mining company. Ona was forced to leave the mine, but refused to abandon his desire to find the sacred diamonds. His thoughts turned to Erasto, and he became driven to find him. Ona could not stop thinking about what had happened the day Erasto fell into that mysterious chamber. The boy was the only person who was able to go down the shaft and into the chamber without it collapsing on him! Why? Ona also suspected that Erasto would be able to find the exact location of the tunnel. If only he could get back into the pit with Erasto and force the boy to show him the spot where the tunnel was located!

Ona tossed and turned in his bed, night after night, blood diamonds in his dreams. The most beautiful diamonds in the world are in that chamber. Erasto has one, but they should be mine, he thought. Ona's obsession transformed to near insanity, and he vowed to find Erasto, even if it took the rest of his life. He would find him, and force him to help get the diamonds. This would be Ona's lifelong mission, and the faint echoes of the proverb, "greed loses what it has gained," faded from his mind forever.

Chapter Three

Mapping a Plan to Help Africa

While Ona was plotting to find him, Erasto was running. Eventually he found his way to Kenya. He was alone and frightened, but he had to find a way to support himself and be safe from Ona. The only solution seemed to be to join the army, so Erasto joined the Kenyan forces at age 16. To his surprise, he found that he was skilled in weapons, especially rifles. By the time he was 19 years old in 1922, he'd been made a member of an elite regiment, the King's African Rifles.

Erasto treasured the diamond that he had taken from the magical chamber. He always kept it with him in a pocket or a small pouch around his neck that he hid under his clothing. He often thought about Duma and worried about him. He also worried about Ona. Some nights he would wake up, startled. He wasn't able to remember his entire dream, but he recalled enough to know that he had been frantically running through the jungle with Ona close behind him. Sometimes Ona was a giant in his dreams, sometimes a lion. Erasto shook off the nightmares as best he could and went back to sleep.

Better dreams were those in which he had baskets full of diamonds. In those dreams he would reach into the baskets and scoop handfuls of the precious stones for Duma, his mother, and the hard-working, beaten-down people of his tribe. He shook those dreams off too, however, and went back to sleep.

No use in dreaming about the diamonds until he could figure out a way to get them.

After all the cave-ins, the north wall of the south diamond pit was left alone, and soon the entire pit was depleted of diamonds and abandoned. Eventually, in 1923, the mine owners decided they had gotten everything they could out of the Kilimanjaro mine and the people they enslaved to extract the diamonds. They moved back to the bigger mines in South Africa. The elephants slowly came back to the area and again used it for their final resting place.

Erasto's people did not forget about the day he fled. Anyone who had been there remembered how Erasto had been the only person to go into the shaft and see the chamber. Duma told a few trusted people that Erasto really had found diamonds in the chamber. They swore to keep the secret. The story became a legend in the tribe. Someday, one of their people would return to the mine, get the sacred diamonds and use them to help the people. During the long trip back to South Africa from the Kilimanjaro mine, it was all they talked about.

As his people traveled back to their village and settled in again, Erasto became used to army life. He was a good soldier. After only a few years, he became head of the King's African Rifles and was highly respected by his men. He traveled across the continent, learning much about Africa, its people, its animals and its needs. Army life suited Erasto. His life was satisfying and he almost forgot about the threat of Ona.

In 1933, when Erasto was 30 years old, he was sent to the Kilimanjaro area, close to the old mine, on a military assignment. Erasto excused himself from his men one afternoon and drove a truck over to the mine. He felt drawn to the mine, not just by idle curiosity but by the pull of the sacred diamonds. There was no way he could retrieve the diamonds now, but it made him feel more hopeful to know that he was near them. As he wandered close to the edge of the pit, Erasto heard a voice.

"Hey!" the voice called hoarsely. "Hey," it said again, weakly this time, as if the first call had taken a lot of energy. Erasto turned back toward the direction of the voice. It was coming from a ramshackle equipment shed.

"Hello?" he called. "Is someone there?" Erasto was carrying a handgun, and he prepared to draw. It could be just a drifter, he thought. But it also could be a criminal with a weapon of his own— it could even be Ona. Erasto approached the equipment shed slowly, his gun at the ready.

"Young man," the voice spoke again, now almost a whisper. "I can see you. Please come closer. Please help me."

Erasto heard the desperation in the man's voice. This wasn't Ona. This was someone who needed his help. He walked up to the door of the shed, opened it and stepped in. A very old man was inside, sitting on a blanket in the corner. Late afternoon light streamed in between the cracked and broken boards to illuminate his face, wrinkled and full of sorrow and pain. Erasto couldn't believe his eyes. It was Duma.

"I am very thirsty," the old man whispered in a hoarse voice. "Do you have any water? I felt too ill to go to the well today." Duma did not recognize Erasto, as he was standing in the shadow at the doorway.

Shocked and distressed, Erasto fumbled for his canteen, opened it and offered it to Duma. "Here," he said. "Drink slowly. Take only a few sips. I will hold the canteen until you are ready to drink again."

The old man reached for the canteen. Recognition flashed across his face. "Your voice," he said. "I recognize your voice. Am I dreaming, or is it you, Erasto?"

"It is I. I cannot believe I have found you, Duma, my father. Why are you here? Why are you not back home?"

THE LIFE CHEST : AFRICA

"It was Ona's revenge. When the mine was abandoned, Ona forced me to stay here. He said I was too old to make the trip and I might as well die here. I've managed to survive as long as I have only by the grace of the gods and our ancestors."

"And it was their grace that brought me here to you," said Erasto, tears rising in his eyes. "Can you stand? Here, take some more water and come with me. Ona, that evil man, meant for you to die here, but I will see to it that you get home to our village."

Duma smiled up at his adopted son. "I never thought I would see you again," he said, and with shaking hands reached for a canvas bag. "But I did keep your few possessions safe. I've held on to them since the day you fled from Ona." Erasto took the bag and looked inside. It contained the small ebony bust of his mother, a rhino horn trumpet, and a necklace made of seeds.

Erasto helped Duma to his feet and led him to his vehicle. Duma was 90 years old now, and almost a walking skeleton. He'd been slowly dying over the years in the camp, but reuniting with Erasto had given him hope. That hope would keep him alive a while longer.

Erasto took Duma to a hotel, arranged for a leave from his army duties, and planned to start back to South Africa with his foster father after a few days. As Duma recovered, he and Erasto talked. They talked about Erasto's career in the army. They reminisced about the old days in the village. And they talked about the sacred diamonds.

Erasto recalled being surrounded by diamonds in the chamber and the feeling he had gotten that ancient ancestors meant for those diamonds to help the African people. "I just had to lie to Ona about the diamonds," he said. "I couldn't let him know they were there. Those diamonds are destined to help the people, not be blood diamonds."

"Yes, I believe that to be the truth," agreed Duma, looking out the window of their hotel room at a magnificent baobab tree.

"One of the things that kept me alive these past years was the hope the sacred diamonds have given me. Just knowing they are there and being guarded by our ancestors." Duma turned from the window to face Erasto. "The pit that holds the sacred diamonds is still open," Duma told Erasto. "Do you remember where the tunnel was?"

"I do, exactly," Erasto reassured the old man. "I made sure to commit to memory that exact spot on the wall. I feel as you do, Duma. I often think of the diamonds. Picturing the chamber in my mind gives me hope. I am discouraged as often as I am hopeful, though. How are we to get the diamonds?"

"Take me there," said Duma. "We will talk on the way."

"Do you have the strength?" asked Erasto.

"I will summon the strength," answered Duma. "If it is the last thing I do, I want to mark the spot where the diamonds are."

They drove to the diamond pit and parked Erasto's vehicle on the north side. Erasto walked to the edge of the huge pit and peered down. "Some of the scaffolding is still in place," he said, surprised. "Look. There's a section wide enough for two men to walk on." He pointed to the spot. "The tunnel was there. If you were standing on the floor of the pit and looking up on the north wall, it was the one on the topmost far right."

Duma walked closer to the edge, toward where Erasto was pointing. "Just below where I'm standing here?" he asked. Erasto nodded. "Then we can mark it fairly easily," said Duma.

Erasto trotted back to the vehicle to get a length of rope. He called back over his shoulder as he ran. "Mark it with what, though?" he asked. "Paint or chalk would wear off." Not watching where he was going, Erasto stumbled over something in the grass. He stopped and looked. It was an elephant bone. This gave Erasto an idea. When he brought the rope back to where Duma was waiting, he also carried with him the little tiger's eye elephant figurine that Duma had made and given him so long ago.

They tied the rope to a nearby tree. Erasto lowered himself down the rope to the scaffolding. When he got to the spot where the tunnel had been, he rested his weight on the wood but kept the rope around him in case it gave way. Erasto then took a folding knife from his pocket and carved a hole in the dry dirt of the wall. He put the elephant trinket into the hole and filled it with enough dirt so that only the elephant's head and ears were showing. He climbed back up the rope and smiled as he grasped Duma's wrinkled hands. "The spot is marked," Erasto said. "And along with that little elephant is a promise. Right now I must take care of you, my old friend. But someday I'll gather the men and the supplies I need to return and retrieve the diamonds for our people."

Duma smiled and nodded. His strength was failing, but he was happy. Satisfied, the two men returned to the hotel. Duma needed to rest before they began the journey back to South Africa the next morning.

"Ah, if we only had the sacred diamonds!" sighed Erasto as he pulled into the parking lot of the rooming house in Manyara, Tanzania, where they would stay on their first night. "We could do so much good with them. Did you see the art museum we passed? It was boarded up. The people here need funds to create art and share it with the coming generations."

Erasto glanced up at the Union Jack that was flying from the porch of the boarding house. "The British control just about everything now, but they won't forever," he said grimly. "These African nations will become independent. Their heritage needs to be honored and preserved."

"There are many ways the sacred diamonds will help the people," Duma agreed. "And someday they will."

Duma and Erasto had many such conversations during the week-long trip back to South Africa. They drove through large cities, small towns, primitive villages and wilderness areas. They spoke of the struggles and the challenges they observed across the continent, and seemed to encounter a different problem in each place they passed through.

In the Pwani region of Tanzania, they saw hungry families begging for food. In Chitipa, Malawi, they saw children in the streets with no school to attend. Injured elephants and giraffes who had been victims of poaching attempts wandered, dying, on the outskirts of Mzimba. When they passed through Lusaka, Zambia, they were harassed by street gangs. In Harare, Zimbabwe, they talked in a restaurant with a young overworked doctor who was concerned about the lack of medical care in the area.

That day in Harare, as they left the restaurant, Duma stopped to talk to a street vendor. He purchased a comb made of rhino horn. One end of the comb was shaped like a rhino's head. Erasto was puzzled. "Duma," he said, "My friend, you have no hair. Why are you buying a comb?"

Duma laughed. "You are not very observant," he chided Erasto. "I bought a little trinket from every stop we made. What's important about this one is not that it is a comb, but that it represents the rhinoceros." Back in the car, Duma reached into a knapsack to show Erasto the rest of his trinkets. He had a teakwood zebra figurine, a brass key in the shape of a giraffe, a bowl decorated with a carved cheetah, a horn whistle in the shape of a buffalo head, and a leopard charm on a chain.

"I didn't know you were so sentimental," remarked Erasto, shaking his head.

"Oh, there's much more to it than that," said Duma. Erasto didn't ask any more questions. He knew the old shaman would explain himself in time.

The final stop they made was in the Kruger National Park, established less than 10 years earlier. They camped under the stars, marveling at a beautiful sunset and the noises of animals and birds all around them. At sunrise the next morning, Erasto was again dreaming of diamonds when Duma gently shook him awake. "Get up, quietly!" the old man whispered urgently. "Come with me! Quickly!"

Erasto rubbed his eyes and silently followed Duma to the top of a ridge. The shaman said nothing but pointed across the savannah. A pride of lions was moving through the grasses on a hunt. Leading them was a lioness. That was not unusual, but the lioness herself was. She was pure white. "A white lion— it's unbelievable," Erasto whispered.

"They exist, and not only in legend," said Duma. "It is a great omen. The white lion is a sign from heaven. She shows herself to give us hope." They stared in silence, watching the pride and its white queen move across the savannah until they were out of sight. Then Duma spread his arms wide and turned in a circle, holding his face up to the rising sun. "This place is now blessed," he said solemnly. "This area of the national park will be known as Timbavati. In the ancient language, Timbavati means, 'the place where something sacred came down to earth.' Never forget, Erasto. Never forget this sacred vision and what it means. The people of Africa will prevail. Good things will come to the cities and towns we traveled through. The white lion is our promise."

Duma and Erasto stood and marveled for a few more moments at what they had seen before they walked back to camp and began the last leg of their journey home.

There was great rejoicing in the village a few days later when Erasto arrived with Duma. The shaman was made comfortable in his old hut. He was happy and content to be home, but it soon became apparent that he was weakening fast. Erasto sat with him one afternoon to talk.

"I can see that you survived in the mining camp and the trip home in order to die in your own village," said Erasto.

"It is true," agreed Duma. "I'm content now to die and join my ancestors. But let me show you this first." Duma picked up something that had been lying next to his bed. It was a large piece of canvas. He smiled. "Even though I am weak, I keep busy," he said.

He unrolled the canvas to show Erasto. It was a map of sorts. There were winding paths drawn on the map, a sketch of Mount Kilimanjaro, drawings of several different animals, and other symbols. He handed it to Erasto while he reached into his knapsack for the trinkets he had acquired on the trip home.

"Spread the map out here on the floor," he said. The shaman laid each animal trinket on the map, on top of the sketch of the same animal. Next to the animal sketches, names of the places through which they had traveled were written on the winding paths, along with phrases that represented the hopes which Erasto and Duma had expressed for each.

The last sketch that the shaman had drawn was a sketch of two majestic lions and the word "Timbavati". He laid a gold coin stamped with the head of a lion on top of that sketch. "Here is the last trinket," he said. "I found it among some of my own talismans right here in my hut. Gold is a symbol of the majesty of the lions but it is also a symbol of greed. Be careful, Erasto. Greed loses what it has gained, and greed must never be a part of this mission."

"It never will be, Duma," promised Erasto.

The old man sighed with fatigue and lay back onto his bed. "My part of the mission is almost finished, but before I die I will perform one last ceremony. It must be done before the sun sets. These trinkets will become powerful talismans. They will help accomplish the goals in each of their cities. I must be alone now. Do not forget what I have told you, Erasto. Keep the map with you always. It will be a puzzle to everyone but you. It is to remind you of our goal. The diamonds will eventually be found, and they will not be blood diamonds. They will be used to help the people. Guard the map and the talismans. Keep the dream alive and the people of Africa will be blessed."

THE LIFE CHEST : AFRICA

Erasto left the old man alone to perform the talisman ceremony as the afternoon shadows lengthened. When he returned to the dark, quiet hut a few hours later, Duma was dead. Erasto sat next to his bed for a long time, saddened but grateful for the time he'd been able to spend with this man who had meant so much to him. He gathered the map and the talismans, carefully stored them in the knapsack, and left the hut to call the elders.

After Duma's burial, Erasto traveled back to his military quarters in Kenya. He was glad to be on familiar ground, and the first thing he did after he settled in was open his Freedom chest. This was a beautiful wooden chest he had received during his advanced rifle training. When he took the final skill test to join the King's African Rifles, Erasto had scored the highest of any soldier in the history of the army. The Freedom chest was his prize, and he treasured it. The chest was a rectangular shape, charcoal black and decorated with metal rivets along the top edge. On each of the longer sides were three inserts made to hold pictures. Erasto had filled the inserts with photographs of himself, his men, and African animals.

General Erasto's original Freedom chest

Although his career was in the army, Erasto never considered himself a fighter. Rather, he thought of himself as a soldier who spent his life striving for freedom. Freedom for himself, for oppressed people, and for the animals of Africa. As he thought about Duma and the sacred diamonds, Erasto lovingly unpacked the items he had received from the shaman. The ebony bust of his mother, a rhino horn trumpet, and the animal talismans all were safely placed in the Freedom chest. Erasto also created a false bottom for the chest, underneath which he hid the puzzle map and his diamond. Ona's obsession with tracking him down was never far from Erasto's mind.

As the years passed, however, Erasto managed to steer clear of Ona. When he was 40 years old in 1943, he became the only native African soldier promoted to Major General of the King's African Rifles. His successful career continued, and he became the general in charge of officer training. In the spring of 1964, when Erasto was 61 years old, he found himself in a Kenyan army camp, training young officers for the King's African Rifles.

One of the most promising men was a 24-year-old British soldier named Simon Lyons, who was born in England but had lived most of his life in Kenya. He was a pilot as well as a skilled rifleman. General Erasto discovered another passion of Simon's quite by accident. Erasto was walking to the mess hall at dinnertime one evening and almost tripped over the young Simon, who was lying on his stomach in the middle of the path.

"What in the world? Soldier!" said General Erasto sternly.

Simon scrambled to his feet and saluted. "Sir, excuse me," he stammered.

"What were you doing?" the general asked. "Are you injured?"

"Oh, no, Sir," Simon answered. "I was drawing that baobab tree and was trying to get it from just the right perspective. I want the picture to be from the point of view of a lion cub."

THE LIFE CHEST : AFRICA

Erasto then noticed the sketchbook and pencil in the young man's hand. "Drawing in your spare time is admirable," he said. "But I suggest you find a spot to plant yourself that is somewhere other than the middle of the path."

"Yes, Sir. Thank you, Sir. I apologize, Sir." Simon saluted again.

"You are dismissed," said Erasto, stifling a smile. "Wait," he added. "Walk with me to the mess hall. I'd like to hear about how you became an artist. May I see some of your drawings?"

Relieved at not being more harshly disciplined, Simon began to eagerly talk with the general about art and Africa. He loved his adopted country of Kenya. Drawing animals, people, and the landscapes of the savannahs was his way of expressing that love. He was quite talented too, Erasto decided, after seeing several of Simon's sketch books.

Simon Lyons in uniform

General Erasto became a mentor and friend to Simon Lyons. He told the young man many stories as they sat around the campfire on cool evenings. They shared their mutual hope for the well-being of the African people as nation after nation struggled for independence. They expressed their concern about preserving Africa's heritage and protecting its animals. Erasto often took items from his Freedom chest to show Simon, and the keepsakes prompted some of his most fascinating stories. Simon heard about Erasto's youth and his people being forced to work in the mines. He heard stories of Duma and how the shaman had taken Erasto under his wing. Erasto told Simon of the evil Ona and how he had betrayed their people.

The general sharing the secrets of the African puzzle map with Simon

Erasto came to trust Simon like a son, and he told him about the sacred diamonds. He showed Simon the diamond that he had taken from the chamber, told him the story of marking the spot where the tunnel was located, and one night even showed him Duma's puzzle map and the talismans.

Erasto and Simon talked that night till the fire was fading to coals. "My dearest wish is that I could get together a group of trusted men to dig for the sacred diamonds," said Erasto. "They would all have to be committed to the cause of helping the African people, and not in it for their own gain."

"Greed loses what it has gained." Simon repeated the proverb thoughtfully. "It's possible, isn't it?" he asked. "Once you retire, Sir, and my time in the army is over, we could gather the people together."

"You are right," agreed Erasto. "I must plan, if it is ever going to happen."

But the planning was not destined to occur that night. Erasto put the talismans back in their small knapsack. As he stood to roll up the puzzle map, he heard a noise that didn't sound right. "Quiet," he said to Simon. "Listen."

"It's just an animal, isn't it?" asked Simon.

"No," said Erasto. "The foot is too heavy. Draw your gun." Both soldiers turned toward the noise, guns drawn. They heard a rustling in the underbrush, and a shot rang out. Erasto fell to the ground with a horrifying yell. He had been wounded in the leg. Simon stood above him, trying to protect him and at the same time looking into the underbrush for the shooter.

"Don't shoot," said a voice, and a man stepped into the fading firelight. It was Ona.

"Hello, Erasto," he said with a grim smile, looking down at his foe. "I failed at surprising you tonight. Next time my man won't trip over his own feet and accidentally fire his gun. But consider this a warning. Next time I will get what I want. I will eventually force you to tell me where the diamonds are. And then I will kill you." Ona turned and swiftly disappeared into the darkness.

Other soldiers came running. Simon pointed to where Ona had gone and several soldiers ran in that direction. A few more soldiers helped Simon with the injured general.

Erasto had suffered a severe leg wound which required surgery. Simon visited him in the hospital tent the next morning. As the young man pulled up a chair to sit next to the bed, Erasto could see that he was still shaken over what had happened.

He put his hand on Simon's shoulder. "Relax," he said. "Ona's been tracking me for years. I see him now and again. He is as determined to find the sacred diamonds as I am. But I have good on my side. I have the promise of the white lion."

"What will you do now?" asked Simon.

"It is inconvenient," admitted Erasto. "I need to move to another location as soon as I'm able. Luckily, in my position with the army, I can come and go as I please. So we must say goodbye soon, at least for now."

"I'm sorry about that," said Simon, shaking the general's hand. "But I want you to be safe. I'll visit you every day while you're recuperating."

"Thank you," said Erasto with a smile. "I'm afraid we won't be able to write after I leave. I can't let anyone know where I'm going. It's the only way to keep Ona off my trail."

"Won't you stop running at some point?" asked Simon.

"Yes, of course," said Erasto. "I'll retire, and find an out-of-the-way hut somewhere in the jungle." He smiled, but looked at Simon with certainty. "As I told you," said the general with confidence, "good will prevail in the end."

Whenever that is, Simon thought glumly to himself.

After several more operations, it was determined that the general's leg could not be saved, and it was amputated just above the knee. Confined to a wheelchair, Erasto struggled to stay positive. How could he possibly retrieve the diamonds now?

His answer, and a good deal of comfort, came to him one night. Erasto saw Duma in a dream. The old shaman spoke, telling Erasto that the sacred diamonds would be found, but not by him. "Many people will help in the mission," he said. "Even people that you do not know, people who are not born yet. Good will prevail. You have the promise of the white lion."

Erasto awoke from the dream with new hope, and also a sense of urgency. I am the only one who knows all the information that is needed to find the sacred diamonds, he thought to himself. I must pass along the knowledge somehow. But there must be a secret to it—a puzzle—something that keeps Ona from getting the information.

After a few days of thought, Erasto had an idea. The first thing he did was make another map: the diamond map. Using pictures and instructions, it detailed exactly where the tunnel to the sacred diamonds was located, and would lead whoever followed the map to the little tiger's eye elephant stuck in the wall of the pit. The diamond map contained seven sketches: Mount Kilimanjaro; three diamond pits; the south pit, which was where the diamonds were located; the north wall of the pit; the 12 tunnels on the north wall, with the elephant figurine marked; the nine shafts in the tunnel; and the final location, the shaft which led to the diamond chamber.

Finally, Erasto had the information written down which was previously only in his head. The next step would be to keep this information safe from Ona. Erasto carefully tore the map into its seven parts. The parts would need to be hidden and stored separately. He would be the only person who knew where they all were.

The next part of Erasto's plan involved Duma's puzzle map, and several of Erasto's soldiers. Many regiments of the King's African Rifles were disbanding as country after country declared independence. There were many soldiers who were being forced to leave the army, some at a young age. A few days before he was to retire in 1969 and leave his current base at Nakuru, Erasto studied the ranks of his men carefully. Under the guise of exit interviews, he called several soldiers to his office for meetings. At these meetings, Erasto assessed the character, abilities and passions of these men. He chose six. One had a passion for medical work. One had a passion for teaching leadership skills to children through playing football. Another wanted to become a veterinarian and work with endangered animals. One man wished to start a school to educate both boys and girls; another wanted to teach people about farming; and the last man Erasto chose wanted to run a center for African culture and arts. These were just the people Erasto needed.

Sitting in his office with the final soldier he interviewed, Erasto told him the plan, as he had done with the others. He was extra cautious, though, and the men did not know who else was in on the plan. "I want you to travel to Tanzania," he told the man who was interested in the cultural center. "There is an art museum in the Manyara region that has been closed. It could be reopened as a cultural center. I'm able to give you some funds for seed money, but you will be responsible for raising money and public interest in the project. You also need to take this." Erasto gave the man piece number six of the diamond map.

"Build a chest to honor the leopard. Use a leopard motif in every way you can at the cultural center. Hide this map piece in the leopard chest, and this leopard charm as well. It has been blessed by a Zulu shaman. The map is part of the key to a great treasure. There is a store of sacred diamonds that I've seen with my own eyes. Someday they will be mined. I know they are meant to help the people of Africa. Be faithful in your part of the mission and develop the cultural center. I don't know when, but someone will come to you and ask for your piece of the map. They will be on a mission to collect the map pieces and retrieve the sacred diamonds. You are to give them the map piece when they tell you the proverb 'greed loses what it has gained.' Eventually you will be rewarded with a share of the diamonds, but the profit from them is meant to benefit the people through art, music and dance. The diamonds are not for anyone's personal benefit, yours or mine. Remember, greed loses what it has gained."

Erasto also showed each man his Freedom chest. He explained to them that storing his precious keepsakes in the chest had helped to give his life purpose and focus. He encouraged them

THE LIFE CHEST : AFRICA

to do the same with the chests they would build. The rhino, zebra, giraffe, cheetah, Cape buffalo and leopard would all have beautiful chests built in their honor.

"Your chest doesn't have to hold only the map piece and the talisman," he told each of the men. "Fill it with the treasures of your life as well. Your motives are good and your life is worth living. Take joy in your life! Record your joys— and your sorrows as well— in your animal chest."

Erasto had the trust and respect of his soldiers. The ones who were chosen for this project were eager to start their new lives. They would build the chests, guard the map pieces and the talismans, serve the people, and wait for the adventurer who would come to claim their part of the map.

The diamond map with seven pieces outlined

After meeting with the last soldier, Erasto was satisfied. He could retire and move on with his life. Erasto's plan was to move to the Timbavati region of Kruger National Park. He would start a safari camp, and work for the ethical treatment of the animals that were the treasure of Africa. His piece of the map was #1, a sketch of the base of Mount Kilimanjaro. Now every location on the puzzle map had a protector. Every cause had a champion. Somehow he would find a person to take up the mission of finding the sacred diamonds.

Lastly, Erasto added information to Duma's puzzle map. He wrote on the map that each location must be visited, in order, to get the clues to the location of the diamonds. Each clue was hidden in an animal chest at each city. He also wrote the proverb "greed loses what it has gained" at the top of the map.

After he finished, Erasto suddenly had second thoughts. Did he put too much information on the puzzle map? What if Ona got his hands on it? Hastily, Erasto rubbed out two of the clues in the center of the puzzle map: the pictures of the giraffes and the cheetah, and the causes they represented. I'll remember those clues myself for now, he thought, and find someone I trust to pass them on to.

Erasto must have sensed Ona's presence, because Ona had indeed found him at the Nakuru army base. The years had not lessened Ona's greed, and even at the age of 75, he was as determined as ever to find a way to get the sacred diamonds for himself. He had been snooping around for a few days, searching for Erasto's office. As he snuck down a hallway on the second afternoon, he heard Erasto's voice and stopped. This was it! Ona overheard Erasto talking about a cultural center and then— his ears perked up— a map. A map piece? He couldn't be sure, but he wasn't going to let this opportunity go by. Ona heard footsteps approach the door from inside the office, and hid around the corner until the man leaving Erasto's office had reached the stairwell and started up to the second floor.

Erasto had given away all the map pieces except the one he was planning to keep: the sketch of the base of Mount Kilimanjaro. He was about to roll it up when the door burst open and he saw his old nemesis, again waving a gun at him. "Give me that map!" Ona snarled.

THE LIFE CHEST : AFRICA

Erasto handed it over. "It is of no use to you," he said quietly. "That is only one piece of the map. The other pieces are well hidden, scattered over many miles."

"That will not stop me," said Ona. "Haven't I found you wherever you go? Wherever the army hides you, I show up. I have many spies in many places. Now I know that a map exists," he said as he waved the map piece in the air, "I don't even need you anymore. I will find the rest of this map. You are just a useless old cripple now. You cannot stop me."

Ona laughed and slipped out of the room. Erasto sighed. The piece of the map that Ona took gave him no information he didn't already have. Ona already knew the diamond pit was somewhere at the foot of Mount Kilimanjaro, and that's the only thing the piece indicated. But Erasto was discouraged. He *was* a cripple. He couldn't retrieve the diamonds himself. He had to find someone who would be willing to take on the mission— and he didn't know who that would be. But for now, Erasto decided, he would continue with his plan: the safari camp.

Simon Lyons painting

By 1970, Tanda Tula, Erasto's safari camp, was up and running. He added the words "Tanda Tula Safari Camp and Oasis" next to the picture of the lions on the puzzle map. And just as he had instructed his soldiers to do, he built an animal chest. His map piece was gone, but he still had the lion talisman—the gold coin—and he kept it in the lion chest. He still kept the puzzle map hidden in the false bottom of the Freedom chest.

Other safari camps began to spring up in the area throughout the 1970s. Ona, still tracking Erasto, worked with his nephew to open a safari camp close to Tanda Tula, named Royal Camp. Erasto knew the camp was Ona's, but he never encountered his enemy again. In 1974, he saw a funeral procession leave Royal Camp and read in the newspaper that Ona had died. Was this the end of Ona's quest or would his nephew carry it on? Erasto wondered.

Tanda Tula attracted tourists and photographers. It also attracted artists. One of those artists was Simon Lyons. Simon left the army in 1972 and became a full-time painter. He created beautiful landscapes of the savannahs and striking images of African animals, especially lions and elephants. It was a very happy day in 1975 when Simon, visiting Tanda Tula to get inspiration for a painting, met the owner— who turned out to be his old friend General Erasto. After that, Simon made a point of visiting Tanda Tula every year. He loved working on paintings there, and it was always a highlight to spend time with Erasto.

Many people came and went at Tanda Tula, as guests and workers. In 1982, Erasto met a young married couple at an army base he was visiting in Kenya. They were Somali refugees, desperate for freedom. Their plight touched Erasto's heart, and he offered them jobs at Tanda Tula. They were grateful for the opportunity to work, and became like a son and daughter to Erasto. He shared much of his story with them, showing them the Freedom chest and telling tales of army life.

THE LIFE CHEST : AFRICA

In 1989, the couple had a son, whom they named Senwe. It was an amazing day all around on the game reserve. Eight different animals were born on the same day as little Senwe: a lion, a rhino, a zebra, a giraffe, a cheetah, a Cape buffalo, a leopard, and an elephant. Erasto was amazed when he heard the news. These were the same animals that were sketched on Duma's puzzle map! It had to be a sign— a sign that the pieces of the diamond map would soon be put together and the diamonds found, maybe in this generation!

Erasto decided to tell Senwe's parents about the sacred diamonds. He showed them the lion chest and the lion trinket. He told them the whole story of finding the diamonds, Duma's puzzle map and his diamond map. He explained to them how he divided up the diamond map and sent his soldiers out to improve the lives of the people while they waited for the map to be put together and the diamonds found. Senwe's father got a pen and a journal. "This story is important," he insisted. "It must be written down. We will keep the journal in the lion chest."

"And we will guard it in our hearts as well," said his wife.

"You will be keepers of the lion chest," said Erasto. "Keep the story alive, and keep your own memories and keepsakes— and that of your little son— in the chest." Erasto chuckled. "Being born on the same day as all the animals on the puzzle map! I think he will prove to be quite a special child."

"But who will retrieve the diamonds?" asked Senwe's father. "We have neither the resources nor the skills."

"I've been promised that it will happen," said Erasto. "All I can do is trust in that fact."

Soon after little Senwe was born, Simon Lyons arrived at Tanda Tula for his yearly visit. He reminisced with Erasto about their old days in the army and the night Erasto was shot by Ona's henchman. "The sacred diamonds," Simon sighed. "If only we could have found them."

Baby Senwe and the eight baby animals

Erasto stared hard at Simon, a new light in his eyes. "We still can," he said. "Or at least you could."

"I could?" asked Simon. "What do you mean?"

"I trust you, Simon," said General Erasto. "You are not African, but you love Africa. I must pass on this information to someone who might actually be able to carry out the mission. You are a traveler; you move freely around the continent creating your paintings. You have all the knowledge and skills you learned in the army. You could get the diamonds." Erasto excitedly wheeled his chair to the corner of the room where he kept his Freedom chest. "Remember the puzzle map? I still have it. It's one of the keys to finding the diamonds. Sit down, Simon, and I'll tell you the rest of the story."

Erasto told Simon how he created the diamond map, divided it into seven pieces, and placed each piece in one of the cities that he and Duma had chosen long ago. He explained to Simon about the plan to put the map back together, piece by piece, to find the exact location of the diamonds. He also told Simon about the two clues on the puzzle map he had rubbed out: the giraffe and the cheetah. He showed Simon the proverb written on the map.

As he talked, Erasto became more and more excited, until he started to get short of breath. "You're not well, my friend," said Simon worriedly. "I promise you I will do everything I can to find the diamonds, but you must rest."

"I cannot," wheezed Erasto. "Not until I'm sure you understand everything. I want you to be the keeper of my Freedom chest. It will be yours after I die. Now I must tell you one more thing. My old enemy, Ona, is nearby. I mean his nephew is. He runs the safari camp nearest to this one. It is called Royal Camp. The sole purpose of it is to spy on me here. But I'm an old cripple. I don't think they get much from spying on me." Erasto tried to laugh, but it turned into a cough. He was finally satisfied that Simon understood the whole story, so he agreed to drink some tea and go to bed.

The cough, however, became pneumonia, and within a week, Erasto was on his deathbed. One afternoon, while waiting for the doctor, Simon talked with Senwe's parents. They showed Simon the lion chest and the journal in which Senwe's father had written the story of the diamonds.

The day of Erasto's death at age 86 was a sad one for everyone at Tanda Tula. Simon remained at the safari camp for a month, grieving his friend and working on paintings. He decided to display several of the items from the Freedom chest in the Great Hall at Tanda Tula in Erasto's honor, including the ebony bust of Erasto's mother. Simon planned to leave the Freedom chest at Tanda Tula, but worried about the safety of the puzzle map. Who knew what the spies were up to at Royal Camp?

Simon Lyons hiding the map behind his painting

After a few days of worrying, Simon found a painter's solution to the problem. He painted a large landscape that he called Migration of the Wildebeest. He made it just the right size: a little bigger than the puzzle map. Simon framed the painting with the map behind it, and hung it above the fireplace in the Great Hall. He felt satisfied that no one would disturb it. It will be safe there, hanging high above the mantel, he thought to himself. Half the people who walk by probably won't notice it. It's a blow to my ego, he chuckled to himself, but that's all right.

Just before Simon left Tanda Tula to go home to Kenya, he had one final conversation with Senwe's parents. He told them that he might be back to start the journey to retrieve the diamonds. "I'll try to get the money, the resources and people together," he assured them. "But I just don't know when." Simon thanked Senwe's parents for helping to run Tanda Tula, and patted baby

Senwe on the head. After going back to his home in Kenya, Simon traveled throughout Africa for the next several years, painting and periodically visiting Tanda Tula.

10 years went by peacefully at Tanda Tula. Senwe grew into a lively child who loved animals, which was no surprise to his parents. Senwe and Simon played games together when Simon came to visit, and Senwe loved to watch Simon paint lions, elephants and leopards. The only thing that Senwe loved as much as animals was money. Frankly, he was a little profiteer. He sold everything he could find to the tourists at Tanda Tula. Senwe could pick up a rock off the ground and sell it to a tourist as a stone from an ancient temple!

Once, Senwe was so eager to sell something to Simon that he grabbed a beaded necklace off a counter at the information desk and started to make up a story about it belonging to a Zulu princess. Simon laughed and took the necklace from the boy. "Senwe!" he scolded. "That necklace came from the general's Freedom chest. I believe his grandmother made it, and she was not a Zulu princess. Stop trying to sell me things I already own!" he said, rubbing Senwe's head and giving him a friendly shove.

"Well, I was just practicing on you, Simon," laughed Senwe.

"You're a good salesman, all right," agreed Simon. "I guess any money you can make for Tanda Tula is fine with me."

Senwe took those words to heart, and when his parents left him in charge of the gift shop that day in 2002 when Kim Yost and his friends walked in, he sold up a storm. Senwe was a good salesman, and Kim was a savvy buyer. He bought the necklace, a rhino horn trumpet, and the ebony bust. Flush with the success of these purchases, Kim looked above the fireplace in the Great Hall and saw Simon's painting, Migration of the Wildebeest. It didn't take long before Senwe had $500 and Kim had the painting. Simon wasn't around to object to the sale, and neither Kim nor 11-year-old Senwe knew that the precious puzzle map was hidden behind the painting, and on its way to Kim's home in Canada.

"There was some really neat stuff in the Freedom chest, Grandpa," said April. "I wonder if Senwe used the rhino horn trumpet to call animals. I would," she said confidently. "I'd be like the Pied Piper!"

"You'd love all the animals in the safari camp, Blossom," said Josh. "We saw some pretty great sights there, didn't we, Bernie?" he asked his cousin.

"Absolutely," answered Bernie. "And the food wasn't bad, either."

"Wait a minute!" said April. "Grandpa? Uncle Bernie? You really went to Africa? You didn't just talk about it?"

"We sure did, Blossom!" laughed Josh. "And what an adventure it was!"

"Tell me!" insisted April. "I want to hear the story!"

"Now just wait, Blossom. We'll tell you all about it after you take your nap, okay?"

"Do I have to take a nap?" whined April. "Now?"

"It's no use complaining, April," warned Bernie. "Your old grandpa is the one that really wants to nap."

"Hey, grandpas need rest, too! And so do great-uncles. I see you yawning," said Josh.

"Fine," said Bernie. "Let's get our beauty rest, everybody."

THE LIFE CHEST : AFRICA

Chapter Four

Bernie and Josh: On the Road Again

Bernie handed April a glass of juice and joined her at the kitchen table with one of his own. "Good nap!" he said as he stretched.

April disagreed. "I hate naps." She frowned. "I keep telling my mom I'm too old for them. Hey, let's go wake up Grandpa!"

"Let him sleep a little longer, April," said her great-uncle. "I want him to be in a good mood when he wakes up. You don't want to deal with him when he's grumpy."

Bernie smiled, and April wasn't sure if he was kidding. "I've never seen him grumpy," she said. "Uncle Bernie, did you and Grandpa ever get grumpy and fight when you were younger?"

"Sure, sometimes," admitted Bernie. "I guess everybody in a family does. But families are strong. It's like a proverb I heard in Africa. 'A family tie is like a tree; it can bend but it cannot break.' Your grandpa and I have always been there for each other, even when the going got tough."

"Did the going get tough in Africa?" asked April.

Josh appeared in the doorway, laughing. "Bernie had it tough, Blossom. Like when he stepped on diamonds and thought he was going to break them!"

"Hey!" said Bernie. "I've got plenty of stories about you too, you know."

"I want to hear all of them!" said April as she bounced up and down.

"Let me get a glass of juice," said Josh as he opened the refrigerator. "Got any chips in your house, Doc?"

"Look in that cupboard above the cooktop," answered Bernie. He turned to his great-niece. "Before we could go to Africa, we had a lot of planning to do, April. It was a pretty complicated trip. We figured out that we could use the information on the puzzle map and the plate, but there was still a lot we didn't know."

"It was Christmastime when we found the map and the plate in the life chests at Bernie's folks' house," said Josh as he sat at the table with a bag of potato chips. "We had to go home at the end of the week, so we came back in February to plan the trip. Your mom and grandma came too, Blossom. And your mom was almost the same age you are right now."

"Was my mom like me when she was little?" asked April.

"She was," answered Josh. "She got into so much trouble, Blossom. Just like you," he teased.

"Grandpa!" protested April. "I don't get in trouble!"

"No, you don't, April," reassured Bernie. "Quit teasing the kid, Grandpa, or I'll take away your chips."

Josh laughed, spraying crumbs. "Just kidding, Blossom. You do look a lot like your mom, though. Same smile. And she was full of questions when she was little, just like you. I had to explain all our Africa plans to her step-by-step."

"Me too! You have to explain them to me too!" said April.

"Yes, ma'am," answered Josh. "Let's see. I was 32, and your uncle Bernie was an old man of 33. Your aunt Li had just married him, which was strange, because she was usually so sensible."

"Hold it right there," said Bernie. "April, wouldn't you rather have me tell the story? I have a much better memory."

April giggled. "Take turns," she suggested.

"All right," said Bernie. "My turn," he said, grinning at Josh. "Your grandpa and grandma and your mom came out to see Chen Li and me in New York City. We were living in an apartment in Midtown. The life chests were still kept at my parents' house in Brooklyn, but I had Gramps' Traveler chest and the map and plate. So we got down to business planning our trip."

Leah ran her hand over the old canvas puzzle map, which was spread out on Chen Li's dining room table. "It's amazing that the ink hasn't faded much," she said, tracing the paths with her finger.

"The drawings are beautiful. It's like a piece of artwork," mused Chen Li. "Here's the plate," she said, setting it in its place in the middle of the map. "Do you want to wake up your husband? Bernie and Meg will be back in a few minutes with Josh's favorite doughnuts."

"Yeah, I'll go kick him out of bed," laughed Leah. "Since we got in so late last night, he'll blame it on jet lag, but the truth is that he doesn't get enough sleep at home. He works harder now running the foundation and monitoring our investments than he ever did when he had a regular job."

"The foundation he set up with his mom is a wonderful cause," said Chen Li. "They're helping a lot of kids stay in school."

"And it makes Josh so happy to use our money to improve inner city school programs," said Leah.

Meg burst in the door, followed by Bernie with a box of doughnuts. "Dad's not up? I'll take him a doughnut!" Meg grabbed a chocolate one from the box and ran down the hall.

"We got the last dozen of the morning batch," Bernie said. "I hope Josh appreciates the trek I made to score his favorite kind."

Chen Li shook her head. "You complain about walking four blocks to the bakery?" she said. "How will you ever survive in Africa?"

"That'll be different," laughed Bernie. "When I'm in Africa I expect I'll be running from lions."

"Thanks for breakfast, Doc," said Josh, walking into the kitchen with Meg. "How many chocolate ones did you get?" he asked, digging in the doughnut box.

"Only two more, and one of those is mine," warned Bernie.

"Gotcha, Doc." Josh fished out a cherry doughnut with sprinkles, handed it to Meg, and helped himself to some coffee. "Ah," he sighed, settling down in a chair. "Now I can start to wake up. I hate jet lag." Leah stole a look at Chen Li and they both stifled laughter.

"Let's get started, then," said Bernie. "Just keep your coffee away from the map. Look here. I've got a map of Africa on my tablet. Let's see if we can find the locations on the puzzle map. They might not have the same names now."

"How about if you finish your doughnut and come with us, Meg?" Leah asked her daughter. "You can help Aunt Li and I find some information on the computer in the office. We can look at pictures of African animals too."

"Okay," said Meg. "I want to see giraffes and lions!"

They all spent the rest of the morning hard at work. Bernie and Josh worked at deciphering the puzzle map and planning their route. Leah helped by researching nearby areas when a cause and a city didn't match up. Chen Li found flights and accommodations. After lunch, they sat down in the living room to compare notes.

"I think we're in good shape. I'm pretty sure we understand everything on the map," said Bernie.

"We're making progress," agreed Leah. "I had to do a little digging, but I'm pretty sure we have all the right locations now. For some reason, the two in Tanzania have moved, but I found a center for the arts in Babati, and a community farm that fits the description which is in the Kilombero Valley."

"Good work, Babe," said Josh, kissing his wife on the neck. "Wow," he added. "I'm starting to realize what a lot of driving this is going to be."

"Are you going to have a car, Dad?" asked Meg.

"Yes, probably a Land Rover," answered Josh.

"The thing is," put in Bernie, "It's going to be a pretty daunting task even after we find all the clues and get to the diamond mine. We're going to need a lot more than a shovel and a pickax. In China all we did was walk up to the spot on the Great Wall and start digging. This is a lot more complicated."

"And dangerous," said Chen Li. "My mother's death was a result of her recklessness. But you could be as careful as possible and still get hurt in an old mine like that."

"I know," said Bernie, putting his arm around his wife's shoulders. "We'll have to hire some people— experts— to make sure we're doing everything right."

"What kind of people would those be?" asked Leah.

"Explosive experts, I guess for one," said Bernie. "And somebody who knows enough to keep Josh away from the dynamite."

"Hey!" countered Josh. "I only blow things up in video games." Then he noticed Leah's worried face. "Honey," he said. "I would never do anything stupid, knowing that you and Meg are back at home waiting for me."

"Good," said Leah, smiling. "Let's make a list. Number one: Don't do anything stupid. Number two: Get help with explosives and excavating."

"What does a diamond look like?" interrupted Meg. She took her mom's hand and peered closely at the rings on Leah's finger. "Shiny like this?"

"Actually, no," answered her mom. "Not at first. They get polished and cut like this after they've been taken out of the ground."

"So how do you know when you found a real diamond, and not just a stone?" asked Meg.

"They still look like diamonds," said Bernie. "But Meg brings up a good point. I think we might need a diamond expert along with us."

"Whatever you say, Doc," agreed Josh. "How are we going to find one?"

"I know a gemologist at the university who's been to Africa," said Bernie. "I'll get in touch with her to start with."

"Speaking of starting," said Leah. "Where do you think you'll fly into? Cape Town?"

"Yeah," said Josh. "We can't go to Africa without spending at least a few hours there. I even splurged and had Chen Li book us a room at the Cape Grace."

"It's right on the waterfront," added Bernie. "I'm looking forward to watching the sunset and drinking a glass of wine before I collapse with exhaustion."

"You just better stay in your room," teased Chen Li. "It sounds like a party city!"

Before Bernie had a chance to defend himself, Meg interrupted. "Where do you go after that?" she asked.

"The first place we have to go to is a safari camp called Tanda Tula," answered her dad." I hope it's still there."

"It is," said Leah, scrolling down a page on her tablet screen. "I just looked it up. Wow! Meg, look at this photo of all these lions."

"The lion is symbol number one," said Josh as he looked over Leah's shoulder at the photos of Tanda Tula. "Hopefully we'll find someone there to show us the lion chest and give us the first clue."

"What are the clues? Do you know?" asked Meg.

"No, we don't," answered Josh. "It doesn't say anywhere what the clues actually are. But they're supposed to get us to the mine and show us exactly where the diamonds are located."

Bernie looked up from a book he was paging through. He sighed. "You know, there's a lot of ifs and maybes we're facing," he said. "I hope it's going to be worth it."

"It will be worth it, Doc," said Josh, punching Bernie on the shoulder. "We're young! We're smart! We'll find those diamonds!"

"One of us is getting sick of being punched," said Bernie, rubbing his arm. "Leah, can you teach your husband some manners?"

"No," said Leah simply. "That's why I love him."

"I'll never win," said Bernie.

"You speak the truth, cousin," laughed Josh. He glanced at his daughter, who was laughing too. "Oh, Meg– um, don't punch your friends in the arm, okay?"

"Don't worry, Dad. I don't punch my friends. I punch the bullies," said Meg.

"What?" said Leah in surprise. "Josh, let's have a talk with your daughter about conflict resolution, all right?"

"Sure, honey," said Josh sheepishly. "How about if we go for a walk? Come on, Meg. Get your coat. I want to hear about these bullies."

After they left, Chen Li turned to Bernie. "I think Meg's fine," she said. "I did the same thing when I was a little girl."

"Well, that's different," her husband said. He smiled teasingly. "You grew up in such an uncivilized country."

His joke got him a punch on the shoulder. "Yup," he said as he rubbed his arm. "I'll never win."

Bernie and Josh fit Simon's plate onto the map

After several more days of planning and research, Josh and Bernie were ready to go to Africa. They made reservations at Tanda Tula and arranged for a diamond expert named Gogo Okonjo and a former soldier and munitions expert named Effiom Boro to join them at the safari camp. The two men had agreed to travel all the way to Tanzania with Josh and Bernie. They would use their expertise to help find the diamonds and also act as guide and bodyguard on the trip.

The day before Leah and Meg had to return to California, the two cousins sat in the kitchen, going over their checklist one more time. "Should we try to talk to someone at each of the stops and explain what we're doing beforehand?" asked Josh as he calculated the distance between Cape Town and the safari camp on his comm.

"I don't know," said Bernie. "Maybe not. For one thing, it might be hard to get people to even understand what we're talking about. Besides, I want to be there when I tell them the story. Who knows? One of these people might hear the word 'diamonds,' keep their clue from us, and try to get the diamonds for themselves."

"That makes sense," said Josh. "Okay. We'll take our chances on finding the right people when we get there."

Chen Li came into the kitchen and leaned against a counter. "Bernie, you just got a message from the department head. He approved your leave of absence for next semester," she said.

"Excellent," said Bernie. "I wish I didn't have to take the whole semester off, though. This trip should only take a couple of weeks."

"I'm glad you're off the whole term," said his wife. "I'll get to spend more time with you when you get back. Besides, it's good that you have the time if you need it."

"Yup," agreed Josh. "Who knows how long it'll take to blast those diamonds out?"

"If it takes as long as it did for you to blast your way through that last video game level, then we're in trouble," laughed Bernie.

"Stop!" warned Chen Li as Josh raised his fist. "No punching! Here comes Leah and Meg!"

Bernie grinned at Josh as he lowered his arm. "Hi, ladies!" he said to Meg and Leah as they came in, arms full. "What do you have there?"

"We took some things from Gramps' chest to look at," said Leah, setting down the ebony bust of an African woman.

"The African things," added Meg. "See this little man with the shield and spear? Mom said he's a Zulu warrior."

"This woman's face is so well done," said Chen Li, studying the ebony head. "She looks wise and sad at the same time."

"I suppose there were a lot of things for her to be sad about," said Bernie. "I believe that bust was made during the time when thousands of African people were forced to work in the diamond mines."

"That's why we're going to Africa," said Josh. "Remember what Gramps said in his journal? He and Simon Lyons wanted to finish the mission that General Erasto started: to help the people and the animals of Africa with the diamonds. We've got the map and the plate. It's up to us now!"

THE LIFE CHEST : AFRICA

Part Two

Quest For The Diamonds

AFRICA

THE LIFE CHEST : AFRICA

Chapter Five

The Lion Chest: The Puzzle Comes Together

"Are we there yet?" groaned Josh from behind his eye mask. "I've been trying to sleep, but I just can't."

Bernie turned from gazing out of the window of the plane to smile at his cousin. "You know, I think your eight-year-old daughter is more patient than you are. Next thing you know, you'll be asking for ice cream."

Josh sat up excitedly, lifting off the eye mask. "Is there ice cream?" he asked.

Bernie noticed flight attendants moving carts at the front of the cabin area. "As a matter of fact, they are starting to serve food," he said. "Hang in there, Josh. We're more than halfway to Cape Town. When we get there– let's see– it will be about three in the afternoon. Our flight to the airport near Tanda Tula is early the next morning. So we'll have a little time to get over the jet lag and enjoy Cape Town."

"Good," said Josh. "I like to be fresh as a daisy when I start my adventures."

"A shower is all I ask," countered Bernie, laughing. "Good thing the weather won't be too hot. May is a nice mild month in Africa. We're lucky it coincided with the end of my semester."

"Here comes dinner," said Josh, glancing down the aisle. "Hope I can get some vanilla ice cream with chocolate sauce."

After the long flight and their night in Cape Town, Bernie and Josh were ready to board the 50-seat plane that would take them on the last leg of their trip. They were headed to Tanda Tula Safari Camp in the Timbavati Game Reserve, which was part of the Kruger National Forest.

"What a great old plane," said Bernie as they crossed the tarmac with the other passengers traveling north. "Hold it. I want to take a picture. Let me get one of you with the plane in the background. Smile, Josh!"

"You're not in a museum, Bernie," said Josh through gritted teeth as Bernie took the picture. "We're really going to fly in this antique!"

"I know!" said Bernie. "Isn't it exciting? Come on!" They climbed aboard and took their seats. Bernie's enthusiasm was dampened a little when the plane started to shake as it picked up speed, but he didn't let on.

Josh, however, was vocal in his disapproval. "Is this thing going to rattle the whole time we're in the air?" He looked out the window. "I half expect to see parts falling off."

"I thought you liked old things," countered Bernie. "You're always saying you wish you had one of Gramps' antique cars."

"That's different!" insisted Josh.

"You know," said Bernie, "I bet this is the same type of plane Gramps flew when he was in Africa."

"You're probably right," Josh agreed. "It might even be the same exact plane." He glanced out the window as the plane climbed. "Check this out, Bernie! We're going right over Table Mountain. It's so flat. It looks like the mountaintop was cut off with a knife."

"I heard there's a cable car you can ride at the mountain," said Bernie. "It takes about five minutes to get to the top, and the view is just amazing."

"Let's put that on our list for the next time we're here," Josh said. "Our families would love it, too." He settled back in his seat and looked around at the old jet's interior. "I hope they replaced the engines. It doesn't look like they upgraded the inside at all."

"We're at cruising altitude now," said Bernie. "I think the shaking is subsiding. Hopefully this baby will stay in one piece the rest of the trip."

Josh sighed in relief. "Yeah, it's better now. I thought my teeth were going to fall out." He closed his eyes and tried to picture their destination. "Tanda Tula, here we come!"

"I'd be excited for the safari camp even if we weren't going treasure hunting," said Bernie as he paged through a Tanda Tula brochure. "Look at these photos. This is a beautiful place, and since it's in the middle of the game reserve, there are animals all around."

"I'm glad people only shoot the animals with cameras now," said Josh. "It's terrible to think how animals used to be shot just for sport, or for their ivory, like the elephants."

"And a lot of species were hunted to extinction or near extinction," agreed Bernie. "Thank goodness for protected areas like the game reserves."

"Excuse me, but I'm afraid it's still going on." The speaker was a poised middle-aged woman sitting in the row ahead of Josh and Bernie. "I don't mean to eavesdrop, but I couldn't help overhearing," she said, turning to face them. "I'm going to the Timbavati myself. My name is Lucy Mayo. I'm with an organization in London that's trying to prevent poaching of the protected animals in Kruger National Park."

"And you say that animals are still being poached? In this day and age?" asked Bernie in surprise.

"I'm afraid so," the woman answered. "Greed never goes away."

"Neither does disregard for the welfare of animals," sighed Bernie.

Josh and Bernie introduced themselves, and they spent the rest of the two-hour trip discussing the beautiful national park and game reserve where the safari camp was located.

"Your camp is called Tanda Tula?" asked Lucy, looking at Bernie's brochure. "I'm staying nearby at Royal Camp for a few days. It was a little cheaper," she shrugged.

"I'm sure we'll be looking at the same lions," said Josh.

The pilot announced their approach to the East Gate airport. "Good luck keeping an eye on those poachers," said Bernie to Lucy as the passengers fastened their seatbelts. "Maybe we'll see you around."

The old plane started to shake again as it approached the airport, but Josh didn't notice it this time. He was looking at herds of impalas running through the grasses next to the runway. "What a sight!" he said to his cousin. "Hundreds of impalas! They're so graceful. It's like watching a living river."

"There's a herd of wildebeests over here," said Bernie, looking out the other window. "It's unreal!"

When the plane landed at the East Gate airport, Josh and Bernie were met by a driver from Tanda Tula, who directed them to the Land Rover that would take them to the camp.

"Sweet!" said Josh excitedly as they were loading their luggage into the vehicle. "It's not a levicar! We get to feel the rubber meet the road!"

"We do have some levicars at Tanda Tula," said the driver apologetically. "They were all checked out when I went to pick up a Land Rover."

"Don't worry," said Josh. "This is great!" He jumped into the back of the Land Rover, grinning.

The drive took about an hour, and along the way Bernie and Josh got their first taste of Africa from the ground. The scrubby shrubs and small trees with branches broken and chewed on by elephants, the starkness of bare leadwood trees silhouetted against the blue sky, and the towering termite mounds were part of a world that was different from anything they had experienced before. They heard the cries of wild dogs, noticed birds large and small, and saw a family of warthogs trot through a ditch at the side of the road. They were both completely in love with Africa even before pulling up to the gates of the safari camp.

Josh stretched and couldn't help grimacing a little as he climbed out of the Land Rover. "I saw that," said Bernie. "Are you still glad we didn't have a levicar?"

"You bet," insisted Josh. "Maybe I can talk them into letting me drive one of these."

A half hour after arriving, Josh and Bernie put their feet up in a spacious, airy tent, located near Tanda Tula's oasis. "This is the life," sighed Josh. "Leah could hardly believe my description of the place when we called home. She told me I wasn't going on any more adventures without her!"

"Chen Li said the same thing," nodded Bernie. "She loves to travel."

Josh sat up and peered through the canvas opening. "Listen to those birds! This place is teeming with life. I'm really looking forward to our safari tonight."

"Me too," said Bernie. Then he frowned. "But what next? About our mission, I mean? Tomorrow will be our second full day in Africa. We're here, and we're ready to find the diamonds. What do we do now? Who do we talk to?"

Josh stretched out on his bed. "Well, we've got the three C's to accomplish. Cause, chest, clue. We know that the first

THE LIFE CHEST : AFRICA

cause is protecting animals, here at Tanda Tula. That's the first step. The second step is to find the chest." Josh paused to think and then continued. "Let's take a walk around camp. Get a feel for the place, meet some of the people. Then we start asking around about the chest. Who knows? Maybe we'll even see it somewhere."

"Okay. Sounds like a plan," agreed Bernie. "Our guides are meeting us here later this afternoon. I sure would like to have that clue in hand before we sit down to plan the trip with them."

"Do you think we should take the map with us?" asked Josh.

"No, let's not," said Bernie. "It's in my locked briefcase. I'll stash it under the bed for now."

After hiding the briefcase, Bernie and Josh explored the camp, accompanied by Brian, an armed guide. "Animals often wander into camp," the guide explained. "Usually harmless ones like monkeys or impala. But this morning we had a leopard walk through. So I'll stay with you for a bit on your stroll."

Tanda Tula through Josh and Bernie's eyes

"Good idea!" Josh agreed, scanning the path for animals. A young warthog trotted by, but nothing more dangerous.

"That warthog is on his way to the oasis," said Brian. "The oasis here attracts animals of many species." He laughed and pointed to a low branch in a nearby tree. "There's Cayar. Better watch out for him."

Bernie and Josh looked up to see a small vervet monkey, silvery-gray except for its black face, gazing intently at them from the leafy branch. "Cayar?" Josh asked.

"It's short for 'little pest' in Somali," explained Brian. "Make sure you keep the door panels in your tent zipped up tight and locked. The monkeys love to get inside the tents. They'll steal anything that's not nailed down, and Cayar's the smartest one."

"He does look like he's plotting something," agreed Bernie as they continued down the path.

"Tanda Tula is also next to an elephant trail," added the guide. "You may think you feel an earthquake some morning, but it's probably a huge herd of elephants passing by. I can show it to you later. It's so wide it looks like a dry riverbed."

Their walk through the camp took them past a dozen tents, several lounging areas, and an open-air market. Levicar Land Rovers hummed by, driven by guides carrying rifles. All sorts of people, from families to scientists, visited Tanda Tula. Brian left Bernie and Josh safely in the Great Hall.

"The chest could be in here," said Bernie as they entered the spacious hall. Some of the canvas walls were rolled up to take advantage of the cool breeze.

"Look down at this end," said Josh as he walked toward the large stone fireplace flanked with African decorations of shields and spears. "Above the fireplace mantel here. This has to be the spot where Simon Lyons' painting used to be."

"Migration of the Wildebeest?" asked Bernie. "The painting that he hid the map behind? Wow." He shook his head in disbelief. "Just think of Gramps buying that painting right off the wall."

"And not knowing anything about the map," added Josh. "What crazy luck."

After a few more minutes of looking around the Great Hall, Bernie and Josh saw nothing that looked like it could be a lion chest, and decided to head over to the reservation office.

A pleasant young woman greeted them at the front desk. "Our great-great-grandfather was here back in the year 2002," Bernie explained. "He wrote in his journal that he saw a beautiful chest decorated with a lion on the front. Do you know if it's still here anywhere? We'd sure love to see it."

"I don't remember seeing a chest like that anywhere," said the young woman. "Maybe Miss Afiya knows. Kosey!" she called to a young man ambling toward the door with a bowl of food in his hands. "Where's your grandmother?"

"She's at the tour station outside," said the young man without smiling. "I was just going to take her some lunch."

"Okay, follow Kosey," the young woman said to Josh and Bernie. "He'll introduce you to Miss Afiya and you can ask her about the chest." Josh and Bernie hurried to catch up to Kosey, who was already out the door and walking down the path.

"Your name is Kosey? I'm Josh and this is Bernie," said Josh, holding out his hand.

"Sorry. Bowl." Kosey indicated that he was unable to shake hands.

Josh didn't speak, but gave Bernie a look that said, "Friendly fellow, huh?" They walked through the busy camp in silence. As they approached the tour station, Kosey trotted ahead. He put the bowl in front of his grandmother at the counter, pointed to Josh and Bernie, spoke a few words, and disappeared behind the building.

Kosey and Afiya

Afiya studied the two young men. All Kosey had said was that they wanted to ask her about a chest. What could they mean? The Freedom chest and the lion chest were both in her apartment. No one had seen them for years. She couldn't remember the last time she had opened one of them. At 90 years old, I guess my memory is a little faulty, she smiled to herself, but that doesn't mean I've forgotten the story.

Afiya was the daughter of Senwe, who had sold Simon Lyons' painting— and the map— to Kim Yost all those years ago.

She was the keeper of the chests and the only person living who knew the entire story of the diamonds. Afiya decided to be cautious with these strangers and not give anything away. Not yet. The spies from Royal Camp had tried repeatedly over the years to get information from her, but lately they seemed to have given up. Who knows? They could be trying again, she thought.

Josh stopped Bernie before they got close enough for Afiya to hear, and whispered in his ear. "Hey, remember the proverb? Maybe we should start by saying that."

"I feel like I'm in a spy movie, but okay," agreed Bernie. "Let's do it." He walked up to Afiya and shook her hand. "I'm Bernie, and this is my cousin Josh," he said.

"Hi. Um, greed loses what it has gained, uh, wouldn't you say'?" stammered Josh, suddenly thinking that he sounded really stupid.

Afiya's eyes narrowed, but her heart leapt. The proverb! Could these young men be here to get the clues to the sacred diamonds?

"Yes, I agree, and I have said those words many times, mostly to my grandson. How do you know that proverb?" she asked.

"From our great-great-grandfather's journal," said Bernie.

"And his map!" Josh burst out. "The puzzle map. We have it."

"I am not sure I know what you mean," said Afiya. She was getting more excited with every word, but still maintained a cautious demeanor. "Please tell me more."

Bernie and Josh told Afiya the whole story, from reading Gramps' journals to finding the map and the plate, to planning the journey to find the diamonds. After a few minutes, Afiya let her guard down, and after a half hour of talking, all three were laughing and hugging with joy and excitement.

"It is so hard to believe," said Afiya. "That someone would finally be here with a plan to recover the diamonds. I learned the story when I was a little girl, and have been waiting for someone to come for the clue ever since."

"I hope we can do it," said Bernie. "We're going to need a lot of help. I hope you don't mind— we have two local guides coming to meet us here this afternoon. Would you like to meet them too?"

"Yes. Thank you for the offer," said Afiya. "You can't be too careful. The people at Royal Camp nearby know about the diamonds. You have to be sure the people you have hired aren't their spies."

"We did background checks on them before we left," said Bernie. "And if you give them your seal of approval, that's all we need."

"How about if we go get the map and the plate?" asked Josh.

"Please do," said Afiya. "I'm very anxious to see them. I'll get Kosey to mind the booth and we can go to my apartment to examine them."

When Josh and Bernie came back to the tour station with the briefcase, Kosey was behind the counter reading a magazine. They were several yards away but they could hear Afiya's voice. "Pay attention! There is a large group checking in this afternoon and they want to go on a drive right away. Make sure their guide is here." She turned to Josh and Bernie when she saw them approaching. "Come with me," she said. She started down the path and turned to scold her grandson one more time. "Kosey, don't fall asleep!" she called.

Afiya's colorful apartment was filled with African fabrics and decorations. Josh and Bernie sat on the sofa and took the map from the briefcase while Afiya started tea in the kitchen. She came back into the living room and sat in a chair across from the sofa while Bernie and Josh spread the map out on a low table. Her eyes were shining.

THE LIFE CHEST : AFRICA

"It's so wonderful to see this," she said, running her wrinkled fingers over the drawing on the canvas. "When you walked up and said the proverb, I could hardly believe it. You really do have the map. But the blank spot in the middle— does the plate help decipher it?"

"Yes," said Bernie as he lifted the plate from the briefcase and placed it in the middle of the map. "We're lucky that Simon Lyons painted the clues on it before he died. He was the only person Erasto related the clues to."

"Ah, I see it now," said Afiya. "All the cities are in place."

"And the animals, and the causes they represent," added Josh.

Afiya looked up at Josh and Bernie. "The causes are very important," she said. "If you want to retrieve the diamonds, I will help you. But only if you are doing it for the right reasons. You know that these diamonds are sacred and should help the African people, don't you?"

Yes," Bernie assured her. "All the stories of General Erasto and the old shaman, Duma, are about giving the wealth from the diamonds to the people in the cities on the map. Believe me, that's our mission too."

"Ah, you know about Erasto! He was like a father to my grandparents," smiled Afiya. "He is the one who made the diamond map, tore it into pieces and had the pieces hidden in the animal chests in each city on the puzzle map."

"Is that what the clues in the chests are?" asked Josh excitedly. "Pieces of a map? We knew we would be looking for clues, but we didn't know what the clues were."

"Yes, the clues are pieces of the diamond map," answered Afiya. "The diamonds are somewhere in a mine at the foot of Mount Kilimanjaro, where Erasto's people were forced to work, and where they were tortured to the point of death. Erasto realized toward the end of his life that he was the only person alive who knew exactly where the diamonds were in that mine. He then made the diamond map. It has seven pieces, and each piece shows a more detailed description of the path to the chamber where the sacred diamonds lie."

Afiya stopped for a moment to think of the next detail of the story, then continued. "Erasto sent six of his former soldiers to the locations on the puzzle map to start ventures that would help the African people. Each of the soldiers was told to make a chest that honored his location's chosen animal. Erasto gave each soldier a piece of the diamond map and told him to hide the piece in his animal chest. He told the men that someone would eventually come and ask for the piece, reciting the proverb to prove they knew the story. Their descendants should still be waiting for someone to come and retrieve the map pieces, just as I have waited."

"Pretty smart," said Bernie in admiration. "I suppose you have to get all the pieces of the map before you can use it."

"The map is useless without all the pieces," agreed Afiya. "Erasto was worried about his old enemy, Ona, getting the map and stealing the diamonds for himself. That's why he spread the pieces all over Africa. He even kept the details of the plans from his soldiers. None of them knew who the other chest keepers were, or where they lived." Afiya shook her head, smiling. "You're going to have quite an adventure finding the chests and the clues."

"I hope they're all still there," said Josh. "The animal chests and the map pieces."

Map piece number one, stolen by Ona

THE LIFE CHEST : AFRICA

"You have more to worry about than that," said Afiya. "Ona's descendants and followers are still around to this day. He and his nephew started Royal Camp nearby, soon after Erasto founded Tanda Tula. But Ona wasn't interested in animal conservation. He only wanted a chance to find out where the diamonds were. You see, Ona stole one of the map pieces; the one that was supposed to go into the lion chest that I have here at Tanda Tula."

"But can we still find the diamonds, even with that piece missing?" asked Bernie.

"Luckily, the piece Ona stole was the first piece of the map," answered Afiya. "It only showed the base of Mount Kilimanjaro. We already know you have to go there. It's the rest of the pieces that will give you the crucial information you need."

"That's lucky," said Josh.

"But Ona's greed was fueled when he stole the map piece," said Afiya. "He lusted after those diamonds to his dying day, and there are people at Royal Camp even now who have inherited his greed. You must watch out for them. I was afraid you might have been spies from Royal Camp when I first met you. The proverb reassured me, and now I trust you with the whole story. An old lady can't help you much on the trip, but I'll make sure you have the supplies you need, and you'll go with my blessing."

Afiya ran her hand over the puzzle map again, tracing the path from the lions at Tanda Tula to the next stop. "I wish my father Senwe could have seen this," she said, softly laughing. "The story is a family legend now: how my father sold the painting with this map behind it to the Canadian man. He was just a little boy of 11, but when Simon Lyons found out about it, my father got the tongue lashing of his life."

"Poor kid," said Josh. "When I was a kid I always hated it when my mom gave me a piece of her mind."

"Oh, he didn't let it upset him," said Afiya. "My father could charm anyone. He talked Simon out of being angry soon enough; once he heard that the Canadians were planning to help find the diamonds. He convinced Simon that it was all for the best!"

They all laughed at Senwe's cleverness, but then Afiya's smile became a frown. "That was the last time my father saw Simon Lyons. Simon went back to his home in Kenya. Everyone was shocked when they heard he was killed by a rogue Cape buffalo just a few months later. It was a terrible loss."

The old woman sighed again. "My grandparents grieved for Simon but they were also disappointed that there would be no diamond expedition. They made sure my father knew the whole story, and he passed it on to me. I was beginning to think the story would die when I died, because my grandson has no interest in it."

"That's Kosey, right?" asked Josh. "Where are his parents?"

Afiya didn't answer right away. "I'm sorry," said Josh. "I didn't mean to bring up something you might not want to talk about."

"It is hard, but I will tell you," said Afiya. Her face, although wrinkled and weathered, still betrayed her grief. "My son and his wife were conservationists. One spring when Kosey was still very young, they took a Land Rover out to the game reserve, meaning to spend a few days observing the lions. They wanted to count new births in the prides. But they never came back. After a week, their bodies were found under a pile of brush in an acacia grove. Both of them had been shot."

Afiya stopped speaking. The memory seemed to be too much for the old woman. She leaned back in her chair, and a tear appeared in the corner of one of her closed eyes.

"I'm so sorry," said Bernie.

Afiya spoke again, her head still resting against the back of her chair. "The authorities thought they must have accidentally stumbled on poachers in the act of killing elephants for their ivory. Their murderers were never caught, but I believe it was the evil men from Royal Camp. I know them. I know what they are capable of doing."

The old, wise woman sat up as straight as she could and looked sternly at the cousins. "I tell you this story not so you will feel sorry for me, but so you will know how dangerous your mission is. You may want to rethink this trip. If the people at Royal Camp find out you are planning a mission to find the diamonds, they will try to stop you. They may even attempt to kill you."

Bernie and Josh looked at each other soberly. There really were poachers and thieves out there, and they were capable of murder. If they would kill innocent people over elephant ivory, how quickly would they kill to get the sacred diamonds?

Afiya continued her warning. "Africa has been a volatile continent since the beginning of time. Besides the poachers and thieves, there are other dangers. Tribal wars escalate without warning. Travelers never know when they might find themselves in the middle of one."

Josh took a deep breath. "We've come this far," he said. "I guess we're not quitting now, huh, Bernie?"

"Absolutely not," agreed Bernie. "We'll have protection. One of the men we hired has military and bodyguard experience. We won't let anyone keep us from this mission, Afiya. The diamonds should help Africa— both the people and the animals."

"My father would be thankful to hear you say that," smiled Afiya. "He loved the animals more than anything. Did you know he worked as a safari guide here? He was the very best. Let me pour some tea and I will tell you the story. It started the day my father Senwe was born."

Afiya went into her small kitchen and came back with a tea tray. "I have chai tea and biscuits," she said. "I also have some Amarula. It is a South African drink made from the fruit of the elephant tree. I enjoy it every day at teatime."

Bernie and Josh tried the sweet, strong liqueur. "It has an interesting taste," said Bernie. "Caramel with a hint of fruit."

"But you prefer tea?" asked Afiya.

"Yes, thanks," said Bernie. "How about you, Josh?" he asked.

"We better have tea this afternoon," Josh agreed. "It'll help us stay awake."

Afiya filled their cups with the fragrant chai and began the story of her father.

"Of course, there are often days when many animals are born in the game reserve. But the day my father arrived, eight other babies were born, right here at Tanda Tula, all different. A lion, an elephant, a Cape buffalo, a giraffe, a zebra, a rhino, a leopard, and a cheetah were all born the same day. It was quite a time at Tanda Tula. My grandparents thought it was a sign. They filled my father's nursery with little toys of each of the animals."

"That's quite a coincidence!" smiled Bernie.

"It might sound silly to you, but there was something to it," said Afiya. "My father did love animals. They were his playmates as he was growing up and they trusted him more than anyone else. Everyone knew my father would be a safari guide as soon as he was old enough."

Afiya paused to sip her liqueur. Josh asked, "When did he become a guide?"

"At 18 years old," the old woman answered proudly. "He was one of the best safari guides the area has ever seen. Guests would ask for him specifically, because he seemed to know where the animals would be. It was almost as if they came to greet him on his safari drives."

Afiya smiled at her memory. "He used to take me with him sometimes when I was young. It was amazing to see how unafraid the animals were around him."

"It's wonderful to have that natural ability to understand and appreciate animals," said Josh.

Afiya frowned. "I can't say the same for the guides at Royal Camp," she said. "They have never been as good as ours. They even tried to sabotage my father's tours because they were jealous. Tanda Tula has always been a more popular safari camp than Royal Camp."

"That's rotten. What did they do?" asked Bernie.

"Sometimes they strung wire across the road or tried to chase the animals away, but they never succeeded in spoiling my father's safaris. He had a sense of when they were around, just like a zebra or kudu can sense when its enemy is near. He would just change his route and avoid them."

"Does Royal Camp have much business these days?" wondered Josh.

"They don't go on many safaris. There has always been suspicion that they kill animals for sport, but they have never been caught."

"Is there any evidence?" asked Bernie.

"Indirectly, yes," answered Afiya. "There are so many animal skins and mounted trophies displayed at Royal Camp. Many more than here at Tanda Tula, and newer ones."

Josh was puzzled. "Newer ones? What do you mean?"

"African animals haven't always been endangered," Afiya explained. "In the past, we often used animals for food and for their hides. When an animal was killed, we gave thanks for it, and used every part of its body. The hides you see on the walls at Tanda Tula were hung there long ago. In developed areas of Africa, we now protect the animals and only shoot them with cameras."

"I understand," said Josh, nodding. "Seeing a new hide or piece of ivory would mean that it had been taken illegally."

The lion chest

"Yes," said Afiya. "My father would be heartbroken to see it." Afiya's eyes then brightened with a new thought. "I have some pictures of my father," she said. "Would you like to see them? They are in the lion chest. Come with me; I'll show you the lion chest and General Erasto's Freedom chest."

They walked to the rear of Afiya's apartment, where she got out a key and unlocked a door. "I keep the chests in a locked room," she said. "I wish I didn't have to, but they hold treasures that my enemies would kill for."

Bernie and Josh were sobered by this statement, but were still excited to see the chests they had read so much about. The Freedom chest, worn but still handsome, sat in an honored place on a table in the corner of the room. Its picture frames held old photos of the general, some with his soldiers and one with Simon Lyons.

The lion chest was magnificent. It had been well cared for over the years, and the patterned squares of inlaid wood were beautifully offset by polished metal trim and a large figure of a lion, front and center on the chest.

THE LIFE CHEST : AFRICA

The lion trinket

"We have chests like these in the United States, too," said Bernie, running his hand over the top of the lion chest. "We call them life chests. My parents gave me one when I was six years old."

"I didn't get mine until I was 19," said Josh. "Bernie's parents were responsible for that one too." He smiled and gave his cousin an affectionate punch on the shoulder. "And my wife and I surprised Bernie with one when he got married."

"Well I was surprised, but my wife wasn't," laughed Bernie. "They had her pick it out. Chen Li and I each have our own life chest, so the one we got for our wedding is a smaller one. We're going to put keepsakes in it that relate to our life together, like our marriage certificate, a flower from our wedding, and the first letter she sent me from China."

Josh and Bernie spent the next hour looking at treasures. Afiya's family's legacy was kept in the lion chest, and she showed them photos of Senwe as a little boy and as a safari guide with Afiya on his lap in a Land Rover. Lastly, the old woman took what looked to be a large coin, stamped with the head of a proud male lion, from a leather case. It was the lion trinket, blessed by Duma long ago. "The shaman Duma had great hopes for the diamonds to help the African people," said Afiya. "And Erasto carried on that hope. Let's look in his chest now."

General Erasto's original Freedom Chest

General Erasto's Freedom chest held medals, diaries, and keepsakes from his travels. "I have one last thing to show you from Erasto's Freedom chest," said Afiya after they had admired the photos of his regiment. "Take everything out of the chest," she said as she checked to make sure the door was locked. Bernie and Josh removed the last few items from the Freedom chest, looking at each other questioningly. Afiya reached in and lifted out a false bottom. Underneath the false bottom was a small velvet bag. The old woman opened it and took out a heavy grayish stone the size of a walnut, jagged and glinting in the lamplight. She was holding in her hand the diamond that Erasto had taken from the sacred diamond chamber.

"This is the diamond that started it all," Afiya said solemnly. "The chamber that you will search for is lined with millions of these from top to bottom, according to what Erasto said."

Bernie and Josh each held the diamond for a silent moment.

Afiya spoke again. "This diamond represents many years of suffering. You are here to help bring joy and a measure of justice to offset that suffering. This is something you must never forget as you travel. The diamonds are to benefit the African people."

"We'll do everything we can," said Bernie. "I hope we can help."

"Our team should be here pretty soon," Josh reminded Bernie. "The guys we hired are meeting us at the front desk. I sure am glad that one of them is a bodyguard."

Afiya put the diamond back in the velvet bag and placed it in her pocket. Josh and Bernie helped replace the rest of the items in the Freedom chest.

"Would you come with us, Afiya?" asked Bernie as they left the room. "I'd like you to meet them too."

"Yes," said Afiya. "I want to make sure they have honorable intentions." She locked the door behind them, and they made their way to the front gate.

Kosey met them on the path. "Grandmother, two people are looking for these guys," he said, pointing at Josh and Bernie. "They're at the registration office," he added as he ambled off.

Afiya looked at her grandson, and then turned back to Josh and Bernie. "I apologize for my grandson," she said. "He is not a happy boy. He does the work I ask him to do, but his spirit is lost. He has not found his way in life yet."

"How old is he?" asked Josh. "About 18?"

"He is 17 years old," said Afiya.

"Yeah, I figured," said Josh. "I can relate. I was a lot like that when I was his age. Hopefully he'll find his way."

Bernie waved at the two men standing at the front desk as they approached the registration office. One was tall and muscular, the other short and thin.

"Gogo Okonjo? Effiom Boro?" Bernie called.

"Just call me Effie," said the larger man, giving Bernie a firm handshake.

"That would make you Gogo, I guess," said Josh to the smaller man.

"Yes, that's me," he said shyly.

Introductions were made all around and the group decided to meet in the Great Hall to talk over their plans. "Afiya is the matriarch of Tanda Tula," explained Josh as they walked. "She's been the keeper of the diamond story for many years."

"And the keeper of the chests that hold the stories," added Bernie.

"It sounds fascinating," said Gogo. "I hope to use my expertise as a gemologist to help as much as I can."

"I'm not really interested in stories," interrupted Effie bluntly. "I'm a military man and a fighter. All I know is that we're going to get a Land Rover and travel north for a few weeks. Then we're going to look for some diamonds. Just tell me who I'm protecting and what you want me to blow up and I'll do my job."

As they found chairs in the lounge, Afiya told Effie about the owners of Royal Camp. "Their names are Agnes and Aaron Bradley," she said. "They pretend to run a safari camp, but the main reason they have the camp is to try to find information about the diamonds. I don't hire many people here. I'm always afraid someone who walks in asking for a job is one of their spies. Keep an eye out for them now, but hopefully they won't be a problem once you start on your trip."

"Got it. Anybody else?" asked Effie.

"I've seen their bodyguard," answered Afiya. "His name is Abdi Kalu. He's easy to recognize. There is a large scar running down the left side of his face, and his left ear is half gone."

"Sounds like a tough guy," observed Josh. "What happened to him?"

"He was attacked by a lioness," answered Afiya. "He barely escaped with his life. Lions can be unpredictable. A tourist was killed recently in Kenya by a lion that jumped in the open window of a safari van. I am sorry for innocent people who are hurt by lions, but Abdi is no saint. He was attacked because he tried to take cubs away from a mother." The old woman clucked in disapproval. "Abdi Kalu is an evil man with no shame. He is a descendent of Ona Madaki, who was the first person obsessed with greed for the sacred diamonds."

"And that desire has stayed alive for so many generations?" asked Gogo. "That is hard to believe."

Bernie and Josh looked at each other, silently recalling their trip to China, where they encountered Chen Mara and her legacy of greed. "It's not as unusual as you might think," said Josh grimly.

"How about you, Gogo?" asked Bernie. "Do you have any questions?"

"I grew up in Tanzania and I've heard the legend of the sacred diamonds," said Gogo. "From our emails and conversations, I think I have a clear idea of what the mission is. I've been studying and teaching gemology for several years and I'm very familiar with the old mines around Kilimanjaro."

"Good," said Bernie. "We'll need your expertise when we get to the mine."

"And here is what you will find," said Afiya. She opened the drawstring of the small velvet bag that she had brought with her. "This is one of the sacred diamonds. The only one that has ever been taken from the chamber."

Gogo held it first. "It's amazing. I can't believe I'm really looking at one of the sacred diamonds," he whispered before handing it to Effie.

"It's quite a stone," agreed Effie.

"You may encounter many dangers on your trip," warned Afiya as she placed the diamond back in the velvet bag. "Are you certain about going?" she asked Gogo and Effie. "Are you willing to take these risks to find the diamonds and help your people with them?"

Gogo took a deep breath. "I won't say that I'm not scared," he admitted. "But I feel as if my life has been leading toward this. I must do it, no matter how nervous I am."

"I'm in," said Effie. "It beats being a security guard at the Pretoria Mall." He looked at the others sheepishly. "That's the only other job offer I've had lately," he said. "I need something with more action."

"Then we're all set," said Josh. "Can you two go over our supply list and make sure we have everything we need? Bernie and I are going on a night safari and then we'll leave first thing in the morning."

"We'll have everything ready," Effie assured him.

"Let's walk back to your apartment," said Bernie to Afiya. "We'll help you make sure that the diamond gets put away safely."

The group dispersed, and after dinner Josh and Bernie enjoyed an amazing night safari. After watching a beautiful sunset and enjoying a "sundowner" drink, they set off with Brian in a Land Rover equipped with a powerful spotlight. The sounds of animals and birds were everywhere, and with the aid of the spotlight, they saw hyenas and a leopard.

"It's pretty quiet tonight," remarked their guide as the Land Rover approached the oasis where they hoped to see a large male lion.

"Quiet?" asked Josh. "I've never experienced such a noisy night in my life!"

"I don't mean the animals," Brian explained. "I mean the gunfire. The guides at Royal Camp shoot into the air to try to flush the animals out of the brush. Very stupid. An animal ends up dead as often as not, and they always claim it was an accident." He shook his head. "Poachers. That's what they are. They're slippery, but some day they'll get caught." He shined the spotlight at the water's edge. "There's the big guy."

Josh and Bernie stared in wonder at the huge tawny lion, relaxing on the sand with the breeze ruffling his dark mane.

"He ate a kudu yesterday, and he's still pretty mellow," Brian remarked. Then he noticed Josh leaning over the side of the truck to get a good camera shot. "I wouldn't get out and rub his belly, though," he warned, only half joking. "Let's head back."

After the safari, Josh and Bernie returned to their tent and settled in for the night, with the noises of the African bush still surrounding them. "Amazing," said Bernie. "The wildlife that you can hear all around us!"

"And they're all sounds that you'd only hear in a zoo back home," said Josh. "But there are no fences here. It's like we're in the middle of a zoo with no bars!"

"Pretty cool, huh?" asked Bernie as he climbed into bed.

"I guess," agreed Josh reluctantly, peering out into the darkness. "I just never had a hyena sing me to sleep before, and then threaten to eat me for breakfast."

They both settled in, but Josh was startled by a very close noise just a few minutes later. He sat up. "Hey! Bernie? Is that you?"

"Huh?" answered his cousin groggily. "I just fell asleep. What's the deal?"

Josh jumped out of bed and grabbed a flashlight. "I think I forgot to latch the door," he groaned. "We have a visitor. Cayar unzipped the panel!" His flashlight beam found the monkey, happily snacking on the bag of banana chips Josh had left on a chair.

"Out!" Josh scolded. "No more freebies for you!"

Cayar stayed put, however, until Bernie tossed another bag of snacks out the door. The little monkey skittered outside, and Bernie secured the door panel tightly.

"Hey! Were those my macadamia nuts?" asked Josh, shining the flashlight at the retreating intruder.

"Yes," answered his cousin. "Better he took a few snacks than a comm device or my glasses!"

"That's true," agreed Josh, climbing back into bed. "Little pest is right." He yawned and closed his eyes, sliding into dreams of lunching with monkeys and hyenas.

The next morning, Afiya sat down with Josh and Bernie as they were finishing their breakfast. She looked concerned. "I have something important to talk to you about," she said. Before Josh or Bernie had a chance to ask what it was, she continued. "You must take Kosey with you on the trip," she said.

"What? Your grandson? Why?" asked Josh.

"My family has been keeping the story of the diamonds alive for many years," Afiya answered. "It is only right that someone from the family should be there when the diamonds are found. And my grandson needs a mission like this. He needs to understand his heritage. I want him to have an appreciation of Africa and see what his ancestors experienced in the mines."

Josh and Bernie weren't sure what to say. How could this sullen teenager be of any help to them? Bernie spoke up. "Give us a few minutes to talk about it, if you would," he said, standing up.

"All right," said Afiya. "Let me know soon. I will go and talk to Kosey now, and tell him the plan." Afiya left the dining hall and soon found Kosey. He was leaning against the counter at the tour station, listening to music on a comm device. Kosey didn't react well when Afiya explained how she wanted him to spend the next several weeks.

"You have got to be kidding me, Grandmother!" Kosey said angrily. "We don't know these people! Why would you send me away with them to who knows where? To do what? Take orders from them and be their water boy? Besides, who would take care of you?"

"I'm sure you would enjoy having a break from your old grandmother," said Afiya wryly. "But don't you see, Kosey? This is our family's legacy. Your great-great-grandparents made a promise to General Erasto that someone from our family would help find the sacred diamonds."

"Maybe they did," answered Kosey. "But I didn't make any promise. Don't put this on me."

He turned and walked away from his distraught grandmother as she called to him, "Please! Kosey, this is your destiny."

The words had no effect on her grandson. Afiya dropped her head in despair for a moment, but then stood tall. I won't give up, she thought to herself as she followed Kosey down the path. I will make him understand.

In the meantime, Bernie and Josh had left the dining hall and walked down the path toward the front gate. "What do you think, Josh?" said Bernie. "Should we take Kosey with us? It seems that this kid might get in the way more than anything."

"I don't know," said Josh. "He kind of reminds me of me at that age."

"Yeah, that's exactly what I mean," said Bernie, grinning. "But I guess we really can't say no. If it wasn't for Afiya's help, we wouldn't be doing any of this. We wouldn't know what the clues were or how they all fit together."

Their conversation was interrupted by a woman calling from near the front gate "Hello!" she said as she waved. "Remember me?"

As Bernie and Josh got closer, they saw that it was Lucy Mayo, the woman they had met on the plane from Cape Town.

After they greeted each other, Lucy explained. "I just had a taxi drop me off. I couldn't stay at Royal Camp. The place is so poorly run; I don't understand how they stay in business. And besides, I need to write up my report on poaching. Part of it is going to be about their operation and I don't want them looking over my shoulder."

"This is a great place," said Bernie. "You'll like it here much better. We're leaving today, but let's sit down for a cup of tea after you register."

"Sounds fine," said Lucy.

"Wait a minute," said Josh, looking past the front gate. "Friends of yours?" He nodded toward two people who had just gotten out of a levicar and were trotting toward them.

"That's one of the owners of Royal Camp," said Lucy, referring to a woman with stringy blonde hair, dressed in khakis. "And that big guy is always hanging around her and her brother."

"Josh, he's got a gun," said Bernie. "And I see the scar on his face. It's Abdi, their bodyguard."

"Super," said Josh. "Adventure already."

The visitors were Agnes Bradley and her bodyguard Abdi Kalu. Agnes started yelling as they approached. "You! You snuck out early and didn't pay your bill! You can't steal from us!" she yelled at Lucy.

Lucy answered as calmly as she could. "My company is being billed for my stay," she explained. "I gave the person at your front desk all the information she needed to send an invoice."

"Huh," snorted Agnes. "That's what you say. I'll call and check."

"Whatever you like," said Lucy. "Let's go," she said to Josh and Bernie.

"Good idea," said Josh as they walked away.

Agnes, on her comm device, turned and hissed at Abdi. "Stay with them! Keep your eyes open. Something's going on!" Abdi obeyed, walking a few feet behind the trio as they headed back into the camp.

"That guy is following us," said Josh, glancing behind him. "Can we lose him somehow?"

"Quick, he's bending to tie his boot," said Lucy urgently. "Duck into this tent!"

The tent was open on both ends. They managed to slip out the other side onto a more secluded path, and headed the opposite way. When Abdi looked up from his boot, he continued on quickly, thinking that Lucy and the two men with her must have run ahead.

He didn't find them, but he stopped when he heard a heated conversation taking place in the open, echoing Great Hall. Afiya had found Kosey and was pleading with him. "Please!" Abdi heard her say. "You must care about Erasto's legacy. You must help the Americans. They mean well, and their assistants are good people. They have the puzzle map, and they know where to find the pieces of the diamond map. I really believe they can find the diamonds at Mount Kilimanjaro, and you can help them."

Abdi froze. Erasto! The old nemesis of his ancestor Ona! And diamonds? They must be talking about the sacred diamonds! Agnes was right. There is something going on, he thought to himself. He hid behind a pillar and continued to listen.

"Forget it," he heard a young man's voice say. "You can't talk me into it. It's a stupid idea. It sounds even more boring than what you make me do here."

Abdi waited silently to see what would happen next. After a few more minutes, the conversation ended, and a wrinkled old woman walked out of the building. Abdi looked around the corner to see a teenage boy slumped on a couch. He casually walked up to him. "Beautiful day, isn't it?" he said, looking past Kosey at the cloudless morning sky.

"I guess," answered Kosey.

"I just heard you say how bored you are," said Abdi, sitting down in a chair across from Kosey. "I don't see how anyone can be bored in this place, but whatever. Wanna earn some quick money? Then you can go into town and party. It's nothing illegal," he added quickly.

"How?" asked Kosey.

"I'm curious about that old lady you work for," said Abdi. "If she's got a map, I'd sure like to see it. I'm very interested in maps. I'll give you a thousand rand if you can take a photosim of it for me."

"Why don't you just talk to her yourself?" asked Kosey.

"That old hag? I heard the way she yelled at you. What a witch. She'd probably try to put the same ugly spell on me that somebody put on her." Abdi laughed. "So what do you say?"

"What do I say?" Kosey said as he stood up. "I say get out of here before I punch you in the face. You're talking about my grandmother." He got angrier as he spoke. "She raised me. I owe everything to her! Get out, I said!"

Abdi raised his hands. "No problem, no problem," he said as he stood and left the hall. Kosey chased him down the path. "And she's not ugly! She's beautiful!" he yelled.

Kosey stopped to catch his breath and watched Abdi and Agnes get into their car and glide away. What was that all about? Maybe I should tell my grandmother, he thought to himself.

A few minutes later, Kosey found Afiya at the front registration desk, talking to Josh and Effie. "Grandmother—" Kosey began, but Afiya interrupted him. "Don't worry. I just finished telling Josh that you won't be going with them."

"Grandmother, wait," said Kosey. "I owe you an apology. But there's something else." Kosey told them about the man who had asked him to take a picture of the map. Afiya's hands flew to her mouth.

"Oh no!" she said. "It probably was a spy from Royal Camp. He must have heard me scolding you in the Great Hall. How could I have been so foolish? Now they know almost everything."

She began to cry, and Kosey put his arm around her. "It's all right, Grandmother," he said. "They don't have the puzzle map and they'll never get it. I'll guard it with my life on the trip."

Afiya looked up from her grandson's shoulder. "Do you mean that you will go?" she asked.

"Yes, Grandmother," answered Kosey. "I'm sorry for causing you grief. As long as I know that you will be looked after, I'll do everything I can to help find the diamonds. And someday I will punch that guy in the face."

"Good," said Josh. "We'll be happy to have you along."

"Now, Grandson." Afiya put her gnarled hands on Kosey's shoulders. "The old woman looks after the child to grow its teeth and the young one in turn looks after the old woman when she loses her teeth," she said. "Do not forget the old proverb."

"I'll remember, Grandmother," said Kosey. "You won't be left alone."

"But we'll need to change our plans a bit," said Effie. "If those thieves at Royal Camp see us leave today, they'll follow us for sure. We should wait until after dark, and leave at about four in the morning."

"Good idea," said Josh. "I'll go tell the others."

The villains: Abdi Kalu with Agnes and Aaron Bradley

The Bradleys at Royal Camp were excited to hear what Abdi had found out at Tanda Tula. "I knew something was going on!" said Agnes. "I have a sense about these things!"

"We'll get them this time!" said her brother Aaron. "We'll follow them— stay right on their tail— and when it's the right time, we'll ambush them and take the maps."

Aaron ordered Abdi and their other accomplices to load a Land Rover with supplies. Then he and Agnes began drinking to celebrate.

Abdi shook his head as Aaron got out the gin. This never ended well. He knew they would drink into the night and sleep away the morning. They would most definitely not be right on the tail of the Americans and their group from Tanda Tula tomorrow.

Although he was treated as a lackey by the Bradleys, Abdi was the most ambitious and intelligent of the thieves from Royal Camp. He felt driven to prove himself. Abdi grew up tough and street smart. He knew his legacy, too: he was proud of being a descendant of Ona Madaki. He was also glad to have gotten a job with the Bradleys; they were descendants of the mine foreman who had worked with Ona.

However, in Abdi's mind there was an underlying resentment of the Bradleys. He paced outside his tent late that night after his employers had fallen asleep. I do most of the work for them and they treat me like a servant, he thought to himself. When we get the diamonds, I deserve as much of the treasure as Aaron and Agnes. Their ancestor was the mine foreman, but my ancestor was the great Zulu, Ona Madaki. He was the man who was clever enough to follow Erasto all those years and steal that piece of the diamond map. Abdi's bitterness rose in his throat. They sure didn't give me very much recognition for finding out about the map today. I've got to do something to really show them how smart I am. He kicked a stone, and it rolled under the Bradley's Land Rover.

Abdi was skilled in improvising electronics. He often modified comm devices to be used as bugs, and now, seeing the stone roll under the Land Rover, he had another idea. Digging through the tool box he kept in his tent, he found an old GPS device. With a little work, he rigged it so it would attach to the bottom of a vehicle to track and transmit its movements. He then programmed a small receiver that he could keep in his shirt pocket.

Taking the tracking device, Abdi walked the mile to Tanda Tula. He didn't take a car for fear of being seen. After sneaking around the dark camp for several minutes, he spotted an older Land Rover with four or five people gathered around it. They loaded a few boxes into the vehicle and left the area.

This must be the group going out after the diamonds, Abdi thought. I have to move fast. They may be back soon. Abdi smeared a bit of superfast adhesive he had created from acacia tree sap onto the device. He quickly walked to the Land Rover and slid the tracking device underneath the front fender. The homemade adhesive held firmly. Abdi slipped back into the darkness. He walked back to Royal Camp, listening to the sounds of the African night and feeling proud. Now maybe I'll get more respect, he thought.

It wasn't until late the next morning that the Bradleys emerged from their cabins. They found Abdi outside under a sun umbrella, calmly drinking coffee. "Abdi! You fool!" snapped Agnes, kicking the chair the big man was sitting in. "Why didn't you wake us? The Americans are probably long gone by now!"

"I should have gotten rid of you when I fired your lazy friend Dean!" yelled Aaron. "What do you suggest we do?"

Abdi smiled and raised his hands. "Calm down, now. Here is what you do. Sit down and have some coffee. Or maybe you need a hangover remedy?" he said cheerfully.

"Stop joking around!" demanded Aaron, but Agnes sat and put her head in her hands.

"I do have a killer headache," she groaned. "What's up your sleeve, Abdi?"

"It's not up my sleeve. It's in my pocket," said Abdi, taking out the receiver for the tracking device. "We know exactly where the Americans and their friends are. I planted a tracking device on their Land Rover last night."

"Good show! But why didn't you just say so in the first place?" said Aaron.

"That was smart," agreed Agnes. "So now what? We follow and catch up to them?"

"Maybe," answered Abdi. "But we can take our time if we want. Let them get a couple of clues and then ambush them in a few days, farther down the road. We're totally in control of how we do this job."

"You're right," said Aaron. "We don't need to go off half-cocked. We already know to head north to Kilimanjaro, because of the piece we have from the diamond map. And now we can track them step by step. Be sure to keep an eye on that receiver."

Agnes stood and stretched, squinting against the sun. "Good. We don't have to rush. This will give me time to get some breakfast and take a bath. Abdi, tell Rupert and Charlotte to start cooking."

The brother and sister walked away without any more comment, leaving Abdi feeling almost as bitter as he had the night before. I'm still just their flunky, he thought. But they'll appreciate me someday.

Chapter Six

The Rhino Chest: Good Beginnings

The 12-hour drive to Harare was filled with tension at the outset. Everyone was silent and watchful as they climbed into the Land Rover and pulled away from the front gate at Tanda Tula. Gogo turned out the headlights and drove as quietly as he could, while Effie, with his gun drawn, kept an eye out behind them. Their goal was to give the Bradleys at Royal Camp no indication that they had left to begin the search for the diamonds.

No one dared to speak, but Gogo couldn't help whispering to Effie, "A levicar Land Rover would've been quieter."

"I like these old trucks better," answered Effie. "No turbines to clog with dust."

The group began to relax after about a half hour on the road. Effie holstered his gun. Bernie passed around a thermos of coffee and Josh struck up a conversation with Kosey about working at Tanda Tula.

"I help out wherever my grandmother needs me. You know, to get ready for safaris. I don't mind it too much," admitted Kosey. "It's just all I've ever known. I'm done with school and I don't really know what to do now. A lot of my friends go into town to dance and drink. I like doing that sometimes, but they keep getting into trouble. My best friend got arrested last month."

"The trouble with trouble is, it starts out as fun," said Josh. "I don't know who coined that phrase, but believe me, it's true. I know from experience."

Kosey nodded, but didn't talk for a few minutes. Josh spoke up again. "Do you think you might want to be a safari guide?" asked Josh. "Your great-grandfather was one of the best."

"Yeah," agreed Kosey. "He's a hard act to follow, though." Kosey sighed and faced the window. "My grandmother always talks about my potential and I feel guilty for not living up to it. I hate it when people do that." He quickly turned back to Josh. "I didn't mean you guys. It's pretty cool to be on this trip and help you out. It's important to my grandmother, anyway," he finished with a shrug.

Josh didn't push the subject. The last five minutes was the most he had ever heard Kosey talk, and he was happy with that for the time being.

"Anybody hungry? I'm feeling kind of hollow," offered Bernie.

"This guy," said Josh, thumbing his chest. "I could eat a buffalo."

"I've got some protein bars in that pack over there," said Gogo over his shoulder. "I figured we'd make a quick stop for lunch later. We have to get some miles in this morning."

"Yeah," agreed Effie. "I want to put as much distance as possible between Royal Camp and us before they realize we're gone."

"My sentiments exactly," agreed Josh, digging through the pack. "Drive on, sir!"

The sky began to lighten, and the sunrise over the plains and rolling hills was rich and golden. A crisp, clear morning followed and Josh and Bernie continued to marvel at the sights and sounds of Africa. Noisy birds, thorn-covered trees, elephants and giraffes wandering along the roadside: it was all so different from anything they had experienced before. After a quick stop at a roadside café halfway to Harare, the group stretched their legs for a few minutes and then climbed back into the Land Rover with Effie in the driver's seat. "This is so awesome that we got a wheeled Land Rover," said Josh. "You gonna let me drive sometime, Effie?"

"Maybe, when I get tired," answered the big man behind the wheel. "You ever driven anything besides a levicar? I didn't get this rig for fun. I got it because it's more reliable on dirt roads. The levis are quieter for safaris, but they need their turbines cleaned of dust twice a day."

"Well, sure, I know. But it's not that different from a levi, is it?" asked Josh, hanging onto the roll bar as Effie navigated a tight corner.

"Oh, you'll see," laughed Effie. He apparently didn't trust Josh's driving ability, because even though they stopped a few more times during the day, Effie jumped behind the wheel every time.

After one of those short stops, Gogo spoke up. "We're going to be traveling by the Great Zimbabwe National Monument!" he declared. "It would be a shame not to stop and see it."

"What? That broken down old city?" said Effie. "We're not tourists!"

"Aw, come on, Boss," said Josh. "Just for an hour, okay? It sounds interesting."

Effie reluctantly agreed and the group took a short tour of the Great Zimbabwe Ruins. Gogo explained the history as they walked the grounds. "This was an ancient city, built between the 11th and 15th centuries," he said. "There's a lot of mystery about it. No one really knows its exact function. Some of the walls are 11 meters high and 800 meters long. Why? Nobody knows."

Josh and Bernie gazed in amazement at the huge granite walls and turrets. "It reminds me of the Great Wall of China!" said Josh.

"Chinese artifacts have been found here," said Gogo. "There was definitely a trading relationship between these people and the Chinese."

"Wow," breathed Bernie, snapping pictures with his comm. "Human ingenuity never ceases to amaze me!"

Effie, walking up to the group, managed a smile. "It does make a guy proud, I guess," he said. "But your hour is up." He turned and jogged toward the Land Rover. "Back on the road, tourists!"

They still had a half day's drive to their destination. Late in the afternoon, Effie stopped at a traffic light and turned to Gogo. "Coming into Harare," he announced. "Anybody know where we're going?"

"Well, yes and no," said Bernie. "All we know is what's on the puzzle map."

"I got it right here, Bernie," said Kosey, tracing the path with his finger from Tanda Tula to Harare on the puzzle map. "Cause, chest, clue, right? The cause is the hospital, and we're supposed to find a rhino someplace. There isn't anything called a rhino hospital, is there?" he asked skeptically.

Bernie checked the information on his comm. "There's no hospital with the word rhino in its name, if that's what you mean. There's a big public hospital in the middle of town, and another one on the outskirts. We're going to pass the public hospital in a few minutes."

After a few more miles navigating the city streets, they drove past the entrance to the large government hospital. "I don't see a rhino anywhere," Josh said, squinting into the distance.

"Should we drive past the other one?" asked Gogo. "Yeah," answered Bernie. "It's just a few miles from here."

The town's other hospital was down a small side street lined with trees. "The hospital is at the end of this road," said Bernie.

"Hey, look at the sign!" said Kosey excitedly. "There's a picture of a rhino on it!"

"Bingo!" shouted Josh with a fist pump. "Clue number two, here we come!"

Effie stopped the Land Rover near the door at the end of the drive. Josh and Kosey hopped out. Before they could even turn off the vehicle, though, the entrance doors of the hospital slid open and a young woman came storming out. A man pushing a gurney followed her.

"Hey! You can't park here!" she yelled, hitting the side of the Land Rover with her clipboard. "Move your truck! Right now!" She ended her speech by kicking a tire.

"Ukuzola, be calm," grumbled Effie as he put the Land Rover into reverse and backed down the drive.

The wail of a siren added to the commotion. "Hurry!" said the young woman. "There's a parking lot on the side of the building. You need to get out of the way of the ambulance!"

As Effie moved to the parking lot, an ambulance pulled up to the front door. An attendant jumped from the back and loaded the patient onto the waiting gurney. The young woman let out a sigh of relief as the patient was wheeled inside. She turned to Josh and Kosey as Effie, Gogo and Bernie walked up to join them.

"I apologize for shouting at you," she said. "But you can see it was an emergency, and your truck was blocking the entrance to the hospital."

"I understand," said Josh. "No need to apologize."

"I don't know," whispered Kosey to Effie as the rest of the group moved through the door. "I thought she was kind of harsh."

"And she hit my truck," agreed Effie.

Gogo turned around from the doorway. "Come on," he said. "She said we could come in."

"My name is Winna Sylla," the young woman was saying. "Come into the waiting area and sit down. How can I help you?"

Now that the crisis with the ambulance was over, she relaxed. Her gracious smile caught Kosey off guard. Maybe she's not so harsh after all, he thought.

Josh and Bernie looked at each other for a minute before answering Winna. Here we go again, they both thought. How do we start telling this complicated story? The proverb?

To their surprise, Kosey jumped in. He had been emboldened by Winna's smile. "We're on a mission," he announced.

"A mission?" Winna looked puzzled. "Like a scavenger hunt?" she asked.

"No, this is serious," said Kosey. "We found the cause: your hospital. We know it's the right one because of the rhino. Now we need to find the chest."

"Hang on, Kosey," interrupted Josh. "You *are* making it sound like a scavenger hunt. Tell us about the hospital," he said to Winna. "Why is there a rhino on the sign out front?"

"I don't know," said Winna. "I think it's always been there. I never really thought about it before." She stopped and sighed. "The person who could probably tell you is gone. She died suddenly a few months ago. She was the head of the hospital, and my mentor. I've gone through two years of nursing school but I want to become a doctor." Winna stood up. "Her grandfather founded this hospital. Take a look at this memorial she had made in his honor."

The group walked toward the wall where a large plaque hung. It contained a photograph of a soldier in uniform. Underneath the photograph was an engraving of a rhinoceros.

"Looks like our man," said Effie.

"Yes," agreed Bernie. "He must be Erasto's soldier!"

"And there's another picture of a rhino," added Josh, pointing to the framed etching. "With some writing under it. 'A friend is someone to share the path with.' "

"That's an old African proverb," said Winna. "It's sort of the mission of the hospital. Everyone who comes down the path to the door of this hospital is taken care of. You saw that ambulance come in. The doctors are taking care of that patient now. Only when he's stable will they ask if he has money to pay. No one is turned away. We're all sharing the same path."

"That must be hard on the hospital's finances," said Bernie.

"It is," agreed Winna. "There is so much need and so few resources. But the tradition of charity was started by the founder of the hospital, and we've always done it. His granddaughter, my mentor, told me that she hoped the hospital would receive a large endowment. Then we could afford to upgrade equipment, hire more staff and really help all the people in the community, even the ones who can't pay."

"Where did she expect the endowment from?" asked Bernie.

"I don't know," answered Winna. "But for some reason, she always held out hope for it."

"She was right to have hope," said Kosey excitedly. "That's why we're here."

"I wish we had cash in hand to give to you," put in Bernie quickly. "But it's a little more complicated than that."

"What do you mean?" asked Winna.

"We can explain it after we find something," said Josh. "Your mentor may have had a chest, decorated with rhino horns. Have you ever seen it?"

"Yes, I think so," answered Winna hesitantly. "We haven't cleaned out her office yet. It may be in there. Come with me."

THE LIFE CHEST : AFRICA

The group followed Winna down a hall and Josh thought of something else. "There's another African proverb," he said. "Greed loses what it has gained. Have you ever heard that one?"

"No," said Winna. "But I like it." They reached the office. "Go ahead and look around," she said.

"Here it is," said Kosey, after a few minutes of searching. The chest was behind the sofa, with several medical books stacked on top. "Can we move it out to get a closer look?" asked Bernie.

"I guess so," said Winna. "Just be careful." Effie moved the sofa and Bernie and Gogo pulled the chest out into the middle of the room.

The rhino chest

The rhino chest was dusty, but still beautiful. Rhino horns formed handles on the sides, and the front of the teak chest was carved with a scene of two rhinos at an oasis, gazing into the trees.

"Well, here it is," said Winna, moving the stacks of books to the desk. "Now tell me– why do you want the chest, and how did you know it was here?"

"The man who started your hospital was a soldier under a general named Erasto, back in the 20th century," explained

Bernie. "He knew of a secret chamber of diamonds in a mine at Mount Kilimanjaro. This hospital is one of the causes he wanted to benefit from the diamonds if they were ever found."

"And we're trying to find them," added Kosey. "He put clues along the road from South Africa to Kilimanjaro, in seven different places."

"What are the clues?" asked Winna.

"Pieces of a map," answered Gogo. "Each map piece was put in a handmade animal chest like this one. Can we open it?"

Winna felt a bit overwhelmed. "I don't know what to think," she said. Looking from one face to another, she tried to distinguish truth in what these strangers had told her.

Kosey understood. Impulsively, he took Winna's hands in his. "I know what you're thinking," he said. "I only met these guys a few days ago myself. But they're the real thing. My great-great-grandparents knew Erasto, the man who discovered the diamond chamber. He wanted the diamonds to benefit the African people and not become blood diamonds. This isn't a scavenger hunt or a trick to steal something from you. There is treasure out there, and we need your help to find it."

"Okay," said Winna, smiling. Kosey's earnestness and sincerity had won her over. And he had nice hands. "Let's see if we can find your map piece."

The rhino chest held many treasures that had been carefully placed in it over the generations. Gifts from patients, graduation certificates and birth and death records passed through Winna's hands as she searched through the chest. "Look at this," she said as she picked up a comb with a rhino head carved on one end. "This is really old, isn't it?"

"There's a tag attached to it," said Effie. "What does it say?"

Winna read the faded writing on the paper. "Blessed by the shaman Dumaka Dia for the success of this venture."

THE LIFE CHEST : AFRICA

The rhino trinket

"The shaman was Erasto's friend," said Josh excitedly. "He's the one who drew the puzzle map!"

"But we took everything out of the chest, and I don't see a piece of a map in here," said Winna.

"It may be in a secret compartment," said Bernie. "It could be on the bottom, or maybe the inside of the lid. See if the lid slides or moves in some way."

Sure enough, a panel in the lid slid open and Winna reached in to pull out the treasure they were looking for. A cheer went up from the group.

"That's it!" said Josh.

Winna handed Bernie the scrap of canvas. It was map piece #2, showing Mount Kilimanjaro with three diamond pits at its base on the south side. "Does it tell you where to go to get the next clue?" she asked.

Map piece number two

"No, that information is on a different map: the puzzle map that Josh mentioned," answered Bernie. "I'll get it out of my briefcase to show you. This piece we just found will help us find the diamonds when we get to Mount Kilimanjaro. Can you sit down with us for a few minutes? Maybe have a cup of coffee? We'll explain the whole thing."

Winna looked at her comm. "I need to check in and do my rounds," she said. "I'd like to join you in about an hour if that's all right. There's a small café here in the hospital. I can meet you there."

"Sounds good," said Josh. "Do you mind if we take the map piece with us to the café?"

"All right," answered Winna. "I'll walk you over to the café, and then I'll see you in an hour."

"One down," said Effie as he sat down a few minutes later with a steaming cup of coffee. "And five to go."

"This is quite helpful," said Gogo, looking closely at piece #2 of the diamond map. "I'm familiar with this area at the base of the mountain. I know right where these three pits are."

"Does the map show which pit the diamonds are in?" asked Kosey, drinking a soda as he looked over Gogo's shoulder.

"No," answered Gogo. "I suppose that information will be on the next piece we find."

Bernie looked up from his comm. "I found a place to stay for the night," he said. "It's not far from here."

"I need a good night's sleep," said Effie. "We've got another long drive tomorrow."

"Don't forget, Boss," said Josh. "I'll drive anytime."

"Believe me, I haven't forgotten," said Effie. "You keep reminding me."

The group laughed as Winna approached. "Good joke?" she asked.

"Not really," said Bernie. "Josh is more pathetic than funny."

"You only say that because I can't reach across the table to punch you," said Josh, grinning. Then he added, "Don't worry, guys. We talk like this all the time. Only rarely do I actually punch him."

They laughed again, Kosey the loudest. He was beginning to feel comfortable in the group, and enjoyed watching Bernie and Josh's good-natured ribbing.

"Winna, sit here," said Gogo, bringing another chair to the table and placing it next to Kosey.

"Thanks." Winna sat down. "So," she began, "I know you're looking for diamonds, and this map piece will help you find them. But there's another map too? And how did you learn about this treasure in the first place?"

"You might need a cup of coffee for the whole story," said Bernie.

"I'll get it," said Kosey, jumping up.

During the next half hour, Winna heard the story of Duma, Erasto, and Simon Lyons; the puzzle map, the plate, the diamond map; and the hope that the legend of the sacred diamonds held for the people and animals of Africa. Explaining it all again, Bernie and Josh were re-energized for the rest of the trip and Effie and Gogo found new inspiration. Kosey just found himself staring at Winna's dark eyes and wavy auburn hair.

"It's incredible, isn't it?" said Winna, gazing at the details on the puzzle map. "It says 'Harare' right here on the map. It has a picture of a rhino and the word 'hospital'. This hospital was planned so long ago, and most of us who work here don't know its history. I started here a year ago, just after I turned nineteen. I had no idea of the significance of the rhino chest, and what it held."

"Maybe your mentor was planning to tell you, and she didn't get the chance," said Kosey.

"Yes," agreed Winna, holding back tears. "Her heart problem came on very quickly."

"We're very sorry for your loss," said Bernie. "But will you let us take the map piece?"

"Of course," said Winna. "If you find the diamonds, it will benefit so many. I'll do everything I can to help. Part of me wishes I could go with you."

"I wish you could too!" said Kosey enthusiastically. "Well," he said in answer to the amused looks from the others, "we don't have a medical professional."

Winna stood up quickly. "Back to work for me. Good luck to you," she said, shaking hands all around. "Maybe during the trip you can let me know how it's going," she said to Kosey.

"Sure," Kosey answered. He was embarrassed now and tried to act casual. "If we have time."

Winna smiled and waved as she walked off. Bernie started to say something to Kosey about having a crush, and got a punch in the shoulder from Josh. He looked at his cousin quizzically.

While the others settled in at the hotel, Effie fueled up the Land Rover and did a maintenance check on it. He returned with sandwiches, and they ate on the hotel's porch, watching the beautiful African sunset blaze and then fade.

"Six-hour drive tomorrow," said Effie, standing and stretching his huge frame. "I'm going to get some sleep."

"I guess we all better do that," said Bernie." I know who you're going to dream about, Koscy," he said with a grin.

"No idea what you're talking about," muttered Kosey, quickly going inside.

"Don't embarrass the kid, Bernie." said Josh to his cousin. "Have you totally forgotten what it was like to be 17?"

"I've been trying to forget for a long time," said Bernie. "But okay, I'll quit teasing him."

At breakfast the next morning, Josh was in the middle of describing one of Gramps' antique cars when Winna walked up to the table, carrying a box.

"I'm glad I caught you before you left," she said. "I put together some first aid supplies I thought you might be able to use. It has anti-malaria pills and histamine blockers for allergic reactions, plus the usual bandages and creams." She handed the box to Kosey and smiled.

"Thanks a lot," said Kosey. "That was really kind of you."

"Well, I said I wanted to help," said Winna. "This isn't much; it only took a few minutes to put together. We can go back to the hospital and get some water jugs too, if you can use them. "

"Yes, we can," said Gogo. "They'll come in handy."

"Would you like to sit down?" asked Josh. "Join us for a few minutes. Bernie, let's go put this kit in the Land Rover. Effie, you got everything packed up?"

Winna and Kosey with the water jugs

"Yeah, but I want to stretch my legs before we start," said Effie. "I gotta keep an eye out for those Royal Camp fellas, too, just in case."

Gogo excused himself to use the restroom. Kosey started to get up too, but Josh stopped him. "Have another cup of coffee with Winna. You did your share of work this morning bringing our suitcases down."

After he reached the door, Josh turned and smiled at the two young people chatting away. "Relax, Boss!" he called to Effie, who was pulling the Land Rover up to the hotel entrance. "The adventure can wait another 15 minutes, right? Take a peek inside," he said, pointing to Kosey and Winna. "Don't they look good together?"

"I'd rather get out of here before any romance starts," grumbled Effie. He leaned on the horn, and Kosey jumped up from the table. "Oops! Accident!" the big man said to Josh, laughing.

Chapter Seven

The Zebra Chest: Shaking Off Trouble

"OK, we have a few hours, so let's figure out this problem," said Bernie as the group in the Land Rover settled in for the six-hour drive to Lusaka.

"What problem?" asked Josh, stuffing a doughnut into his mouth.

"I say let's talk about the problem of you leaving crumbs all over the truck," grumbled Effie.

"That too, but I meant the problem of what we say when we get to each of the stops," explained Bernie. "So far it's been pretty awkward. We're not sure where to begin, we don't know if they know the proverb, and we're not sure who to talk to."

"Yeah," said Kosey. He shook his head. "At the hospital, I made it sound like we were on a scavenger hunt. It was pretty dumb."

"It wasn't so bad, but what you need is an elevator speech," said Gogo.

"What's that?" asked Kosey.

"Think of it as a way you can explain the mission in the time it takes for an elevator ride," explained Gogo. "You touch on the main points in less than a minute."

"Good idea," said Josh. "My mom and Leah have an elevator speech for the nonprofit we run. Anybody they talk to might be a potential donor, so they're always ready with the speech when somebody asks them what they do. That reminds me," he added, clicking on his comm. "I need to call home. We've been gone five days now, and it's been a few days since I checked in."

"I talked to Chen Li this morning," said Bernie. "You better step up your game. Oh, and ask Leah for some elevator speech ideas while you're at it."

After a short conversation with Leah and a long-distance hug from little Meg, Josh turned back to the group.

"Okay," said Bernie. "Did Leah give you some good ideas?"

"She agreed with Gogo. Touch on the main points: cause, chest, clue," said Josh.

"And we're looking for zebras," added Kosey.

"Yes, but I think we still need to ease into that somehow," said Bernie. "And try to figure out who the best person is to ask about the cause, the chest, and the clue."

Gogo had another idea. "How about asking to speak to the person who knows the most about the history of the organization?"

"Sounds like that would be a good place to start," agreed Bernie. "The next place we're going is the football club. Who wants to be the spokesman?"

"Kosey and I will do it," volunteered Josh. "Okay, Kosey?"

"Sure," said Kosey. "I won't make it sound like we're on a scavenger hunt, I promise."

"I gotta say something," Effie put in. "You know that we're talking about real football here, not that game you Americans play that you call football, right? I never could figure out why you would call it football. You hardly ever use your feet."

"True enough," admitted Josh. "I don't know why we call it football either. Or where the word soccer comes from."

"People think it's American, but soccer is actually a British term from the early 20th century," explained Gogo. "It was short for association football, which is more like soccer. They called it that to distinguish it from rugby football, which is more like American football."

"Thanks, Gogo, but now my head's spinning," said Josh, laughing. "Do we know where this football club is in Lusaka?"

"I've been looking online," answered Bernie, scrolling through pages on his tablet. "I think we're in luck. There are half a dozen football academies around the city, but here's one called Zebra Stripe Football Club."

"That's got to be it!" said Kosey excitedly.

"Yup," said Bernie. "I just hope our luck holds out once we get there."

The group reached Lusaka after lunch. On the outskirts of the city, they saw many well-manicured playing fields and lots of kids and coaches. Zebra Stripe Football Club, however, was in the heart of the city. Next to a sign showing a football decorated with zebra stripes was an older school building and a weedy playing field that had seen better days. Happy shouts came from football players on the field, though, and as soon as the Land Rover pulled up to the school, Josh and Kosey jumped out to watch. Gogo, Bernie and Effie climbed out of the truck and shook their heads as they watched Josh and Kosey get invited to join the game.

"I thought those two were in charge of the elevator speech today," grunted Effie.

"I guess they forgot," sighed Gogo.

"We might as well start over there," said Bernie. "Let's go join them."

They walked toward the bench, and talked to a coach sitting there. Bernie asked her if she knew of anyone who was familiar with the history of the organization or had heard of the founder. She pointed to an equipment shed on the other end of the field and said they should talk to the young man there, who was repairing a net. "His name is Geteye Kalu," the coach said. "I think he's related to the man who founded Zebra Stripe."

"Josh!" called Bernie as they headed down the sidelines to the equipment shed. "We found somebody to talk to! Come on, guys!"

"Okay, Doc," said Josh. "Guess we gotta go, Kosey."

"See you later, kids!" called Kosey as he kicked the ball to the goalie. "You guys are pretty good!"

By the time Josh and Kosey had caught up with the others, they were already in the middle of a conversation with Geteye.

"Yes, I've heard of the sacred diamonds," he was saying. "My mother mentioned them now and then. I thought it was just a legend."

"How did your mother know about the diamonds?" asked Gogo.

"Her great-uncle was the founder of this football school," answered Geteye. "But what does a diamond mine at Mount Kilimanjaro have to do with this little place?"

The football club players and coaches

"Let me ask you a question first," said Bernie. "And then I can answer yours better. Is there a chest here? Decorated like a zebra?"

"Yes!" said Geteye in surprise. "It's in the lobby. My mother's great-uncle put zebras everywhere. I guess it was his favorite animal," he said with a shrug.

"There's more to it than that," said Josh. "Can we go look at it? Like Bernie said, if we find what we're looking for in the chest, we can answer a lot of your questions."

"Of course. Follow me." As they walked across the field, Geteye talked about his work at the football club. He was a coach and teacher whose heart went out to the kids growing up in the city. A lot of them were bored, aimless, and unsupervised, he explained. The area had been rife with crime for years, and these kids were often coerced into joining gangs.

"Gangs?" whispered Gogo anxiously to Effie, glancing around.

"It's a rough place. I was raised here myself," said Geteye. "So I know what it's like. Being able to come here and play football after school and in the summer gives them something fun to do. That's part of it. We also teach leadership classes, and we have projects to help benefit the community. Neighborhood cleanups, things like that. And we get social services for the kids who need it, too."

"Has it been effective?" asked Bernie. "Have you seen crime go down?"

"I've been working here five years, since I turned 20 years old, and I think it makes a real difference," answered Geteye. "We're keeping kids off the streets and the gangs are shrinking. That's what my friends on the police force tell me."

They reached the school building and entered the lobby. "We have an office here, a couple of classrooms, a gym, and locker rooms," said Geteye. He gestured around the lobby. "And zebras everywhere, as you can see."

He was right. There was a mural of zebras painted on the wall, a wallpaper border of zebra striped soccer balls, zebra stripe pillows on the couches, and zebra stripe rugs.

"And this must be the chest you're looking for," Geteye said, leading the group to a trophy case on one wall. Underneath the case was the zebra chest.

"Wow," said Kosey. "It's beautiful." He ran his hand over the polished inlaid wood on the lid of the chest. The curved strips of inlaid wood were stained black and white to resemble a zebra hide. The black and white stripes covered the entire chest except for a border surrounding each side, which was golden teak laid in a zigzag pattern.

The zebra chest

"So," said Geteye, trying to understand. "The founder of Zebra Stripe had this chest made? And he had something in it that's a clue to where these diamonds are?"

Just then, the front door opened and a group of laughing boys and girls burst into the lobby.

A girl of about 12 years old ran up to Geteye. "Coach! I stopped three goals in the practice game! You should've seen me!"

"That's great, Anya!" Geteye said enthusiastically. "You said you wanted to be keeper, and I knew you'd make a good one if you stuck to it and faced your fears. Congratulations!"

He turned to the other kids, some of whom were kicking a ball around in the lobby. "Hey! Get to the locker rooms!" He pointed to the boy who brought in the ball. "Two demerits for your team, and don't complain. You know footballs are only allowed on the field and in the gym. Hand it over."

The boy tossed the ball to Geteye and trotted off to the locker room with the others. "The beginner teams are going to be arriving in a few minutes," Geteye said. "And they're even noisier. How about if we take the chest to the coaches' office to look for that clue?"

"Good idea," said Effie. "How heavy is it?" he asked, standing up.

Bernie stood up too. "I bet you and I can handle it," he said.

"It's down this way." Geteye led the group toward a hall on the other side of the lobby from the locker rooms.

"Oof! What's in this thing?" asked Bernie as he attempted to lift one end of the chest.

"I honestly don't know everything that's in it," admitted Geteye.

"Step aside, Bernie," said Effie. "I got this." The big man put both arms around the chest, lifted it up and hoisted it onto his shoulder. "Let's go," he said.

Bernie shook his head in admiration. Geteye led the way to the coaches' office with Effie and the chest bringing up the rear. Inside, Effie grunted as he carefully lowered the chest to the floor. "There you go," he said. He smiled, betraying his pride in his strength.

"That's impressive, Effie," said Josh. "How much can you lift?"

"Whatever needs to be lifted," said Effie, back to his gruff self. They turned to the zebra chest. "Is it locked?" asked Gogo worriedly.

Geteye tried the lid. "Nope," he said as he lifted it. "Now let's see what's in here." He handed a trophy to Kosey. "I forgot about these trophies that we rotated out of the display case." He picked out a shoe with broken cleats and sighed. "Some of the stuff is just junk that the kids have thrown in here," he said. "I guess I should keep it locked. I think the key is in the coaches' desk."

Geteye reached further into the chest. "Wow," he said. "This is a picture of Zebra Stripe's founder and the first group of kids he coached! I think I'll frame it and hang it on the wall."

After lifting out more trophies, a deflated ball, and some old class schedules, the chest was nearly empty. "You said the clue was part of a map?" asked Geteye. "I don't see anything like that in here."

"This is what I'm good at," said Bernie. "Looking for secret compartments. Step aside," he added, glancing at Effie and grinning. Effie shook his head and rolled his eyes, but he smiled too.

Bernie felt along the lid, sides and bottom of the chest. "Right here," he said, sliding open a side panel. Two items dropped into the chest from the secret compartment. Bernie picked them up. "The map piece!" he said triumphantly, handing it to Gogo. "And look at this, Geteye," he said, giving the coach a small figurine.

It was a zebra, made of teakwood and carved with expert and loving detail from the stripes to the tail. "The old shaman who made the puzzle map created a talisman for each city on the map," explained Bernie. "Erasto gave them to his soldiers to keep with their pieces of the diamond map." He gestured to the little teak zebra. "So there's a good luck charm for Zebra Stripe Football Club. You better keep that safe, too."

THE LIFE CHEST : AFRICA

The zebra trinket

Map piece number three

"It's map piece #3 all right," said Gogo, examining the small piece of canvas. "See? It shows the three diamond pits that were on map piece #2."

"But there's a star on this one," said Kosey, pointing. "That's the south pit," said Gogo.

"So we got one more hint," said Effie. "Now we know which pit to go to. I wonder how hard it will be to find the right spot in the pit. Maybe I'll have to do some blasting."

"We won't know until get the next clue," said Josh.

"Where do you go for the next clue?" asked Geteye. "Mzimba, Malawi," answered Effie. "It's about 10 hours from here. That reminds me; I need to check the tire pressure on the Land Rover."

"I'll come with you," said Josh.

"I'm not letting you drive yet," said Effie.

After they walked out the door, Josh could be heard complaining from down the hall. "Aw, how about just a spin around the parking lot?"

"Is Josh a good driver?" Gogo asked Bernie. "He seems a little—I don't know— impulsive."

Bernie laughed. "Yeah, he's a pretty good driver in a levicar, but don't worry. I think Effie's got a handle on the situation."

Bernie kept the briefcase with the puzzle map in it by his side wherever they went. He opened the case and took the map out to show Geteye. "Here's the whole route," he said.

Geteye admired the intricate artwork on the map, and pointed to the proverb at the top. "What's this?" he asked. "Greed loses what it has gained?"

"That's an African proverb," answered Bernie. "Erasto figured that the person who was retrieving the map pieces would recite the proverb to the chest keeper as kind of a password. But so many generations have gone by. I don't know if anyone knows the proverb anymore."

"I sure didn't," said Geteye. "But I'll use it now. It's a great thing to teach the kids, especially when I see how little they have. They want things that their parents can't afford, and a lot of them think success is only measured by possessions. They don't have the skills or the resources to learn how to work toward a goal. That's when they start stealing. Trying to teach them what is really valuable in life— teamwork, pride in your own efforts— it's hard sometimes."

"If we find the diamonds— I mean *when* we find the diamonds," said Kosey, "you'll have a lot more money. That'll help, won't it?"

"Yeah," said Geteye, brightening a little. "We'll be able to hire more coaches and pay them better. We'll have more leadership classes and be able to get more kids off the street."

"Here's another thing you can do," said Bernie. "Use the zebra chest. It shouldn't be a footlocker or a junk box. Put it in a place of honor, and use it to store the things that you and the kids are most proud of. I have a chest like this too, and that's what I do with it. My family and I store things in our life chests that remind us of the past, celebrate the present, and inspire us for the future." Geteye looked at the photograph of Zebra Stripe's founder, and thought for a moment. "The chest really is a good metaphor for life," he mused. The young coach looked up at Bernie. "I guess that's why you call them life chests, huh?"

Bernie nodded, and Geteye was quiet for another moment, an idea forming in his head. "I think I'll take the zebra chest back out to the lobby and have a stand built for it. I'll talk about the founder in our next leadership class and have the kids help me figure out what they want to store in the chest. Actually, I could probably do an entire leadership class about the zebra life chest!" he said excitedly.

"That's an excellent idea, Geteye," said Bernie. "The kids will really feel connected to Zebra Stripe and what it stands for." He rolled up the puzzle map and put it back into the briefcase. "Can I take the diamond map piece?" he asked. "We'll need to put all the pieces together when we get to the mine at Kilimanjaro."

"Sure," said Geteye. "Is there anything else I can do for you?"

"Got another football lying around?" asked Kosey. "I'd love to kick one around some more."

"No problem," answered Geteye. "Here, take this one," he said as he tossed Kosey the football he had confiscated earlier.

Kosey jumped up and started dribbling it down the hall as Bernie, Gogo and Geteye followed. Kosey and Geteye got in a few passes before Bernie teased, "Hey! Two demerits for your team!"

"Whoops," said Geteye, picking up the ball. "I guess I better follow my own rules." He hung on to the ball until they left the building, and then tossed it to Kosey again.

"You're welcome to stay the night," Geteye offered as they walked to the playing field. "We have a small dormitory room and kitchen that we use for overnight leadership camps."

"We'll take you up on that," said Bernie. "Okay with you, Gogo?" he asked.

"Fine," said Gogo, but he was hesitant. He hoped there were secure locks on the doors. The comments about crime and gangs still had him worried.

THE LIFE CHEST : AFRICA

The night went by without incident, and the group slept comfortably in the dorm, except for Effie's snoring. Gogo grumbled the next morning about investing in earplugs.

Geteye arrived early with eggs, bread, fruit and coffee, and they chatted while he made breakfast in the kitchen.

The coach shook his head in amazement at the whole story, from the history of the sacred diamonds to where they were now, generations later, hoping to find them at last.

"I'll be rooting for you to succeed," he said, setting a plate of flatbread on the table as the group dug into scrambled eggs. "I guess I can't do much to help, but I wish I could."

"You're doing plenty," said Josh, his mouth full. "Thanks a lot for breakfast."

"And for helping us find the map piece," said Kosey.

"Here's something, anyway," said Geteye. "I just remembered I had these." He reached into a cabinet above the refrigerator and took out a mesh bag filled with about 30 colorful hacky sacks. "Take these," he said, handing the bag to Kosey. "Give them out to kids, or anybody who wants to play."

"Thanks," said Bernie. "Who knows? We might need a goodwill gesture at some point."

"I'll make sure you have a zebra striped football to take with you, too," said Geteye.

"Sweet," said Josh. "Thanks again."

After cleaning up the breakfast dishes, the group headed out to the parking lot, and Geteye went with them to say goodbye. It was Saturday, and kids were already starting to gather on the playing field. Effie and Gogo spread the puzzle map out on the hood of the Land Rover to check their route to Mzimba against the GPS.

After tossing a zebra striped football to Josh, Geteye looked past the Land Rover to the playing field where warm-ups were starting.

"Mzimba is the next stop," said Effie to Gogo. "But this is the section of the map that got rubbed out. What do we need to know about Mzimba?" He turned to ask Bernie. "Can you get the plate out?"

Before Bernie could open the briefcase again, Geteye interrupted them. "Excuse me a minute," he said. "There's a person over there I don't know. Sometimes gang members come around, trying to get the kids to rejoin. I better go check it out." He jogged toward the field, a worried look on his face.

"Think I should go with him?" asked Effie, cracking his knuckles.

"Just wait," answered Gogo. "We don't want to start a fight. It's probably nothing."

Geteye trotted toward the figure standing on the edge of the field. When he got close enough to call out hello, the woman turned and ran. Bernie had his high-powered binoculars trained on her as she jumped into a Land Rover and glided away. "Oh, no," he said quietly.

Geteye trotted back to the group. "I don't know who she was," the coach said. "She ran when I called to her. Maybe she was looking for gang recruits."

"She's from a gang all right," said Bernie grimly, lowering the binoculars. "But she's not after your kids. I saw the decal on the side of the Land Rover she got into. It's from Royal Camp."

189

Gogo turned pale and Effie slammed his fist into his hand. "I should've gone after them!" he muttered.

"They haven't done anything yet," said Josh, quickly rolling up the map and putting it in Bernie's briefcase.

"But they know where we are! They could try to kill us any time!" said a shaken Gogo. "How did they find us?"

"Who are they?" asked Geteye. Kosey took him aside to explain the history of Tanda Tula and Royal Camp and how they were hoping to retrieve the diamonds without the Bradleys' knowledge.

While they talked, the rest of the group made a plan. "We've got to lose them," said Effie. "Somehow they got lucky and found us here, but they can't know where we're going next, so we need to throw them off. Let's not head straight to Mzimba."

"Yeah," said Josh. "We should backtrack or go in a different direction or something. Get them off the track."

"That's the idea," said Effie.

"Gogo," said Bernie. "Let's you and I look at our maps and figure out a route that will be nice and confusing. We can lead them on a wild goose chase for a day."

"All right. I hope it works," sighed Gogo, still nervous. "I just can't figure out how they found us." Gogo tried to calm himself down as Bernie looked through his backpack for his tablet. Breathe, Gogo told himself. Breathe! Still shaking as he tried to access the maps on his tablet, he dropped his comm device. It bounced underneath the Land Rover. Sighing, Gogo knelt down to reach for it. As he did so, he noticed a small flash from under the fender. The red light flashed again. Gogo laid flat on his back and slid under the truck. Looking up, he saw the tracking device Abdi had placed there.

"Bernie!" he called urgently. "Bernie, are you still there?"

"Yeah," answered Bernie. "What are you doing?"

Gogo tried to pull the tracking device loose but it wouldn't budge. "I need an army knife!" he called from under the Land Rover.

"I think Josh has one." Bernie was puzzled, but he called Josh over, got the knife and handed it to Gogo. The cousins both listened as Gogo talked to himself under the car.

"Careful— don't want to break it," he muttered. "There!" Gogo slid out from under the Land Rover and stood, brushing the dust from his clothes. "Take a look at that!" he said, handing the flashing device, covered in semi-hardened sap, to Bernie. "They planted a tracking device on us! That's how they knew we were in Lusaka!"

By now the entire group had crowded around. "Wow," said Josh. "Those guys mean business."

"Good job finding that thing, Gogo," said Effie. "Now we can really throw them off."

"Should we bust it up?" asked Kosey.

"I have a better idea," smiled Effie. "We won't have to go on a detour to throw them off. I'll put this thing on a different car. They'll follow it, and it should take them quite a while to figure out that it's not us."

"Awesome," agreed Josh. "How about sticking it to a garbage truck?" he laughed.

"That would be great, but there's not one here," said Geteye. He thought for a moment. "We just had a delivery of some donated equipment. They're going to be heading to Lubumbashi. That's north, but it's way off your path. How about putting the device on that truck?"

"Good plan, Geteye. Consider it done," said Effie.

"But will the driver be in danger?" asked Gogo.

"I don't think so," said Geteye. "It's a rental truck that he's dropping off as soon as he gets to town."

"They weren't following us closely. From what I can tell, they were hours behind us," said Effie. "By the time they catch up to the truck in Lubumbashi, the driver will be long gone."

The device was quickly planted, goodbyes were said, and the group climbed into the Land Rover for another leg of the journey. They would be able to throw Royal Camp off their trail for now, but knowing that they had been followed still worried them. This would be a tense trip, without the jokes and optimism of the past few days. The only reassurance they had was that the tracking device would throw their enemies off their trail. If they could keep them guessing, all would be well again.

It's true that the Bradleys and their henchmen had been foiled for the time being. They would waste an entire day following a delivery truck to the wrong city. But once they discovered the ruse, they would have something to fall back on. Agnes Bradley had a photosim of the puzzle map. She had taken it with a high-powered camera while Gogo had it spread out on the hood of their Land Rover. The villains were still in the game.

Chapter Eight

The Giraffe Chest: Unexpected Help

Agnes opened the curtain in her brother's motel room, letting the late morning light stream in. "Wake up," she said, nudging Aaron in the ribs. "The goody-two-shoes gang left. They're on the way to their next stop."

"Stop nagging me," muttered Aaron. "I was just trying to take a little nap. We don't have to worry as long as Abdi is monitoring the tracking device. That makes things pretty easy for us."

"How about giving me some credit, too?" asked Agnes. "I got a picture of their weird map. If I zoom in on it I can read some of the words."

"Don't even bother," said her brother. "Just use the tracking device. Did anybody get breakfast yet?"

"You missed it," said Agnes. "I'll ask Charlotte if there is any left."

Charlotte Scott, Agnes' friend, was an expert with small arms. Besides her and Abdi, the Bradleys had recruited Rupert Turner, a former army officer, and Jamila Tinibu, a skilled hand-to-hand fighter.

The group started on their day's journey after Aaron had coffee. Rupert drove the levicar Land Rover, with Abdi giving him directions based on the information from the tracking device receiver.

"This trip is boring," complained Agnes, stretching in the back seat. "I'm going to listen to music on my comm."

"No, you can't," said Abdi. "Not with the way I've configured this tracking device. It would give too much interference."

"Why not just sing a song for us?" asked her brother sarcastically. "You always wanted to be a rock star."

"Nobody would want to hear that," said Charlotte.

"Shut up," said Agnes. "But don't worry. Nobody's singing in this car, believe me."

They rode in silence after that, keeping several miles behind what they thought was the Land Rover from Tanda Tula. After about seven hours, they found themselves in the city of Lubumbashi, Congo. Abdi drove down the narrow streets slowly. "Hey, everybody. Keep your eyes open for their truck," he said. "It should be somewhere on this block, according to the tracking device. I want to see them before they see us."

"I wonder what all these stops they're making are for?" asked Jamila as Abdi pulled into a parking garage.

"They're picking up clues to where the diamonds are, stupid," said Agnes. "There was an old diamond map that got torn into pieces and given to a bunch of different people. They're trying to collect all the pieces."

"I know they're putting together a map, idiot," retorted Jamila. "I just wonder what the significance of all these different places is."

"Who cares?" asked Agnes. "Once they get all the pieces, we jump them and take the map. Then we get rid of them for good. That will be fun. No more loose ends. And no more Tanda Tula."

"Where are they, Abdi?" asked Aaron, looking over Abdi's shoulder at the receiver.

"According to this, they're just across the street from this garage," answered Abdi.

"Well, let's do something, then," said Aaron testily. "I want to keep an eye on what they're up to. Agnes, you go with Abdi and search around the block."

"Why me? You want to take another nap?" asked his sister scornfully. "I can't believe how lazy you are!"

"We don't want all of us tromping around the place!" argued Aaron. "Someone has to stay and watch the truck, anyway." With that, he put his hat over his eyes and his feet up on the dashboard, ending the conversation. Agnes stomped away, followed by Abdi.

After about 40 minutes, Agnes and Abdi's voices could be heard in the echoing parking ramp long before they reached the Land Rover. They were both furious. "How could you be so stupid?" yelled Agnes.

"There was nothing I could've done about it!" said Abdi. "How could I have known they found the tracking device?"

"What's going on? What happened?" asked Aaron as the two got closer.

"We've been following a delivery truck all day!" explained Agnes angrily. "We went to the exact spot where their Land Rover should have been, but we couldn't find it anywhere. The receiver kept taking us back to a delivery truck."

"They really got us," admitted Abdi. "I finally realized they must have found the tracking device and stuck it on the delivery truck to throw us off track. I looked underneath the back fender and sure enough, there it was." He opened his hand to show the small device to the others. It was the same piece of equipment that he had built and originally put underneath the Tanda Tula Land Rover.

"Oh, no," groaned Jamila.

"Oh, yes," said Rupert. "So what are we going to do now?"

"I just remembered!" said Agnes excitedly "Now you'll be glad I took that photosim of their map." She scrolled through the pictures on her comm, found the photosim of the puzzle map and zoomed in on it. "Look!" she said. "It's right here. We were just at Lusaka. See, it says 'Lusaka' on the map. All we have to do is check the next place they're going."

Aaron looked over her shoulder. "Something's wrong with your picture taking skills. There's a section of the middle of the map that looks out of focus. I can't see anything on that part."

"The picture's fine," snapped Agnes, looking closer. "It's the map. The middle section is gone. It looks like it was rubbed out. What rotten luck. I can't believe it!"

"So now we don't know where to go next? What do you think it means?" asked Jamila.

"I guess they kept part of the map secret, in case somebody tried to sneak a picture of it. They're way ahead of you, Sis," said Aaron.

"Well, can we get anything from this?" asked Rupert, taking the comm from Agnes. "It looks like they're going to Chitipa," he added.

"Yeah, but *where* in Chitipa?" snapped Agnes. "The other towns had places to go to, like a hospital, or that football school we found them at."

Aaron grabbed the comm impatiently. "Forget Chitipa then. The next one says 'agriculture school,' right here by Pwani, Tanzania."

Abdi shook his head. "Not anymore. Remember that bad drought? All those farmers moved to the Kilombero Valley years ago. Let's head that way."

"But they could have been there and gone already. We have no idea!" said Jamila.

"All the more reason to stop arguing and head to Kilombero now. Let's go," insisted Abdi, getting in the truck and pushing Aaron over to the passenger seat. He pulled the Land Rover out of the parking garage and headed north.

"We have to drive all night?" complained Charlotte.

"Shut up and get me a water bottle," demanded Aaron. He turned to Abdi. "I hope you know what you're doing. This isn't much to go on."

"We'll find it," said Abdi, bearing down on the accelerator. "They got past my tracking device but they can't lose me that easy."

The Tanda Tula Land Rover rolled on toward Mzimba and the animal rehab center, their next stop. Kosey sat up front, helping Effie navigate. "Another long drive," sighed Gogo from the back seat. "Yup. Ten hours," grunted Effie. "You complaining?"

"Oh, no," said Gogo quickly. "In fact— um— I was just thinking what a good thing it is that we all get along so well." He glanced at Bernie and Josh, who sat on each side of him, guns at the ready, keeping watch. Hopefully they weren't being followed, but Effie had said to keep alert. They'd be going through a lot of sparsely populated areas. The landscapes were beautiful, but the long stretches between towns were also the places where tribal skirmishes flared up.

"Sure, Gogo," said Bernie. "I can't chat right now, though. I want to concentrate."

"Sorry. I just feel pretty useless," said Gogo. "I don't know how to handle a gun, and even if I did, my hands shake so much I wouldn't be able to use it."

"It's all right, Gogo," said Bernie. "You and Kosey are extra sets of eyes. That helps. And you can punch me if I start to fall asleep. Josh can't, but you can."

Gogo grinned in spite of his fear. "All right, it's a deal," he said.

It was a beautiful morning, and everyone relaxed a bit as the hours wore on. Gogo, Kosey and Bernie fell asleep in spite of themselves. Josh asked Effie, "Hey, Boss. What would you do if they did follow us again?"

"I'd love to see their headlights in the rearview mirror," admitted Effie. "I know how to lose a pursuit car. Now that's fun."

"I bet it is," smiled Josh. "But it doesn't look like we'll be doing that tonight. So now what?"

"I guess you can find a place to stay," answered Effie. "I'll put the Land Rover in a parking garage and stay with it for the night. I'm still not completely sure we won't be ambushed."

"I'll stay with you," offered Josh. "That way we can take turns, and you can get some sleep."

"I'll take you up on that," said Effie. "Thanks."

Once they heard the plan, everyone else offered to stay with the Land Rover, too. Josh and Effie convinced them that somebody in the group should get a decent night's sleep, so Kosey, Gogo and Bernie found a hotel for the night.

The next morning, with no sign of their pursuers, they completed the drive to Mzimba, starting out before sunup. There are worse places to be running from bad guys, Josh thought to himself, watching the sun come up over the horizon as the Land Rover bumped along. A flock of herons ran through a field next to the road. All of a sudden they rose into the air *en masse,* wings flashing in the growing sunlight. Africa really is the most beautiful place on earth, he decided.

Effie drove on side roads and out-of-the-way paths as much as possible in case the Bradleys were following them. This route had the added benefit of being closer to many more animals and birds than they would have seen on the busier roads.

Josh saw a mass of animals approaching on the savannah and poked Bernie, who had fallen asleep. "Bernie! Bernie, you have to see this!" he said to his cousin, pointing. "Look over there!" Bernie rubbed his eyes and squinted. Not far from the two-lane road they were on was a herd of wildebeest, running in the same direction as they were driving. They all watched for several minutes while the herd thundered past, kicking up dust and snorting.

"What an incredible sight," said Gogo. "I don't think I've ever seen a migration this close. Do you see the young animals?" he asked. "They're always flanked by adults, to keep them safe. These migrations provide many meals for the predators. Any animal who can't keep up is fair game. You know, I've lived here all my life and the beauty and grandeur of Africa will always amaze me." They continued to watch in silence until the herd finally thinned out.

Seeing the animals made everyone, even Effie, feel hopeful again. Maybe they had lost the Bradleys and their henchmen for good. Conversation began to flow. Gogo and Bernie traded university stories. Josh and Kosey joked around, and Effie told tales of the army.

When they reached Mzimba, Bernie looked up from his tablet to give Effie directions to the rehab center. "There are a few veterinary hospitals in the city," he said. "But only one that calls itself an endangered species rehab center. I hope that's the place were looking for."

"I'll do the talking today," offered Gogo as they found a parking space on the road next to the center. "I've felt kind of useless the past few days. I need to do something more to earn my keep."

"You're not useless," said Josh. "You found the tracking device, remember? But don't worry. You'll be plenty busy once we get to the diamond mine."

The group entered the cool, airy lobby of the rehab center and looked around. "I don't see any giraffes," said Kosey. "The football club was full of zebra decorations. This place doesn't have anything."

"Yeah. It's not a good sign," agreed Josh. The lobby was neat and tidy, but devoid of giraffes. An old man dressed in a blue work jumpsuit dusted the vertical blinds on the large windows behind the front desk. Completing his task, he twisted a rod, allowing the warm afternoon sunlight to stream in from between the slats of the blinds.

"Well, we won't know anything until we find the right person to talk to," said Gogo. "I'll head over to the reception area."

The others waited by the door while Gogo made his way to the desk. He talked to a young man for a moment, waited while the man made a short phone call, and then came back to the group. "I asked to see the veterinarian who's worked here the longest," said Gogo. "She's just finishing up surgery and will come out to talk to us when she's done."

"Look at this over here," called Kosey to the rest of the group. He had walked over to a photosim display on the wall opposite the registration desk. "It's a whole display of success stories of animals that the rehab center has saved."

"Wow," said Josh. "There are still a lot of endangered species in Africa, despite all the conservation efforts."

"Yeah," agreed Bernie, examining the display. "And they also save animals that have been injured by poachers' traps or hit by cars. Look at this cute baby rhino!"

"It looks like this place does great work. But I hope it's not a dead end," said Gogo. "What if there's no chest and no clue here? So far we know which diamond pit to go to. But that's not enough."

"Let's not worry about it yet, okay?" said Bernie. "Geteye didn't know anything about the clue in the zebra chest and we still found it. There's something magical about the animal chests and Duma's talismans. Somehow they help keep the dream alive, even after all these years. I really think we're going to find all the chests, the clues, and the diamonds too."

Gogo shook his head. "I hope so," he said. The rest of the group seemed discouraged as well. Bernie was about to say something else to try to lift their spirits when a tall African woman wearing a colorful head wrap and surgeon's scrubs came through the double doors leading from the operating rooms.

"Hello. I am Dr. Boro. You wanted to speak with me? I only have a few minutes until my next surgery." Her manner was brisk and efficient, but friendly.

"Thank you for seeing us," said Gogo, shaking her hand. "It looks like you do some wonderful work here for the animals of Africa."

"We do what we can," said Dr. Boro. "I have my own veterinary practice, and I come here a few times a week to do surgeries at no charge. The center has been through some rough times. We almost had to close it more than once for lack of money. But somehow it survives. The founder was quite a visionary in setting up this rehab center long before the general public was aware of the problems of endangered species."

"We're looking for information about the founding of this center," said Gogo. "Do you know anything about its history? I realize you work with many endangered species here, but wasn't it originally dedicated to giraffes?"

"I've been here about 30 years," answered Dr. Boro. "We focus on saving and rehabilitating animals from the most endangered species. We've been pretty lucky with giraffes. They're not as sought after by poachers as elephants and rhinos are."

"We're specifically looking for a chest the founder had made when the center first opened. It may have been decorated with giraffe hide," Gogo explained.

"We thought the whole center would be decorated with a giraffe motif," interrupted Kosey. "Maybe this isn't the place after all," he said to Gogo.

"Wait," said Dr. Boro. "There did used to be a giraffe motif here. We got a small grant a few years ago, and besides updating the surgical suites, they did a bit of redecorating. The giraffe decorations were taken down."

They were in the right place after all!

"Was there a giraffe chest?" asked Gogo. "Where do you think it is now?"

"Oh, yes. Now that you mention it, I think there was a chest decorated with giraffe hide. It used to sit here in the lobby." Dr. Boro looked around. "Right over there," she said as she pointed. "On that wall underneath the picture display. It must have been removed when the place was redecorated. All the giraffe items were given away or sold. If I had known that the chest had a connection to the founder, I would have kept it."

"So you don't know anything else about the chest? Do you know what might have been inside it?" asked Gogo.

"I'm afraid not," answered Dr. Boro.

"Would someone else know anything about the founder or the chest?" asked Josh.

Dr. Boro thought for a minute. "I don't think so," she said. "As I said, I've been volunteering here for about 30 years and I'm the veterinarian who has been here the longest, by far."

"Thank you," said Gogo, shaking Dr. Boro's hand. "We appreciate your time. I suppose we should let you get back to your work."

"Yes," said the veterinarian. "We are trying to save a zebra with a gunshot wound. The animal should be prepped for surgery now, so I'd better go."

Everyone smiled at Dr. Boro and thanked her again, but after she had gone, despair settled on the group.

"Just what I was afraid of," said Josh. "The chest is gone. We're missing a clue."

"Shouldn't we try to find it?" asked Kosey.

"How?" said Josh. "Knock on doors around town and ask who was at the rehab center's garage sale? There's no way to know."

"We've got to move on anyway," said Effie. "The longer we stay in any one place, the better chance the Bradleys will catch up to us."

"Let's just go, then," said Josh. "We can talk about it in the truck. I guess finding all the clues was too much to hope for."

The others, dejected, began to walk toward the door, but Bernie stopped Josh, grabbing his arm and pulling him into a hallway. "Josh," he said. "You're usually building everyone up and now you're so negative. This isn't like you. What's wrong?"

"I guess I'm losing faith in the adventure," said Josh. "Maybe we didn't think it through enough. Here we are, traveling across the continent, dragging these other people with us, without any guarantee that we'll find what we're looking for. This thing was my dumb idea. I'm sorry I talked you into it."

"You didn't talk me into anything," said Bernie. "I wanted to come on this adventure as much as you did. I suppose we didn't stop to think about what we would do if we couldn't find one of the clues. But we'll figure something out. Maybe we can still find the diamonds without the clue from the giraffe chest. We've just got to stay positive, for everybody's sake."

"You're right," said Josh. "Thanks for the pep talk, Bernie. You're pretty good at those."

"I learned it from my dad. It's the magic of the life chest, cousin," said Bernie. "Wonderful and crazy things happen when you have a life chest. You know that!"

"So true!" said Josh. "Thanks for reminding me. There are so many amazing life chest stories. Let's share some with the others."

"Good idea," said Bernie. "We can tell them the story of finding ourselves in Gramps' book, and some of the lessons we learned from all the *Pumptitude* books. Remember, Josh? Attitude determines altitude! Crank up that attitude, cousin!"

"Yeah, you're right," said Josh, nodding. "My attitude adjustment starts right now! And after that, I'll tell them how your life chest brought you your ideal girl," he added, grinning. "That should entertain them while we drive to the next stop."

"I guess I can tell my love story if it will lighten the mood," agreed Bernie reluctantly. "But hang on. I just remembered something. We didn't recite the proverb to Dr. Boro. Do you think that would've made a difference? Should we go find her?"

"I don't know," said Josh. "Probably not. She didn't seem to know anything about the story, and she's in surgery now anyway."

"Yeah, I guess you're right," said Bernie. He started down the hallway toward the lobby again when they passed an open doorway and heard a voice coming from inside. It was an old man's voice, quiet but confident.

"Greed loses what it has gained," the voice said.

Bernie and Josh stopped in their tracks. The old man who had been dusting the blinds stepped into the doorway and said again, "Greed loses what it has gained. That's the proverb you're talking about, isn't it?"

"Yes! Yes, it is!" said Josh excitedly. "You know the proverb! Do you know the story of the diamonds?"

"I do," said the old man. "And I heard most of the conversation you had with Dr. Boro. She's the doctor who has been here the longest, but I'm the janitor who has been here even longer."

"I'm sorry," said Bernie. "How stupid of us to think that only the doctors would know the story."

"It's all right," said the man. "People don't pay much attention to me here, and I'm used to it. I do my job and get along."

The rest of the group came down the hallway to look for Josh and Bernie. "What's going on?" asked Effie. "We better get going."

"Great news!" said Josh. "We found the chest! Wait– do you have the chest, Mister–?"

"My name is Asante Mensah," the old man said. "Please call me Asa. And yes, I do have the giraffe chest."

The group made introductions all around. They told Asa of their search to find the diamonds and to fulfill Erasto's dream of helping the people and animals of Africa with them. "I'm so glad we found you!" said Josh. "Or that you found us, I mean. We were beginning to give up hope for the giraffe chest."

"I am very happy as well," said Asa. "I too had almost given up hope that someone would come to retrieve the clue in my lifetime. This is a joyful day." Asa's voice, already hoarse, turned into a dry whisper as he finished his sentence.

"Let's go sit down," said Bernie, leading the old man toward the chairs in the lobby. "We want to hear your whole story, Asa."

"I'll get him a bottle of water from the Land Rover," volunteered Kosey, sprinting to the door.

Asa, with information about the chest

After sitting down, Asa told the story of how he became the chest keeper. "My grandfather was the soldier who founded this rehab center," he explained. "He showed me the map piece and told me about General Erasto. I heard the story of the diamonds many times as a child. I hope you can find them. There's so much work to be done here, and the center is low on funds."

"You've seen the map piece?" asked Josh eagerly. "Yes," said Asa, standing. "Let's go get it now."

THE LIFE CHEST : AFRICA

He explained further as they walked back down the hall. "So many years had passed and no one came for the clue. When they redecorated I took the giraffe chest." He laughed softly. "No one really cared that the janitor kept the old thing. They don't pay much attention to me around here. There's not that much for me to do. I had to stay around, though, to meet you when you finally arrived."

They stopped at the door of a storage closet. "I keep the chest in here," Asa said. He opened the door, and Effie and Kosey pulled the chest out. It was covered with a blanket, and Asa took it off to reveal a polished well-kept chest. The front was covered in giraffe hide and flanked with graceful carvings of two majestic, long-necked giraffes.

The giraffe chest

The giraffe trinket

Asa lifted the lid, but it didn't budge. "Is it locked, or stuck?" asked Kosey.

Asa chuckled. "I'm getting old," he said. "I forgot. I have the key right here." He pulled a heavy key ring from his pocket. The ring held several keys to doors in the rehab center, and also an old brass key in the shape of a giraffe. "Ah, here it is," said Asa. He put the head of the giraffe in the lock and the chest clicked open.

"This key was tooled especially for the giraffe chest, blessed by a shaman." said Asa, holding it up. "My grandfather told me it's a good luck charm."

"It brought us good luck today, finding you," said Josh. "Yes," agreed Asa. "Now let's find your clue."

The chest was full of keepsakes and artifacts from generations past: diaries and journals, newspaper articles, photographs and medical records. Asa took a wooden box from the bottom of the chest. Inside the box was map piece #4. He handed it to Gogo.

"Here it is!" said Gogo excitedly. "It shows the south pit, and look! It says 'north wall' right here."

THE LIFE CHEST : AFRICA

"So it's the north wall of the south pit that the diamond tunnel is on," said Josh. "I sure am glad we found this clue. I don't know how we could find the right tunnel without this map piece."

"Asa, this is fantastic," said Bernie. "Thank you so much for helping us. Will you let us take the map piece with us?"

Map piece number four

"Yes, take it," said Asa. "That's what it was kept here for. To help find the diamonds. I wish you safety and good fortune on your journey."

"Thanks," said Josh. "And we'll bring the good fortune back to you. We want all the organizations on the puzzle map to benefit from the diamonds. Rehab centers like this are really important to save endangered animals and help make people aware of the trouble they're in."

Bernie opened his briefcase, put the diamond map piece in it, and took out the puzzle map to show Asa. "Where are you going next?" asked the old man. "And why is this part of the map rubbed out?"

Bernie almost started to tell Asa that they were on their way to Chitipa, but he had a troubling thought. What if the Bradleys were close by? What if they came to the rehab center and started questioning the people here? Would any of their new friends be in danger?

"General Erasto didn't want all the information in one place, in case his enemy Ona was able to get the map." Bernie explained. "We need to keep it secret, too. I don't want to frighten you, but we're being followed by people who would do anything to get the map and the diamonds. I don't want to put you in danger, Asa."

"I understand," said Asa. "My grandfather told me all about Ona and how he would stop at nothing. If his descendants are as ruthless as he was, then you need to be very careful."

"Yes," agreed Bernie. "They are ruthless, and clever. Don't worry. We're on our guard."

"I'm glad we found the map piece, but we've talked enough. We have to keep moving," said Effie. "Let's get a bite to eat and get back on the road. If Gogo and I take turns, we can drive through the night. If the Bradleys are following us, it will help throw them off."

"I can drive too, Boss," Josh reminded Effie. "Just give me the word."

Effie smiled. Finding the giraffe chest had lifted everybody's spirits, even his. "Maybe on the way back, after we get the diamonds," he said, clapping his hand on Josh's shoulder.

Asa walked with the group to the Land Rover and bid them farewell. "I hope to see you before too long, and hear the story of your successful journey," he said.

"And hopefully more than stories," said Gogo as he shook Asa's hand. "The money from the diamonds will help fund the center."

"And then we should tell the whole town about General Erasto, and the founder of the center, and the giraffe chest," said Kosey. "Everybody should know the story."

"That's true, young man," said Asa. "I kept the story to myself for too long. I'll talk to the director of the center and get him to display the giraffe chest again. By the time you come back, it will be in a place of honor."

"We'll be looking forward to it!" called Josh, waving to the old man as they drove off.

Chapter Nine

The Cheetah Chest: Kosey Gets Schooled

"What a way to mark our first week in Africa, Bernie," said Josh contentedly, as he relaxed in a camp chair facing the quiet lake. The water glowed red and orange with the reflected colors of the sunset. "This was a darn good idea, Effie."

"Well, it's not far to Chitipa. I figured this would be a good way to relax a bit," said Effie, yawning and stretching between satisfying gulps of hot coffee.

The group had stopped to camp for the night at Lake Malawi in Nyika National Park. They had connected a tarp to the side of the Land Rover and held it up with bamboo poles to provide some shade. Kosey tended a campfire as Bernie and Gogo got out sleeping bags.

"Effie, what's your take on the Bradleys and their thugs?" asked Bernie, stretching out on his sleeping bag. "Do you think we've lost them for good?"

"I don't know, to be honest," admitted Effie. "If they were following us, we sure haven't seen them. And they haven't tried anything. I wish I knew what they were up to."

"Maybe they've given up," said Gogo hopefully. "Maybe they lost track of us and just turned around and went home."

Josh shook his head. "Don't count on it," he said. "As badly as they want the diamonds? It's been their goal for generations. If I wasn't so tired right now, I'd tell you the story of a very similar lady we met in China. They're not going to give up that easily."

Kosey agreed. "I've heard stories about Ona's descendants and their partners all my life. And that big guy who tried to bribe me into taking a photosim of the diamond map— he seemed pretty hard core."

"It's tiring and stressful to always be on our guard," said Bernie. "But I guess we still need to be. I'll take the first watch tonight."

"We'll all take a shift," agreed Josh.

The sounds of the African night took the place of conversation for the next several minutes. Hyenas, birds, and even lions and elephants talked back and forth while everyone listened and finally settled down to sleep.

The next morning, they finished their drive to Chitipa and stopped for breakfast at a local café. "It might take a while to find the school we're looking for," said Bernie. "I've got a list of the schools in town. I guess we'll just have to start at the top and visit them one by one."

Kosey looked up from reading a flyer he had picked up when they came into the restaurant. "What about this?" he asked. "It's a sports schedule for the local schools. This one here— the Chitipa Coed Primary School— their mascot is the cheetah."

"That could be it!" said Gogo. "Good job, Kosey. We'll start at that school, anyway."

Bernie, who had been looking at the puzzle map and the plate, began to put them carefully back in his briefcase. He held the painted plate up before wrapping it in a protective cloth. "Wow," he said. "Thank goodness Simon Lyons didn't keep these two clues to himself. It's tragic that he died when he did, but it was so fortunate that he painted the giraffe and the cheetah cities on this plate and gave it to Gramps."

"That's for sure," agreed Josh. "No one ever would have known where those clues were if it wasn't for the plate. No plate, no diamonds!"

"But we have the plate," said Gogo. "So let's pay the bill and head out to our cheetah stop!"

The group was soon on their way to Chitipa Coed Primary School, and Bernie volunteered to be the spokesperson. They saw a busy place as they entered. Sounds of talking, singing and laughing children came from several classrooms. A group of what looked like six-year-olds ran past, all carrying picture books, apparently on their way to the library.

"Lots of kids," observed Josh.

"Yeah, and really noisy," said Gogo. "I wonder if it's always this loud and chaotic here. I can't imagine they get much work done."

After standing in the lobby for a few minutes watching kids and teachers running back and forth, a man approached them. "How can I help you?" he asked.

"We would like to see the principal, if possible," said Bernie, shaking the man's hand.

"Sure. Follow me and I'll take you to her office." The man introduced himself as they walked. "My name is Mr. Uba. I'm a reading teacher here."

"How does any reading get done in such a noisy place?" asked Gogo, dodging to avoid two boys running past them in the hall.

"It's difficult," admitted Mr. Uba. "The school is overcrowded. I'm glad parents are sending their children here, especially the girls. For so many years girls weren't allowed to go to school at all. Once they learn to read and write, they can see a much brighter future for themselves. But as you noticed, it does make it harder to teach when the place is bursting at the seams."

He stopped at a door marked Principal. "Our principal's name is Tabia Turay," he said. "Just go in and tell her secretary that you would like to meet with her. Are you teachers?" he asked.

"I am," said Bernie. "But I don't teach young children. I admire you for having the patience and the skill."

"I love teaching the little ones," said Mr. Uba. "It's my privilege to help them discover the joy of reading. When each generation has more educated people, it improves life for everyone, don't you think?"

"Yes," agreed Gogo. "We are not teachers ourselves, except for Bernie, but we're very interested in education and in this school in particular."

"I'm glad to hear it," said Mr. Uba. "I better get back to my classroom. The children will be returning from the library soon. Good luck in your meeting. I hope you find Ms. Turay in a good mood."

"That's an odd thing to say. I wonder if she's often in a bad mood," said Bernie.

They filed into the office and asked if Ms. Turay was free. The secretary said she would be soon, and asked them to sit and wait, pointing to a long bench facing the door to the hallway. Over the next 20 minutes, they saw half a dozen boys and girls go in and out of the principal's office, obviously there because they had broken a rule. Most of them looked downcast and guilty, but a few were defiant as they walked in to see Ms. Turay.

One girl, who seemed to be about 10, came out of the office looking even tougher than when she had gone in.

"I feel sorry for those kids," said Kosey, shaking his head. "I spent a lot of time in the principal's office when I was in school, too."

"Yeah," agreed Josh. "It kind of feels like we're next in line to get a lecture."

The door opened to the principal's inner office again. A little boy came out, followed by Ms. Turay. "Don't worry," she said to the boy. "We don't tolerate bullying here. I'll see to it that those children don't tease you again."

The boy left the office and Ms. Turay looked up to see her next appointment: a group that was much taller than her usual students. "I only have a few minutes before my staff meeting. Come in," she said, turning back into her office. Josh, Bernie and the rest stood up and followed her.

"What can I do for you?" the principal said from behind her desk as they all found chairs. "If you are salesmen, you won't get far. Our school has very little money."

"No, we're not selling anything," said Bernie. "We're looking for something. We saw that your school mascot is a cheetah. Do you know about a large chest with cheetah decorations? Is it here at the school? Its story is part of the founding of the school and it's very important to us."

Ms. Turay sighed and rolled her eyes. "You're not talking about that old legend, are you? The story of the sacred diamonds? I don't have time for fairy tales. I'm too busy trying to run this school."

"So you've heard the story?" asked Kosey. "You know about the diamonds and the animal chests? Then you must know where

THE LIFE CHEST : AFRICA

the chest is, right? We need to get the clue out of the cheetah chest to help us find the diamonds."

Ms. Turay nodded. "Yes, my predecessor told me the story. But as I said, I have no time for such nonsense. It's just an old fable. If there ever was a chest here, I have no idea where it could be. You're wasting my time and yours."

Kosey started to feel angry. The legend of the sacred diamonds was part of his family heritage, and this woman was saying that it was nonsense! He wanted to tell her how insulting she was being, but he paused, and took a breath before he spoke. "Ma'am, I understand that you are very busy," he began. "But my ancestors knew the man who discovered the sacred diamonds and hid the clues to their location in six different animal chests. The story really is true, and we want to find the diamonds so we can help your school with them. Do you have any idea where the cheetah chest might be?"

The principal seemed to soften a bit after listening to Kosey's earnest request, but she still shook her head. "No, I'm sorry. My predecessor might've known where it was but frankly I just didn't believe the story when he told me. I've never seen a cheetah chest and I certainly haven't time to look for one." Ms. Turay was back to her no-nonsense self.

"Now I must ask you to go," she said, standing. "I suggest that you spend your time finding ways to really help the children here instead of chasing after old legends. My teachers are overworked and underpaid. I don't need promises of diamonds. I need funding and supplies, and a bigger building. This is the only school in the area that accepts both boys and girls and educates them equally, and I have my hands full preparing them for secondary school. Now if you will excuse me, I have a staff meeting to run. I meet with the teachers every day while the children are eating lunch."

"I understand," said Bernie, extending his hand to the principal. "Thank you for your time. I wish we could do more for you now. But we need to find cheetah chest first."

"Couldn't we search the school for it?" asked Josh as they walked toward the door.

Ms. Turay stopped them and raised her hand. "No," she said. "I won't have strangers wandering around while school is in session. We take a semester break in a few weeks. I suppose I could let you come back then if I can convince a staff member to accompany you around the school. But we are done for today, and I will say goodbye," she said firmly.

"Goodbye, and thank you again," said Bernie as they left her office.

The group was silent for a few moments as they walked back toward the entrance. Then Gogo spoke. "A few weeks? What should we do? Just wait here?"

"We could move on and find more of the clues, and then come back here," suggested Effie.

"That's what we might have to do," agreed Josh.

"What did you say?" asked Bernie as they passed the cafeteria. "I didn't hear you, Josh. It's even noisier now, at lunchtime, than it was before."

"Let's go outside and talk," said Gogo. "We'll be able to hear each other, and I don't want to get in trouble with the principal again."

The group went outside, all except Kosey. He had stopped to look at the scene in the cafeteria. It wasn't long ago that he had been running around primary school like these kids, getting in trouble, having fun and even occasionally learning something. He chuckled to himself as he watched the kids at the long cafeteria tables eating and talking. Some were eating food they had brought from home, and others were buying flatbread sandwiches and fruit, waiting in line to pay a stern white-haired woman who sat on a short bench behind a folding table. Kosey leaned against the doorframe, reminiscing. That lunch lady looks just like the one from my old school, he thought to himself. I wonder if there's a cloning factory that makes lunch ladies. They all look alike.

Two little boys, impatient from having to wait in line, started pushing each other. The lunch lady sighed. As she walked over to the boys to break up their quarrel, the folded blanket that had covered the bench slipped off. Kosey stared at what the blanket revealed. The lunch lady hadn't been sitting on a bench. Her seat was a chest. He couldn't believe his eyes. It was the cheetah chest! What should he do? The chest was just a few yards from him! He had to get it. But how could he? Ms. Turay had ordered them off the property.

Kosey looked again at the lunch lady and the quarreling kids. The argument had escalated and now a half dozen boys and girls were being scolded by the lunch lady. Kosey had an idea and he acted on it quickly. There was an abandoned lunch next to him on a table. He picked up a bread roll and chucked it hard at the loudest kid.

"Hey," the boy yelled, glancing around the room. "Who threw that?" His eyes fell on another boy at a nearby table, laughing. "I'll get you for that," he said, picking up a half-eaten pear from someone else's plate and throwing it. The pear hit the other boy square in the chest.

"That was mine!" said a girl, standing up. Another piece of fruit was thrown, then a sandwich, then a carton of juice, and soon the cafeteria had erupted into a full-fledged food fight.

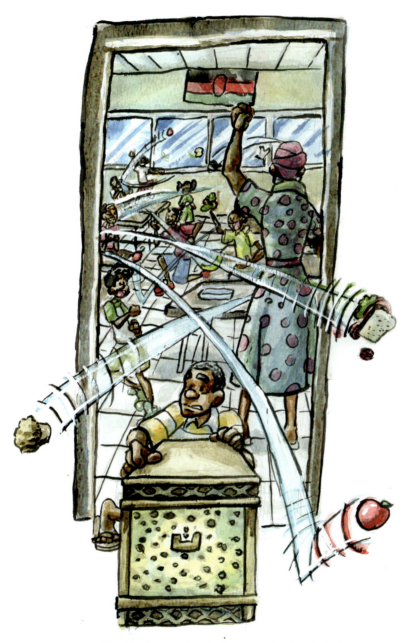

A food fight at the school distracts the lunch lady
as Kosey steals away with the chest

THE LIFE CHEST : AFRICA

Just what I hoped for, thought Kosey, as he quickly moved toward the chest. The lunch lady had her back to him as she shouted at the children to behave themselves. Having reached the chest, Kosey pushed it toward a door that had been opened to let in fresh air. Cake and fruit flew past him as he ducked, pushing the heavy chest as fast as he could through the doorway.

Once outside, he leaned against the wall and sighed in relief. He had done it! Kosey took a moment to look at the chest. It was beautiful. Intricately carved wooden trim surrounded the chest, and the front was decorated with smooth cheetah skin. Please don't be locked, Kosey breathed as he tried the lid. To his relief, it opened. There were awards, letters and pictures in the chest but he didn't have time to look at them. He had to find the secret compartment that held the map piece.

The cheetah chest

As Kosey was lifting items out of the chest, he noticed someone beside him. "What are you doing?" said a voice. Kosey looked up. It was a little girl; one of the kids who had been in the principal's office earlier. In fact, it was the one Kosey had noticed for her defiance.

"Never mind," said Kosey impatiently. "Get out of here. Go back inside."

"You can't tell me what to do," said the girl, hands on her hips. She watched Kosey for a moment as he searched through the chest. "Are you stealing something? I'll tell on you. Unless you share it with me."

Kosey stopped searching and looked up at the little girl. She had wild hair and dirty clothes but she radiated confidence. Smart kid, thought Kosey to himself.

"I'm not stealing," he said. "Not really, anyway. I don't have time to explain; but if you help me, I will share a treasure with you."

"Oh, yeah? What?" the little girl asked.

"Look at this," said Kosey, pointing to one of the inside walls of the chest. He had found the secret compartment, a narrow slot built into the side of the chest. He could see the map piece in it, but he couldn't fit his hand inside.

"There's a piece of canvas down there that I need," he said, pointing to the compartment. "My hand won't fit. Can you get it?"

"Okay," said the girl. She reached into the narrow compartment, pulled out the map piece, and handed it to Kosey.

It was piece #5. The drawing was 12 tunnels on the south wall. The tunnel in the top right corner had the head of an elephant sketched over it. That must be the tunnel we're looking for, thought Kosey to himself. "Thank you! This is fantastic!" he said to the girl as he stood up.

THE LIFE CHEST : AFRICA

Map piece number five

Just then the Land Rover skidded around the corner. "Kosey!" yelled Effie. "Where have you been, kid? We've been looking all over for you, but they wouldn't let us back into the school."

"I got it, guys!" called Kosey, waving the map piece. "I found the chest!" He trotted toward the Land Rover, but the little girl followed him.

"Hey, wait a minute!" the little girl said. "Where's my cut?"

Kosey stopped and turned to her. "What?"

"You said you were going to share with me. Where's my cut?" she repeated.

Kosey thought for a second, and then had an idea. "Hang on. I'll be right back, I promise." He ran to the Land Rover, and dug through the luggage and supplies in the back. After a moment he found the bag of hacky sacks that Geteye had given them at the soccer school. "Give me a few minutes," he said to Effie. "I've got a diplomatic mission here."

Kosey held up the bag as he trotted back to the little girl. "Here's your share," he said. She reached for the bag, but Kosey held on to it for a moment. "I'm Kosey. What's your name?" he asked, crouching down to her level.

"Deka," she answered.

"I have to tell you something first, Deka," Kosey said. "You need to remember this. It's a proverb. Greed loses what it has gained. I'm sharing with you, and now I want you to share with the other kids too."

"How?" Deka asked.

"Your teachers are doing the best they can, but they need help," answered Kosey. "You're lucky that you have this school. The things you're learning here are really important."

He handed her the bag of hacky sacks. "Take one for yourself and give the others away, but only to kids who are studying hard and trying to obey the rules, okay? That's how you can help your teachers. Think you can do it?"

"Sure," Deka said. "It'll be kind of fun." She looked at the cheetah chest. "Are you going to take this chest?"

"No," said Kosey. "It belongs to your school. I just needed that map inside it." He peeked through the doorway. "Everybody's gone. I hope they're not all in the principal's office."

THE LIFE CHEST : AFRICA

"Nah," said Deka. "We had a food fight last week, too. They just send everyone back to class."

"You better go then," said Kosey.

"I'll help you with this first," offered Deka, gathering items to put back in the cheetah chest. She picked up a small wooden bowl. "Look at this, Kosey. It has a cheetah on it."

Kosey examined it carefully. The smooth teak was decorated with a carving of a cheetah that wound cleverly around the outside of the bowl. "This is a special bowl, Deka," he told the little girl. "It was made by a Zulu shaman. It's a good luck charm for your school."

The cheetah trinket

"Wow," said Deka. "What should we do with it?"

"Let's put it back for now," answered Kosey. "Can you help me push the chest back inside? I don't want your lunch lady to have nowhere to sit." They pushed the chest back into the lunchroom and spread the blanket over it.

"The chest is special, too," said Kosey. "But keep that a secret between the two of us for now. I'm going to come back in a week or so. I'll tell you more then. In fact, I'll tell the whole school the story of this cheetah chest. Keep watch over it until then, okay?"

"Okay," agreed Deka. "It's pretty safe anyway, with Miss Lerato sitting on it all the time. When you come back, can you bring more hacky sacks?"

Kosey laughed. "I can bring a lot more than that. What do you think you'd like the most that you don't have here at school?"

"I want new playground equipment," said Deka. "They tore down our climbing gym because it was falling apart. Oh, and my teacher's always wishing she had a new computer."

"We'll see what we can do about that," said Kosey. They walked outside where the Land Rover was waiting. "But you help me out too, right?" said Kosey as he climbed in.

"I will!" Deka called, waving as the truck backed off the grass. "See you later!"

Effie pulled onto the road and headed north again. Kosey handed the map piece to Gogo as the others looked at him in wonderment. "Where did you find it? How did you do it?" they asked in amazement.

Kosey smiled with great satisfaction. "Never underestimate the power of a food fight!" he laughed.

Kosey enjoyed the remainder of the day's drive, as he related the story of how he found the cheetah chest and got the map piece. When they were about halfway to Kilombero, the group stopped for the night. "Five hours on the road tomorrow and we'll be at the next stop," announced Effie as they found their hotel rooms.

"And Kosey can tell us the story all over again!" chuckled Josh. "I can just picture that lunch lady's face. Good work, kid," he added, shaking Kosey's hand and then impulsively pulling him into a hug.

"Thanks, Josh," stammered Kosey. He wasn't used to feeling this good about himself, much less having others praise him, but he decided he liked it.

Chapter Ten

The Buffalo Chest: A Narrow Escape

Aaron Bradley piloted the Land Rover to the gate of Freedom Farm and set it to hover. "I don't see their old truck anywhere around," he said. "Let's lay low for a while." He glided into a grove of trees outside the gate. "We'll be able to see anybody coming and going from here," he said.

After a few hours of waiting, the group began to get restless. "They could've already been here and left," said Jamila. "Or maybe this isn't even the right place."

"I sure wish they hadn't discovered the tracking device," said Rupert.

"I found the place without it! It's the only agriculture school in the area," bragged Abdi.

"You all make me sick. Quit complaining." Said Agnes

Aaron adjusted the controls and moved toward the gate of Freedom Farm. "Agnes is right. I should fire you all," he said. "Let's just go and find out if they've been here yet or not."

"Good," said Abdi, cracking his knuckles. "I want to do something, not just sit around."

"Fine," agreed Aaron. "Have your guns ready, but keep them hidden." He settled into a parking space next to a trailer with a sign that said Administration Building.

"I'll go in with Abdi and Jamila," he said. "The rest of you stay out here. Don't fall asleep on me. Stay alert."

"You're the one who's always falling asleep on the job," snapped Agnes.

Aaron answered by slamming the door as hard as he could. The trio walked up a short flight of stairs and into the trailer that served as the office space for Freedom Farm.

Jira was seated on a tall stool behind a long counter. She was a short, muscular woman in her mid-30s. Living at Freedom Farm with her father most of her life and working with local growers and families had nurtured her open, friendly personality. She loved the outdoors and was never happier than when she was digging in dirt and working with plants.

"Hello!" she said cheerfully as the group walked in the door. "Are you here for the natural fertilizer workshop?"

"No, not us," said Aaron. "We're looking for a map. Actually, we're wondering if some people came by earlier— maybe yesterday— looking for a piece of a map."

"A map?" said Jira.

"Yes, an old hand-drawn map; or rather, a piece of it. Do you know its story?"

Jira's face brightened even more. "Yes, I do, but you'll have to excuse me a minute. Let me get my father. I'll be right back."

The group waited nervously but Jira returned in a few moments with Jomo, her father. Jomo was a man in his 60s who had worked outdoors his entire life. His manner was strong and assertive, but he possessed the gentleness of someone who knew how to nurture both animals and plants.

"Hello, hello!" he said, extending both his hands to shake Aaron's, then Abdi's and Jamila's. "This is unbelievable. It's wonderful to see you! We didn't know if anyone would ever come for the map piece since we had to relocate. I was starting to think that no one cared anymore."

"Oh, we care a great deal," said Jamila with a smile.

"Good, good," said Jomo, smiling back. "Let me lock up the office and I'll take you to— "

"Wait, father," said Jira, touching his arm. "Excuse me for interrupting, but there's something— Excuse me a minute," she said to the visitors as she pulled her father to one side. They whispered together for a few moments.

While the father and daughter were talking, Jamila gathered her cohorts in a corner. "Well, we found out what we needed to know," she hissed. "Obviously nobody's come by yet for the map."

"But what should we do?" asked Aaron. "They want to give it to us!"

"Take it. What else?" insisted Abdi. "It will give us leverage. We won't give it to the Americans until they agree to share the diamonds with us."

"I'm not sharing any diamonds," snapped Aaron.

"Oh, don't worry," said Abdi with an evil grin. "I said we'd agree to share. I didn't say we actually would."

"Good," said Aaron. "That bunch from Tanda Tula is going to suffer the same fate those conservationists did when they got in our way."

Jira and Jomo returned to the front of the office. Jomo spoke, still smiling. "My daughter reminded me of something we need to do. I'm sure it's just a formality but— um— the proverb? Do you happen to know the proverb? I really can't give you the map piece until we recite the proverb. Silly, I suppose, but it's part of the process."

"Proverb? What proverb are you talking about?" asked Aaron. "What does that have to do with the map?"

"It's a saying on the puzzle map." Jomo was a bit confused now. This wasn't how the conversation was supposed to go when the seekers came to get the map piece.

"He must be talking about the map that Agnes took the photosim of," offered Jamila.

"That thing again? Puzzle maps, diamond maps, proverbs? I don't have time for this, old man," said Aaron curtly.

"Don't speak to my father that way," said Jira protectively. "You know what? We changed our minds. There's nothing here for you."

"You're not going to start playing games with me now," said Aaron. "It's obvious you have the map piece. Let's go get it."

Abdi pulled his gun from his pocket and pointed it at Jomo and Jira. No one was smiling anymore. Jira clung to her father's arm.

"Come on," said Abdi menacingly. "Move it. You're going to get that map piece and give it to us."

"No," said Jomo firmly. "You're not getting it. You're not the people who should have it. I don't know how you found out about it, but we're not giving it to you."

"Have it your way," said Abdi. He nodded to Jamila, who sprang into action. She moved swiftly behind the counter and grabbed Jira, dragging her to the middle of the room.

"Father!" cried Jira.

"Do what I tell you. Give us the map piece. You don't want your daughter to get hurt, do you?" said Abdi. Jamila wrenched Jira's arm behind her back, making her cry out in pain.

Jomo ran to his daughter's defense. "No!" he yelled, trying to pull her away from Jamila.

Abdi stepped in between them and knocked Jomo to the ground. "I can hurt you as much as I need to. I could even kill you, no problem. And we would just ransack this place until we found the map piece. Either way, we're going to get it."

Jomo lay on the floor, gasping for breath. "Father," cried Jira again, still in Jamila's grasp. She turned to the woman. "Please, he can't breathe. Let me go to him. He may die!" Jamila shrugged and let go. Jira sprinted for the door and made it outside before they could stop her.

"Dammit!" said Jamila. "I didn't think she looked that smart."

"You sing pretty good for a little guy, Gogo," said Effie after Gogo finished a Tanzanian folk song. "And you can even drive and sing at the same time."

"Thanks, I think," said Gogo. "Now how about an American song?" he said to Bernie and Josh.

"Aw, you don't want to hear me sing," said Josh.

"You're not so bad," said Bernie. "Come on. Let's sing Swing Low, Sweet Chariot."

They began singing with gusto, if not skill. "I've heard that song," said Gogo. He started to sing along. After a few moments, to everyone's surprise, Effie joined in, adding a hearty bass part. Josh and Bernie stopped singing to listen to the two African men, so different in almost every way, harmonize perfectly on the song.

When it was over, everyone applauded. "You guys should go on tour!" said Kosey. "You sound great together."

Effie laughed. "I sang in church choir my whole life," he explained.

"Me too," said Gogo. "What do you know, Effie! We have something in common."

"I think we're all a good team, you guys," said Josh. "It was a great idea to put the tracking device on a delivery truck that was leaving the rehab center."

"Yeah," said Kosey. "That truck was headed up to Lubumbashi. It should buy us enough time to throw them way off our track."

"But the truck is still going north, so they won't get too suspicious," added Josh. "Hopefully they'll follow it for at least a day. I really think we lost them. Don't you, Effie?"

Effie clenched his fists. "I hope so. We can't be sure, but I hope so."

"When do you think we will be in Kilombero?" asked Bernie.

"What's the matter, Bernie?" joked Gogo. "You don't like our singing?"

"I like it fine," answered Bernie. "I'm just trying to find the farming school on this map."

"Another few miles," said Gogo. "Does the place have a name?"

"I'm pretty sure it's this one," said Bernie, pointing to the location on his tablet. "Freedom Farm. Their website says they work with local people to improve agricultural conditions and teach sustainable farming. The date they were founded coincides with when Erasto's soldiers would've gone to their cities."

He pushed a button on his comm device. "It's run these days by a father and daughter: Jomo and Jira Jaja. I'll give them a call. See if I can arrange to have someone meet us there. It might be good for them to have a heads up."

After a minute, however, Bernie closed his comm device. "That's funny," he said. "It says on their website that they have office hours today. Someone should be answering the phone, but nobody is. Oh, well. I guess we'll just do what we've always done and find the right person to talk to when we get there."

"That will be okay," said Josh. "We're five-for-five, so far. Hopefully it won't be hard to track down the buffalo chest. And since it looks like we got the goons from Royal Camp off our trail, I'd say we're doing pretty well." Josh started to sing again and soon the others joined in, all except for Effie. The big man was deep in thought. He knew Josh was trying to keep everyone's spirits up, but for some reason he had a feeling that things were not going to go as easily as they hoped.

After Jira ran out of the trailer, Abdi and Aaron dragged Jomo out too. "Stop her!" Abdi called to Rupert and the women in the Land Rover.

Nobody moved fast enough, and Jira ran out of the gate. "Well, she has nowhere to go," said Agnes, still sitting in the back seat. "There isn't anything outside this farm for miles. Did she have a comm device?"

"No," said Aaron. "You still shouldn't have let her get away!" he scolded Jamila.

"We've got her father, anyway," said Jamila. "She'll be back for him."

Abdi threw Jomo to the ground. "We're gonna just keep making it worse on you till you give us what we want," he growled.

When they pulled close to the gate of Freedom Farm, Kosey saw a sign with a picture of a middle-aged man standing next to a Cape buffalo. "Hooray!" he cheered, his arms in the air. "This is the place, all right! Woo hoo!" He stopped yelling when he saw a woman running toward them.

"Help! Help!" she shouted. "You've got to help me!" Gogo brought the car to a screeching halt and jumped out.

Effie got out the passenger side, gun at the ready. "What's going on, Miss?" he asked.

"They've got my father!" she gasped. "They asked about a map– but we wouldn't give it to them." She tried to collect herself. "They hurt my father, and they've got guns!"

"Let's go, fast!" said Effie. "Gogo, stay here with the young lady. It's the Bradleys and their goons. They caught up to us again somehow. Bernie, Josh— you have your guns?"

"Sure do, Boss," said Josh. "What's the plan?"

I won't know till we get in there," said Effie. "Just do what I say as quickly as you can." He got into the driver's seat.

"No," said Jira, who had caught her breath. "I'm not staying here! My father is hurt and he may be killed."

She jumped into the back of the Land Rover, as did Gogo. "We're all going, Effie," said Gogo. "Step on it."

Effie shook his head and drove through the gate.

Aaron kicked Jomo again. He had raised his foot for a third blow when a noise rose up from the entrance to the farm. It was the tires of the old Tanda Tula Land Rover skidding on the gravel as it roared through the gate.

Effie assessed the situation with a professional eye. Four people in or near a vehicle, and a white guy standing over an older man on the ground who looked like he'd been beaten. The big bodyguard looked like the only one who had a gun drawn.

"Josh!" Effie yelled. "The big guy! Shoot the gun out of his hand!" Josh aimed and fired. The bullet lodged in Abdi's right arm. The big man yelled out and dropped his gun.

Effie drove straight at the group in the Land Rover. None of them had time to grab their guns. "Wanna play chicken?" Effie yelled. They did not. Charlotte and Jamila ran. Rupert and Agnes were still in the truck. Effie slowed down just enough to bump the vehicle and shove it into a tree, then backed up with a screech and stopped.

Aaron rushed to the wounded Abdi, and Jomo managed to crawl away from him. He leaned against the trailer's stoop, gasping. Kosey ran to the old farmer. He reached under his shoulders and tried to lift him. "Can you stand?" he asked.

Jamila was nearby. She took the opportunity to punch Kosey in the gut as he helped Jomo. Kosey staggered, but didn't drop the old man. Jamila then kicked Kosey in the face and stood back to laugh as he struggled to help Jomo to the steps.

Effie jumped out of the car and looked around again. Kosey and Jomo were at the steps of the trailer with a sneering Jamila nearby. Aaron, a few yards in front of the trailer, had crouched down next to Abdi to check his injury. Abdi was bleeding badly, and probably going into shock. Agnes and Rupert were in their vehicle, trying to get it started.

Bernie and Josh both had their guns drawn. Josh was approaching Aaron and Abdi, and Bernie was headed for Agnes and Rupert. Gogo and Jira were safe in the Land Rover behind him. None of the villains had a gun drawn on any of his people. We've got the advantage, Effie thought.

He relaxed for a moment and lowered his gun; but he had forgotten about Charlotte Scott. Charlotte had jumped out of the Royal Camp Land Rover just before Effie had pushed it into the tree. Drawing her gun, she snuck around behind Effie.

The only person who noticed her was Gogo. He was staying with Jira, trying to keep her from getting out of the Land Rover to go to her father. Out of the corner of his eye, Gogo saw Charlotte sneak around behind the Tanda Tula Land Rover, gun drawn. Crouching down, she was getting in position to shoot. Effie, his back to Charlotte, was in her sights.

The Land Rover was running and Gogo hopped into the driver's seat. The little man came to a quick decision. "Hang on," he said to Jira, as he threw the Land Rover into reverse and stepped on the gas. The rear bumper hit Charlotte hard. She fell to the ground, dropping her gun.

Gogo hit the brakes and jumped out of the car. He ran to grab Charlotte's gun but slipped and fell on the gravel. Charlotte reached the gun before he did. With both of them on the ground, she lifted the gun, rose to her knees, and aimed it at Gogo's head. "I'll get you for that," she hissed in pain. Gogo desperately scrambled to his feet, knowing he wouldn't be able to get away before she fired. He heard the shot all right, but he didn't feel it. It hadn't come from her gun. Charlotte collapsed in a heap.

Hearing the commotion behind him, Effie had turned and fired. Charlotte was dead.

The gunshot got everyone's attention. Josh and Bernie froze in horror, lowering their guns. But Agnes, who had gotten their Land Rover running, jumped into action. She wasn't interested in any more shooting. She just wanted to get out of there. Agnes glided the truck up to Aaron, who helped Abdi get in the vehicle. Aaron pointed his gun at Effie, but his sister knocked his hand away. "No more shooting!" she yelled. "Do you want to get us all killed?"

Jamila gave Kosey one last sneer before she jumped in the Land Rover. Agnes steered toward the gate. "Get Charlotte!" called Agnes as she paused at the woman's body. Rupert and Aaron quickly loaded Charlotte into the truck. They sped away.

Jira ran to her father and Kosey, with the others following. There was silence in the farmyard for a moment. Then Effie spoke, matter-of-factly. "Gogo, are you all right?" Gogo nodded. Effie turned to Jira and Jomo. "Let's get this man some first aid," he said. "You too, Kosey."

Josh and Bernie quickly walked to the Land Rover for the first aid kit as the others helped Kosey and Jomo to the trailer. "Wow," said Josh to his cousin as he dug through the supply bin. "I guess this is all in a day's work for Effie, huh?"

"I don't know," answered Bernie. "He probably gets more shook up than he lets on."

"Well, I'm a little rattled," Josh admitted. "We got shot at in China, and Chen Mara was crushed to death, but I've never seen someone shot at close range before."

"Me neither. Uh oh. We've been gone almost 10 days, and I promised Chen Li I'd call her today," Bernie remembered. "Let's not tell anyone back home about what happened just now, okay?"

"No arguments here," Josh agreed. "Leah would freak out!" He moved a blanket and found the first aid kit. "Here it is."

The cousins hurried back to the group. Kosey insisted he was fine, but took the ice that was offered and held it to his face. Jira bandaged her father's head as the group talked. "Thank you for rescuing us," said Jira. "I don't know how you happened to come along when you did."

"Well, we meant to get here before those guys did," said Bernie. "They've been following us. I don't know how they managed to figure out where we were going next, much less get here before us."

"Wait," said Jira suspiciously. "Are you here for the map piece, too? Don't even bother asking. I'm not letting my father get killed over a map. Look what just happened when they came in and asked for the map piece. When we found out they didn't know the proverb, all hell broke loose!"

"I understand how you feel. But we do know the proverb," said Bernie. "Greed loses what it has gained. We're not after the diamonds for ourselves. We're here to fulfill General Erasto's dream. We want to use the diamonds to help the people of Africa."

Jira visibly relaxed, and Jomo, who had been leaning back in a chair with his eyes closed, sat up excitedly. "Yes! That's it!" he said. "That's the proverb. Jira, they're the right ones! Don't worry. We can give the map piece to them."

"All right. If you say so, Father," said Jira, patting his hand. "Don't get excited. You need to rest." She looked up and smiled at the group. "Thank you again. Really. After my father has rested a few more minutes, we will take you to our cottage. That's where we have the buffalo chest and the map piece."

"What about the Royal Camp guys?" asked Kosey. "They got away. Do you think they're going to come back?"

"No, they won't," answered Effie. "One of their gang is dead and Abdi Kalu is pretty badly wounded from what I could see. That will slow them down for a while."

"Who are they?" asked Jira. "How do you know them?"

"I'm ready to walk to the cottage," interrupted Jomo. "I'd like to have a drink and get more comfortable. Let's go. We can talk there."

The group walked to Jomo and Jira's homey cottage at the edge of the farm. It was a small, round building, terra cotta colored, with a pointed, thatched roof. After she helped Jomo get comfortable in his favorite chair, Jira made coffee and gave her father a glass of brandy.

They spent the next hour talking about the search for the diamonds. "We've waited for someone to come for the map piece ever since the story was told to us," said Jira. "My greatest hope was that someone would come while my father was still alive. We're so happy that you are here."

"I'm sorry that we weren't able to protect you from danger," said Effie. "My job is to keep people from getting hurt."

"I'm fine," said Jomo. "You did your job well."

"He sure did," said Gogo. "I call saving my life doing your job very well!"

"We're even," said Effie gruffly. "You stuck your neck out for me first, Gogo. Now what about that map piece? We need to move on before the Royal Camp people have a chance to regroup."

The buffalo chest

"The buffalo chest is in my father's bedroom," said Jira. "Come with me." The chest was covered in smooth buffalo hide and trimmed with notched, painted wood. Jira unlatched the leather straps that bound the chest from front to back. The lock's metal trim resembled buffalo horns.

The buffalo trinket

The first thing Jira lifted out of the chest was a whistle, made of buffalo horn and decorated with the head of a buffalo. She laughed as she showed it to the group. "I think this whistle was put into the buffalo chest by the founder of Freedom Farm," she said. "Father used it to call me in from the fields when I was little."

"It's a talisman," explained Bernie. Jira handed the whistle to him. "Erasto's mentor and foster father was a shaman named Duma," he continued. "He blessed a trinket for every city that the diamonds would benefit. Erasto gave those animal trinkets to the soldiers he sent to each city and told them to keep the trinkets in their animal chests. They were meant to be good luck for the organizations the soldiers developed, like your farm."

Bernie turned the whistle over in his hand. "When we first came to Africa to look for the chests and the map pieces, we were afraid they might have disappeared, but we have found every one so far," he said. "All the organizations are struggling for money, but they have survived. That proves to me that there is magic in the talismans."

"I believe it," said Jomo. "Freedom Farm has struggled now and then, but we do survive and grow. And we help many people learn how to produce their own food and sustain their families. That help is desperately needed in a country where so many are hungry, and even starving."

"That's right," said Jira. "And look at what happened today. The fact that you came along when you did— that was good luck if I've ever seen it."

Josh peered into the chest. "What else do you keep in here?" he asked.

Jira lifted out a photograph of a young woman. "We keep a lot of family memories in the buffalo chest," she said. "This is a picture of my mother. She passed away when I was young. But I have strong memories of her, partly because of the pictures father kept. But especially this." She showed the group a small journal. "My mother had a lingering disease. When she knew that she would die from it, she started writing letters to me in this journal, and kept it safe in the buffalo chest. She wrote me a weekly letter for more than a year. And when she did pass away, my father gave me the journal. It's one of my most treasured possessions."

"I'm sorry about the loss of your mother," said Kosey. "My parents passed away when I was young, too. My grandmother raised me, and she helped keep their memory alive for me. We have one of the animal chests, too. The lion chest. I keep a lot of my parents' things in it, like their wedding rings."

"A chest like that really helps you focus on what's important in life," said Bernie. "In America we call them life chests."

"That's very nice," said Jomo.

"And here is what we've all been waiting for," Jira said jokingly, speaking in a deep voice like an announcer. She opened a small sliding door in the inside lid of the chest and took out a small folded piece of canvas.

Gogo examined it eagerly. "It's map piece #6, all right. Look, it shows nine holes in the tunnel floor."

Map piece number six

"Which one is the hole we go into to find the sacred diamond chamber?" asked Kosey, peering at the canvas.

"I don't know," admitted Gogo. "Maybe it's this one, with the bones drawn on top."

"I sure hope so," said Kosey, shaking his head. "I'd hate to be stuck at that point."

Effie stood up. "If you folks think you're okay, we better get moving," he said to the farmers. "I'll contact the local authorities before we go and get someone to come by and check on you. But I don't think those goons will come back."

"Thank you, and good luck," said Jomo. "I hope you are able to get the diamonds without any more interference."

"I don't know if we can hope for that," said Effie with a wry smile. "We'll get the diamonds all right, but I'm prepared for plenty more interference."

They shook hands all around, and thanked the farmers again. "We will be back in a few weeks," said Josh. "The revenue from Freedom Farm's share of the diamonds will help the farm grow and prosper. Just hang on to that good luck charm."

"I will," said Jira. "Thank you again. Stay safe."

Back in the Land Rover, Effie was more talkative. "I didn't want to say it in front of the farmers, but now you see how vicious and desperate that bunch from Royal Camp can be. One of their people almost killed Gogo. And now she's dead— but it could just have easily been one of us. If anybody wants to back out of the trip now, go ahead. I think we would all understand."

"Don't you think they might give up?" asked Gogo. "You had them running pretty scared."

"We can't count on that," said Josh. "They want the diamonds as badly as we do. And we've seen what they're willing to do to get them."

"That's right," said Effie. "I don't think they'll come back here, but we've got to keep an eye out for them as we move on. I don't know how they knew to find us at Kilombero. That worries me."

"Do you think they put another tracking device on the Land Rover?" asked Bernie.

"No. I checked it thoroughly," said Effie, shaking his head. "Like I said, decide if you want to bail. Are these diamonds worth it? What if one of you gets killed next time?"

There was silence in the Land Rover. Josh and Bernie thought about their families. Kosey remembered his promise to his grandmother to come back. Was the risk worth it? The unspoken questions and worries filled their minds as the truck rolled on.

"Grandpa, that's terrible!" said April. "It was dangerous in Africa! Why did you even go? Grandma and Aunt Li must have been so worried about you."

"Well, Blossom, we were pretty young," said Josh. "I'll admit that we didn't totally know what we were getting into. But I think even if we did, we would have gone anyway. We really wanted to help people by finding those diamonds. It's like this African proverb I heard: 'Courage is the father of success.' And you know me and your uncle Bernie. We love adventure. Right, cousin?"

"Absolutely," agreed Bernie. "April, I think almost everything worth doing requires at least a little bit of courage."

"I guess so," said April. "I know you have to be brave to go on adventures." She yawned and stretched. "Is Aunt Li around? She said she'd watch my favorite cartoon with me."

Bernie smiled and stood. "Let's go get her," he said. April skipped out of the room and Bernie followed.

Josh shook his head. "Cartoons just beat out one of my stories?" he said to the empty room. "Guess I better step up my game!"

Part Three

Battle For The Diamonds

AFRICA

THE LIFE CHEST : AFRICA

Chapter Eleven

The Leopard Chest: The Clues Are Complete

On the next day of their visit to Bernie and Chen Li's home, the family went to the zoo. "We're gonna see some real neat animals today, Blossom!" said Josh as he looked at the zoo map. "Where do you want to go first?"

"I want to see the farm animals, Grandpa," announced April. "Especially the horses."

"I guess that's not too far away from this entrance," said Nathan, April's dad. "We don't want to tire your grandpa out with too much walking, April."

Josh peered over his glasses at his son-in-law. "Don't put me in a wheelchair just yet, youngster!" he said in a mock-threatening tone.

Bernie and Chen Li joined the group. "There you are," said Bernie. "We were just checking to see what time the zookeeper presentation is."

"But where's my wheelchair?" asked Josh, with a sideways smile at Nathan. "Don't you know my feeble old legs are giving out?"

"You're kidding, right?" said Chen Li. "Just this morning, you and April were dancing like the Rockettes!"

Josh laughed. "Yeah, I'm just giving Nathan a hard time. But maybe those high kicks weren't such a good idea," he said, rubbing his back.

"Come on, everybody!" called April from down the path. "The horse barn is this way!"

After visiting the farm animals, the lions were next. "Wow," said April as they watched two big cats, a male and a female, stretch and yawn in the sun. "They sort of remind me of my cat at home, but gianter!"

"I don't think that's a word, but I know what you mean," said her dad. "They sure are big and powerful looking."

"You saw lions up close when you were in Africa, didn't you, Bernie?" asked Chen Li.

"We sure did," he answered. "On safari. They were beautiful and frightening at the same time."

"Lions, and leopards, and elephants, and rhinos and warthogs too," said Josh. "And the occasional mongoose."

"Africa can be a pretty dangerous place," said Chen Li.

"Well, the mongooses weren't real threatening. But you're right. We faced a lot of danger there."

April remembered where Josh's Africa story had left off. "What about the bad guys you fought with? They were pretty dangerous. What happened after you got away from them?"

"You want to hear the story now, Blossom?" asked Josh.

"It is close to lunchtime," suggested Nathan. "We could sit down at the café and hear the story there. Sound like a good idea?" Bernie and Chen Li nodded.

"Sure," agreed Josh. "But I'm taking a break to tell the story, not because I'm tired!"

They were a little more than 100 kilometers out from Freedom Farm when Effie stopped in the small town of Mikumi. Gogo, who had been dozing in the passenger seat next to Effie, looked around hazily as Effie pulled up to a small hotel. "Where are we? What's up, Effie?" he asked.

"I think we need to rest," said Effie, shutting off the ignition and stretching. "All of us."

"It has been a rough couple of days," agreed Gogo. "But we've only got one more animal chest to find before we have the entire diamond map. We've been lucky in that respect, anyway." He took a deep breath as he thought about the danger they had escaped from. "Besides that, we're lucky that none of us got hurt any worse than we did today, or even killed."

Josh spoke up from the back seat. "It wasn't just luck. I really believe the talismans are leading us to the chests. And it was because of you two that none of us got killed back there at the farm. Thanks for having our backs."

Effie got out of the Land Rover to collect luggage. "Just doing my job," he said as he gathered duffel bags. Josh could tell he was proud, though, by the way he swung the heaviest bag up onto his shoulder as he walked toward the hotel.

Effie was right. The group was exhausted and needed to rest. They were excited about finding the last map piece and going to Mount Kilimanjaro, but the events of the previous day were still heavy on their minds. After a quick meal, everyone turned in early and got a good night's sleep. What they dreamed about was anybody's guess. Diamonds? Gunfire? Family at home?

Early the next morning at breakfast became the official time to reassess. "Okay," said Effie, his mouth full of bread. "You all had time to think about it. Anyone dropping out?"

A momentary silence greeted his question. It would be disappointing if anyone decided to go home. Everyone had proven to be a valuable asset to the group, but besides that, they had all become trusted friends. On the other hand, they were in ongoing danger. The Royal Camp group was capable of murder, and the only thing that had stopped them yesterday was Josh wounding Abdi Kalu and Effie killing Charlotte Scott.

Thoughts and worries hung heavy in the air. Bernie and Josh had families to consider. Kosey had promised to return and take care of his grandmother. They had all seen up close how much danger was involved. They may have been on a treasure hunt, but this was no game.

Effie spoke up again. He knew what everyone was thinking. "I'm a family man, too," he said. "I got two kids, living in Johannesburg with their mom. I want to be there for them while they're growing up." He turned to his partner. "What about you, Gogo?"

"I take care of my mother, like you take care of your grandmother, Kosey," said Gogo. "I've also got a girlfriend in Nairobi. We'd like to get married in a year or two. She wants to have a lot of kids."

"So. We all have families and people who love us. We all have commitments and responsibilities," said Josh. "But I don't see anybody getting up from this table. Are we all in? Everyone's staying?"

There was another short silence, but it was broken by little Gogo. "I want us all to go on together," he said. "On the first few days of this trip, I wasn't sure I'd made the right decision. And yesterday— I've never been so terrified. But Effie saved my life and we're all okay." He smiled at the big man before he continued.

"We're close to making this happen. We can find those diamonds! The hospital, the football club and the school, the rehab center, the game reserve, the farm, and now the cultural center— the wealth of the diamonds is going to revitalize these places and make a huge difference to our people. I'm still in. I'm doing this."

"That goes for me too," said Kosey.

"And me," added Bernie.

"Gogo convinced me too," said Josh with a smile. "I guess that does it then, huh?"

"Yup. We got a five-hour drive. Let's pack up and head for that artsy place," said Effie, downing the last of his coffee and standing.

"It's an African cultural center, Effie," said Bernie. "Gogo and I have been reading about it online. The original building burned down and the grandson of the founder began again here in Babati."

The Babati Center for the Arts was an impressive building. It was made of glass and steel, but still had an African sense to it with its combination of modern architecture and traditional African design.

Pulling into the drive, the Land Rover rolled past a construction area with a large half-finished building. The sign in front of it said "New theater and exhibit hall: Completion 2112."

"2112? Wow, they're a little behind," said Kosey. "That was two years ago."

This place must have the same money problems as the other organizations we visited," said Josh. "It's too bad."

"Okay, Effie," said Bernie as they drove past the unfinished theater. "Pull up right here in the visitors' parking lot, will you? I sent a message this morning and arranged for us to get a tour. Someone should be waiting for us in the lobby."

"All right," sighed Effie. "This artsy stuff isn't my thing, though."

"Just try to roll with it, Boss," laughed Josh.

"Wait a minute," said Gogo. "What do you mean artsy stuff isn't your thing? I've heard you sing like an angel."

"I don't think any angels look like me," countered Effie.

"When you saved my life, I found out that angels come in all shapes and sizes," insisted Gogo as they walked down the sidewalk to the main building.

The lobby was spacious and colorful. Everything had an African flair, from the lobby furniture to the patterned tile on the kiosks. Light flowed through skylights and illuminated beautiful African artwork on every wall. The floor was painted with a leopard motif, with swirls and angular patterns surrounding abstract renderings of the beautiful animals running through grasses and lounging in trees. The group was still taking it all in when they were approached by a stately dark-skinned woman with long black braids wrapped around her head. She wore a colorful orange and green floor-length dress in a traditional African pattern.

"Welcome to the Babati Center for the Arts," she said, extending her hand. "Are you the group that called for a tour?"

"Yes," said Bernie. "We're excited to see everything the center has to offer the local community."

"Come with me and I'll be happy to show you," she said. "My name is Bibi. I'm a volunteer, and an artist. One of my paintings is hanging right there." She pointed at a portrait of a mother and child. "I also conduct tours and lecture on the history of African women artists."

After admiring Bibi's painting, the group looked around at the rest of the lobby gallery. Josh was drawn to a large painting on a wall by itself, and called Bernie over to see it. "Look, Bernie! It's a Simon Lyons painting!"

Bernie trotted to where his cousin was closely examining the painting, which showed a group of elephants at a watering hole.

"It's called Swamp Kings," said Josh. "Isn't it magnificent? Look at the detail of the elephants' hides, and the light and shadow."

"It is beautiful," agreed Bernie. "I'm a little surprised that this center would have a painting by a white artist, though."

Bibi joined them at the wall. "Simon Lyons donated that painting to the center," she explained. "Most of the work here is by native artists, but he had such love for our animals that many considered him an adopted African!"

"Simon did love Africa," said Josh. "You can see it in all his art."

Bibi then took the group to see exhibits of African musical instruments and traditional African fashions. "The mission of the cultural center is to preserve all types of African arts that might otherwise be lost," explained their guide.

"I thought art meant just pictures on the walls," remarked Kosey to Effie as they left the fashion gallery. "This was pretty cool."

"I guess," said Effie. He leaned over and whispered to Kosey. "It's more interesting than I thought it would be, anyway."

"Oh, we're just in time," said Bibi excitedly as they approached the entrance to the auditorium. "We're previewing a new piece this week, and there's a performance starting in a few minutes. It's really just a dress rehearsal but we'd love to have you see it."

"It sounds wonderful," said Gogo. He practically sprinted into the auditorium, so the others followed.

"What are we watching?" Effie whispered to Josh as they took their seats.

"A dance performance," said Josh.

"We had some dancers perform at Tanda Tula for the tourists a few years ago," said Kosey. "I liked it."

They got comfortable in their seats in the cool auditorium as the house lights dimmed and the stage lights came up.

THE LIFE CHEST : AFRICA

The dance was a representation of the circle of life. Layers of gauzy curtains hung interspersed with hanging vines. The lights gave the impression of a golden African sunrise. Men and women in colorful costumes leapt across the stage, moving in front of and behind the fabric and vines. Musicians played haunting tunes on flutes and banged out percussive rhythms on drums.

A few minutes into the performance, two male dancers entered, carrying a large box which they carefully placed center stage. A female dancer opened the lid of the box. Josh squinted to look more closely at the prop. His eyes widened and he nudged Bernie.

"Bernie!" he hissed.

"What?" said his cousin. "Josh, you know you're not supposed to talk during a performance."

"This is kind of important," said Josh. "Look at that box on stage. Bernie, it's the chest!" He tried to keep his voice down to a whisper, but he was too excited. "It's covered with leopard skin. It's the leopard chest!"

"They're using the leopard chest in their dance performance!" said Bernie, amazed. "That's great! What an awesome artistic statement!"

"Yeah," said Josh. "Not to mention the fact that we just found the chest. That's kind of what I meant."

They continued to watch the performance. A dancer mimed cradling a baby in her arms as another performer reached into the chest. This dancer was a tall man with a confident, athletic air. His role in the dance was to lift imaginary items out of the chest; items that represented life's passages.

The other dancers became young children as he tossed them an imaginary ball from the chest. They grew to school age when he took out a book. They paired up as couples when he mimed smelling a flower. They danced together as families as he mimed stirring a pot of soup. When he pulled an imaginary walking stick from the chest, the dancers became elderly. For a few moments, their movements became slow and stiff, then they sank to the ground as the lights changed from yellow to blue. In the final moments of the dance, a small child entered the stage, circled the chest, opened it and peered inside with a smile as the lights dimmed.

The colorful dance performance

Excitement ran through the group as the house lights came up. "Did you see it?" Kosey asked. "It was the leopard chest, wasn't it?"

"I'm sure it was. Don't you think so, Bernie?" asked Gogo.

"Absolutely," he answered. "Now let's go see it up close. We'll get backstage somehow."

"I hope it still has the clue in it after becoming a prop for a dance," said Josh.

They found Bibi waiting for them in the lobby. "Did you enjoy the show?" she asked.

"It was good," said Effie. "Don't get me wrong," he whispered to Kosey. "I liked it, but you wouldn't catch me doing something like that in a million years."

Kosey nodded in agreement, and then noticed a family coming out of another door of the auditorium. He saw a young woman and did a double take. It was Winna! What was she doing here? "Excuse me a minute," he called back to Effie as he sprinted toward the group she was walking with. They were about to leave the building. "Winna? Winna!"

The young woman turned to see Kosey. When he caught her eye, he slowed down to his more typical ambling walk. I look like an idiot, he thought, running at her like that.

"Kosey?" Winna said in surprise. "Is that you?"

"Yeah," Kosey said, having caught up to her. "Crazy, huh, us running into each other again?"

"It sure is," agreed Winna. Then she got a good look at Kosey's face. "What happened to you?" she said in horror. Kosey was confused but then remembered his injuries. He'd gotten beaten up just the day before yesterday! His nose was still very swollen, he had two black eyes, and his forehead and one cheek had dark red scabs that stood out from his brown skin. His hands went to his face. I must look awful, he thought.

Winna saw Kosey's embarrassment. "Oh, that was rude of me. I'm sorry." She turned to the people standing beside her. "Mom, Dad, this is my friend Kosey. I met him at the hospital last week. Kosey, these are my parents, Mr. and Mrs. Sylla."

"Nice to meet you," said Kosey shyly.

"So how do you know each other?" asked Winna's mother. "Did Winna treat you in the emergency room?"

"Um, no," answered Kosey. "This happened just a couple days ago."

"Kosey and his friends knew about the rhino chest that was in Ms. Moller's office," explained Winna. "They found a piece of a map in it, which is going to help them find a stash of diamonds in a mine. The hospital's going to get a share of some of the money from the diamonds."

"It's kind of a complicated story," Kosey said apologetically.

"Would you excuse us for a minute to talk?" Winna asked her parents. "You don't mind, do you?"

"No, go ahead," said her father. "We'll be in the gift shop."

Winna pulled Kosey over to a bench. Pushing on his shoulders, she forced him to sit while she peered into his face. "Wow," she said. "You really got beat up. Does it still hurt?"

"A little," admitted Kosey. "When I breathe."

"Is your nose broken? Have you seen a doctor?"

"No, it didn't even occur to me. We had to keep moving. I can tough it out. Ow," he said as she pressed her finger against the side of his nose.

"Stop squirming. Let me take a look at it." Winna examined Kosey's nose while he sat as still as possible. Even with the pain, he felt a surge of happiness at having her so close to him.

"I guess it isn't broken," she announced. "It's still in one piece. You're only bruised."

"That's good," he smiled. "How come it still hurts so bad, though?"

"It's going to hurt for a while. And be swollen," said Winna. "But eventually you'll return to your normal cute self," she smiled, sitting down next to him on the bench.

She thinks I'm cute, thought Kosey. Even with a beat up face! That's a good sign. "But will I be able to play the piano, Doc?" he joked.

"Of course. Why wouldn't you?"

"Hey, that's great! I never could before!" laughed Kosey.

Winna groaned. "I can't believe I fell for that old joke! I hope you don't play the nose flute, though. That might be a problem."

"No, I'm more of a ukulele guy," said Kosey. The two young people smiled at each other.

"Have you put anything on the broken skin?" asked Winna, standing again. "Let's go get your first aid kit and find some antibiotic cream."

While Winna and Kosey were getting reacquainted, the rest of the group continued to talk to Bibi. "The dance really was wonderful," said Bernie. "Thank you for letting us watch it. I have a question, though. That chest they used in the dance—do you know where it came from?"

"Let me think," said Bibi. "I can ask Chatha Eze, our lead dancer. He created the dance. I think he got the idea for it from that old chest."

"Was he the dancer who took the things out of the chest?" asked Bernie.

"Yes, that's him," said Bibi. "We should be able to find him before he goes home. He'll be happy to meet you. He loves to talk about the dances he's choreographed. Come this way."

They walked by stagehands and dancers packing up to leave the theater. The tall dancer came out of the dressing room dressed in sweats and carrying a duffel bag and a bottle of water.

"This is Chatha Eze," said Bibi. "Congratulations on a fine performance, Chaty. These folks were in the audience. Do you have time to talk to them for a few minutes?"

"Sure," he said. "Call me Chaty." After shaking hands all around, he turned to Bibi. "I'll walk them back to the lobby if you have to go, Bibi."

"Thanks. I do have to meet another tour group," she said as she headed to another exit. "Goodbye!"

"Goodbye, Bibi! And thanks!" called Josh.

The dancer turned back to the visitors. "I'm glad you could see the show. Are you from around here?"

"No, we're on a trip of sorts," said Bernie. "It's kind of a mission, actually. It has to do with the leopard skin chest you were using as part of the dance."

"Isn't it a cool piece?" asked Chaty as they walked. "The founder of the arts center built it, and it's always been handed down to the lead dancer. It became mine a few years ago, and I decided to use it in a dance. Do you think it worked?"

"Yeah. It was a fascinating dance," said Bernie.

"Thanks. We keep a lot of mementos in it; pretty much the whole history of the cultural center is in the chest. That's what gave me the idea to use it as a metaphor for the journey of life. I emptied it out for the performances, but all the keepsakes will go back in later."

"Are you sure you took everything out of the leopard chest?" asked Josh.

"Yes," answered Chaty, puzzled. "Why? And what did you mean when you said your trip had something to do with the chest?"

"We're looking for something that was hidden in it," explained Gogo. "Do you know any more of the history of the chest, such as why the founder built it?"

"I didn't think he had any particular reason," said Chaty. "And I didn't know there was anything hidden in it. What is it?"

"It's kind of a long story," put in Bernie.

Just as they re-entered the lobby, Kosey trotted up to the group with Winna and her parents. "Hey," he said. "Look who I found!"

"What a nice coincidence to see you all here," said Winna. "I'm visiting my parents and we decided to spend the day at the cultural center. It's one of my favorite places."

"I have an idea," said Josh after the group made introductions. "Why don't we all have dinner together?"

"That sounds nice. Is it all right with you?" asked Winna, turning to her parents.

"Sure," her mother said, nodding in approval.

"Kosey, you go ahead and make the plans with Winna's parents," suggested Josh. "We'll see you back here in a few minutes."

He turned toward Chaty. "We really need to take a look at that leopard chest," he said. "Can we do it right now?"

"Yep. It's backstage on a prop table," said Chaty.

"Great," said Josh. "We'll start to explain the story to you on the way. Lead on."

While they walked to the backstage area, Chaty heard the story of the sacred diamond mine, General Erasto and his soldiers, and the founding of the organizations that would benefit from the diamonds.

"You know, I have heard that diamond story before," remarked Chaty. "The story of the sacred stash of diamonds at Mount Kilimanjaro that no one can find! I thought it was just a folktale."

"It sounds like a folktale, I admit," said Effie. "It took a little convincing to get me to believe it, but it really is true."

Chaty flipped on the light over the prop table. "Here it is," he said. "But I know it's empty. You say there's a piece of the diamond map inside somewhere?"

"Yes. There should be a secret compartment," said Josh, opening up the lid. "Bernie? Wanna check?"

The leopard chest

Bernie ran his hand along the inside of the chest and the lid. "I'm not coming up with anything," he said. "Maybe it's in the bottom. Effie, help me turn it over."

They carefully tipped the leopard chest and examined the bottom. "Here it is," said Bernie. "There's a sliding door right here." He opened it and took out map piece #7. "And here's our last map piece. We did it!"

"We got all of them!" said Effie, clapping Gogo hard on the back. The smaller man coughed, but smiled.

"I knew we would," said Josh. "It's the luck of the talismans."

"Hey, what about the talisman?" asked Gogo. "Shouldn't there be some kind of leopard trinket?"

THE LIFE CHEST : AFRICA

"That's right," said Josh. He turned to Chaty. "You took everything out of the chest. Was there a figurine of a leopard, or a painting or something? It would have been put in the chest by the founder."

"Hmm." As he thought, Chaty fingered the necklace he always wore.

"There's your talisman." Effie pointed to Chaty's neck. "He's wearing it!"

The leopard trinket, a necklace

He was indeed. The leopard trinket was a brass charm in the shape of a stalking leopard, strung on a leather cord.

"Of course. I forgot," laughed Chaty. "When the leopard chest was handed down to me, I received this necklace. It belonged to the founder as well?"

"Yes," said Josh. "It was made by an old shaman to bless the arts center. I'm glad you still have it."

"So am I!" said Chaty. "Maybe it helps me dance better, too!" They laughed and Chaty continued. "So do you have everything you need to find the sacred diamond chamber?"

"I think we do," answered Effie. "Now we can drive to Kilimanjaro and start searching there. This piece will point us to the exact spot where the chamber is."

"We don't know what condition the pit will be in," said Gogo. "We don't even know if all those tunnels on the map still exist. It's been so many years since that map was drawn. The weather and erosion in an open pit like that could have totally obscured them."

"And don't forget elephant stampedes," added Effie.

"Well, that's why we brought you, Boss," said Josh, punching the big man in the shoulder. "Effie's our explosives expert," he explained to Chaty as he rubbed his hand.

"Whoa," said Chaty. "This sounds like a complicated undertaking."

"It is complicated," said Effie. "And dangerous, too. But it's about time that diamonds are used to help Africa instead of funding wars. So it's worth it. Right, Josh?" Effie moved to hit Josh in the shoulder but pulled his punch and laughed when Josh ducked.

"I'm too fast for you, Boss. Hey, let's find Kosey and his girl," Josh said. "He'll be excited to see the map piece, too."

They walked back to the lobby. Winna's parents had chosen a restaurant down the street and the group made their way there, excitedly talking on the way.

During dinner, the story was explained further and everyone examined the map piece. "This is piece #7," explained Kosey to Winna and her folks. "It shows the shaft that goes down into the diamond chamber. That's where the jackpot will be."

THE LIFE CHEST : AFRICA

Map piece number seven

"Chaty, what's the story of that half-done building we passed on the way in?" asked Bernie.

"The economy took a turn for the worse a few years ago," explained Chaty with a sigh. "We had several investors, but they weren't able to fully fund the project. So there it sits— a new exhibition space and concert hall waiting to be completed."

Kosey tried to lift Chaty's spirits. "When we get the diamonds and sell them, you'll have the money you need to finish the building. And I'll come see the first concert you have there. How about you, Winna?" he asked the young lady at his side.

"Sure," said Winna, smiling back at Kosey. "It's a date."

After dessert, Bernie addressed his friends. "I made a reservation at a guesthouse near here. We should be turning in pretty soon. We've got to rest, and there's planning to do before we're ready to go to the mountain."

"That's right," said Effie. "I want to make sure all our ducks are in a row."

"And all our i's are dotted and t's are crossed," said Gogo.

Effie turned to him, puzzled. "Isn't that what I said?"

"Yeah," laughed Gogo. "I was just agreeing with you."

"Well, it was really great to meet everyone," said Josh to Winna's parents.

"Yes, it was a pleasure to spend the evening together," said Bernie. He nodded at Kosey and Winna, who only had eyes for each other.

Winna blushed when she noticed everyone was looking at them. She hurriedly told her parents, "Kosey is going to walk me back to our hotel. We won't be out long." The two young people quickly said their goodbyes and walked out the door.

"I'm not usually afraid of anything," said Winna to Kosey as they strolled down the sidewalk hand in hand. "But I'm worried about you on this trip now. I'd like to see you again— with your face looking normal."

"I'd like to see you again, too," said Kosey. "And my grandmother needs me back home. Now I've got two good reasons to want to stay safe. You'll see me in a week or so when I bring a check to the hospital."

"Come back even if you don't have a check for the hospital, okay?" asked Winna. She stopped and leaned toward Kosey, impulsively kissing him.

"Ow!" Kosey said, in spite of enjoying the kiss.

"Oh— your nose! I forgot!" said Winna.

"It's okay, really. Here," he said, taking her shoulders. "Let's try again."

A few minutes later, the rest of the group approached the two young people, who were still on the sidewalk, embracing. Josh nudged Bernie and they crossed the street to walk on the other side.

"Wait! Is that Winna?" asked her father, peering into the darkness.

"Yes, dear," said his wife. "Come on, now. She's grown and she knows her own mind." She pulled her husband along, smiling.

"I can vouch for Kosey. He's a good guy," Josh assured them.

Gogo shook his head and chuckled. "I guess we'll plan the assault on Kilimanjaro in the morning."

"Better to do it with a pot of coffee, anyway," grunted Effie.

Chapter Twelve

Mount Kilimanjaro: The Dream Within Sight

Kosey opened the door of the small guesthouse and saw Effie sitting on the patio at a picnic table, drinking coffee. "Winna's parents invited us to have breakfast with them at their hotel this morning," he said, standing on the threshold. "Do you think that will be okay?"

"Sure, kid," said Effie. "Let's get everybody else out of bed and get moving. We have a lot to do today."

An hour later, Kosey and Winna were gazing at each other over rice cakes and chai tea while the others showed the maps to Winna's parents. Chaty, the dancer from the arts center, had also joined them.

"This is just amazing," said Winna's mother as she looked at how the diamond map fit together. "It's wonderful that you were able to find all the map pieces. General Erasto was certainly a man with a vision."

"He was," said Bernie. "I just hope we can make his vision a reality. It's been almost 150 years since this map was made. I hope it has all the information we need."

"The location of the pit and the indication of the north wall are clear," Gobo reassured him. "And it shouldn't be too hard to find the area where the tunnel is on the north wall, even if some of the tunnels have been obscured over time."

"We've had good luck up until now," agreed Josh. "I'm itching to finally get to Kilimanjaro and find the sacred diamond chamber."

"I'm sure you will find the diamonds," said Winna. She tried to keep her tone casual. "But what about…" She looked at Kosey and her voice trailed off. Kosey reached for her hand under the table and held it tightly.

"I know. The Bradleys," sighed Josh. "How much danger do you think we're still in, Effie?"

The big man shrugged, but concern showed on his face. "They know we mean business," he answered Josh. "You injured Abdi Kalu pretty bad."

"And you killed another one of their bunch!" said Kosey enthusiastically.

"I'm not proud of that," said Effie quietly. "No good soldier kills for fun. I only did what I had to do to save little Gogo."

Kosey's face flushed. "I didn't mean— I'm sorry!"

"It's okay, kid," said Effie, putting a hand on Kosey's shoulder. "I just hope you never have to make that kind of choice." He turned back to the group and continued. "I'm not sure what to expect from them now. Abdi was their best fighter. They're not much without him. It might buy us some time if they wait for him to heal up or look for someone else to hire."

"Don't forget their ninja," said Kosey grimly, touching his bruised face. "She's got quite a roundhouse kick."

"No kidding," said Effie sympathetically. "I guess we have to be ready for anything."

"I agree," said Gogo, nodding seriously. "I'm just glad we had you with us, Effie."

"That's for sure," said Josh. "But let me ask you something, Effie. Do you think we can do this? Should we go on? What's your expert opinion?"

Effie didn't hesitate. "Yes," he said. "Between the five of us, we have the brains and the skills we need. Even if the Bradleys catch up to us and we have to fight them again, I think it's worth it."

"Good," said Josh. "I'm glad to hear you say that."

"Oh, we can do it all right," said the big man. "But we can't go until we're ready, and there's a lot to do. Come on, Gogo. Let's go over the supply list and make sure everything's in the Land Rover." Effie stood, brushed the crumbs off his lap and turned to go.

"I've got the list here on my tablet," said Gogo, following him.

"Okay, Boss," called Josh. "Thanks. We'll join you in a few minutes."

"It's checkout time, and we need to be going. I'd like to wish you good luck," said Winna's father. "We certainly appreciate everything you're doing."

"The hospital and the other organizations will be greatly helped," added Winna's mother as she shook Kosey's hand.

"We'll say a prayer for you every day," said Chaty. "But I wish there was more I could do to help." He touched the leopard charm around his neck and then had an idea. "Say— these trinkets that General Erasto put in all the animal chests— are they supposed to be good luck talismans?"

"Yes," said Bernie. "They were blessed by his mentor, the old shaman Duma."

"Well, how about this?" said Chaty, unlatching the necklace. "You need a talisman more than I do right now." He handed the leopard charm on its leather cord to Kosey. "Will you wear it?"

"Sure. It would be an honor!" said Kosey. He examined the charm before putting it on. "I'll keep it safe, and I'll give it back to you when we return. Its home should be near the leopard chest."

"That's great, Chaty," said Josh. "Thanks. I guess we better get moving, though. Effie and Gogo are probably ready to go."

The group walked out to the parking lot to say their goodbyes, with Winna and Kosey holding back a little. Kosey didn't jump into the Land Rover until Effie honked the horn, interrupting his last kiss with Winna. He waved goodbye until he could no longer see her, then sighed and turned away.

"Now we're on the home stretch," grinned Effie as he picked up speed along the road.

"The closest place to the mountain is a little village called Marangu," announced Gogo. "We can set up a base camp outside of town, but it should be inconspicuous."

"It'll be more than that," said Effie. "I'll have it downright camouflaged, don't worry."

Bernie looked up from his comm. "We'll be there in about four hours. What do you think we should do first?"

"I'd like to drive right up to the pits," said Gogo. "We should be able to find the three pits on map piece #2 pretty easily. The pit we want is going to be the southernmost one. Once we identify it, we can see how difficult it's going to be from that point on."

Gogo spoke confidently. He was in his element: these diamond mines were where he grew up. He was excited to revisit his childhood home with the prospect of finding real treasure.

"Did you learn about the diamond mine at Kilimanjaro when you were young?" asked Kosey.

"Yes, and it always has fascinated me," answered Gogo. "Even though we were forbidden to go near the pits, my friends and I would explore the area whenever we could get away with it. Once, we lowered a rope down one of the pits and found our way into a tunnel." He laughed and shook his head at the memory. "Those tunnels were very unstable. We were lucky to get out alive. Thank goodness my parents never found out about it. But I transformed that curiosity into my passion. I've been studying the abandoned mine at Kilimanjaro and the diamonds that it produced for years now."

"All the better for us," said Josh. "Between your expertise and Effie's, we're in good shape."

Effie frowned. "We'll be in better shape when we get inside that pit," he said. "The longer we're above ground the more chance the Bradleys will see us."

"If they do catch up to us at all," said Bernie. "But you're right, Effie. The quicker we can make this happen the better."

The conversation waned as the truck bumped along. Kosey's mind went back to Winna. I wonder if she really does care, he thought. I think she likes me. She sure seemed worried about me when we left. The Land Rover hit a pothole and Kosey's stomach jumped. He felt nervous, but he wasn't certain what he was nervous about. Sure, they were finally going to get to their destination and dig for the diamonds, hopefully without interference. But thoughts of Winna were all mixed up in there too. He liked her so much. Her confidence, her intelligence, her sense of humor and her beautiful eyes— she was the most amazing girl he had ever met. I guess I want her to be proud of me, Kosey thought. Funny. I'm worried more about Winna than running into that chick with the roundhouse kick again.

Josh's elbow in Kosey's ribs brought him back to reality. "Look!" Josh said. Kosey gazed in the direction Josh was pointing, as did everyone else in the truck. "It's Kilimanjaro!" continued Josh. "Isn't it incredible?"

The mountain rose up before them in the distance. The warm afternoon sun, glinting through the trees and tall grasses of the surrounding savannahs and forests, cast a golden light on its western side. "I grew up in the shadow of this mountain, and I will always be amazed at its beauty," said Gogo reverently.

"It's pretty, all right," said Effie. "But let's get down to business and make sure we're on the right road."

Map piece number two

Using piece #2 of the diamond map and the GPS on Bernie's comm device, Gogo helped Effie navigate. They made their way slowly through the little-used winding roads which led to the diamond pits at the foot of the mountain. "Check out the birds-eye view on my comm and compare it to the diamond map," Bernie instructed Gogo. "How does it look?"

"This is the place, all right," said Gogo excitedly. "And right there," he pointed to one of the pits on the screen. "Is the south pit. Kosey, do you have the third map piece?"

Map piece number three

"Yes, right here," said Kosey, handing it to him.

Effie stopped the Land Rover. Piling out of the vehicle, they transferred their gaze from the maps to the real thing. It was incredible. The pits were several hundred yards away, and the mountain was further in the distance. But before them were bones. Elephant bones, large and small. Skulls and skeletons and even some pieces of ivory, scattered across the grassy expanse. The sight stunned them into silence.

Effie finally spoke. "It's an elephant graveyard."

"Yes," said Gogo. "When this area was being mined, the elephants were driven off. They could no longer access their sacred burial ground. It made them restless and angry, and there were stampedes for a time. Then they stopped coming for the most part. When an elephant did appear, it was killed for its ivory, and eventually they disappeared altogether."

Approaching the elephant graveyard

"But they came back. They must've come back," whispered Kosey. "Look at all these bones!"

"They did, when the mine was abandoned. Now it's sacred ground again, and we might see elephants," said Gogo. "But remember: no picking up ivory for souvenirs, no disturbing any of the bones."

"No problem," said Josh. "It's not what we're here for."

Bernie nodded. "Africa has enough problems with poachers," he said.

"I feel kind of weird walking past all these elephant bones to get to the pit," said Kosey. "But I guess we have to."

"Let's do it," said Effie. "We're not here to disturb the elephants' graveyard or hurt anyone."

"That's right," said Josh. "One of the reasons we want to get the sacred diamonds is to give money to Tanda Tula to help fight poaching. I'm sure the elephant spirits are cool with that."

The group walked carefully through the field of elephant bones until they got to the edge of the south pit. Gogo pulled out map piece #4, which marked the north wall of the pit, as the others gazed across the dark expanse.

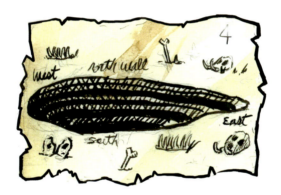

Map piece number four

"The light isn't great right now," said Effie. "We'll be able to see a lot better in the morning. But I can still get a pretty good idea of what that wall looks like. Show me map piece #5, will you, Gogo?" he asked.

Effie and Gogo examined the map piece, which showed 12 tunnels in the north wall. Gogo pointed to the top right corner. "Right here is the spot we need to find," he said. "The spot that's marked by an elephant head in the drawing."

Effie squinted into the distance. "I don't see much of an opening there. Let's take the dynamite in case we have to blast our way in."

THE LIFE CHEST : AFRICA

Map piece number five

"How are we going to get to the tunnel?" Kosey asked. "I think I see a couple of ladders on the ledge, and scaffolding."

"There was a whole system of ladders and scaffolding that was used when the pit was being mined," answered Gogo. "Most of it is gone now. What's left will be very unsafe to use."

"Yup," agreed Effie. "We've got good rope ladders with us. I got a boatswain's chair, too. That should be all we need. Now let's get out of here and find a place to camp for the night. We should get everything ready to go and move out at daylight."

There was a grove of acacia trees nearby, with a huge baobab tree in the center. Effie parked the Land Rover on the side of the baobab tree that hid it from the road. Kosey and Josh cut a few leafy acacia branches to cover the Land Rover while Gogo and Bernie set up camp for the night.

"These baobabs are really amazing, aren't they?" said Bernie in admiration of the giant tree.

"The baobab is the tree of Africa," nodded Effie. "It's a symbol of the resilience of the African people— always finding a way to survive. The fruit, the water inside, the bark, the leaves, and the seeds— every part of the baobab is useful for something."

"It's even used for shelter," agreed Gogo. "The people and animals of Africa could not have survived all these thousands of years without it. In fact, this very tree may be thousands of years old. Some say the baobab was the tree of life in the Garden of Eden."

"It sure is big enough for shelter," said Bernie. "I've heard of people hollowing out baobab trees and living inside them." He began to walk around the giant, bulbous trunk. "Hey, there's an opening right here! If it was a little larger I could fit in it!" Bernie peered inside the large hole in the tree's trunk.

"Yeah, but you might not want to—" before Effie could finish the sentence, Bernie had stuck his head inside the tree. He came out again, fast, along with three tawny-colored bats, which flapped their leathery wings in his face before flying up into the branches.

"Whoa!" Bernie backed away in haste. He lost his footing and fell on his backside.

Effie couldn't help laughing. "I was about to tell you that bats and birds live inside a lot of these baobab trees," he chuckled. "Are you okay?"

"Yeah, sure," said Bernie sheepishly, standing and brushing off his pants. "That was pretty silly of me."

"Everything all right?" asked Josh as he and Kosey came around from the other side of the tree.

"Yeah," said Effie. "Bernie's just learning a little bit about baobab trees."

"And fruit bats," added Bernie. "I just invaded their privacy," he explained, pointing at the hole in the tree.

"Bats?" said Josh worriedly. "I've never been up close and personal with a bat."

"Fruit bats are harmless," Gogo assured him. "Bernie just scared them."

"Yeah, that mug coming at me in the dark would scare me, too," laughed Josh, punching Bernie in the shoulder.

"Ow," said Bernie, rubbing his shoulder. "Thanks for the insult and the injury."

Kosey watched the cousins joking around and smiled to himself. He could see the affection between Josh and Bernie and admired the way they could good-naturedly tease each other. I guess that's something you can do when you know for sure how the other person feels about you, he thought to himself. That's a good kind of relationship to have.

Once the group settled in their tents for the night, the conversations subsided and the noises of the African bush took over. The chorus of insects was constant and soothing. Nocturnal birds cooed and called, and bats could even be heard echo-locating. Just as he was about to drop off to sleep, Josh thought he heard a distant rumbling. Bernie heard it too. "Elephants," he whispered. Josh gave in to sleep, and his dreams would be filled with the lumbering giants, grazing and marching down the wide elephant trails.

An elephant stampede woke Josh and he bolted upright in his sleeping bag. He was about to yell "Run for your life!" when he realized the roaring noise he had heard was just the engine of the Land Rover.

Effie and Kosey had already made a trip to the edge of the pit and back, hauling supplies and equipment. "One more load and then I'll come back for the rest of you lot," said Effie to Josh, who had come out of the tent, squinting in the bright sunlight.

"It's a marvelous day for it," said Bernie enthusiastically, handing Josh a cup of coffee. "Sunny, but not too hot. Diamonds, here we come!" he finished, tapping his coffee cup against Josh's for a toast. As long as we don't get visited by a herd of elephants, thought Josh, still groggy from his dream.

A half hour later they had the camp packed up. Everyone hopped into the Land Rover for the short drive to the edge of the pit. They could have walked, but Effie had decided he wanted the Land Rover close by in case they needed it for a quick getaway. The Bradleys were still on his mind. He had his gun loaded and handy and made sure Josh and Bernie had theirs as well.

Bernie and Gogo checked the GPS and directed Effie around to the north side of the south pit. Effie found a small grove of trees and hid the Land Rover there. They walked a few hundred meters to the pit and looked over the edge. The depth of the huge hole was dark, but bright sunlight illuminated the upper third.

"How deep do you think this hole is?" asked Kosey, peering down.

"About 100 meters," answered Gogo.

Kosey let out a long, low whistle. "That's quite a pit," he said.

"Yes," agreed Gogo. "And much of it was dug by hand. Our ancestors were literally worked to death for these diamonds."

His words reminded the group of a sober reality. They stood in silence for a moment, staring into the pit. Then Kosey spoke. "We're doing this for them," he said quietly. "The sacred diamonds will be their legacy."

"Let's get down there and make it happen," said Effie. "Is this the right spot, Gogo?" he asked.

"As far as I can tell, we're right above the spot where the tunnel leading to the sacred chamber originally was," answered Gogo. "I don't know for sure, though. The pit doesn't have square corners, so it's hard to tell where the north wall actually intersects the east wall. We've used both the GPS and an old-fashioned compass. I guess we'll have to just make our best guess."

"The scaffolding just below us looks pretty rotted and broken down," said Bernie.

"I wouldn't trust it," agreed Effie. But there's a piece further down that's more solid. It looks like it was built on an earthen ledge."

"How do you know for sure that it's solid?" asked Josh.

"I don't," answered Effie. "Help me set up the rig to anchor this boatswain's chair. Lower me down in it and I'll test the scaffolding. If it fails I'll still be harnessed in. If it holds me, it'll hold any of us."

Bernie and Kosey had already set up the anchor pegs and crank mechanism, and Effie climbed into the boatswain's chair: a harness and seat contraption. It reminded Josh of the rigs that window washers used on skyscrapers. They lowered Effie down till his entire weight was resting on the scaffolding. It held the big man, and Effie came back up smiling.

Gogo was lowered down next to check out the tunnel opening. "I wish I knew for sure that this was the right spot," he muttered to himself as he hung in the boatswain's chair. Gogo took some measurements, glanced down at his instruments and then back up at the wall. He noticed an object glinting in the sunlight. "Hey," he called to the group. "Pull me up a little— three or four meters. And slide the chair over to the left— no, my left— stop! That's it!"

An elephant in the wall

"What?" asked Effie. "What's going on? What do you see?"

"There's something stuck in the wall!" answered Gogo excitedly. "Hang on— there! I've got it! Pull me up!"

Effie hauled the boatswain's chair up as quickly as he could, and took the object from Gogo's outstretched hand as soon as it appeared above the lip of the pit. "It's a little statue," he said, turning it over in his hands and handing it to Kosey, who stood near him. "What do you think it means?" the big man asked.

"It's a sign!" answered Kosey. "It must mark where the tunnel is. Now I remember; General Erasto wrote about it. You did find the right spot, Gogo!" he said to the little man hanging in the boatswain's chair.

"That's great," said Gogo. "Now could you finish the job and get me out? I'm a bit dizzy hanging here."

THE LIFE CHEST : AFRICA

"Whoops! Sure thing," said Bernie. He rushed to finish cranking up the chair. Kosey handed the figurine back to Effie and ran to help.

"The tunnel is still viable," Gogo said as he climbed out of the harness. "The thickness gauge on my surveying instrument showed that it's only closed up about 10 meters in. Typical erosion."

Gogo turned to Effie. "Do you think you could do a small, controlled blast just to get rid of the debris at the mouth of the tunnel?" he asked. "It's loose enough to dig but it would take half a day."

Effie rubbed his hands together in anticipation. "That's what I'm here for," he said. "Help me get the explosives together and I'll make it happen. Is the debris dry or wet?" he asked Gogo as they began to sort through the supplies.

Within an hour it was done. Everyone cheered when the smoke cleared after the explosion, revealing an open tunnel. There was a section of scaffolding just below the opening that was sturdy enough to walk on. "We'll wait a few minutes for the dust to settle," cautioned Effie. "Let's take a lunch break. Then we'll start lowering the digging equipment."

After a few hours, the group was ready to look for the diamonds. They had lowered picks, shovels, ladders and containers to the tunnel entrance. They dismantled the boatswain's chair and hid it with the Land Rover. Two ropes tied to stakes in the ground would suffice for climbing in and out of the pit now. Finally, the hopeful adventurers slid down the ropes and walked into the large, broad tunnel. They could hardly contain their excitement.

"I can't believe how close we are," said Josh to Bernie, shining his flashlight down the tunnel. "I wonder how far in we're going to have to go?"

Map piece number six

Bernie looked up from the map piece he was studying with his own flashlight. "I've got the next clue here," he said. "Map piece #6. These circles— I guess they are holes in the ground. Maybe we'll come to a bigger cave where these holes were dug. Gogo, what's your opinion?"

"I think that's right," answered Gogo. He held up the last piece of the map. "See? Once we find those nine holes, one of them will lead to the sacred diamond chamber." Gogo and Bernie continued to study the map pieces.

"Come on," said Josh to Kosey. He trotted further down the tunnel, his excitement getting the better of him. "Let them look at the map. Let's keep going."

Effie, cautious as ever, brought up the rear. The rest of the group was getting diamond fever but the bodyguard's mind was on the ever-present danger of being discovered by the Bradleys. He kept his eye on the mouth of the tunnel and listened intently for any noise from outside.

Kosey sprinted ahead of Josh. "I'll find the diamonds before you, old man!" he joked. The tunnel widened and Kosey disappeared around a corner.

THE LIFE CHEST : AFRICA

Josh almost ran into him. "Hey, what's the idea?" he said. "You almost caused a pile-up." Then he saw what had made Kosey stop short. "This is it!" said Josh. "The diamond chamber! Guys! Come here quick!"

Bernie and Gogo joined them in the small round cave, where the tunnel seemed to end. "Is this it? Is this the diamond chamber?" asked Bernie. He shined his flashlight around. "Where are the diamonds?"

Kosey kneeled down and picked up a small object. "How about this?" he asked, handing it to Gogo.

"Yes, this is a diamond!" said Gogo.

"But that's all?" asked Bernie, scanning the walls with his flashlight. "Someone else must've been here before us and found the diamonds. There's nothing here!"

There was silence for a moment. Was this the end of the adventure? No diamonds after all? There was never any guarantee that they would find the sacred diamonds, but their luck had been pretty good up until now. Nobody could believe it was over.

Gogo, fumbling for his flashlight and the map pieces, broke the silence. "No! You forgot. There's one more map piece. Look!"

The others gathered around him. "You hold the map," said Bernie. "We'll use our flashlights."

"Here's map piece #6," explained Gogo, smoothing it out. "That's where we are now. In this little cave with nine shafts dug in it." Kosey shined his flashlight around the perimeter of the room. He counted nine holes, some partially filled in.

Map piece number seven

"Look at this hole on the map," said Gogo. "There's a drawing of a little tunnel leading off from it. Bernie, will you give me map piece #7?" Bernie unfolded the last piece of the diamond map and held it up next to #6, which Gogo held.

"See how they line up?" said Gogo. "One of the nine holes in this room leads into a shaft that goes down into the sacred diamond chamber. That's where we will find the jackpot."

"Fantastic!" said Josh. "But how do we know which hole it is? Do we need to dig down into all nine of them?"

Kosey, who had been scanning the room with his flashlight, spoke up. "I don't think we'll have to do that," he said. "Look at this." He shined his flashlight on one of the holes. It had been filled in with dirt, apparently from a cave-in. And sticking out of the hole were human bones; two lower legs and part of a foot.
"I guess we should start here," said Kosey quietly. "It looks like this guy tried to get down the shaft, and it caved in on him."

"Wasn't it part of the legend of the diamond chamber that nobody could get into it without being crushed in a cave-in?" asked Josh.

"Yes, except for Erasto," said Bernie. "It looks like this is the shaft. Let's get digging."

Nobody moved. "What do we do about the bones?" asked Kosey.

"I'll dig them out," volunteered Josh. "It isn't the first time I've had to handle human bones. We found some inside the Great Wall of China."

"Yup," said Bernie. "That was an unexpected discovery, too. I'll help you, Josh."

The bones were carefully moved and they began to dig. It wasn't long before the shaft opened up beneath them.

"I wasn't sure how far we'd have to dig," admitted Gogo. "In fact, I was worried that we wouldn't be able to open up this shaft at all."

"Our luck has held out so far," grinned Josh, wiping his brow with a grimy hand. "Look at how narrow the shaft is, though. Can any of us get down into it?"

"I can. I'm sure I can," said Kosey, peering into the shaft. "I'm the smallest one here."

"But what about the shaft? It might cave in on you!" said Gogo anxiously. "No one but Erasto ever got down there!"

Kosey touched the leopard charm on his neck. "Ah, but you forget!" he said with a grin. "I have a talisman. Lower the ladder, fellas. I'm going in!"

Even as he spoke, Kosey began to get nervous. He thought to himself, this is crazy! My stomach is jumping into my throat! What if the tunnel caves in after all? But I'm going to do this to make my grandmother and Winna proud of me.

With a deep breath, Kosey started down the ladder. The others waited breathlessly as Kosey disappeared into the dark. "The shaft is pretty narrow at first," he called. "But now it's opening up. If you hold your breath for the first part, I think everybody can get down here. Except maybe Effie." Kosey laughed. There was no other sound for a few moments, but then his voice came up again from the depths. "I reached the end of the ladder," Kosey said. He shined his flashlight below. "It's only another meter or so," he said. "I'm going to jump down."

Another 30 seconds passed, but it seemed like 30 minutes. "Kosey!" called Gogo. "What's going on? Answer me, please!"

"I can't believe it!" came Kosey's voice from the chamber. "Diamonds! They're all around me! Get down here! You gotta see it!"

Bernie and Gogo eagerly squeezed into the chamber. "I knew it! I knew it!" cried Bernie as he clambered down the ladder. "We found the sacred diamonds! Come on, Josh! Where's Effie?"

Josh didn't answer. He was as excited about finding the diamonds as his cousin, but he was suddenly worried. Where was Effie? Had the Bradleys caught up to them? Josh decided to double back and find their bodyguard. "I'm sure he's right behind us," he called down into the shaft. "Be right back!" Josh trotted toward the tunnel entrance, hoping his concern was unfounded.

"Hurry up! There's diamonds everywhere!" Bernie yelled. The trio in the diamond chamber shone their flashlights all around. Everywhere the light hit, diamonds glittered above, around and below. It feels like being inside a disco ball, thought Bernie.

And the colors! "Gogo, are these all really diamonds?" asked Kosey, shining his flashlight on a wall of rose colored stones. "Some are pink, and yellow!"

THE LIFE CHEST : AFRICA

Kosey, Bernie and Gogo in the diamond chamber

"They're diamonds, all right," answered Gogo. "Sometimes they are different colors. And these are the most perfect ones I've ever seen."

"Wow," breathed Bernie. Then he looked down and yelled, "I'm even stepping on diamonds! I can't help it!"

Gogo laughed. "Don't worry, Bernie. They're diamonds! They won't break!" The little gemologist reached down and picked up a greenish-yellow stone the size of a baseball. "Look at this!" he said in amazement. "What a fantastic specimen! I wonder if there are even bigger ones!"

"How does this happen, Gogo?" asked Bernie. "So many diamonds in one place?"

"Volcanic activity pushes the diamonds up in pipe-like rock formations under the surface," answered the gemologist. "So they do tend to be concentrated in tunnel-like areas. But this really is the biggest deposit I've ever seen."

"No wonder Erasto's dream was to come back for these diamonds," said Kosey, shining his flashlight on the glittering ceiling above. "It's breathtaking."

Meanwhile, near the entrance of the tunnel, Effie paced back and forth. I'm worrying for nothing, he told himself. Abdi is probably still in the hospital. They wouldn't try to attack us without him. Then Effie's keen ears picked up a sound he did not want to hear: voices from outside the tunnel and up above. The big man stopped short. He turned and saw a figure walking toward him from within the tunnel. "Josh?" he whispered urgently. "C'mere!"

"Yeah, it's me," said Josh, trotting up to him. "What's going on?"

Effie's hand went up. "Shh," he said. "People up above. I just heard somebody say Agnes. It's gotta be the Bradleys."

THE LIFE CHEST : AFRICA

The villains approach

"They found us?" whispered Josh in dismay.

Effie nodded. "Follow me. And don't make a sound." The two men quickly and quietly approached the mouth of the tunnel, pressing themselves against the wall. The voices were just above them. They belonged to Agnes and Aaron Bradley.

"I see tracks from their Land Rover!" Agnes said in frustration. "But where are they?"

"Effie, this is bad! What should we do?" said Josh, trying to keep his voice low.

"Nothing, for now. There's scaffolding above us," Effie hissed. "They can't see us or our equipment."

The conversation continued above. "Let's keep driving around," suggested Aaron. "Maybe they're at a different pit."

"Fine with me," answered Agnes. "It's too hot to be wandering around in this sun." The voices faded, and Josh and Effie heard a vehicle hum away.

"Here's the plan," Effie said, turning to Josh. "Once they get around to the other side of the pit, they'll be able to see that we've blasted open this tunnel. So let's get our equipment inside. Then you go back and tell the others. I'll stay here and keep my gun drawn."

After quickly hiding the equipment, Josh shook Effie's hand. "Okay, Boss," he said. "We'll be back in a flash." Josh hurried back down the tunnel. When he reached the shaft to the diamond chamber, he saw Bernie poke his head up from the hole. I'd laugh if things weren't so serious, Josh thought. My cousin looks like a redheaded prairie dog!

THE LIFE CHEST : AFRICA

"Hey!" said Bernie. "What's going on? Don't you want to see the diamonds? We really hit the jackpot!"

"That's awesome," said Josh. "But we've got visitors. The Bradleys are wandering around up above. Quick, climb out so we can make a plan. Effie's back at the tunnel entrance and it won't be long before those goons figure out where we are."

"Oh, no!" said Bernie in dismay. "I'll tell the others!"

Josh started back, and then heard gunshots. "Effie!" Josh yelled. "Effie!" He ran faster, pulling his gun from its holster.

April took the last sip from her soft drink with a loud slurp. "That sounds like a hippo, Blossom!" said Josh, and glanced at his comm. "Look at the time! Bernie, weren't you going to take us to a baseball game tonight?" he asked.

"That's right," answered his cousin. "The Bisons are my favorite minor league team, and they're heading for the playoffs. Let's go." He stood and drained his coffee cup. "I don't want to miss the first inning. Pigeon-Toe Murray's at the top of the batting order!"

"Uncle Bernie!" cried April. "What about the story? Grandpa was just getting to a real exciting part!"

"I don't mind," laughed Bernie, ruffling April's hair. "I know how it ends!"

"But I don't!" insisted April. "What happens to Effie? Does he get hurt? I like him!"

"Now stop teasing her, you two," said Chen Li gently. "April, I know you'll enjoy the baseball game. Grandpa and Uncle Bernie will finish the story tomorrow." She looked up at her husband and his cousin. "Won't you?"

"Sure, Blossom," said Josh. "First thing."

"Okay," said April grudgingly. "I'll go if I can have cotton candy. But your timing is terrible, Grandpa. I want to know if the bad guys get the diamonds! And if Kosey kisses Winna again!"

"Everything turns out fine, honey. Don't worry," said Nathan, holding April's hand.

"Wait till you see Pigeon-Toe Murray run the bases! He's the fastest guy in the league!" said Bernie to Josh as they walked to the car.

"I bet I was faster when I ran from those elephants in Africa," laughed Josh.

"Save it till tomorrow," advised Bernie. "Or we'll never get to the game."

THE LIFE CHEST : AFRICA

Chapter Thirteen

Greed Loses What it Has Gained

April sighed. It was morning. The sun was up. She had been sitting outside the bedroom door for what seemed like forever, and Grandpa was not up yet! Old people sleep too much, she thought to herself. It's boring.

Nathan came around the corner with a cup of coffee and smiled at his daughter. "Grandpa still asleep?"

"Yes, Daddy," said April. "And I really want to hear the rest of the story! I want to know what happens to Grandpa and Uncle Bernie and Effie and everybody else."

"I understand," said Nathan. "Let's try something." He opened the bedroom door just enough to slide in his arm holding the coffee cup. "Rise and shine!" he said in a singsong voice. "Time to wake up and smell the coffee! You do smell the coffee, don't you?"

"Yes! I smell it but I can't reach it!" said Josh from his bed. "Coffee— so— close! Must— have— coffee!" he joked.

Nathan retreated with the coffee and laughed at his father-in-law. Even at 8 o'clock in the morning, Josh was in a good humor.

April wasn't happy, though. "Don't give it to him!" she insisted. "Tell him he has to promise to get up and finish the story before he gets any coffee!"

"I heard that," said Josh. "Blossom, are you trying to kill me?"

"Oh Grandpa, just please please please get up!" said April, jumping up and down. "I had bad dreams all night about elephant ghosts and bad guys chasing you with guns. Uncle Bernie's in the kitchen eating breakfast. He said you got away from the bad guys but he can't finish the story without you."

Josh appeared in the doorway, tying the belt on his robe. "Of course we got away from the bad guys. I'm standing here, aren't I?" he grinned.

"I know, I know," said April. "But I want to know how you got away and what happened to everybody else." She grabbed Josh's hand and started pulling him down the hall toward the kitchen. "Come on, Grandpa!"

"Lead on! But get some coffee in me," said Josh. "I won't be able to remember anything until I'm caffeinated!"

Effie waited just inside the entrance to the tunnel. He was ready. Any minute now he might have to pull his gun. He and Josh had attached two ropes at the edge of the pit on each side of the tunnel so they could climb back up. The Bradleys could use those ropes too.

Sure enough, a vehicle glided up a few minutes after Josh left. A voice called out. "I saw movement just below here!" It was Agnes. "Come on, Rupert! There's a rope you can climb down."

"You better be right behind me, Aaron," said Rupert Turner as he began to lower himself down. "There's another rope over there." Aaron grudgingly followed suit.

"Do you see anyone?" Jamila yelled down at the men.

Effie heard the activity above and readied his gun. Pressed against the inside wall of the tunnel, he pictured the two men climbing down on both sides of the tunnel opening and wondered which man would get to the ledge first. I got a 50-50 chance of turning the right way, he thought. Let's do this thing.

Effie burst out of the tunnel and turned to the left, hoping to be face-to-face with one of his foes, but Aaron was still not even halfway down the wall. Before Effie could turn around to the other rope, he felt a bullet whiz past his head. The shooter was Rupert, who had rappelled quickly and was about to jump off the rope onto the lower scaffolding. Swiveling to his right, Effie took aim and fired at almost the same instant. The bullet hit Rupert in the shoulder. Rupert let go of the rope and lurched forward as he fell, missing the scaffolding and toppling into the pit.

The 100-meter fall would have killed him sure enough, but fate (or maybe the elephant ghosts) offered up a more grisly death. The rocky, uneven wall of the pit was riddled with elephant bones, some embedded in the rock and dirt, and some protruding out. Halfway to the bottom, Rupert yelled as he fell, but his descent was stopped by a large tusk extending from the wall. He was impaled on the sharp piece of ivory, and his yells subsided as the tusk went through his heart. It was probably the most beautiful piece of ivory he would ever see, if he had been able to see it.

Effie didn't stop to look at what happened to Rupert. He turned his gun back toward Aaron, who was still climbing down the rope. Effie decided to fire a warning shot at Aaron, but his gun jammed. Josh burst out of the tunnel as Effie turned back to examine his gun. They almost ran into each other.

"Boss! What's wrong?" panted Josh.

"Gun jammed," explained Effie, opening up the revolver to check for spent casings. "Bradley's on his way down. The other guy's out of commission. Shot him."

They heard Agnes yelling from the edge of the pit, "Rupert! Rupert! Damn you!"

Josh wondered for a fleeting moment if she was cursing Effie for shooting Rupert, or Rupert himself for managing to get killed. Could be either one, he thought. Then he stepped out of the tunnel and turned his attention to Aaron.

"Thanks for finding the diamonds for us," called Aaron from his perch on the wall when he saw Josh. "We'll take over from you amateurs now."

"In your dreams!" retorted Josh, striding up to Aaron. "Are you gonna hang there forever? Or are you ready to fight?"

In reply, Aaron slid further down the rope and tried to kick Josh in the face. Josh dodged Aaron's foot and grabbed the end of the rope, yanking it back and forth. Aaron held on for dear life as Bernie, Kosey and Gogo emerged from the tunnel.

"Start climbing back up and I'll quit shaking the rope!" Josh called to the frightened Aaron. "Get out of here and tell your sister that you've lost."

"I'm going!" yelled Aaron desperately. "Stop shaking the rope," he begged as he climbed back up. "I'll fall into the pit!"

"We haven't lost! Not by a long shot!" came another voice from up above. It was Jamila, who was rappelling down the wall on the rope that Rupert had used on the other side of the tunnel.

"How could you forget about me?" she cried gleefully as she jumped onto the upper scaffolding. Her triumph didn't last long. The rotten wood gave way and she came crashing through the boards onto the more stable scaffolding below. She landed near the edge and began to lose her balance. Kosey was nearest the spot where she fell. He instinctively ran to help her, reaching out to pull her up more fully onto the ledge. Jamila steadied herself, looked up at Kosey and smiled. "Gee thanks, kid," she said. "You got a good heart." Then she kicked him in the groin.

"Whoa!" Kosey stumbled backward and fell. Gogo helped him up as Jamila stood, laughing.

"That didn't hurt too much, did it?" Jamila laughed. "I'm not ready to take you out just yet. You're too much fun to fight with."

Up above, Aaron yelled at his sister. "I'm not going back down there again!" he said angrily. "You try climbing down that rope!"

Effie and Bernie talked hastily just inside the mouth of the tunnel. "What should we do now?" Bernie asked.

"They're backing off." answered Effie. "Agnes and Aaron are too cowardly to come down here and fight us. Jamila is tough, but she's all they got left."

"I'll stay here to help Kosey with Jamila," said Bernie. "You and Josh climb back up and take care of the Bradleys."

In the meantime, Jamila continued to laugh at Kosey while he caught his breath. He wanted to punch her in the face, but how could he? She's a girl, he thought as he gasped for air.

Bernie appeared next to Kosey and Gogo. "You okay?" he asked.

"C'mon," Jamila sneered at Kosey. "Too scared to fight?"

Bernie stepped forward. "Leave him alone," Bernie said. "Can't you see he's hurt?"

"Yeah, I kind of meant to do that. I guess that's all the little baby can take." Jamila reached out and grabbed Bernie by the shirt collar, pulling his face close to hers. "How about you and I fight?" she said. "Come on, it'll be fun." She pushed him backward and he slammed into the rocky wall of the pit.

THE LIFE CHEST : AFRICA

Kosey had now recovered enough to jump back into the fray. "Stay here!" Gogo called as Kosey moved toward Jamila.

"Nope," said the young man. "This is my fight."

Hearing him approach, Jamila turned and tried to punch Kosey in the face. He dodged her fist and came back with a punch of his own to her stomach. Girl or not, it didn't matter. What mattered was keeping his friends and the diamonds safe.

There wasn't room on the scaffolding for Bernie or Gogo to join in the struggle. They had to watch while Kosey fought Jamila.

As they punched and kicked, Kosey fought with all his might. He took a couple of good hits, but so did Jamila. After dodging one of Kosey's blows, Jamila laughed and backed up a step to take a breath. Not realizing how close she was to the edge, she slipped and stumbled over. Her quick reactions and toned muscles enabled her to catch herself. Instead of falling into the deep pit she clung to its lip, her fingers grasping at loose rocks and rotting boards, as Kosey, Gogo and Bernie watched with horror.

A fight on the scaffolding

Kosey began to move toward her but hesitated when Jamila spoke. "Help," Jamila called. "Help me!" Kosey had been stopped, not by Jamila's words but by the strange gleam he saw in her eyes. I don't dare help her! he thought. She'll pull me off the ledge! I know she will!

Bernie, however, didn't see the evil in Jamila's eyes. "We can't let her fall!" he said as he hurried to the edge of the scaffolding and reached for Jamila, grabbing both her arms so she could use the strength in her legs to climb to safety. Jamila scrambled up and got her upper body onto the ledge. She pulled one leg up, then the other— and Kosey knew. He saw in an instant that Jamila, as she disengaged from Bernie's grasp and regained her balance, was turning to kick Bernie off the edge of the scaffolding into the pit. Kosey leapt into action. There was only time to do one thing. As Jamila reached out with her kick, Kosey grabbed her leg and pushed it away from Bernie, still crouching at the edge of the pit. Jamila screamed— a long, desperate wail— as she fell the 100 meters to the bottom and her death.

"Kosey!" gasped Bernie, realizing what had happened. "You— you saved my life! That was incredible!"

In response, Kosey turned toward the wall and vomited. Effie's right, he thought. Taking someone's life is nothing to be proud of.

While this was happening, Effie and Josh had climbed the ropes and emerged from the pit. Agnes and Aaron were still standing by their Land Rover, arguing. Effie and Josh were able to easily sneak up on them and draw their guns.

"Hello again," said Josh, holding his gun on the brother and sister as they raised their hands. "Can we agree that this is over now?" he asked. "I think we got you beat."

"No, you don't," came a voice from the other side of the Bradley's Land Rover. A man had been sitting behind the truck. He rose up to his full height, came around the corner of the Land Rover, and turned to point a pistol at Josh and Effie. It was Abdi.

His injured shoulder was bandaged but he held the gun steady and grinned. "Bet you didn't expect to see me here," he said. "I heal fast. Must be the Zulu in me."

"Keep your gun on those two, Josh," said Effie, not taking his eyes off Abdi. "I'll handle this guy." He took a step toward Abdi. "I guess we have a standoff."

"I'll drop my gun if you will," said Abdi. "Even with this arm bandaged up I could still beat you to a pulp."

"You think so?" asked Effie. The two big men stared at each other, anger and hatred in their eyes. Effie paused for a moment and looked Abdi up and down. His anger softened momentarily and was replaced with frustration.

"Abdi Kalu, this makes no sense!" Effie said. "You and I are both Zulus! We are tribal brothers!" He nodded in the Bradleys' direction. "These people you work for— they are descendants of the same people who exploited our tribe when diamonds were first discovered in Africa. Why are you working for them? What are you getting out of this?"

Abdi hesitated. Were the words sinking in? wondered Effie.

"What do I get out of it? What everybody wants. Money!" answered Abdi impatiently. "What else is there?" He threw down his gun and lunged at Effie.

"What else is there? Lots, but you'll never know," said Effie. He threw down his gun as well and the two men met in hand-to-hand combat.

Even with Abdi's arm injury, they were an even match. Frustration, anger, envy and regret all came into play as they fought. The others watched in frozen silence, unable to intervene. These two modern Zulu warriors were from the same tribe but different worlds, and those worlds were colliding. Whoever won this fight would win the sacred diamonds.

Abdi threw a punch with his good hand and Effie staggered as it hit his jaw. He recovered and struck back, landing a blow in Abdi's midsection. He was hesitant to hit Abdi on his injured shoulder. He wanted to fight fair. Abdi fell back, and it seemed as if he was beaten, but only for a moment. With a yell, he rushed head down at Effie, slamming into him like a TV wrestler. The pain from his gunshot wound made his head spin, and fed his anger.

Josh, still holding his gun on the Bradleys, felt helpless watching his friend in this desperate fight. He briefly glanced up, and saw something that puzzled him. There seemed to be a cloud in the distance, hugging a hill on the horizon. Aaron and Agnes saw it too, and it grew bigger and bigger as they watched. A sound rose up to match the cloud. Was it thunder? Josh wondered. Then he heard a trumpeting: the cry of an elephant. The trumpeting increased, getting louder and louder as the cloud grew. He suddenly realized what was happening, and seeing scores of hulking gray bodies come into focus confirmed it.

"Stampede! It's an elephant stampede!" he yelled. The ground began to shake. The pounding of heavy feet and fierce trumpeting became almost deafening. An elephant herd was lumbering straight at them in a tightly packed group, all flapping ears, waving trunks and powerful stomping limbs.

The elephants had indeed returned to their ancient burial ground, thinking that the humans had finally left for good. Hearing explosions and gunshots, however, had excited them to fear and anger. They were not going to let their land be taken again.

THE LIFE CHEST : AFRICA

The elephant stampede

Josh faced the thunderous elephant herd. To his left was the pit and to his right was the Bradley's Land Rover. The others assessed the situation as well, and everyone jumped into action. Abdi and Effie stopped fighting and got to their feet. Aaron called to his sister. "Get to the truck!" he yelled as he ran toward their Land Rover. Agnes frantically tried to catch up to him.

With the elephants coming straight at them, Josh, Abdi and Effie ran to the pit. The rope! Where's the rope? thought Josh, terrified. Then he saw the stake driven into the ground which held one of the climbing ropes. He lowered himself over the edge, and hung on to the rope. Effie and Abdi were both closer to the other rope. Abdi got there first and began to lower himself down as the ground shook above him.

"Keep going! Climb all the way down!" yelled Effie. Abdi had stopped moving and was hanging desperately onto the rope a few meters below the edge of the pit. "I can't move! I'll fall! I'll fall into the pit!" screamed the terrified man over the din of the trumpeting elephants. He hung on to the rope for dear life. The ground continued to shake and made climbing dangerous, but Josh got down his rope as best he could. Dust filled his eyes and mouth as the roar of the stampede seemed to shake the entire earth.

Josh reached the bottom of the rope and dropped off onto the ledge. "Effie! Effie!" he called, seeing his friend up above. "Quick, use this rope! Over here!"

Meanwhile, the Bradleys tried frantically to reach their Land Rover as the elephants got closer. The roaring of the great beasts and the thundering of their huge limbs was deafening. "Hurry! Hurry!" gasped Agnes as she stumbled across the rough terrain. Suddenly, a group of about 20 elephants peeled off from the herd, getting in between the humans and the truck. They seemed to be deliberately surrounding these people who had invaded their sacred graveyard and poached their ivory. A 5000 kilogram bull elephant can run 40 kilometers an hour. Once the elephants decided to go after the Bradleys, they didn't have a chance.

On the ledge in the pit below, Josh could hear Agnes' and Aarons' screams mingled in with the elephants' trumpeting. He closed his eyes tight and tried not to picture what was going on up above. But he couldn't help imagining it. Limbs mangled, skulls crushed, bloody bodies pounded into the ground. There was no way the Bradleys could have survived. Or Effie, if he was still up there.

After a few more minutes, the pounding and the trumpeting began to subside. The elephants moved on. The prediction that Duma had made to Ona all those years ago had come true. Evil had been punished, and greed lost what it had gained.

Eventually an eerie silence settled over the scene as the dust began to settle. All that could be heard was gasping from the choking dust. Bernie, Kosey and Gogo had taken shelter inside the mouth of the tunnel, and they now emerged, rubbing their eyes.

"Josh! You're all right!" gasped Bernie as he hugged his cousin.

Josh hugged him back, but he had to find their bodyguard. "Effie! Where's Effie?" he asked.

Everyone took up the cry and yelled the big man's name, looking up to the edge of the pit and calling with all their might. No answer. They finally stopped in exhaustion.

"You're shaking, Josh," said Bernie. "Stay here. I'll climb up and look for Effie."

Josh leaned against the wall of the pit and sunk to the ground. Gogo came over to share a bottle of water. As Josh drank, he turned and saw Abdi. He had been standing off to one side, but such a big man couldn't remain inconspicuous.

"You," said Josh. "Effie couldn't get down the rope because of you!"

"I froze. I couldn't jump," Abdi tried to explain. His voice trailed off.

"How about if you jump now?" came a voice from behind Josh. He turned to look at Gogo. Anger flashed from the eyes of the little man. "Effie deserves to live— not you! He let you go down the rope first?" Abdi nodded. "And you just hung on while he was caught in the elephant stampede!" yelled Gogo. "Effie was my best friend, and you killed him!"

Gogo lunged toward Abdi, intending to push him off the ledge into the pit. Josh easily caught the little man and held him back.

Kosey stepped forward. "Don't do it, Gogo. Even if he deserves to die, you don't want another man's blood on your hands. It's not worth it."

Josh agreed. "Effie wouldn't want that. This guy is one of his countrymen."

Gogo backed off, stifling a sob as he pushed away from Josh and Kosey. "Just keep me away from him. I don't want to see his face," he blurted out.

Bernie gave up calling for Effie and yelled down to the others. "Come on up here, you guys. The elephants really did a number on the place. And I don't see Effie anywhere," he added sadly.

Turning their backs on Abdi, Gogo, Kosey and Josh climbed out of the pit and looked around. The few scraggly trees that had been at the edge of the pit had been trampled. The Bradley's Land Rover was in scattered pieces. The gas tank had burst and started a small fire which was smoldering. Dust was still in the air but some remains of the Bradleys could be seen. Aaron's pith helmet and Agnes's sunglasses lay near a twisted door panel from their vehicle. Kosey reached down and picked up a necklace. Still attached to it was a pendant, now bloody, made from elephant ivory. "The elephants got their revenge on those poachers," said Kosey grimly.

"I guess they also got Effie," sighed Josh. "It's my fault. I should've made sure he got down into the pit. I don't know..." he trailed off.

"It's not your fault," said Gogo. His eyes stung with tears. "It's his," he said, nodding toward the pit. Abdi was still down there on the scaffolding.

"Effie's really gone?" asked Kosey. "I can't believe it." Tears began to run down his face. The two cousins wept as well and they all stood in silence, trying to understand the loss of the big no-nonsense bodyguard who had become their friend.

Josh blew his nose on his handkerchief and held his hand up to shield his eyes from the setting sun, which cast a golden-orange glow on the clouds of dust still surrounding them.

He saw something dark move toward them and wiped his eyes. He punched his cousin on the shoulder. "Ow," said Bernie. "What's wrong?"

"Look," said Josh, pointing to the dark mass in the middle of the cloud of dust. "What is that? It's too small to be an elephant." Bernie looked. So did Gogo and Kosey. The figure silently walked toward them, and spoke.

"Not an elephant. Just me," said a voice as the figure emerged from the dusty golden cloud.

It was Effie. Slightly limping, bleeding from the head, but alive. And smiling.

The others were flabbergasted, all motionless, except Gogo. He launched himself at Effie and enveloped him in a bear hug, as much as a short skinny guy can envelop a six-foot-two bodybuilder.

"Oof!" said Effie as he let himself be hugged. "Careful there, buddy. I might have a couple cracked ribs." Effie laughed and then caught his breath in pain. At the sound of his familiar chuckle, tears came again from everyone, but they were tears of joy. There were hugs all around, this time careful of Effie's sore ribs. And everyone talked at once.

"Wait, wait," said Effie, holding up his hands. "Everyone's okay? You're all here?"

"We're all fine," said Kosey. "But the Bradleys weren't so lucky. They got trampled by the elephants." He held up the bloody pendant.

"That takes care of them. But what about Abdi?" asked Effie, the smile gone from his face. "Where is he?"

"On the ledge down there," said Josh, pointing to the pit. "Since he's the only one left from the Bradley gang, we shouldn't have too much trouble taking him to the police."

Effie didn't answer, but walked over to the edge of the pit and crouched down. Through a broken section of the scaffolding he spotted Abdi sitting against the wall of the pit with his head in his hands.

"Abdi!" he called. No answer. "Abdi!" he said again. "Look up!"

Abdi gazed up, startled by the voice. "Is it really you?" Abdi asked. "You're not dead?"

"I came close, but no," laughed Effie. He lay on his stomach and reached his arms down into the pit. "Brother," he said. "Come on up. Let's talk."

"But I'm not your brother," said Abdi softly. "I left you to die."

"Do I look dead?" countered Effie. "I'm alive, but I don't have the strength to climb down there and get you. You'll have to come up on your own." He glanced at Abdi's gunshot wound, which had begun to bleed under the bandages. "Can you make it by yourself? Please try."

Abdi stood. "I will," he agreed. Silently he made his way to the rope and climbed up, betraying his pain with an occasional grunt. Bernie and Josh helped him over the edge and Abdi stood before the group.

"You better not try anything," said Gogo. "Somebody give me a gun, so I can hold it on him."

"No, Gogo. It's not necessary," said Effie. "I'm not even sure where any of our guns are." He reached into his pocket. "All I have is this little elephant."

"It's the talisman! You have the elephant talisman!" said Bernie.

"I guess that's what saved me," said Effie in wonderment, turning the little stone elephant over in his hand. "I gotta admit, I never really believed in the power of these things. But it was incredible. I was near the edge of the pit. I dropped to the ground and covered my head with my arms. I could hear and feel the elephants right behind me and I prayed for death to come quickly. But nothing happened. I wasn't trampled. I just felt air rushing past. It was like the elephants were deliberately going around me!"

"That little elephant held on to Duma's blessing all these years," said Kosey in wonder.

"As did all the other talismans that were stored in the animal chests," agreed Bernie. "They're life chests, really, and they carry the same magic."

"I've been blessed, that's for sure," said Effie. "Feels like I got a second chance at life." He glanced at Abdi, his Zulu kinsman. "It can be a second chance for you as well," he said.

Abdi looked into Effie's eyes and saw forgiveness and acceptance. It gave him hope, but he still wasn't sure. "I don't know," Abdi said. "I see now that I was a fool to align myself with such evil people as the Bradleys. I betrayed myself and my countrymen."

"Let's forgive," said Effie. "New beginnings," he said, as he extended his hand to Abdi. Abdi hesitated for only a second, then shook it heartily. Effie pulled him in for a hug, but was careful of both men's injuries.

"Hey, let's get out of here," said Josh. "We need to patch the two of you up and all of us need to clean up and get some rest."

"I'll make the necessary calls to the authorities," said Gogo. "And in the morning, we can start the process of extracting the diamonds."

The group started for their Land Rover, which had been spared in the elephant stampede. "Lucky we've still got a truck," said Kosey.

"The elephants seem to be on our side," agreed Bernie.

The rest of the evening was spent recovering from the day's ordeal and informing the authorities of everything that had happened. Gogo took charge, filling out reports and speaking for the group when they met with the police. When he told the story of the Bradleys and their henchmen, he left Abdi off the list. "There were six of us and five of them," he told the officers.

Later, Abdi stopped Gogo, who was leaving the hotel restaurant after dinner. "I appreciate what you did," he said to Gogo. "Now I won't be arrested. But I want to pay for the wrongs I committed. How can I be forgiven otherwise?"

"Like Effie said, it's a second chance," answered Gogo. "Effie has forgiven you, and all of us have as well."

"Thank you. I won't let you down," said Abdi, shaking Gogo's hand. "I'll figure out some way to repay you all to make up for what I've done."

"You're a good man. I can see that," said Gogo. "If you remember that yourself, it's an excellent start."

Gogo stayed busy the rest of the evening and into the next day making arrangements with a company he had contacted earlier about extracting the diamonds from the chamber. He also talked to a man who would be cutting and brokering the diamonds for sale. The broker handling the sales transactions worked for a government-sponsored diamond exchange. They made certain that the diamonds would be sold to legitimate business interests and would not end up on the black market or be used to finance wars or purchase weapons. Once the diamonds were sold, the proceeds would be divided up into equal amounts for each of the organizations that General Erasto had designated. In addition, a portion of the diamonds would go to a museum.

While Effie and Abdi were recovering from their injuries and Gogo was handling the business end of things, Bernie and Josh updated their families back home. Everyone had gathered at Bernie's parents' house in preparation for Bernie and Josh's flight back to New York. Ruby put them on speakerphone when they called. Everyone was relieved to know that Bernie and Josh were safe and they were excited to hear what had happened at the diamond mine.

"The magic of the life chest is alive and well in Africa!" said Josh triumphantly. He explained how the animal chests had now become like life chests for their keepers, and the wealth from the sacred diamonds would continue to preserve the legacy of the chest keepers, protect the animals of Africa, and make life better for all. Josh and Bernie relayed some of the exciting parts of their adventure, but they had agreed beforehand to leave out the elephant stampede and a few other gory details. "We can fill in the gaps of the story after we get home safely," said Bernie. Josh nodded his agreement.

"After the diamonds are sold, it will be another week before we start for home," explained Bernie on the speakerphone. "We've got to retrace our steps to go back to all the places we stopped at."

Josh chimed in. "This time instead of trying to find a map piece, we'll be walking in with a check. That's gonna feel really good!" The family congratulated Josh and Bernie on their success, and said goodbye, for now.

The youngest member of the expedition was a little bit at loose ends that night. Kosey hadn't been able to reach his grandmother to tell her the good news. He'd try again in the morning. Walking by Josh and Bernie's hotel room, Kosey heard laughter coming from inside. He felt a twinge of envy, but quickly pushed it aside. They've got a great family, he thought. But I do too, even though it's just my grandmother and me. I want to remember every day to tell her how much I love and admire her. Kosey smiled as he reached his room and unlocked the door. And Winna, he thought. Maybe someday I'll be able to tell her the same thing.

THE LIFE CHEST : AFRICA

Chapter Fourteen

Hard-Won Rewards

Josh and Bernie went out with Gogo to the diamond pit to watch the third day of excavation. An expert team of miners had set up new scaffolding and were bringing load after load of diamonds out of the tunnel. A security team was in place to guard the mine, and even Josh and Bernie had to show ID to get into the area where the diamonds were being sorted and packed.

"They're even more beautiful out here in the daylight than they were in the chamber," said Bernie, scooping the rough stones out of a pail with his hands and letting them run through his fingers.

"They're dividing them up by size," said Josh, walking over to a flatbed truck already loaded with boxes of diamonds. "Look over here." The lid of one of the boxes was open and Bernie peered in. "Wow. These are almost as big as that baseball-sized one we found."

He turned to Gogo, who was walking up to them after talking with a government official. "What's going to happen to all these diamonds, Gogo?" he asked.

"The government's helping me negotiate their sale," said Gogo. "Some of the less perfect ones will be used for industrial applications, but most will be used for jewelry. Remember that big one? It's going to the national museum here in Tanzania."

"The diamonds are going to help all the causes so much," said Josh. "Gogo, when will we be able to take them their money? And how much will it be?"

"I've been thinking about that," said Gogo. "I've got an idea that I think is good, but it's too involved to explain right here. Let's talk to the others about it. The mining is almost done for the day. They'll guard the mine overnight and start again in the morning."

"Okay," said Josh. "I want to get back and see how Kosey's convalescent patients are doing."

"Yeah," agreed Bernie. "Effie is a tough guy, but after the elephant stampede he was hurt a little more than he let on. And the doctor is coming over this evening to re-bandage Abdi's gunshot wound."

"We better start back then," said Gogo. "It will take us a few minutes to get through security. Poor Kosey's got his hands full trying to keep those guys quiet so they can get better."

When the mining started, Kosey had gone out to the pit a few times to watch the operation. It was exciting to watch the diamonds emerge from the tunnel, and it was gratifying to see the fruits of their labor. But Kosey didn't spend as much time at the mine as he thought he would. What he found that he really wanted to do was spend time with Effie and Abdi. Kosey waited on the men as they recuperated, cooking for them and trying to get them to take it easy.

He also listened to their stories. Effie told Kosey about his childhood, his family, and the time he spent in the military. It was harder to get Abdi to open up. It was only a few days since he'd been trying to kill Effie, and although he was beginning to trust his new friends, he didn't feel quite comfortable baring his soul. Kosey and Effie managed to get a few stories out of him, however. It turned out that Abdi had served in the army too, for a brief period of time. The prospect of making fast money in black market ivory had lured him away from the military and got him mixed up with the Bradleys. Abdi was deeply ashamed of this, and even though Kosey and Effie tried to convince him that he could start a new life, he spent long periods of time on his own, walking and thinking.

When Josh, Bernie and Gogo got back to the hotel, Effie and Abdi were engaged in a lively game of chess. Kosey was making chai tea and poured some for everyone. "They're arguing," said Kosey. "But at least they're sitting down." The last chess match was a draw, so the players put away the board to listen to what Gogo had to say.

"The mining is going well," said Gogo, sipping his tea. "There are more diamonds than even I imagined there would be, and they are very high quality. When they are sold there will be plenty of money to make improvements in all the organizations that General Erasto wanted to help. In fact, there's too much money."

"Too much money? What do you mean?" asked Kosey.

"Don't worry. It's a good problem to have," said Gogo. "There's going to be enough money to get everyone off to a good start on their improvements, but I'd like to set up an endowment fund with some of it. Then the organizations will have more than just a one-time gift. They'll be able to access funds periodically and have a good source of income for future projects."

"It's a phenomenal idea," said Bernie. "It's nice to know that the diamonds will be helping to build a better Africa for a long time into the future."

"That's exactly right," said Gogo. "I hope I can get the government to agree. I have a call in to a friend of mine who's with the cultural ministry here in Tanzania. I'm going to meet with her tomorrow. I hope I'll be able to get the government to sponsor a nonprofit organization to manage these funds."

Josh spoke up. "My mom runs a nonprofit out in California. My wife Leah works with her, and I know a little bit about it too. How about if I come with you to your meeting?"

"Sure," said Gogo. "That would be very helpful."

"Little Gogo's got some great big ideas," said Effie admiringly.

"Well, I'm not great in a fight, but put me in front of a bureaucrat and I can hold my own," laughed Gogo.

"It's a really good plan," said Kosey. "But you guys must be hungry. I ordered in some curry with beans and rice. Let's get ready to eat."

It took a few more days for everything to come together. Most of the diamonds were mined, and a good portion had been cut, appraised and sold through Gogo's diamond broker. Abdi and Effie were well enough to travel, and Gogo was hopeful that he would receive the go-ahead to start up a nonprofit organization to manage the endowment fund created by the sale of the diamonds.

On the 21st morning of their adventure, Josh and Bernie were packing up the Land Rover. Bernie's briefcase, which still held the puzzle map, the pieces of the diamond map and the plate, now also contained checks written out to each of the recipients and special uncut diamonds to be given along with them.

"What a trip this is going to be," said Josh as Bernie stowed the briefcase safely under his seat. "I can't wait to see everyone's faces."

"Who are you most excited about giving the money to?" asked his cousin.

"I'm not sure," answered Josh. "Maybe that principal at the primary school who kicked us out. She's gonna be pretty surprised."

The uncut diamond and check

"Well, we're not exactly going to surprise them this time," cautioned Bernie. "We called ahead to each place to tell them we're coming."

"I guess that makes sense," said Josh. "I can't wait to see a smile on that lady's face, though."

"We're ready to go when everyone gets here," said Bernie. "Here comes Gogo."

Gogo approached the Land Rover quickly, running as fast as his short legs could carry him. "I've got really good news!" he called. "The foundation has been approved!"

"Congratulations!" said Josh.

"That is good news," agreed Bernie.

"But that's not all," added Gogo breathlessly. "They've asked me to run it! My full-time job will be managing the funds from the diamonds."

Effie, Abdi and Kosey joined the group, carrying their luggage. Gogo continued the story once they were all in the Land Rover and started off.

"It'll be an honor to run the foundation," said Gogo.

"You're the perfect person for it," said Effie. "You were a big part of this expedition. You know the whole story of the diamonds and General Erasto's dream."

"Thanks," said Gogo. "You were all part of this expedition too, of course. It couldn't have happened without all of us. In fact, I've got a message to you from the government minister I met with. She wants to give each of you a reward for your part in finding the diamonds. Kosey, I'm sure your grandmother could use the funds. She's got to be thinking about retiring pretty soon."

"Yeah," said Kosey. "Some extra money would help as she gets older."

"It's a nice gesture, but Bernie and I don't need the money," said Josh.

"That's right," agreed Bernie.

"What about your mother's nonprofit?" Gogo asked Josh. "You could donate the money to that."

"Good idea," said Josh. "They do literacy work with kids in the inner city. Maybe she'll want to start an African heritage program."

"My father is a police officer," said Bernie. "I'd love to be able to donate some money to their fund for the families of officers killed or wounded in the line of duty."

"I'm not sure what I'll do with my reward," said Effie, steering the Land Rover onto the main highway from a dirt road. "It would be nice to have some extra money, but since you folks are being so generous, I might have to follow suit. I'll think about it for a while."

The group then turned to look at Abdi, and everyone felt slightly embarrassed. He broke the silence. "Don't worry," said Abdi, shaking his head. "I don't expect any kind of reward. If I'm able to spend the rest of my life working to make up for my mistakes, then I will feel very lucky."

Effie turned to smile at the big man in the back seat. "Good things are ahead for you, brother," he assured his kinsman. "You and I have both been spared death more than once, so there's got to be a reason we're still here."

"One reason you're still here is to make me miserable," said Josh to Effie, lightening the mood. "You keep promising to let me drive this bucket, but I still haven't had a chance to get behind the wheel."

"You're persistent," laughed Effie. "Tomorrow, maybe."

It was a festive atmosphere at the cultural center in Babati when they arrived. There was music and drumming, dancing, singing, and food and drink. The board of directors of the center was on hand to accept the check and the diamond. The crowd that had gathered in the auditorium cheered when Chaty put the diamond in the leopard chest and announced that the chest would be displayed in a special place in the lobby.

Kosey returned the leopard charm to Chaty, and it went in the leopard chest as well. Chaty told the audience that replicas of the leopard charm were being made that would be sold in the cultural center gift shop. The money would go to a scholarship fund for music and dance classes for young people.

"We've got to bring up the next generation to appreciate the arts and culture of Africa, right?" said Chaty with a smile. "Knowing the whole story of General Erasto, the diamonds, and the leopard chest makes our mission here that much more special."

He turned to Kosey and the others, who had come up on stage. "Thank you for fulfilling Erasto's mission by finding the diamonds. We will be able to finish our new concert hall and fund several programs we have been planning. One of them is to take a group of African musicians and dancers into the schools to do presentations and workshops on our cultural heritage. Thanks to you, our artists and our patrons, African culture will stay alive and thrive."

Chaty turned back to the crowd for a final announcement. "The leopard chest represents the past legacy of the Center. But it also inspires us to work toward a better future, one that encourages new artistic expression for a new Africa."

The next stop was the farm and agricultural school at Kilombero. As they were approaching Freedom Farm, Bernie mentioned that he had not actually talked to anyone there. "I left a message for them," he said. "But I didn't hear back. I'm not sure if they know we're coming."

"Well, they should be glad to see us," said Kosey.

"I hope so," said Josh. "Last time we were here, it was not the most pleasant experience."

Jomo and Jira working at the agricultural school

"Maybe I'll stay in the truck," offered Abdi. "If they see me, they might think the Bradleys are back."

"You don't have to hide," insisted Effie. "I'll go in first and explain things to them."

When the Land Rover pulled into the driveway of the farm, no one was around. However, the place wasn't deserted; there were cars and trucks in the parking lot and they could hear voices coming from a field close by.

"Huh," said Gogo. "I wonder where they are."

"Let's follow the direction of the voices. I think they're in that field behind the barn," said Effie.

The group tromped over, with Gogo carrying the check and the souvenir diamond. As they approached the field, they could see a dozen people working with baskets and wheelbarrows.

"There's Jira," said Kosey. He waved and shouted. "Hello!"

The young woman looked up and came jogging over. "Is that who I think it is?" she said, her hand shading her eyes from the sun. "You're back!"

"Did you get my message?" asked Bernie. "I called yesterday."

"No, I'm sorry," answered Jira. "We have been out in the field from morning until night the last few days. We're harvesting green amaranth this week."

Jomo walked up and stood at his daughter's side. Jira smiled at him proudly. "My father developed a variety of amaranth that has almost twice as much protein as the kind we used to grow."

Jomo held up his dirt-covered hands. "I apologize for not being able to shake hands with you," he said. "But I welcome you back to Freedom Farm. It's good to see that you all are safe and looking healthy. We were very worried about you."

Effie took Jomo aside and explained that Abdi was with them, and was a changed man. Jomo walked with Effie back to the Land Rover to greet Abdi and welcome him to the farm.

"Try the amaranth," said Jira to the others. "It's really fresh." She handed some leafy greens to Kosey, who passed them around.

"It's like spinach," said Josh, crunching on the fresh greens.

"I've heard that it's even better for you than spinach," said Bernie. "Popeye should change his diet."

"I guess we should tell you what's going on, since you didn't get Bernie's message," said Gogo. "We found the diamonds, and it's an incredible treasure! I've been authorized by the government to give you a check. It should help run Freedom Farm for quite a while, and you can apply for more money when you need it. I'm starting a foundation to administer money from an endowment fund for all of General Erasto's causes."

"That's wonderful!" exclaimed Jira. "We'll be done harvesting here in a few hours. I'll invite all the workers and volunteers to stay for a meal. We've got to cook up some of this amaranth. After dinner, you can tell everyone about the diamonds, and I'll explain the projects that we will be able to work on with the money. How does that sound?"

Everyone agreed that it sounded good, and Josh had another idea. "How about if we help you finish the harvest? The work will go that much faster, won't it?" he asked.

"Sure! The more hands the better!" said Jira.

As they walked out to the field, Effie and Jomo joined them. They took Jira aside for a moment and told her about Abdi's change of heart and his desire to make up for the wrongs that he had done. "Would it be all right for him to join us?" Effie asked Jira.

Father and daughter looked at each other for a moment and Jira nodded. She turned back to Effie. "Yes," she said. "It's all right. Everything has turned out for the good and there's no reason to hold hate in our hearts."

"Thanks," said Effie as he trotted back to the Land Rover. Abdi was welcomed with open arms and felt grateful for Jomo and Jira's understanding.

The dinner was festive and showcased fresh local food. The volunteers cheered and Jomo shed a tear when Gogo presented him with the check and a large uncut diamond in a beautiful presentation box decorated with African designs. Jira made a speech about General Erasto's hopes for the people of Africa and how Freedom Farm was contributing by empowering people to grow their own food. The funds from the diamonds would go to seeds and supplies as well as research money and instructors to teach sustainable agriculture to the local families. The buffalo chest was on display, and Jira announced that it would continue to be an inspiration for the future of Freedom Farm. Jomo proposed a toast and shouts of "hip hip, hooray!" filled the air.

The primary school in Chitipa, Malawi, was next. "You did talk to someone there, didn't you?" said Kosey nervously to Josh. "I wouldn't want to go in that school again and get the same reception we got before from Ms. Turay."

"Yes, I talked to a secretary. She was very excited. I checked in with them again this morning and they're going to hold a school assembly. They will be ready for us when we get there," said Josh.

When the truck pulled up to the school, they saw a big banner out front reading "WELCOME HEROES." They were greeted by a committee of teachers and students as the rest of the school assembled in the auditorium. The group was escorted onstage to a rousing cheer from the entire school and was met at the podium by Ms. Turay. "There she is," whispered Kosey to Josh as they approached her.

The principal looked rather severe, but as they came closer, she held out her hands and began to smile. Then she actually burst into laughter. "How wonderful it is to see you again!" she said.

"I must say I never thought this day would come! I have to tell you. Something happened to change our students' attitude after the first time you were here. It started with young Deka. She used to be my main troublemaker, but she became a leader! She was such a good example for hard work and respect, and the other students followed her lead. Of course, it did help that somehow she got a bag of hacky sacks. She gave them to children when she saw them obeying the rules!"

Ms. Turay pointed to a row of chairs behind the podium. "Forgive me for rambling on! Please sit down." The principal then stood at the podium and addressed the audience.

"Staff and students, I'm here to say that even a school principal can learn new things. In fact, a smart person learns all her life. I've learned these past few weeks to listen to my students and take the time to appreciate the good things we have here. The people sitting behind me had a dream. That dream was based on an honored legacy, the same legacy that built our school. They believed in that dream and made it happen." She turned around. "Does one of you want to tell the story of how you achieved this dream?"

"I will," volunteered Kosey, standing. "Deka, can you come up on stage?" The little girl bounded up the steps and stood at Kosey's side. Just as he promised her, he told the story of Erasto, the diamonds, the animal chests and the cheetah chest that was the special property of the Chitipa Primary School.

He told the story of Deka helping him find the map piece in the cheetah chest, although he left out the part about who started the food fight. Deka had something to say, too. She grabbed the microphone from Kosey and announced, "Ms. Turay, I don't think Kosey should get in trouble for taking the map piece out of the cheetah chest. I helped him, so you can give me detention if you want to."

THE LIFE CHEST : AFRICA

"I'm not giving anyone detention today," said Ms. Turay. "I'm glad Kosey found the chest and I'm glad you helped him."

The students cheered. "We will move the chest to a display area in the front lobby," announced the principal. "We will display this beautiful diamond and the cheetah bowl as well. The cheetah chest will also inspire our students to do their best and bring honor to our school and community. Oh, and don't worry, Miss Lerato," she said to the lunch lady. "I will get you a nice comfortable chair for the lunch room." Another cheer went up.

"Because of the heroism and selflessness of our friends, we will have money for new books and computers. We will be able to hire more teachers to make our class sizes smaller, and we can get new playground equipment."

"Yay!" yelled Deka. "A new swing set!" She stood up and led the school in the loudest cheer ever.

Pulling up to the animal rehab center in Mzimba the next day, Gogo noticed something different on the sign. "It has a giraffe on it. That wasn't there before, was it?" he asked.

"Not that I remember," said Bernie. "I wonder if there are more giraffe decorations inside."

That question was answered when the group entered the lobby. There were giraffes everywhere: statues, paintings, photographs, giraffe motifs on wallpaper borders, and giraffe stickers on the doctors' name tags. They were greeted right away by Dr. Boro and a few others. "You arrived at just about the time you said you would," said Dr. Boro. "Come into our meeting room. We've got a reception set up for you." They enjoyed punch and cakes, and several photosims were taken of Gogo handing the check and the souvenir diamond to the president of the rehab center's board of directors.

Bernie took Dr. Boro aside when he had a chance. He asked, "But where's Asa? The janitor. He should be here."

Josh overheard and joined them. "Yes, he really made all this possible."

"I wish he could be here," said Dr. Boro sadly. "There hasn't been a good time to tell you since you arrived. Asa died two days ago."

"Oh, no," said Josh. "What happened?"

"He'd been quite ill for about a week and wasn't able to work," said Dr. Boro. "I was visiting him at his home a few days ago, and told him about the call we got saying that we should expect you in a few days with a check for the rehab center. Asa brightened up right away. I hadn't seen him look that lively for months. He sat up in bed and began to talk. He told me the whole story of the diamonds and the giraffe chest. He said he had been foolish to keep it to himself for so many years, and was glad to have a chance to finally pass the story along. I could hardly believe this crazy tale, but Asa convinced me. He told me where to find the giraffe chest, and here it is," she said, gesturing toward the giraffe chest, which was displayed in a corner.

"Asa began to tire after he got the story out," continued Dr. Boro. "His last words before he slipped into a coma were, 'The diamonds are real, and they have been found!'" Dr. Boro sighed. "I wish he could have been here to see you."

"I'm so sorry about Asa," said Bernie.

"What rotten luck," said Josh, pounding his fist into his hand. "He won't be able to see the improvements that the rehab center will make."

"I think he will see it all," said Dr. Boro, looking up through the skylight. "Asa was a great believer in the power of prayer and the ability of loved ones to look down on us with affection and pride. The rehab center will be able to hire more staff and will have resources to be visible in the community. Asa will be with us in spirit."

"Asa was quite a guy," said Josh.

"I agree," said Dr. Boro. "That's why we're renaming the center after him. It will be called the Asante Mensah Animal Rehab Center."

"That's great. I'm so glad he told you the story before he passed away," said Bernie. "It's another reason we need life chests: to make sure these things are written down. Our Gramps always said that the palest of ink is worth a thousand words."

"And those words should go in a life chest," added Josh.

The football school at Lusaka was not exactly abuzz with activity as they pulled up. In fact, it was quiet. "No welcoming committee?" asked Josh. "Do they know we're coming?"

"Yes, they do," answered Gogo. "The coaches didn't want to make a big deal of it. If word got around that the football school was a recipient of a lot of money, they were afraid that it would be an open invitation to gang members, thinking there might be something here they could steal. They're very happy, don't get me wrong. And I'm told that the gang activity is lessening every month. But there's still a small group out there that makes trouble, and the coaches have to be careful."

Inside the building, they found Geteye Kalu, who took them into a meeting room where several other coaches were waiting. The check and the diamond were presented, and there were cheers and hugs all around.

"We're so grateful for all this," said Geteye.

"Yes," agreed another coach. "We're going to be able to get new equipment and uniforms. And we can expand our overnight program into a weeklong summer camp."

Geteye gazed at the yellow colored uncut diamond resting in its presentation box. "I'm really amazed that you were able to find the diamonds. What an adventure! It will be such an inspiring story to tell the kids. Oh, that reminds me! Come and see what we've done with the zebra chest!"

Everyone trooped out to the lobby, where Geteye proudly showed off a waist high platform on which sat the zebra chest. A sign behind it proclaimed the mission of Zebra Stripe Football Club: "To foster leadership and integrity through football." The sign also bore the name of Geteye's great-great-uncle, the founder of the club.

"It looks fantastic," said Bernie. "No more dirty sweat socks in the zebra chest, right?"

"Right!" said Geteye with a laugh. "The zebra chest is going to inspire many generations of young athletes."

"I've got a photosim I want to show you. It's a picture of little Deka, that kid I gave the hacky sacks to," said Kosey. "I think it's in the Land Rover somewhere."

"I know where it is," offered Josh. "Let's run and get it."

Josh and Kosey trotted to the parking lot while the others continued their conversation. At the Land Rover, Kosey dug through a box of supplies looking for the photosim. Josh plopped into the driver's seat and put his hands on the wheel.

"This feels good," he said. "I think I could handle this rig. I don't know if Effie is ever going to let me drive it, though." He sighed and looked up. A boy and a girl, probably about 10 years old, were on the football field kicking around a ball. "It's good that the kids gravitate here instead of places in the city where they might get into trouble," said Josh.

"Yup. Ah, here's the photosim!" said Kosey. "Ready to head back inside?"

"In a minute. I don't know if I will ever get the chance to sit in this driver's seat again," said Josh.

Kosey laughed and shook his head as he turned to walk back to the school building, but stopped when he saw something strange. "Hey, what's going on over there on the field?" he asked. "Looks like trouble."

Josh looked up and saw what Kosey was referring to. A black levicar sedan had hovered right up on to the field. Two men jumped out, grabbed the kids and started hustling them into the car. The kids yelled and struggled but couldn't get away. The men got the boy and girl into the back seat of the levicar and jumped in front.

"They're being kidnapped!" yelled Josh as the levicar began to hover off. "Good thing Effie left the keys in the ignition!" He started up the Land Rover and tried to put it into gear. He had watched Effie drive the truck so many times that he thought it would be easy, but the gears made a terrible grinding sound. The Land Rover didn't move. Josh winced and tried again. This time he managed to jam the transmission into first gear. "Go tell Geteye!" he yelled to Kosey as he spun the truck around. "Call the police!" Kosey ran to the building as Josh drove toward where the sedan was pulling away.

I can't lose them! Josh thought. He lurched the Land Rover right up onto the field in pursuit of the black levicar. He winced as he felt the wheels of the heavy truck dig into the grass. Sorry, but it can't be helped, he thought.

The levicar glided down an alley and pulled onto a city street. Josh hung on to the wheel of the Land Rover for dear life. "Effie was right. This really is different from piloting a levicar," he muttered. He screeched around the corner, still grinding gears. I can't let them get away, he thought. I just hope I don't roll this thing. After a few blocks, Josh started to get the hang of maneuvering the old truck.

The men in the levicar noticed they were being chased and tried to lose him, but Josh stayed right on their tail, managing the turns, braking and shifting with growing confidence. Then the black levicar turned down a gravel road heading into an industrial park. By this time Josh could hear sirens in the background. Good, he thought. I got backup. But I still gotta keep them in sight.

Josh made a hard right turn and the truck drifted, shooting gravel up into the air and through the open window. Gotta be careful, he reminded himself, spitting dirt out of his mouth. "I never knew driving could be so dusty," he said out loud. "That gravel would wreck the turbines on my levicar at home."

Then Josh got an idea, and almost immediately saw his chance to implement it. The black levicar was slowing down. A big supply truck was moving through the intersection they were approaching. Josh put his foot on the gas, blasting more dirt from the tires. "Here we go!" he yelled. He sped up to the left side of the levicar and reached the cross street just as the big truck was leaving the intersection. Before the levicar could move forward, Josh made a fast turn to the right in front of it and braked hard, drifting the truck on purpose this time. Gravel flew up from the dirt road right where he wanted it to: into the turbine fans of the levicar. The shrapnel destroyed the turbine, the fans locked up, and the levicar dropped hard to the ground. Acrid black smoke billowed from the exhaust.

"Yes!" said Josh with a fist pump. But now what? He looked around, hoping to find a weapon of some kind. Most of the guns had been put away, but he remembered that Effie kept a pistol under the front seat. Relief flooded over Josh as he reached under the seat and his hand closed around the gun. *If the cops don't show up soon, I'll have to confront these guys alone. Better out than in,* he thought as he jumped from the truck.

Just then, one of the back doors in the levicar opened and the two kids tumbled out. They fell to the ground but quickly got up and ran. One of the men got out to chase them while the other stayed behind the controls.

Josh positioned himself on the driver's side of the Land Rover, leaned over the hood, readied his gun, and pointed it at the levicar. "Come on out," he muttered. "I'm ready for you."

Josh heard sirens. He knew the police were approaching but didn't take his eyes off the sedan. Three police cruisers glided up. Effie and Geteye climbed out of one and yelled to Josh. "Are you okay?" called Geteye as the officers surrounded the disabled levicar.

"I'm fine," answered Josh, turning to them and lowering his gun. "Glad the cops are here to take over. Officer," he said to the one nearest them. "These guys kidnapped two kids from the football school. The kids escaped and ran down that alley just a minute ago. They got a pretty good head start, but one of the guys went after them."

Two of the officers ran down the alley and another called for backup. "Can we help?" asked Josh to the officer on the comm.

"We've got it covered, thanks," the officer said. "You just stay put. We'll have to get a report from you."

"What happened?" Geteye asked Josh. "Did you ram their levi?"

"And damage Effie's truck?" said Josh. "I would never do that! No, it was pure Yankee ingenuity. I took out their turbine with some carefully placed gravel."

"Pretty clever," said Effie. "I guess you were willing to do anything to drive my Land Rover," he added jokingly.

"It wasn't the ideal situation for my first time. But it was fun," admitted Josh.

The officers who had gone after the kids came back with the boy and girl. The kids were unharmed, and they had the man in handcuffs. The pilot of the levicar emerged with his hands up and was taken into custody. Josh gave a detailed report, and was told he was free to go. Geteye talked to the police as well.

"These kids just recently left a gang," he said. "The gang leaders were afraid the kids would turn them in, so they came after them."

"We'll take the kids in protective custody for now and notify their parents," said the officer. "I'll also get some extra security over at the football school. Once we get these guys put away, we'll have most of their leaders out of commission. Hopefully they won't bother you anymore."

"Thanks for your help," said Geteye. "It's frustrating to see these kids trying to do the right thing but still be in danger."

"We'll keep working together so it happens less and less," said the officer, shaking Geteye's hand. "You do good work on that football field," he added as the patrol cars glided away.

Geteye turned to his companions. "Thanks to you guys, we'll be able to do a lot more work," said the coach. "And hopefully get rid of these gangs for good."

Josh, Effie and Geteye climbed into the Land Rover to head back to the football school. Josh was glad to let Effie take the wheel this time. The big man slid the transmission into first gear with an expert hand. Josh whistled in admiration. "Harder than it looks, huh?" chuckled Effie knowingly.

Kosey started to feel sick to his stomach as they arrived in Harare and approached the hospital. I've ridden in this Land Rover so much, it can't be car sickness, he thought. I guess I'm just nervous about seeing Winna.

Effie stopped for a short break while Bernie called the hospital to let them know they would be there in a few minutes. Josh sat down next to Kosey on a park bench. He saw Kosey's worried face. "Are you anxious about seeing Winna?" he asked.

"I guess I am," answered Kosey. "I know she'll be happy that we found the diamonds, but will she be happy to see me?"
"Why wouldn't she be?" asked Josh.

"I don't know. I haven't done that much for her to be proud of. I guess that's it. She's going to want to hear stories about what happened at the mine. She probably expects me to be a hero, and I'm just not."

"I think you've done some pretty heroic things," countered Josh. "But I don't think Winna expects you to be a hero. She certainly knows you're not perfect. Give her credit for being that smart, anyway," he joked. "I'm pretty sure she likes you just for who you are."

"I hope so. And if she doesn't, someday I'll find a girl who does. I guess that's pretty important— to be yourself and not have to worry if it's good enough."

"Right," agreed Josh. "The person you're with should inspire you to be your best self, but not a different self."

"Being your best self," repeated Kosey thoughtfully. "That's a good goal to have."

Bernie walked up to the bench. "I just talked to Winna," he said. "Everyone at the hospital is excited to see us. Let's go!"

Winna and the hospital staff were waiting at the entrance when the Land Rover pulled up a few minutes later. "This sure is a lot different from the first time we were here," grinned Effie as he hugged Winna.

"Oh, don't remind me of how rude I was," said Winna, embarrassed. "Come and meet the rest of the staff."

As the older folks were making introductions and shaking hands, Winna grabbed Kosey by the arm and pulled him around the corner to a more secluded spot in the lobby. "I'm so happy to see you," she said, studying him for a moment. "And your face is all healed up!" she added before planting a kiss on his lips.

Josh looked around for Kosey. "Where did the kid go?" he asked his cousin.

"Shh," said Bernie, pointing to the two figures partly hidden behind a potted plant.

"Oh," said Josh knowingly. "I guess I'll introduce him to the hospital director later."

THE LIFE CHEST : AFRICA

That evening, the group went out for dinner with Winna and some of the hospital staff. The hospital director explained that they would hire more staff, upgrade equipment, and be able to help more people regardless of their ability to pay. "It's an incredible blessing," said the hospital director. "Some of our staff keep diaries of the patients they see and the stories they tell. I plan on collecting those stories to keep in the rhino chest. It's one of the ways we will continue to honor General Erasto's legacy."

"Where's the rhino chest now?" asked Gogo.

"I'll be keeping the rhino chest in my office, but it will be prominently displayed and well taken care of," answered the director. "I suppose it's a bit unconventional, but from now on, taking care of the rhino chest will be in the hospital director's job description."

"How does it feel to be so close to home?" Effie asked Kosey when they were just a few miles away from Tanda Tula.

"Pretty good!" answered Kosey with a smile. "I can't wait to see my grandmother. She's expecting us, and she knows we're bringing money for Tanda Tula, but I didn't tell her how much. I want to see the look on her face."

"She's planning a pretty big party, isn't she?" asked Josh.

"Yes," said Kosey. "A traditional dinner, with dancing and drumming afterward. I told her about Winna and she invited her too. I hope Grandmother likes her."

"I'm sure she will," said Effie. "Even though she picked you," he joked. Kosey's face flushed red with embarrassment, but after a moment he laughed. This is what family does, he thought. We can joke around, because we know there's love behind it.

"I also told Grandmother about you, Abdi," Kosey said to the former bodyguard. "She understands, and she said you are welcome at Tanda Tula."

"I was worried about that," said Abdi. "Thanks, Kosey. I'll do everything I can to earn her trust."

Their homecoming was everything Kosey had said and more. The travelers were greeted as heroes by the guides and staff at Tanda Tula. Music, food and joyous laughter all contributed to the festive atmosphere. After dinner, Kosey took Winna on a tour of the grounds. She loved seeing him in the place he grew up, watching him interact with his grandmother and the people who worked at the safari camp.

Kosey was sure this was the happiest day of his life. Best of all was the look on Afiya's face when he took her to a quiet corner and handed her the check for Tanda Tula. After Winna helped her sit down to recover from the shock, she began to talk about all the improvements that Tanda Tula would make. "We can hire more staff, and pay them better," she said excitedly. "The Great Hall needs restoration, and we can display the lion chest there."

"Grandmother, that makes me think of something," said Kosey. "I'm going to get Josh. I'd like to talk with both of you about an idea I have."

Afiya smiled as she watched her grandson walk away. Only three weeks had passed, but Kosey had changed so much. He was taller, stronger, and more confident. He looked people in the eye when he talked to them and listened respectfully when they spoke. He had become a man.

Winna was sitting next to her and Afiya patted her hand. She just met this young woman who was in love with her grandson, and she liked her already. If Winna and Kosey ended up marrying, Afiya would not worry about his future. "Do you know what this idea of his is?" she asked.

THE LIFE CHEST : AFRICA

Kosey sharing the check and uncut diamond with Afiya

"He didn't tell me. He's full of surprises," answered Winna. The two women smiled at each other, knowing they had something in common: their love for Kosey.

After a few minutes, Kosey returned with Josh. He sat down next to his grandmother and began to explain his idea. "Here it is," he said. "All of General Erasto's soldiers had an animal chest— a life chest, like you call them, Josh. They kept their memories and their hopes and dreams, too. Josh and Bernie have their life chests back at home. The lion chest is going to be handed down to me from Grandmother. We have the Freedom chest here at Tanda Tula." He paused to collect his thoughts.

"But our friends need a place to hold their memories of our trip and to inspire them to have new adventures. They need life chests, too." Kosey turned to Josh. "Effie and Abdi both served in the military," he said. "I want to give them Freedom chests like General Erasto's. Could you help me figure out how to get them built?"

"Of course," said Josh, smiling. "What a great plan. The life chest tradition will continue with all of you."

"But what about Gogo?" asked Winna.

Afiya spoke up. "Yes, of course. He told me all about the foundation. Gogo needs a life chest as well. He has a great responsibility now, being in charge of the diamond fund. He is the one who is going to keep the story alive. I have made a decision," she said firmly. "I want Gogo to have General Erasto's Freedom chest."

"Are you sure, Grandmother?" Kosey asked.

"Yes," she said. "My grandson, you have the lion chest to hold your legacy. The Freedom chest is going to be Gogo's legacy. He'll honor Erasto's memory and take good care of the chest."

"Whatever you say, Grandmother," said Kosey. "I know Gogo will be honored to have it."

After a few more minutes of conversation about finding a carpenter to build the new chests, Winna left to get Afiya a cold drink. Josh turned to Kosey. "What about a life chest for Winna?"

"I thought of that," answered Kosey. "I want to have a replica of the rhino chest made for her. Can you help me with that, too?"

"Of course," said Josh.

"But don't tell Winna," added Kosey hastily. "I want it to be a surprise."

"I'm going to tell Bernie about the Freedom chests for Effie and Abdi, though," said Josh, rising to go. "Is that cool with you?"

"Sure, Boss," said Kosey. "Knock yourself out."

Kosey and Afiya found themselves alone for the first time that day. Afiya turned to look at her grandson. "I am very proud of you," she said. "You have accomplished a lot in a short time."

"Do you really think so, Grandmother?" asked Kosey. "I feel very different, but in some ways I still feel like my old awkward self."

Afiya laughed. "Your youth will always be a part of you," she said. "But you have gone on quite a journey these last few weeks. Remember how angry you were when I ordered you on this trip?"

"Yes, and I'm not proud of it. I'm sorry for all the times I was so disrespectful to you, Grandmother," said Kosey. "The kids back at the primary school called us heroes, but I don't feel like one. I've made so many mistakes."

"Heroes aren't perfect," Afiya reassured her grandson. "Life is a constant journey. You are a hero when you learn from your mistakes and have the courage to keep going forward, knowing you'll make more mistakes. You went on this journey even though you didn't want to. You learned, you grew, and you changed. It was a hero's journey for you, Kosey." Afiya embraced her grandson and tears wetted the cheeks of both the old woman and the young man.

They rejoined the party with new energy. Josh, Bernie and the others could clearly see the love between Afiya and her grandson as they laughed and shared in the joy of their new beginning.

"Tanda Tula looks different to me now," Kosey confessed as he poured wine for everyone. "It's not just the party decorations. I'm so glad to be back, and I'm seeing it with new eyes."

"You're the one who's different," said Josh. "I think we all are."

"It's true," nodded Bernie. "I thought I would feel proud when we found the diamonds, and I guess I am. But mostly I'm grateful just to be a part of this adventure."

"Duma and Erasto's dream has been fulfilled," said Gogo. "I hope somehow they know."

"With all this noise? How could they not know?" joked Effie. "I'm sure they do," he added more seriously. "We salute you!" he called to the starry sky.

"And Simon Lyons, and Kim Yost," said Josh, raising his glass. "A toast to them all! They paved the way for us to find the sacred diamonds."

Winna smiled and took Kosey's hand. "I know they are proud of all of you," she said. "And so am I."The band burst into a song with a heavy drum beat, drowning out any more conversation. Music and happy laughter filled the square. Everyone joined in, singing, dancing, drinking, or all three. Even the animals seemed to enjoy the festive atmosphere. Cayar, the mischievous monkey, stole a shaker gourd and happily banged it on a log, adding to the noise.

The musicians switched to a rhythmic Juju fusion tune with steel guitar, drum and accordion. Kosey and Winna joined a few other young people who had escaped the crowd and climbed up onto a low roof to dance. They felt as if they could practically touch the stars that shone down on the revelers in the clear night.

The party wound down eventually, but Africa is never completely quiet. The sounds of monkeys, birds and insects continued even after the partygoers drifted off to their homes and tents for a contented sleep.

The group met the next morning for breakfast in the Great Hall. Winna had to get back to work, but she had a few more hours she could spend with Kosey. They planned when they would meet again and Kosey hoped to give Winna her life chest on their next date.

Bernie glanced at the space above the fireplace. "It looks pretty empty up there," he said. "I've got an idea. Let's get the puzzle map framed and hang it above the fireplace where Simon Lyons' painting used to be."

"Where's the painting now?" asked Gogo.

"It's in a museum," answered Josh. "So something needs to go above the mantel in its place. The puzzle map is perfect for that spot. It's another way we'll help keep the memory of our adventure alive for everyone who comes to Tanda Tula. And Josh and I will keep the plate in our Gramps' life chest."

"I'm going to keep the diamond map pieces in General Erasto's Freedom chest," said Gogo. He smiled at Afiya. "It's quite an honor to be entrusted with the care of that chest. It inspires me to be the best steward of the diamond money that I can be."

"I know you will be, Gogo," said Afiya.

"You're definitely the best man for the job," agreed Bernie.

"Speaking of jobs," said Effie, "Abdi and I have an idea. Can we float it by you?"

"We're all ears," said Josh.

"It was mostly Abdi's idea," said Effie, turning to the other man. "You want to start?"

Abdi nodded and began. "I took Effie over to Royal Camp yesterday to show him around. Everybody's gone. The place is deserted now. Effie thought he might use his reward money to buy Royal Camp. I told him we could use it as a base camp to track down poachers."

"Abdi's got some great ideas!" Effie interrupted. "There are places that are using drones to flush out poachers, and Abdi wants to build some that we can use. He's even got a lot of improvements in mind."

"Drones have been effective for stopping poachers," agreed Abdi. "I can build some that will be more accurate and send information faster. The rhino and elephant populations are holding on, but I think we will be able to rid this area of poachers altogether."

"That's fantastic," said Kosey. "I'd love to help you guys out."

"We'll be able to find a job for you, kid. No problem," said Effie, putting an arm around Kosey's shoulder.

"I've got an idea too," said Josh. "Bernie, remember Lucy Mayo, who was investigating the poaching in this area? I've got her contact info. I bet her organization would want to be involved."

Bernie agreed. "Having Lucy as a resource will help a lot," he told Abdi and Effie. "Excuse me a minute," he added as he stood and reached for his comm. "Chen Li's expecting me to call. We already told the family that we were back at Tanda Tula, but I have to let her know when our flight is getting into New York."

"I'm almost done packing," said Josh. "I'll go and finish now. I went to the camp market yesterday and it's going to be a challenge fitting all my new souvenirs into my suitcase."

"I hope you have room in your life chest," said Bernie. "Or are the souvenirs all for little Meg?"

"There's something for everybody," said Josh. "Don't worry. I'll still have plenty of room in my life chest for souvenirs from our next adventure!"

Epilogue

An Appetite for Adventure

"Chen Li, I'm stuffed," said Nathan, waving his white napkin in surrender. "I couldn't eat another bite, thanks."

"Are you sure?" asked Chen Li. "The food on the plane won't be half as good as mine."

"She over-feeds everybody," said Bernie. "Honey, you don't want him to get sick on the plane."

"Are you saying that my special going-away breakfast makes people sick?" asked Chen Li with pretend outrage.

"You're in trouble now, Uncle Bernie!" laughed April.

"Of course not, dear," Bernie reassured his wife. "I just meant he'd be uncomfortable sitting for that long with a full stomach." He looked at Chen Li quizzically. "You're not really mad, are you?"

"No, but I should get an Oscar for that performance!" giggled Chen Li.

Bernie clapped and bowed. "Brava, my dear! Brava!"

"Nobody asked me if I wanted more," said Josh. "Does that mean you all think I'm too fat?"

"No, it just means that I know you'll get up and get whatever you want without being asked," said his cousin.

"Well, I want some more coffee, and I'm getting it," said Josh.

"No, no! Let me," said Chen Li, reaching for the carafe.

"Thanks," said Josh. "I sure wish we didn't have to leave this morning. It's been a great visit."

"I want to stay longer, too," agreed April. "But I'm happy that I get to fly on a plane today. I love airplanes. Grandpa, I remember from the Africa story that you're afraid of airplanes."

"No, I'm not," countered Josh. "Just old rattletrap planes that are about to fall apart. That's common sense."

"I wish our plane was going to Africa and not California," sighed April. "I want to go on an adventure. And not just a little adventure to the zoo, Grandpa. A big adventure."

"I'm sure you will someday," said her father. "But it's California for today. Let's call your mom and grandma to tell them what time to pick us up at the airport."

Nathan punched in the number and Leah picked up the comm. After getting the flight information, she asked to talk to April. "Hi, sweetie," she said to her granddaughter. "Is Grandpa behaving himself?"

"Pretty much," giggled April. "He's been telling me stories about Africa. Do you remember when Grandpa and Uncle Bernie found the sacred diamonds?"

"I certainly do," said Leah. "That was quite an adventure."

"Yeah," said April. "He talked all week long."

April on the comm with Grandma Leah

"Just a minute now!" protested Josh as the grown-ups all laughed.

"Well, he must be pretty tired," said Leah. "April, when Grandpa needs a break from his storytelling, you come to me."

"Do you have stories too, Grandma?" asked April incredulously.

"Do I have stories? Listen to the child." Leah shook her head. "That settles it, then. The next adventure you're going to hear is one of mine."

"I can't wait, Grandma!" said April excitedly. "Can Grandpa listen to the story too?"

"I suppose so," said Leah, smiling. "He was there, after all."

THE LIFE CHEST : AFRICA

Appendices

AFRICA

THE LIFE CHEST : AFRICA

— Appendix A —

African Journey Map

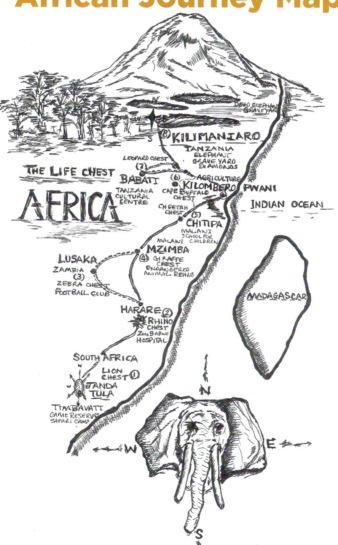

THE LIFE CHEST : AFRICA

— Appendix B —
Character Map

American, Canadian and British Characters

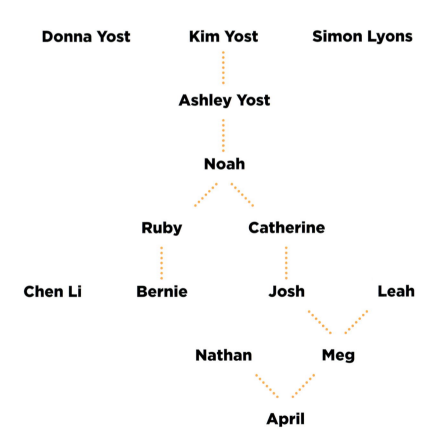

THE LIFE CHEST : AFRICA

African Characters

The "Good" Guys

The Zuma Family

Senwe Zuma

*Dry as a Grain Stalk

Afiya Zuma

*Health

1st Stop
Camp
Tanda Tula, Timbavati
Lion Chest
Lion Trinket

Alfa Zuma

*Leader

Kosey Zuma

*Lion

The Adventure Team

Gogo Okonjo

*Like a Grandfather

Effiom Boro (Effie)

*Crocodile

Winna Sylla

*Friend
2nd Stop
Hospital
Harare, Zimbabwe
Rhino Horn Chest
Rhino Trinket

* Meaning of the character's name

African Characters

The "Good" Guys

Keepers of the Chest/Story

Dumaka Dia (Duma)   **General Erasto Okoro**

*Helping Hand   *Man of Peace

Geteye Kalu
*His Teacher
3rd Stop
Football Club
Lusaka, Zambia
Zebra Chest
Zebra Trinket

Asante Mensah
*Thank You
4th Stop
Endangered Animal Facility
Mzimba, Malawi
Giraffe Chest
Giraffe Trinket

Tabia Turay
*Gifted
5th Stop
School
Chitipa, Malawi
Cheetah Chest
Cheetah Trinket

Jira Jaja
*Related by Blood
6th Stop
Agriculture School
Kilombero, Tanzania
Buffalo Leather Chest
Cape Buffalo Trinket

Jomo Jaja
*Farmer
6th Stop
Agriculture School
Kilombero, Tanzania
Buffalo Leather Chest
Cape Buffalo Trinket

Chatha Eze
*Ending
7th Stop
Cultural Center
Babati, Tanzania
Leopard Chest
Leopard Trinket

THE LIFE CHEST : AFRICA

African Characters

The "Bad" Guys

> ### Past Villain
>
> **Onani Madaki (Ona)**
> *Look

Present Villains

Aaron Bradley

The leader of the villains and descendant of the mine foreman

Agnes Bradley

Aaron's sister and partner in crime

Abdi Kalu

*My Servant

Bradley's top henchman and descendant of Onani Madaki

Rupert Turner

Charlotte Scott

Jamila Tinibu

— Appendix C —
PHOTO ALBUM

THE LIFE CHEST : AFRICA

The game tracker Jack reminded us of Abdi on his way to plant the tracking device.

The African sunset: beautiful throughout time.

A Land Rover from Royal Camp!

What are the villains up to?

Our Cayar: This little monkey and his friends were all over camp!

Photo Album

365

THE LIFE CHEST : AFRICA

Photo Album

THE LIFE CHEST : AFRICA

Photo Album

369

THE LIFE CHEST : AFRICA

Photo Album

371

THE LIFE CHEST : AFRICA

Photo Album

THE LIFE CHEST : AFRICA

Photo Album

375

THE LIFE CHEST : AFRICA

Photo Album

377

THE LIFE CHEST : AFRICA

Photo Album

THE LIFE CHEST : AFRICA

Photo Album

THE LIFE CHEST : AFRICA

Photo Album

383

THE LIFE CHEST : AFRICA

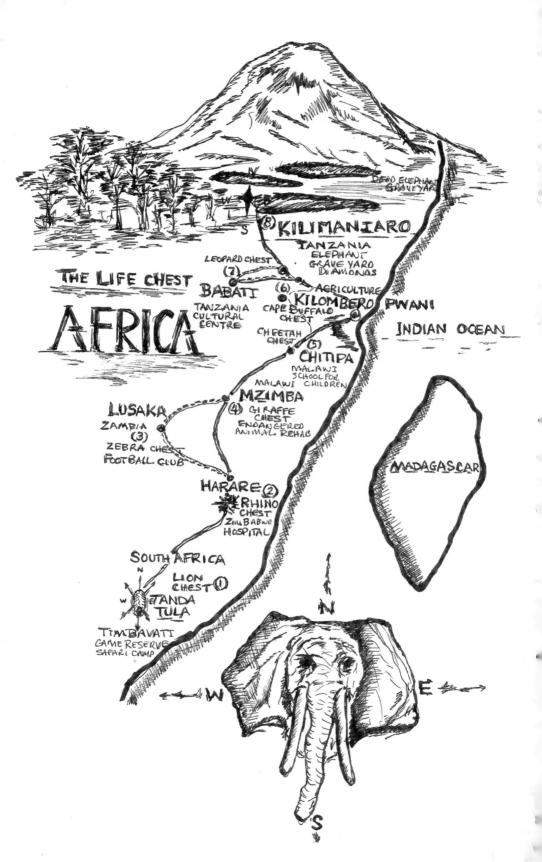